ACCLAIM FOR JAMES W. HALL AND HIS NOVELS

"James Hall's writing is astringent, penetrating, and unfailingly gripping long after you read the last page. Explodes with the brilliance of chain lightning."　　—Dean Koontz

"The king of the Florida-gothic noir."　　—Dennis Lehane

"No writer working today . . . more clearly evokes the shadows and loss that hide within the human heart."
　　—Robert Crais

"James W. Hall's lyrical passion for the Florida Keys, his spare language, and unusual images haunt us long after the story has faded."　　—Sara Paretsky

"A master of suspense . . . James Hall's prose runs as clean and fast as Gulf Stream waters."
　　—*The New York Times Book Review*

"James Hall is a writer I have learned from over the years. His people and places have more brush strokes than a van Gogh. He delivers taut and muscular stories about a place where evil always lurks beneath the surface."
　　—Michael Connelly

HELL'S BAY

"Fast-paced . . . Hall's ability to evoke the deep, primeval essence of the Bay and Glades—the water, air, wildlife, feral excitement—are unmatched . . . All the ingredients for a thoroughly indulgent and hardy stew of a thriller. With his unerring sense of place, and a frighteningly sure grasp of the dark side, nobody cooks it up like Hall."
　　—*Miami Herald*

MORE . . .

groves. Newbies will finish *Hell's Bay* and quickly seek out its predecessors."

—*News & Observer* (Raleigh, North Carolina)

MAGIC CITY

"A gripping tale of dirty politics, love gone wrong, murder for hire, and international intrigue that is impossible to put down. Highly recommended."

—*Library Journal* (starred review)

"Damn good."

—*Miami Sun Post*

"The quintessential South Florida novel."

—*Fort Lauderdale Sun-Sentinel*

"Fast, entertaining . . . Hall offers lively characters, livelier dialogue, and an excellent depiction of contemporary south Florida."

—*Publishers Weekly*

"Another outstanding chapter in one of the genre's most consistently first-rate series."

—*Booklist* (starred review)

"Hall's action scenes are starkly poetic."

—*Baltimore Sun*

"From an opening scene that charges out of the box like a greyhound on amphetamines, to the climactic denouement that will leave the reader as limp as two-month-old kale, the pace . . . never slows."

—*New York Sun*

FORESTS OF THE NIGHT

"Complex . . . chilling . . . [Hall's] prose style becomes almost cinematic . . . don't put this one aside as a beach read. A long winter's night is a better bet."

—*New York Daily News*

"Hall's finest work to date. It's serious, gorgeously written, and deftly plotted. It leaves you wanting another book instantly. Hall's work is being compared to *Cold*

"A suspenseful, sharply detailed blend of history, family drama, and thriller, *Forests of the Night* cuts a wide literary swath, and does it with élan and passion." —Russell Banks

"*Forests of the Night* moves like an arrow—lean and swift—toward its amazing target. James W. Hall is at the top of his form; he's a wonder to watch." —Reynolds Price

"Compelling . . . with action scenes that bristle with visceral intensity . . . nearly everyone has real depth, and the author's appreciation for history and its reverberations adds further complexity." —*Publishers Weekly*

"In the crowded and talented pool of South Florida suspense writers, James Hall pretty much has the deep end to himself. Out of reach for most, it's a place of nameless primal fears and murky evil, from which Hall shapes compelling characters in riveting stories. You get caught up in the light and color, the movement of the unfailingly taut action, but you are always aware of something very old and dark beneath it all. His latest novel is wonderfully disturbing in just this way . . . all of which make the carefully crafted, darkly resonant *Off the Chart* stay with you."

—*Miami Herald*

"After years of tussling with metaphorical pirates of every stripe, fly-tying South Florida swashbuckler Thorn finally gets to go up against the real thing . . . the combination of world-class villainy, exotic locations, quick-march pacing, and studly heroism also suggests Thorn's channeling James Bond." —*Kirkus Reviews*

BONES OF CORAL
"Hall takes this high adventure a step beyond the limits of the traditional action novel . . . a thoughtful, multifaceted novel that should not be missed." —*Library Journal*

"Brilliantly suspenseful . . . Hall raises mystery writing to its rightful place of honor alongside the best of American fiction."
— *San Francisco Chronicle*

BLACKWATER SOUND

"Nautical action sequences [are written] with cinematic vigor."
— *The New York Times*

"Compelling . . . A well-crafted thriller." — *Miami Herald*

"From dramatic beginning to chilling ending, Hall's never been better . . . the result is suspense, entertainment, and high-quality literature." — *Publishers Weekly* (starred review)

"Terrific." — Scott Turow

"I believe no one has written more lyrically of the Gulf Stream since Ernest Hemingway . . . a wonderful reading experience." — James Lee Burke, author of *Bitterroot* and *Purple Cane Road*

"Gorgeous and compelling." — Robert Crais

"Sleek and relentlessly propulsive." — Dennis Lehane

"With beautiful prose and a heavily muscled story, it moves with the grandeur and unpredictability of a hooked marlin. Make that a killer marlin." — Michael Connelly

ROUGH DRAFT

"A thoroughly satisfying thriller . . . Strong and engaging characters." — *The Washington Post Book World*

"Lots of action, some of it gruesome, and an intriguing plot." — *Chicago Tribune*

ALSO BY JAMES W. HALL

HELL'S BAY

BAY

James W. Hall

St. Martin's Paperbacks

This is a work of fiction. All of the characters, organizations, and events portrayed in this novel are either products of the author's imagination or are used fictitiously.

HELL'S BAY

Copyright © 2008 by James W. Hall.

Cover photo montage © Shutterstock

All rights reserved.

For information address St. Martin's Press, 175 Fifth Avenue, New York, NY 10010.

Library of Congress Catalog Card Number: 2007039977

ISBN: 0-312-94417-9
EAN: 978-0-312-94417-9

Printed in the United States of America

St. Martin's Press hardcover edition / February 2008
St. Martin's Paperbacks edition / March 2009

St. Martin's Paperbacks are published by St. Martin's Press, 175 Fifth Avenue, New York, NY 10010.

10 9 8 7 6 5 4 3 2 1

For Geoff Colmes, my guide

We are the children of many sires,
and every drop of blood in us
in its turn . . . betrays its ancestor.

—Ralph Waldo Emerson

JULY

Summerland,
Florida

CHAPTER ONE

Twist for twist, curve for curve, the two-lane road tracked the ancient meander of the Peace River through the sun-battered Florida scrubland. Steering one-handed, Abigail Bates reached up and cocked her rearview mirror off-center to better ignore the white pickup riding her bumper.

She eased back in the leather seat and held the Jaguar to thirty-five and returned to spying on the river through the cypress and pines. In the full sun its dawdling current threw off a silver glow against the riverbank trees and lit the belly of a great blue heron as it slid upstream with ungainly ease. Kingfishers stood watch in the highest branches of the pines, each bird staking out a stretch of water. From the southwest a warm wind breathed through the foliage, shifting leaves and smoothing down the tall grasses.

To her mind, this landscape had a stern grandeur, but go fifty miles west and pluck an average sunbather off the white sands of Siesta Key, drop them on the seat beside her, and most would be hard-pressed to find a trace of beauty in that stark countryside. *Godforsaken* was how she had described it as a defiant teen, seventy years before, serving out her childhood in the land of cattle prairies, citrus groves, pine flatwoods, cypress swamps, and marshes. Back then this wilderness was home to a wealth of scrub jay, sandhill crane, little blue heron, indigo snakes, and any number of species that these days were near extinction. Extinct as well were the leathery cowmen who'd settled that land—roughneck dreamers like her father and his father before him. Although they'd never been glamorized by moviemakers, Florida wranglers like her ancestors were cracking whips over vast herds of cattle a half century before longhorns grazed the prairies of the West.

Despite her youthful scorn of that rugged terrain and its rural isolation, eventually Abigail succumbed to her old man's coaching and learned a measure of appreciation for the hard-scrabble aesthetics of the place.

Apart from the garish aberration of Orlando, the vast interior of the state was thought by most to be a desolate waste-land. Finding champions for those millions of acres of scrub and palmetto and cypress swamp was nearly impossible. Indeed, that lack of care and legal scrutiny was in large measure what allowed Abigail's family to amass their empire.

As she steered the car around another sweeping bend, her foot softened on the gas pedal. On the gravel shoulder a bloated possum lay on its back, its paws reaching skyward as if pleading to the indifferent sun. Unperturbed by Abigail's car, a pair of buzzards plucked at the remains.

If she'd had any sense, she would've braked hard, U-turned, and headed back to the penthouse on Longboat Key. She was a firm believer in omens, and if that possum wasn't one, she didn't know what was.

But damn it, for months she'd promised her granddaughter she'd complete this journey, take a firsthand look at what was at stake. Not that a three-hour paddle down the Peace River was going to alter her decision a whit.

Despite the prickle of unease, she pushed on, and in another ten minutes she saw in the distance her first waypoint, the canoe outfitter's shack.

A good half mile in advance she put on her blinker for the benefit of the yahoo behind her. As she made her turn into the gravel lot, the truck thundered past and she glimpsed the driver, a woman with chalky skin and a long braid.

She parked in front of the dilapidated cabin with a rusty sign over the door: CANOE SAFARI. The man who stuck his head out the doorway at the sound of her car had blond hair that trailed across his shoulders and a scraggle of hair on his chin.

He stepped into the doorway and watched her climb out of the Jaguar. Except for the creaky knees and the steady throb in her left hip, she judged herself as supple as any woman half her age.

For this outing she'd chosen one of her long-departed husband's fly-fishing shirts with all the silly pockets and air vents, a pair of frayed jeans, and pink Keds. She'd pinned her silver hair into a bun and fit a Marlins cap atop. In that getup and the right light she might pass for seventy.

With a squint of wariness the man watched her cross the gravel lot.

"Help you?"

"I'm looking to rent one of your boats."

He gazed at her for several seconds as if waiting for her to break into a grin and admit she was only teasing.

She stepped closer and said, "In case you're wondering, I'm eighty-six. I'm fully insured, but if it'll make you feel easier, I'll sign a release."

The man drew a strand of hair off his cheek and looped it behind his ear.

"What's your fancy? Red boat or one of the yellows?"

It was agreed that the young man, Charlie Kipling, would rendezvous with her downstream at the state park landing at noon and would haul out the canoe and return her to this spot. That would give Abigail a three-hour drift down the Peace, quite enough time to take in the views and remind herself what the fuss was about. All she'd have to do was paddle a few lazy strokes now and then to keep the boat straight.

After she was safely aboard a scarlet beauty, Charlie squatted ankle-deep in the water, holding the stern. He had a simple smile but seemed more weary than a man his age or profession ought to be.

She looked down the corridor of tea-stained water and trickled her fingers through the warm stream. Two canoes slipped past, father and son in one, mother and daughter in the other. The kids chattering to each other while the adults paddled, everyone snug in orange life preservers.

"It's as lovely as I remember."

"Oh, it's picturesque," he said. "For the moment, anyway."

She gripped the paddle, waiting for him to release her into the current.

"But things keep going like they been, won't be long before I'll be shopping for another river."

She held his eyes, and after a few seconds she watched them harden and grow bleak. Once again she'd been recognized.

He licked his lips and licked them again as if fetching for a curse.

"I'll be damned. You're that woman, Bates International."

"That would be me. Abigail Bates. Nice to meet you." She didn't bother holding out a hand.

"Well, goddamn it all to hell."

"Go on," she said. "Say your piece."

"I've seen you at the meetings, sitting with that shithead lawyer, Mosley."

"Nothing's settled yet."

"That's a damn lie. It's a done deal. Train's left the station. It's already chugging down the rails; there's no turning that big-ass monster around. From the governor on down, the fix is in. Permits approved. Those meetings are just for show. Letting people think they got a choice in the matter when we got no choice in hell."

She sighed and shook her head and looked into the river's wavering shine. What he said was true, of course. The meetings were a sham. The people would be patiently listened to, but ultimately the decision was not theirs. Such as it was, such it had always been. The few deciding for the many.

She wanted to reach out and give the young man a reassuring pat but felt sure he'd swat her hand away.

"This river's been taking care of itself for a long, long time."

"Never been any threat like this. Not even close. Already this year it's down another foot. It'll be a dribble before you people are done."

Abigail stared out at the steady current. She'd heard it all before, every dire prediction.

"Anyway, it's more than the damn river," he said. "Way more than that. It's where the river goes, what it does. All the people who depend on it whether they know it or not. Goddammit, I don't believe you just walked right up and thought you could rent one of my canoes."

"Maybe I should've called in advance. You could've written a speech."

"Or brought my gun."

He held her eyes for a moment, then his face went pale and he swung away as if appalled by his own rage.

Abigail bent to her bag and dug out the Beretta.

She gripped it by the barrel and offered it. She'd been shooting all her life but only lately started carrying a pistol as the death threats mounted.

"There's no safety. Just aim and shoot."

Charlie Kipling pivoted back and stared at the pistol. His shoulders shook as if he'd felt a cold draft across his back. He looked into Abigail's eyes. Then with the mix of dread and boldness a man musters to snatch up a snake, he shot out his hand and wrenched the pistol from her grasp. He fumbled with the Beretta briefly before he found the grip.

It surprised her. The young man had struck her as another spineless tree-kisser with no muscle behind his convictions. But as she watched him raise the trembling muzzle and direct it at her body, Abigail drew a resolute breath and saw again that damn possum on the side of the road, a clear warning that any country girl should've taken seriously.

Charlie was panting, a bright sheen of sweat on his cheeks.

"If I took you down, I'd be a hero to a lot of people."

"I'm sure you would."

She watched his eyes flick right and left as if consulting the river spirits.

"If I thought it'd make any difference, I'd do it."

"I'm not trying to talk you out of it," she said.

A gold dragonfly whisked between them.

Over Charlie's shoulder, Abigail saw a minivan pull into

the lot and park beside her Jaguar. After a moment, the side door slid open and three girls leapt out followed by two young mothers in shorts and T-shirts.

Charlie glanced over at the arrivals, keeping his aim fixed on Abigail.

The red-haired woman in the lead noticed the pistol in Charlie's hand and swept up the children and herded them back to the van.

"Hey!" the other woman called out and took a couple of steps toward Abigail. But her friend shouted and she whirled and trotted back to the van.

"You lost some paying customers," Abigail said.

After the van screeched onto the highway, Charlie tipped the pistol toward the muddy bank and fired. Muck spattered the side of the canoe and dotted Abigail's shirtsleeve. He gritted his jaw and squeezed the trigger again and again. When he'd emptied the clip, he dropped her pistol into the shallow water at his feet where it sank to the bottom and gleamed within the swirl of mud like the flash of fish scales.

The glow drained from Kipling's face.

"Noon at the ramp," he said, his voice vacant as a sleepwalker's.

Then he shoved her canoe out into the moving water and Abigail straightened it and felt the current take hold. She tested her stroke, port side then starboard, felt her heart struggling to regain its cadence.

If Kipling didn't show, it was no tragedy. She'd phone her security people in Sarasota to come fetch her. An hour drive, no problem. But she believed Kipling's fury was spent, and he had every intention of keeping the appointment—if only to present his case in a more calculated manner.

A hundred yards downstream she turned and looked back and he was still standing in the shallows watching her go. After a moment, he swatted at a bug near his ear, then turned back to his pine shack.

She traveled almost an hour downstream before her killer appeared.

CHAPTER TWO

By then Abigail Bates had spotted three deer in the brush along the river. An eagle, four osprey, a red-tailed hawk feasting on a plump dove, numerous ibis, a handful of limpkins, and a large creature rooting in the shrubs along a section of private farmland. Probably a feral hog, one of the descendants of the creatures Hernando de Soto's conquistadors introduced centuries before.

Despite the tannic tint, she could see the bottom of the river in most places, twenty to thirty feet deep, and the fish were visible—a snook, one huge catfish, bass, bream, hundreds of minnows flicking by in nervous, synchronized schools.

Because it was midweek and not yet tourist season, the river traffic was light. Only a single kayaker passed her, a stalwart young woman in a skimpy swimsuit who was paddling with the sharp, focused strokes of an athlete in training. The air smelled of snakes and damp mud and an occasional gust of a sharp, insistent citrus scent that made her think of a teenage boy's first cologne.

A few feet ahead the river narrowed and the cypress and pine and flowering shrubs crowded close to the water's edge. Abigail steered the canoe around a tight corner. And there, standing about ten yards to her right on an outcropping of rock, was a woman with flesh so white her body might have been carved from cheap soap.

She was long and bony and wore a green one-piece bathing suit.

Abigail paddled two hard strokes on the starboard side to angle away from the woman's perch on the bank, though at this narrowed spot, the shoreline where she stood was only twenty feet away.

When the canoe was almost abreast of the woman's position, she dove. Five feet down she frog-kicked toward the canoe with powerful strokes.

When she surfaced nearby, a mouthful of water drooled from her lips. She treaded water and gave Abigail a cheerless stare. The woman had heavy eyebrows, a braided rope of coal-black hair, hollow cheeks, and harsh cheekbones. She was in her mid-thirties and had the gaunt look of one who'd known more than her share of rough treatment. Peasant genes. Italian, maybe Greek. A woman who would be a great attraction for certain peckerwoods in the region—men with a fascination for the exotic.

Almost certainly this was the driver of the pickup truck who tailgated her to the canoe shack. After Abigail turned off, she'd driven down the highway until she'd come to this place where the canoe would be pinched between two banks. Perfect spot for an ambush.

No crime of impulse. This was not the sort of woman who carried a swimsuit in her pickup for river frolics. Which meant she'd followed Abigail with full knowledge of her destination and had brought the required equipment. Abigail's lungs hardened. Only one person knew where she was headed today. Only one who might have betrayed her.

For a moment they floated parallel, eyeing each other in silence.

At that juncture, with two solid strokes she could be a boat-length beyond the woman and it would be a race downstream.

But she hesitated, for it had never been Abigail's way to dodge a battle. A fighter as a girl, a fighter still. You didn't swerve from conflict. You took it on and overcame. Those were her daddy's lessons passed on from a long line of hard-ass daddies. Back down once, it becomes a way of life.

She shifted her grip on the paddle, finding a hold that once, many years before, she'd used with a garden spade to hack off a rattler's head.

The swimmer blew a mist from her lips and slid toward the canoe on an angle that would bring her into range in a second or two.

The moment was gone when Abigail might have fled, and a ghost of gloom swelled within her for she saw she'd erred. She should have raced this lanky woman to the next bend, used the river's flow to her advantage. But she'd behaved the way old people so often do. A stubborn attachment to habit. Failure to adapt. She'd made that mistake a lot lately. Treating the new world as if it were still the old.

With two precise strokes the woman closed the gap and her hand shot out for the edge of the canoe. Abigail chopped the paddle blade against her bony wrist and knocked her away. While she recovered just out of range, there was another window for escape. But again Abigail faltered.

Sculling one-handed, the young woman rubbed at her damaged flesh and squinted at Abigail with the stony indifference of one who'd absorbed greater pain than any this old woman could deliver.

"Last chance," Abigail said. "Go back where you came from."

The woman smiled bleakly, then glided to the bow and took hold. With that effortless act, she had Abigail in her control. No way in hell could she work her way forward in that tippy vessel to attack the woman.

"How long can you hold your breath?" The woman's voice had a country flavor.

"What?"

"Thirty seconds, forty? How long?"

The woman rocked the canoe back and forth as if testing its balance. Abigail gripped both gunwales and held on. At each tip she was only a degree or two from going over.

"Tell me what you want. I can make it happen. Whatever it is."

"What I want," she said, "is to see how long you can hold your breath."

Like she was taking down a steer at branding time, the woman slung her arm across the prow and twisted the boat onto its side and Abigail slid across the metal bench and sprawled headlong into the river.

The woman looped an arm around Abigail's waist, securing her with a grip both solid and restrained as if determined to leave no crime-scene bruise. Abigail balled her hands and hammered at the rawboned woman, but she absorbed the blows with the forbearance of a parent enduring a child's tantrum.

Blind beneath the river, all she could make out was a fizz of bubbles as the woman dragged her toward the sandy bottom, ten feet, fifteen, swimming with one arm, the other locked around her waist. Strong as any man her size, this woman seemed at home beneath the surface, knifing down with an easy power.

As they sank, the water cooled. A swirl of dizzy light spun around her, then she released half the air in her lungs, the glittering froth lifting in a cloud to the surface.

Doing that for the woman's benefit. If she could make her body go limp, the woman might mistake her for dead and drop her guard.

Through slitted eyes she saw where the woman was dragging her.

A cypress root that bowed out from the bank like the handle of a large door, the door to a bank or some impressive office building like so many Abigail herself had entered. A woman of authority. Doormen holding them open for her. The long car waiting while she did her business.

Abigail watched the young woman take hold of the root as if she meant to open that door for Abigail, show her into the next world.

Above her the riverbank jutted out and put them in shadows and out of view of any passing paddler. She willed herself motionless, though the pain in her chest was vicious and her consciousness was dimming fast.

After a moment more, the woman relaxed her grip and Abigail thought she'd fallen for her ruse. She jerked hard against the woman's hold, threw an elbow at her face. It missed. She tried a savage kick, but that failed too. The toe of her sneaker wedged in a crevice and came off.

In that spasm of exertion Abigail lost control of her lungs and watched with black horror as a final bubble burped from her mouth, and rose shining toward the sun.

She felt her mouth slacken as the iron in her veins dissolved. Letting go of her ferocious determination, letting go of everything. Her lungs filled and she felt the gentle tug of the current across her flesh. Abigail Bates shivered hard and surrendered.

CHAPTER THREE

Sasha knew the woman was dead but waited just the same, holding the root in one hand, the woman in the other.

The old lady's clothes rippled in the current, and her hair broke from its bun and flowed forward, long and white like a ghost in a windstorm.

Sasha checked the surface and saw nothing passing, then she let the body go. With water heavy in her lungs old lady Bates drifted near the bottom, arms loose by her sides, feet tickling the sandy bottom like a drunk tiptoeing home from an all-nighter.

High in Sasha's throat a knot began to tighten.

It would be as simple as taking a deep swallow. A tempting thought. Sasha and Abigail Bates could go arm in arm on a long death march down the Peace. Miles from here their remains would wash into Charlotte Harbor, spill out into open water, then catch the tide as it fanned into the Gulf of Mexico, and in the following days they'd be swept up in the loop current that filtered south and east through the Keys, then the Gulf Stream would catch them and whisk them along on a long clockwork tour of the globe. The large unfailing mechanisms of the sea churning on, carrying the two of them along for the ride.

That simple. Open her lips and inhale. A beautiful journey.

Sasha watched the dead woman stumble and drift, sunlight rippling along the sandy river bottom before her.

The throb in her throat grew. But no. Sasha wasn't ready to hitch that ride. Soon, perhaps. But now there were promises to keep. Miles to go.

She released her grip on the root and the water lifted and propelled her twenty feet downstream. With a wild gasp she broke through the surface and swam to the bank.

Her tracksuit was tucked under a bush nearby and her Ford F-150 was hidden a half mile away on an abandoned logging road. She dressed and jogged to her truck. She saw no one. When she was back on the highway, she held to the speed limit all the way to work.

In the women's dressing room she changed out of her tracksuit, hanging her damp bra inside the locker on a metal hook to finish drying. Her security jumpsuit was sandy brown, the color of the landscape she would patrol. A camouflage that made her feel invisible as she roamed the property.

Out in the hallway, she nodded hello to the four guys coming out of the men's locker room. Couple of nods in return. Sasha stood to the side and listened to their small talk about the Buccaneers' new quarterback, listened to one guy's racist joke, then walked out to her Jeep Cherokee.

The vehicle was painted the same ashen shade as her uniform, same as the earth and the gray soot that coated the trees and made the sky hazy for miles around. There was real color underneath it all, but it was muted and dull, the way a blackboard gets after years of chalk dust films it over.

She took the access lane for half a mile, went another mile down the public road and parked in the shade of a loblolly pine near the long border of cleared land that ran along the shoulder of the highway.

A mile away the dragline was at work—its massive bucket scooping up tons of earth in single swipes. She felt the thunder rising from the earth, quaking through the frame of the Jeep. She watched her coffee cup tremble in the holder. She rolled up the window, but it did nothing to still the rumble.

Sasha was one of five members of the Bates security team who earned a meager wage making the rounds of the three-thousand-acre mining operation. Her afternoon task was to police the perimeter of #309, one of the gypsum stacks where 80 million tons of toxic sludge were stored. Its earthen walls soared twenty stories and its base covered three hundred acres. Today she was dispatched to check for settling, cracks in the surface of the berm, any sign of a sinkhole opening up or weakening in the structure, and to keep watch for eco-warriors trying to photograph one of the gypsum stacks or climb its banks to take air samples.

Sasha was lean, white-skinned, with eyes the gray-blue of wood smoke. Muscles more solid than most men's. In high school she'd tried out for the wrestling team, pinned every boy in her weight class and ten pounds above. The coach was fine with it, but some fathers protested and she was gone.

Six months after graduating she married C.C. Olsen, eight years older, a science teacher at the high school. Biology, chemistry, physics, whatever needed to be covered, he could do it. Brilliant man, her hero. Wasting his talents in that hick school. But C.C. was dedicated to his hometown, the place that got him started on a life of learning.

First year of marriage, Sasha got pregnant with Griffin. Money tight, they rented a one-bedroom house on Highway 60, dump trucks blasting by day and night, hauling phosphate rock up the road to Tampa to be processed into fertilizer. Sasha spent most of her daylight hours wiping up the gray dust that coated the furniture, the baby's crib, the few plastic toys.

When Griffin was six, heading off to first grade at Pine Tree School, Sasha snuck over to Sarasota and filled out the paperwork for the National Guard. Partly for the spare cash, but mostly to cover tuition to junior college. Study hospitality management, that was her dream. Nab a job in one of those plush beach hotels. She didn't have the brains C.C. had, but hell, she could smile nice, check people in, check them out. She never thought she'd see war.

But as Griffin was turning fifteen, a scrappy kid, and brilliant like his dad, and Sasha was one course shy of her hospitality degree, she got her call-up.

Started out as an eighteen-month rotation, then those eighteen turned into a thirty-month tour. Florida National Guard, 143rd military police, trained to provide battlefield circulation control, area security, prisoner of war and civilian internee operations, and to maintain law and order on the battlefield. Iraq was a dismal place, a gray crumbling country, the devil's sandpit. Savagery and valor. In the end Sasha lost the ability to tell the difference.

She might still be doing an endless hitch, circulating through the western provinces and Baghdad neighborhoods, if C.C. hadn't been struck with lung cancer. The man never smoked his first cigarette, but his disease was so virulent and swift, Sasha's emergency leave barely got her home in time to hold her husband's hand on his deathbed and give him a parting kiss.

Within a week of her return, Logan Hardee, the editor of the *Summerland Times*, got wind of her service record and showed up at her house. He wanted to splash her across the front page: LOCAL WOMAN IS SECRET WAR HERO. He proposed a parade. Whole town could celebrate her heroism—floats, confetti, marching band, speech by the mayor. Put her medal on public display.

Sasha listened in silence, standing on the front porch. When Logan was done, she told him no. She didn't raise her voice. Just a flat no. Now, get off my porch. If I see my name in your paper, I'll track you down and show you a few things I learned in that hellhole.

That was that. Some people gossiped. Versions of her war story made the rounds, a mishmash of bullshit and lies. Didn't matter to her. She had no urge to set the record straight.

After she buried C.C., without any notion how she'd cover next month's rent, out of nowhere the personnel boss at Bates International called and offered work on the security team. She'd be expected to watch for leaks in the slurry pipes, guard the perimeter of the gypsum stack, stay on the lookout for intruders. A nothing job.

Nobody in town could believe Sasha Olsen was drawing a paycheck from her dead husband's sworn enemy.

For while Sasha was in Iraq, C.C. became a crusader. He

got the locals organized, started agitating against Bates. Too many people sick, a cancer cluster a dozen times what was normal. Lung, colon, breast, throat. And Bates was trying to secure permits to double the size of the gypsum stack behind the school and commence mining the pastureland that surrounded the town. A noose tightening around their world.

Sasha hated working for those people, but it was the only game around and she needed something quick, something with a decent health plan because Griffin, in the weeks after she returned, started showing signs of a mystery illness. Which didn't stay mysterious for long. Primary bronchogenic carcinoma, nearly as bad as his daddy's. A tumor restricting the airflow, a main stem lesion shutting down the function of both lungs. The same grim prognosis. As the tumor enlarged, it would invade the lung tissue and perforate a pulmonary artery. Griffin's racking cough would grow worse until one day he would strangle on his own blood.

Mustering energy to begin her drive-around, Sasha idled in the shade, mind blank, body chilled, fingertips still puckered from the long submersion. She was watching a hawk swim lazy circles in the blue vat of air when her son knuckle-tapped her window.

She cranked it down. A foot away Griffin straddled the chromed-up Harley he'd inherited from his dad. Griffin was six-three, thick-chested like C.C. The bristles on his scalp were growing back from the chemo. Faint shadows of eyebrows reappearing, nubby lashes. He had his father's hooded eyes, and before the treatments stole it away, thick luminous hair danced brown against his shoulders.

There was a dark glow in his eyes that shone with chemical heat.

"You get it done?"

Sasha labored to find the words, failed, then simply nodded.

"Any problem?"

She closed her eyes and shook her head.

He set the kickstand and climbed off, leaned closer to the

window. His jeans were baggy, his brown belt cinched to its last hole. Black shapeless T-shirt. Dropped thirty pounds in the last year. Skin with a sallow, pearly sheen, dark hollows under his eyes.

"Well, shit, then this is a red-letter day."

"I guess it is."

"Head of the snake," he said. "Don't forget. Head of the snake."

Sasha nodded.

"Say it. Say the words."

She drew a long breath then spoke their mantra. "Head of the snake."

"You look pale and clammy," he said. "Don't go weak on me, Mama."

He held her eyes.

"Just a little tired," she said.

He lifted a leg and remounted the bike.

"Things'll change now."

"Yeah," she said. "Maybe they will."

They watched a pickup pass. Old man Flannery and the wife heading to town for Thursday groceries. Same people, same routines all her life.

"Purge those doubts," he said. "Fear is acid. It'll eat you up."

He settled his weight on the leather seat.

"Come on now. Gut-check time. You did a good deed."

"You're right."

"Damn right, I'm right."

He scuffed the toe of his shoe in the sandy soil. Reached a hand into his back pocket and pulled out an envelope. Folded and crumpled. She saw the burgundy embossed seal.

"Got another one," he said. "Kind of funny, the timing."

"Which is it?"

"Yale. Full ride. The whole deal."

"Congratulations, Grif."

"I had a bright future," he said. "Back when I had a future."

"Don't talk like that. You got to have hope."

He looked at her for a moment, eyes harsh and steady, then he tore the envelope into confetti and offered it to the breeze. They watched the pieces scatter across the asphalt highway.

"Head of the snake, chop it off, snake dies. Fuck a bunch of Harvards."

Sasha stared at her hands gripping the steering wheel, white and spidery.

"Has something happened, Grif?"

She knew the answer. Had seen it in the gray cast of his flesh.

He drew a white handkerchief from his pocket, pressed it to his mouth, and hocked up a plug of phlegm. He coughed it into the cloth, then held it out so she could view the clots of red. More blood caked his lips.

"Oh, Jesus," she said. "Mother of God."

"Remission's done. Now the fun begins."

He tucked the handkerchief away, and Griffin studied her eyes as he thumped his heart with a fist. Be brave, be strong. Then he smiled. Not a thing bitter in it. A smile from the old days, back before his dad died, before the disease spread its gristly tentacles through their world. A real smile for his mom like the two of them were in on some great joke.

Then he kick-started the bike and roared off into the radioactive air.

CHAPTER FOUR

A steamy night in Key Largo, middle of July. Humidity so thick you could lift a finger and sign your name in the air.

It was the hottest summer anyone could recall. High nineties in the afternoon, dipping only a few sticky degrees by midnight. Not a whisper of breeze off the ocean to cool us off or ignite a thunderstorm. For weeks a heavy lid of high pressure had been clamped over South Florida, and everyone was basting in their own sweat.

Exactly the kind of weather I loved.

I was on the back deck under the single porch light where I'd set up my workbench facing the lagoon, and I was staying busy tying bonefish flies and swatting mosquitoes.

The swatting kept my reflexes sharp, the tying kept me calm. I could've gone inside, switched on the ancient air conditioner, but I relished the heat, always had. And the mosquitoes and I were lifelong rivals. I liked to think I was a legend in their world. Thorn, the big sweaty magnet who wore no shirt, no shoes, and no repellant. The great tempter. I'd been doing this since I was a kid so it was possible thousands of generations of mosquitoes had passed along the word. This one's quick. This one's very quick. Stay clear.

Still, a few hadn't gotten the message. One or two a night made it past my radar, got a taste of my blood, and flew off, but most turned to red goo on my palm. And the smart ones circled close, took a look, and buzzed off.

It was an hour past sunset, the last of the hazy pink after-glow fading. I'd finished two dozen flies since supper and done my part in thinning out the herd of mosquitoes that bloomed in the mangroves south of my house. The Atlantic was spread before me, a vast oily glimmer. Water sloshed against the nearby shore, unceasing in its restlessness.

Living on that sandbar, surrounded by fickle seas, with only the flimsy buffer of mangroves and palms to protect us, gave an edgy zest to daily routines in the Keys. We served at the ocean's pleasure—our moody lover. Forever in her thrall, always alert to her treacherous temper, grateful for the long stretches of peace. This time of year, storm season, we squinted up at the sky with more regularity and monitored the baro-metric fluctuations against the skin for any hint of sinking pressure—a telltale hollowing in the gut, or that sickly yel-low light that warned of some swirling mass beyond the hori-zon. Such fine-tuned weather sense was a critical skill on our island. Deciding when to batten down and when to flee was not a choice most Conchs were willing to entrust to TV fore-casters standing before a flashy array of instruments.

On that airless July night I was finishing up one more of Rick Ruoff's Backcountry bonefish flies. Size 4 hook, rust monocord thread, one-eighth-inch lead weight with painted red-on-yellow eyes. For the tail I used Ruoff's grizzly hackles, splayed to flank eight strands of white Krystal flash. The body was natural tan deer hair, spun and clipped to pear shape, leaving a small shaft of standing fibers as weed or coral guard. Doing it by the book. No variations, nothing creative. Just Rick's recipe for imitating juvenile toadfish. Next was a Bead Minnow, and after that I was planning a Black Urchin and a Bonefish In-Furriator, designs by Phil Chapman.

It had been a long while since I'd tied flies straight from the book. It called for discipline, hard focus. Like a Catholic at his prayers, I found a reliable comfort in the ritual. After all the years of inventing, following my creative impulses, breaking every rule in search of new, original patterns, being locked into such mindless repetition was a sweet relief.

As I was tying off the last knot, I heard Rusty's knock at

the front door. For the last month she'd been knocking on a
fairly regular basis. Three quick knuckle raps, a brief pause,
then three more after that. I didn't get up to let her in. The
door was never locked and she knew it. But Rusty was polite, so she knocked six times before entering. She'd done
that when we were lovers, too. Same six knocks. Back then
they were slower, suggestive. Arousing knocks. Now they
were businesslike. Not hostile or cold. But precise, restrained.

Our fling lasted a few weeks and ended about as well as
breakups can. We're too much alike, she said. That's bad? I
remember asking. According to Rusty, yes, it was, because
when it came to guys, a woman had two choices. There's
your brother or there's the Dark Prince. She'd decided I was
her brother, in fact, her twin. She wanted to try the other.

There was a plentiful selection of Dark Princes sprinkled
around Key Largo, Tavernier, Islamorada, and the rest of the
Upper Keys, and Rusty had spent the last few years sampling the darkest of them. Shit-kickers and shrimpers, deal-
ers of various illegal substances, mad-dog bikers, and oily,
real-estate con men. She'd run through at least a dozen since
we split up.

No hard feelings between us. Still warmth and genuine
affection. We'd both put on some hard miles in the years
since we were lovers. Things neither of us wanted to talk
about.

The floorboards crackled as she walked through the long
living room, and then her rubber soles squeaked across the
tile of the kitchen. I knew Rusty hadn't come calling for ro-
mance. She was on a mission even crazier than that. She
wanted to hire me as her first mate.

She pushed open the screen door and stuck her head out.

"How's it going?"

I waved at the corkboard. "Assembly line's cranking
along."

She stood there for a moment looking at the flies I'd tied
that evening.

"Come in the kitchen," she said. "Something I want to
show you."

I fanned away a final lunatic bug, stood up, and followed her inside.

Rusty looked at me with a tricky smile. A woman with a secret. Decked out in her usual after-work uniform of white T-shirt, khaki shorts, and her one extravagance, Merrell flip-flops.

For as long as I'd known her, she'd worn her blond hair in the same shapeless Huck Finn cut. With that sun-bleached mop and the intense angles of her face and her oversized brown eyes and long, trim frame, at times she resembled a runway model, at others, a card-carrying tomboy.

She was only an inch shy of my six feet, with long, hard-muscled legs and a figure that was holding out nicely against the drag of years. Sometime after she left me she'd gotten a tattoo at the base of her spine, an intricate, swirly Chinese illustration that now and then peeked out above the waistband of her shorts. I was curious, but I hadn't asked what it signified. That seemed a topic too delicate for our present situation.

She was right about our similarities. In many ways she was more than my match. With fly rod or spinning tackle Rusty could out-cast me on accuracy more than half the time, though on my best throws I could beat her in length by a few yards. She knew the backcountry as well as I, and was fearless and deft steering her skiff around the tricky shoals, narrow passes, and coral heads that filled those shallow waters. She could pole the boat for hours without rest, in wind and hard currents. In bright sun or overcast, she could detect the nervous riffles of bonefish or tarpon from fifty yards. She was the only female guide working out of Papa Joe's marina in Islamorada. Nine guys and Rusty.

A few other women guides were sprinkled around the Upper Keys but none with Rusty's reputation for finding fish. She had secret spots, and super secret spots, and a few spots so secret even I didn't know where they were.

On my kitchen table she'd unrolled a three-foot-square laminated sheet. It was an aerial picture of a watery region dotted with islands. She'd set a saltshaker on one corner, pepper on another, and a novel at the bottom.

"What're you reading these days?" she said, tapping the book.

I bent forward to study the chaotic array of islands, inlets, and coves. Creeks threaded like capillaries through marshes and scattered scraps of dry land. It was clearly the Everglades, but it was taking me a minute to get my bearings.

"What is this, Rusty?"

Her lips held a faint smile. I knew the look. She had a fish on—nicely hooked. Now she was letting it run, playing it. A quiet, self-assured expression.

"Title sounds like some kind of thriller."

"Sugarman recommended it. Said it was good."

"Is it?"

I looked back at the photo, a growing awareness starting to warm me.

"Not very."

"What's it about?"

"Come on, Rusty. You don't care about the book."

"What's it about?"

Her smile deepening a degree. So confident.

"Bunch of ex-Navy SEALs and Army Rangers pull off some twisted caper. Our hero whips their asses one by one. White hats, black hats."

"Sounds like your kind of story, Thorn."

"Not really."

"No?"

"I was twelve when I stopped reading comics."

"But Sugarman liked it."

"So he said. I'll have to ask him why."

I looked back at the photo and touched my finger to one of the larger bodies of water.

"Hell's Bay?"

"You got it."

"What is this? A satellite shot of the Glades?"

"Much better," she said. "Satellite photos don't have nearly the detail as this. Plus the stuff you can download, some of the images can be five, ten years old. The rate that mangroves grow, flats and channels shift, it wouldn't do us any good."

"And this?"

"Twenty-three different photographic images spliced together."

I still didn't get it. So she explained about her friend Sherman Beams, how last spring Rusty paid him to fly his Cessna back and forth between Lost Man's Creek and Whitewater Bay for a couple of weeks. Using a belly camera and a wide-angle lens, on successive cloudless days they'd crisscrossed the whole area east of Ponce de Leon Bay and Shark River, laying out meticulous grids across that jumble of islands and winding waterways. When they had all the images collected, Rusty got her brother to dovetail the assorted photos into a single panoramic shot on his computer.

"Teeter did this?"

"Teeter's a genius about some things. When he had it all pieced together in a single image, I took it to the PhotoLab, and they blew it up and laminated it."

My finger was tracing paths through the familiar maze of islands and rivers and networks of channels. Where the peninsula of Florida ended and the Gulf of Mexico and Florida Bay began there was no distinct coastline, but a messy, tattered mix of marsh and mangrove and rivers and bays as if the land at the tip of Florida was unraveling like an old wool scarf.

"What's the idea? Use this as a nautical chart?"

She winked a yes.

"Why?"

"Keep looking, Thorn. Viewing the Glades from the sky, things pop out you wouldn't notice at water level."

It took me another minute before I saw what she was hinting at.

Dotting the northern edge of the photo was a series of small lakes and ponds, each lake rimmed by mangroves. From a passing skiff they would be hidden from view, and I was certain they weren't noted on any of the nautical charts I'd used over the years. Most charts weren't updated for decades, and in the back corners of the constantly changing Everglades, they were virtually worthless. I'd been poking around the Glades all of my life, but I'd never guessed that just behind this or that screen of mangroves were so many lakes.

"So tell me, Thorn, you still don't want that job?"

"You're a wily woman, Rusty Stabler."

"Might require making a few illegal snips in the mangroves. Doing that in a National Park, you could get a hefty fine."

"Still not interested. But I have a good pair of loppers I can loan you."

She groaned and pulled out a kitchen chair and sat down.

After two decades of guiding, she'd managed to put aside enough cash to finance the engineering blueprints for a shallow-draft houseboat of her own design. Then she'd taken the blueprints along with her detailed business plan and laid them before a couple of local attorneys who'd scored millions in real estate.

As luck would have it, Rusty's business model meshed with some obscure tax need of theirs, as well as providing them an excellent venue to entertain clients, so they'd written some hefty checks and given Rusty free reign to have the ship custom built. Somewhere between half a million and a million bucks. A two-story, sixty-five-foot, multi-ton houseboat that drew only twenty-eight inches of water and could reach areas deep into the Everglades far beyond the zones where conventional houseboats would run aground.

The idea was to tow two skiffs behind the houseboat and anchor up as close as she could get to the shallow-water fishing grounds. With a base so far out, there'd be no need to make the long run from the Everglades National Park docks at Flamingo and back again at sunset. That would add several hours to every day of fishing. She could take her time. Use the skiffs to penetrate deep into the backcountry, fish full days, then zip back to the houseboat to indulge in five-star dinners and sleep in air-conditioned comfort. Luxury camping for the well-heeled adventurer. Work the Everglades in the winter when the mosquitoes were hibernating, and in summers do weeklong stretches in the Marquesas.

To make the operation work, Rusty needed a partner who was a reliable handyman and fishing guide and had patience enough to free snagged lures from the mangrove branches for bumbling amateur anglers.

I seriously doubted the patience part, but I hadn't met many machines nautical or otherwise I couldn't jigger into working order, and I'd fished the Glades since I was a kid and knew every creek and tributary from Flamingo at the southern tip all the way north until the navigable rivers ended, and the marsh became impenetrable to anything but kayaks and airboats.

"It's a hell of a photograph," I said. "But these mangroves surrounding the lakes are so thick, it might take weeks to hack through them."

Rusty leaned forward and put her finger on a spot on the photo.

"What do you see?"

Where she was pointing there was a single faint V in the outer rim of the mangroves that surrounded a large oblong lake. At the point of the V an even fainter crooked trail ran from the open water through the mangroves and eventually led into the lake.

"Mouth of an old creek," I said. "Completely overgrown."

I became silent, feeling the hard tug of what she was presenting.

"No way to know how long those creeks have been blocked off," she said. "A century ago that stream could've been twenty feet wide, then year by year the mangroves inched toward the center, eventually sealing it up. Some lakes could've been locked tight since the Civil War. I talked to a marine biology guy at the college who said there's no way to be a hundred percent certain how long they've been cut off. Hurricanes come, destroy new growth, open up the creek again. Sun exposure, disease, tides, currents, lots of variables. But a bunch of creek beds are still there. Enough water to get the skiffs inside."

Rusty was silent while I scanned the photograph. After a couple of minutes I'd counted two dozen hidden lakes, many with the faint remnants of creek mouths. Some of the lakes were tiny, some large, a few were interconnected by narrow channels, and all of them were encircled by mangroves and tucked into the remote fringes of the navigable Everglades.

"So you wedge the skiff beneath the branches, hack your way inside, you're in waters that no one, not even Seminoles, have ever seen."

"Did I bring my pig to a good market?"

I stepped away from the table and looked at her. Her eyes were filled with giddy light.

"Why me? All the guides you know, anybody would jump at this."

"I got my reasons."

"And face it, there's no way to know what you'd find back there. Fish in those lakes would be seriously spooky. Never seen bait. Never seen anglers. One bad cast, the whole exercise is wasted. Don't see another fish all day."

"Exactly," Rusty said. "Extremely spooky. Major challenge."

I walked past her and opened the refrigerator.

"Beer? Rachel ale?"

"Nothing for me."

I opened a Red Stripe and took a seat at the kitchen table. I had a long pull, then nudged the laminated photograph aside and set the bottle down.

"Okay, it's tempting," I said. "Fishing a virgin lake."

"Now you're talking."

"But I got my routines. Being on a houseboat for a week, guiding a bunch of jackasses around the wilderness, that's not my idea of fun."

"Goddammit, Thorn."

I shook my head.

"You got your routines," she said.

"That's right."

"It's those goddamn routines that're killing you."

Rusty cut her eyes away. She hadn't meant to go that far. She clamped her lips and looked at the doorway to the living room, the escape route.

"Never mind. Forget it. I'll find somebody else."

"What's that supposed to mean, 'killing me'?"

She gave her head one small shake. Finished talking.

"You been listening to Sugarman, haven't you? That's what he told you, that I'm withering up, dying. Entropy, a closed system, nothing new coming in the door, I'm starving emotionally. That's his bullshit, isn't it?"

"He's worried about you, Thorn. We all are. You're hunkered down in your bunker, or monastery, whatever the hell it is. Months since you been off your property. You're hiding, Thorn, suffocating. I mean, yeah, I know some ugly shit's come your way. So you retreated and here you are. Making a few dozen flies a day, watching the sun come up, watching it go down. Pretty soon the windows will be plastered over, and you'll be eating nothing but pizza or whatever food they can slide under the door."

I looked down at the sparkle of condensation ringing my beer.

"What if I'm happy with things just like they are?"

"Are you? I remember a different Thorn. A funny guy, lots of friends. Some hilarious nights."

"I can't believe it. You and Sugar, double-teaming me."

"Somebody's got to kick your butt, get you out in the sunlight."

I took another look at the photo. All those hours she'd spent flying over the Glades in a small plane, all that labor. But it had been worth it. Now she could introduce her clients to waters that had never been fished. Sixty, seventy miles as the crow flies from downtown Miami was an unexplored wilderness, a place about as inaccessible as any on earth.

"Give me one trip," Rusty said. "A week out of your life. It doesn't pan out, big deal. You come back to your monastery, I find somebody else. Right now the boat is half done. They've got the hull complete, they're framing the interior and exterior walls, then the trusses for the second level. Exterior skin gets riveted on, windows cut and installed, then the electric and plumbing goes in. Five baths, nine cabins. Completion date: early December. By January, assuming we can rustle up four paying customers, we take our first trip. Hack our way into a couple of those lakes. See how spooky the fish are."

I shook my head. "Thanks, Rusty. But this isn't for me."

She stood up, looked at me for several seconds, then rolled up the laminated photograph and slid it back into the cardboard tube. She walked out of the kitchen without a word and made it halfway across the living room before turning and coming back.

"Let me ask you something, Thorn."

I was silent. I looked out toward the lagoon, my fly-tying bench, the glow of the lightbulb, the whirl of insects.

"Go ahead. Ask your question."

She waited a moment more, staring at me hard.

"Can you remember the last time you blazed a new trail? Did something fresh, something totally new?"

I looked at her but said nothing.

"Think about it," she said, then turned and left.

I did. I thought about it. For weeks I thought about nothing else.

CHAPTER FIVE

Six months later, on a January afternoon, I was kneeling on the rear deck of Rusty's brand-new houseboat, gashing my knuckles against the razory flanges of the water purifier, trying to get the cranky machine into working order. The air was still chilly from the cold front that had passed through earlier that week. The sky was peeled open, exposing its most perfect blue.

Three days earlier from the rooftop of the houseboat, I'd watched thunderheads gather in the northwest as a trough of brisk Canadian air muscled up against the sultry Florida atmosphere. All that morning it grew like a vicious bruise, until at noon the heavens hemorrhaged and a downpour like none we'd seen for months drenched the Upper Keys for most of the day.

Next day, with lows in the forties, my fingers were stiff and toes icy, and the sunlight was so astringent my face grew chapped and took on a ruddy glow. I hauled out a musty sweatshirt and traded my shorts for jeans and brewed pot after pot of coffee just to warm my hands on the mug.

For two days the chill lasted, but now the old marine smells were returning, those lush sulfurous gases rising from the tidal flats and the shadowy waters within the mangroves, the sweet rot of barnacles and spawning shrimp. Hour by hour the air was softening, and the strip of shoreline that had hardened in the cold was turning back to sandy slush. All of it was another reminder of what rude changes regularly race in off the sea. How vulnerable we are on our outcropping of rock, how fully exposed.

It was three in the afternoon and our first two anglers, John Milligan and his daughter, Mona, were due at any moment. Instead of mixing them a welcoming cocktail like a proper host, I was on my knees with my arm poked into the bowels of that water purifier. Before we could set off on our seven-day cruise into the wilderness, I had to get the thing up to speed. I was hoping that could be accomplished by replacing yet again one of its micron filters that was clogged with flecks of broken shell, stringy seaweed, and other rank emulsions of the sea.

The water maker was crucial hardware. Twelve thousand bucks, the size of a small refrigerator. Using a high-pressure pump, it forced seawater through a series of ever finer cylindrical filters, and after cleaning and recleaning the water, the machine finally shot the particle-free water through the main membrane at very high pressure, separating out the salt and funneling the waste back into the ocean. Then the salt-free water passed through two more filters, a charcoal one and finally a UV treatment to kill any residual bacteria. The machine was meant to supply all the needs for the six passengers, four of whom were paying several thousand dollars apiece for the angling adventure and would be expecting freshwater from their shower heads.

Ever since the houseboat had been delivered in December, Rusty and I had been dealing with dozens of glitches, large and small. Breakdowns in the heat pumps and the 15KW Westerbeke generators, shorts inside the wiring harnesses and more shorts in the anchor windless, and plugs and fuses flickering or just going dark. The sewage processor broke down, too, and now the reverse-osmosis water maker was falling far short of delivering the 800 gallons per day the manufacturer promised. The Mothership, as we called her, was one complicated vessel, and I was sure our maiden voyage was about to expose a whole new array of gremlins.

When I finally snapped the micron filter into its slot, I

smoothed its gasket back into the groove. With the socket wrench I tightened the plate and looked up at the sound of a small plane circling overhead.

It was a bright yellow seaplane with bright aluminum pontoons. A Cessna, single-engine, four-seater. The 185 Skywagon, a favorite of Alaskan bush pilots and the barefoot buckaroos who did the run from Key West to the Dry Tortugas three times a day. The Cessna circled overhead then came in for a long smooth landing about two hundred yards east.

For the last half hour Rusty had been idling nearby, awaiting the plane's arrival. I watched her scoot across the shallows to meet up with our guests.

Minutes later she was heading across the light chop toward our vessel. Standing next to Rusty was a tall man with wide shoulders. From a couple of phone conversations with the gentleman, Rusty had learned only that Milligan and his daughter lived upstate on the Gulf coast, that he was an avid fisherman and had found Rusty's houseboat venture on an Internet search. His personal check in the full amount arrived a few weeks back and cleared just fine, and his reservation was set.

The other couple who would share the houseboat for the week were arriving later in the day. Shortly after Milligan booked his trip, Rusty got a call from Annette Gordon, a writer for *Out There* magazine doing a feature on luxury adventure vacations. She was in her late twenties, a New Yorker, and was bringing along one of the magazine's staff photographers, a guy named Holland Green. Rusty was thrilled. Great free promotion. Annette hadn't even asked for a reduced rate. She'd done travel writing all over the world: New Zealand, South America, the Seychelles, Tibet. Rusty thought she sounded low-maintenance, the kind who made it her goal to slip into the background.

As Rusty cut the wheel to dodge a final sandbar, Milligan raised a hand in greeting and I waved back. He looked to be in his middle sixties and just past six feet tall, and even from thirty yards away I could tell he had the shoulders-back, flatbelly physique of a man of high confidence. He wore a red golf shirt that showed off his broad shoulders and the kind of swollen arms I've always associated with one who dug a great many postholes as a boy, strength he'd earned through backbreaking labor in the sun.

Rusty slowed and the boat dropped off plane. Perched on the padded ice chest in front of the console was Mona Milligan. She wore a white fleecy sweatshirt and black jeans, and her auburn hair ran wild in the breeze, tossing like a warning flag as the boat muttered toward the stern platform where I waited.

I tied off the bow line, then leaned over the loading platform to help our first two guests aboard.

Mona looked at my outstretched hand, then met my eyes and held them as she took hold of a bow rail and hauled herself aboard without assistance. Milligan shrugged an apology to me then held out a big paw. I heaved him up, and while he still held my hand, he gave it a firm how-do-you-do.

"Good to meet you, Daniel. Or do they call you Oliver?"

As his words registered, a cold weight shifted within my chest. The man looked at me steadily with a slender smile as though we shared a delicious secret. If I'd followed my instincts, I would've shoved him backward into the choppy sea and hauled the anchor and set out toward the horizon, leaving him to swim the half mile back to shore.

"What's wrong, Daniel? You look ill." A goading tone.

The blood tightened in my veins.

"My name is Thorn," I said.

"Whatever you like," he said, holding to his smile.

As Rusty handed Milligan his duffel and the rest of his gear, I gave him a careful look. Plainly he was an outdoorsman from the melanoma-be-damned school, for the flesh around the open collar of his shirt was as charred as a steak forgotten on the grill. His mustache was barbered so primly it gave his rugged features an air that was faintly unsavory. An echo of Clark Gable as a riverboat gambler. A man who could damn well deal from the bottom of the deck if the spirit moved him.

Rusty gave me a chastising glance and pushed past me to

show the Milligans to their staterooms. My bad manners were already disheartening her. I stood on the rear deck and took careful breaths while I stared out to sea.

It was true my given name was Daniel Oliver. Son of Elizabeth and Quentin Thorn. Born in a hospital in Homestead, Florida, rushed home by my parents in the first twenty-four hours of my life so by local custom I would be officially pronounced a Conch—a title bestowed on those lucky enough to be born in the Florida Keys.

A Conch I was, a Conch I remained. Hard shell, gristly meat, trundling across the floors of silent seas.

Though everyone knew me as Thorn, more than once in private I'd spoken the words *Daniel Oliver* aloud to see how they sounded on my lips. It was a name with some special meaning to my parents, but it was a cipher I'd not broken. I would never know its origin, for my father and mother died in a car crash on the way home from the hospital, a collision that through some supernatural physics their baby boy survived.

The two gentle spirits who adopted me, Kate Truman and Doctor Bill, never spoke of my parents. Trying to spare me, I assumed, from emotional pain. In my teens I spent hours in the courthouse digging through public records without luck. Years later I got my friend Sugarman to run a computer search on their names, but he came up empty. And none of the locals I questioned could provide anything about who Quentin and Elizabeth Thorn were or where they came from. So finally I was forced to invent.

The history I crafted was that my parents, like so many refugees to the Keys, arrived in the islands to escape their pasts and reinvent themselves. I imagined that at the moment of their deaths they were at the awkward juncture when they'd succeeded in wiping out their previous identities but had not yet established new ones.

Beyond that simple fiction I would not let my imagination go. If they had wanted to disappear, then who was I to exhume their remains?

I accepted the idea that my parents, their backgrounds, the

nature of their love affair, their private dreams, and their natural talents would remain a mystery. Though from time to
time when I was praised for my accuracy in casting or dispar-
aged for being such a dogged loner or admired for my surgical precision in fashioning wisps of fur, feather, bead, and
thread into bonefish flies, I attributed those gifts as part of my
birthright from two people I never knew. If I had sometimes
been guilty of excessive introspection, my only defense was
that by looking inward I was hoping to catch some glimpse
of those two ghosts who were harbored in my veins.

Behind me Mona wandered into the galley and sunk down
on one of the couches that faced the satellite TV. The television was Rusty's idea. It seemed bizarre to me that anyone
would go to such expense and trouble to trek into one of the
last wild places on the globe, then sit around and watch
twenty-four-hour cable news instead of climbing up onto the
houseboat roof to listen to the hushed wing beats of thousands of egrets and herons and wood storks heading back to
their roosts and watch the sun melt into the watery horizon
leaving behind eddies of reds, blues, and purples too gaudy
for words.

I made my case, but Rusty overruled me on the TV as she
had on every issue. "People who will pay a thousand dollars
a day to catch tarpon on a fly in some hideaway lake nobody's ever fished before aren't like you and me, Thorn. End
of the day they want their extra-dry martini and stock-market
update."

When Milligan finished stowing his gear in his forward
stateroom, he returned to the galley. As he passed Mona, he
patted his sullen daughter on the shoulder, then came over to
me still wearing that knowing grin. He moved with the loose-
limbed swagger of a barroom tough.

Rusty had climbed up to the wheelhouse to make a cell-
phone call to Annette Gordon to see if her flight had landed
yet at Miami International. On the couch Mona pressed her
chin to her chest, hunched deep in her funk. Since arriving
she had not spoken a word. Nor had she brushed the snarls
from her red hair.

In an earthy, unfussy way, she was quite pretty, though she had the look of a woman who'd been told that far too often and no longer considered it a compliment. Her eyes were opaque blue. A sharp upward jag in her right eyebrow gave her the look of a steadfast skeptic—a woman not easily conned. The eyebrows were thick and a darker shade of red than her hair. Scattered across her forehead was a constellation of tiny freckles. Otherwise her skin was flawlessly sunbronzed, a healthy flush in her cheeks. She wore no watch, no rings or any other jewelry, and her clothes were so lumpy and rumpled she might have slept in them for the last week.

Her expression was fixed in the same harsh squint as it had been when she climbed aboard, an odd mix—part glare, part wince—as though Mona Milligan was hovering indecisively between defiance and desperation.

Milligan slid into my line of sight, his eyes crafty, his head cocked a few degrees to the side like a man sizing up a sparring partner.

"Surely you must be intrigued about how I know your name?"

"I'm trying to contain myself," I said.

"So that's your act, huh, the cool dude?"

"I don't have an act."

Milligan reached into his back pocket, withdrew a photograph, and with a small flourish he lay it on the bar next to me. Then he stepped back and waited with that smile deepening.

I took a look, glanced back at him, then took a longer look.

It was a faded black-and-white snapshot of two teenagers posing in front of an ancient Ford coupe. Behind the car was a section of the veranda of a dignified Victorian home. A handsome older couple sat on the porch swing, engaged in conversation and seemingly oblivious to the photographic record that would include them. There were big oaks shaggy with moss, and runty cabbage palms growing at the edges of the porch. Bougainvillea vines snaked along the eaves and framed the porch in wispy blooms. The place had the look of a plantation constructed far from any village or town, and the people were sun-hardened and squinty in the way of those who've labored in every kind of harsh weather Florida can provide.

The teenage boy had smirking eyes, and his body was as thin and hard as a cypress rail. He'd thrown his arm across the shoulder of the fair-haired girl in a flowered sundress. She had wide shoulders, long slender arms. One hand was lifted up to keep her dense blond hair from blowing across her face. She was a striking girl whose large mouth and bony face gave her a sensuous though slightly mannish aura.

As I stared at her, I heard static growing in my ears, and my throat felt as though it was splitting open. Though I had never seen the woman before, with absolute certainty I recognized her. Her eyes, cheeks, lips, and nose were nearly identical to the ones I saw every morning in my mirror as I shaved.

"Elizabeth Milligan Thorn," the man said. "My sister, your mother."

CHAPTER SIX

"That guy's your uncle?"

"So it appears."

"Well, you're being pretty blasé about the whole thing."

"Stick around. I'm about to dance on the table."

Sugarman poured the rest of his beer into the tall glass and glanced again at Milligan, who stood with the others twenty yards away on the beach. We were sitting outside on the rear porch of the Green Flash Lounge at Morada Bay. Rusty's choice. Upscale joint for her upscale clients. One last meal on land before we set off.

Not the usual Keys tacky nautical décor of glass floats suspended in fishing nets and phony portholes bolted to the walls. The Green Flash was all dark mahogany and heavy leather chesterfield sofas, bookshelves crammed with leather volumes, and plush Oriental carpets spread on the maple floor. Behind the bar were fifty different brands of vodka and a slick bartender who could recite something fancy about each of them. Cigars from around the world were on sale from a locked glass counter. Another Keys establishment trading on the manly fairy dust of Hemingway.

Behind Sugarman the Florida Bay spread out to the western horizon as flat and motionless as a slab of burnished silver. The red disk of sun had dissolved halfway behind the distant mangrove islands and was sending flares of green and blue into the cloudless heavens. Drinks in hand, tourists lounged in the pink-and-pastel-striped Adirondack chairs, watching the dwindling light while they dug their toes into the perfect, imported sand.

I drew the photo from my shirt pocket and lay it in front of Sugar.

Sugarman was my oldest buddy. Former deputy sheriff, now a private investigator working out of an office next to the HairPort up in Key Largo. As a kid, Sugar was deserted by his Jamaican father and Scandinavian mom. All they'd left him was his striking good looks. Quiet, arresting eyes, narrow lips. Most women gave him a second glance, often a lingering third. Behind the sensuous facade, there was something noble in his bearing. He was solid and uncomplicated, blue-collar to the bone, a man of such firm and well-calibrated ethics that even hard-core sinners like me could sense the sharp ping of virtue radiating from him.

"Damn strong resemblance. I'd say it could be your mother, yeah."

I nodded. I had no doubt it was.

"She was a looker. A little countrified, but an eye-catching woman."

"I noticed."

"He laid this on you and you didn't ask him any questions, nothing?"

"He said he'd tracked me down. Wanted to get to know me, maybe offer me an opportunity."

"What kind of opportunity?"

"He didn't say and I didn't ask."

"You didn't ask?"

"He was trying to get a rise out of me. I didn't feel like obliging him."

"Christ, Thorn. You can be so damn pigheaded."

"I'm spending seven days on a houseboat with the guy. I figure we'll get around to it."

Out on the powdery sand, Rusty was making the introductions among Annette Gordon, Holland Green, and Mona and John Milligan. Everybody shaking hands, Milligan joking with the two young people, drawing a laugh from Annette, a gaunt young woman with a brown halo of curls. She was tricked out in an off-white angling outfit so superbly understated it was probably made to order at some Park Avenue haberdashery.

With a camera slung around his neck, Holland was dumpy, mid-thirties, wearing slappy rubber flip-flops, machine-torn jeans, black oily hair to his shoulders.

Hulking just beyond the circle was Rusty's older brother, Teeter. Rusty never volunteered the information, and I never asked the name of his disability. He was six-four and heavyset. His forehead was abnormally broad and his eyes dull and downcast. On the rare occasions when he spoke it was usually no more than a brief mumble. Besides having highly developed computer skills, Teeter was a chef of some renown in the Upper Keys. He had a genius for delicate sauces and eccentric combinations of spices. His yellowtail Matecumbe had earned him a write-up in the Miami paper, which set off a bidding war between two of Key Largo's best eateries for his services.

But Teeter had informed Rusty that he was sick of restaurants. The bickering, the competition, the steamy, obscene stress. So he'd defected from kitchen work and would be assuming culinary duties on the Mothership. He'd also accepted the role of chambermaid and security guard. Each morning when the anglers and guides headed off for the fishing grounds, it would be Teeter's job to clean and straighten the staterooms, wipe down the sinks and showers, make the beds, vacuum, and otherwise stand watch over the empty vessel.

He and I had an awkward relationship. Whenever Teeter was around, he was continually casting looks my way, just as he was doing at that moment from out on the beach. I wasn't sure what his fixation was about, but I'd steeled myself for spending an entire week in close proximity with him, and was pretty sure I'd have to confront him about the behavior if it continued.

"What'd you do to piss that girl off?" Sugarman nodded toward Mona.

"Didn't have a chance. She arrived that way."

"And the kids? That's a majorly weird couple."

"Rusty says they're not an item. Annette's a travel writer, doing a story for *Out There*. The guy's shooting photos."

"Going to make Rusty famous."

"She's hoping."

I watched the light sweeten around us, a last bloom of orange on the horizon. Out over the Gulf some delicate pink clouds tangled their tentacles like mating octopi. A sky that was never still, never lost its power to amaze.

I finished the last of my beer, raised my hand to Tricia Murray, who was waiting on us, and pointed at my glass and Sugar's to save her a trip.

"I don't like this, Sugar. The guy drops the snapshot in front of me, steps back, and gives me a shit-eating grin."

"Granted, it's weird. But consider the bright side: You'll learn who you are, who your parents were. What's wrong with that?"

"I already know who I am."

Tricia brought the beers and fresh frosty glasses and took away the empties. Annette and John Milligan seemed to be hitting it off, laughing at each other's jokes. Holland was shooting film of two local hotties stretched out on lounge chairs in matching thongs. They were drinking margaritas and pretending to ignore Holland, who was a yard away, kneeling and bending at off-kilter angles, focused mainly on their long, tanned legs.

Mona stared out at the last shreds of sunset while Rusty threw anxious looks my way as if I was committing another egregious etiquette error by not coming over and joining in.

"The guy's dicking with me."

"Oh, come on, Thorn. You're working yourself up."

"If it was you, Sugar, is that the way you'd handle this? Zoom in out of the blue, no warning, spring it on a nephew you've never met? Hey, guess who I am? Your freaking uncle. I got an opportunity for you. It's a gotcha thing. A bully-boy trick."

"Overreacting, Thorn. Making a big deal over nothing."

"Would you do it like that, Sugar?"

He shook his head and glanced back at the purpling sky.

"Some people like surprises. Maybe he thought you'd throw your arms around him, give him a big hug."

"I didn't read it that way."

"Oh, man." Sugar sipped his beer, set it down, wiped his lips with his napkin. "Your whole life, you never met any of your own flesh and blood. It's this big missing piece. Then, bam, it happens, and listen to you. You take one look at the guy—your uncle, your mother's little brother—you're around him all of five minutes and you got him pegged as a villain."

I had no answer for that. He was right. My instincts were on red alert. I'd made a career out of reclusiveness, but at all too frequent intervals I'd been dragged into the world by violent men, treacherous women, but most often by my own impetuous folly. More than one innocent life had been damaged or lost because of me. I'd done plenty I wasn't proud of and only a few things I was. Lately I'd reached the point where I was having trouble telling the difference.

Distrust and wariness had become a reflex. In the last year the condition seemed to worsen. At the first sign of trouble, I found myself flinching and turning away. Anything could set it off—a defiant look sent my way across a crowded bar, or a woman's come-on smile. I'd duck my head and hustle back to my burrow, pick up my fly-tying gear, and disappear into the refuge of work. Whole weeks passed without human contact. Until Rusty challenged me that night in July, it suited me fine.

Sugarman claimed it was some version of post-traumatic stress. I'd passed some watershed and was sliding into a new state of mind. One too many catastrophes, too many innocent friends or lovers caught in the crossfire. Now I was shell-shocked down at some cellular level.

Whatever its name, I had grown sick of it. Sick of hiding out, stiff-arming all human contact. So I'd heaved the boulder away from my cave door, staggered out into the sunshine, signed on to be sociable, a certified hale-fellow-well-met. Then John Milligan climbed aboard, laid the photo on the bar, and, Christ Almighty, the whole shitty cycle was starting again.

A short while later we exited the Green Flash Lounge and moved upstairs to Pierre's, the fanciest eatery on the island. As the group waited to be seated, a man appeared in the doorway behind us and Milligan swung around to greet him, then introduced him one by one to the rest of our party.

His name was Carter Mosley, the pilot who'd flown the Milligans down from Sarasota. A short man, not more than five-two, he stood very erect. After he shook hands with each of us, Mosley's pale blue eyes landed on my face and he took a moment to study its angles as if trying to fix me in his memory.

Mosley was silver-haired, mid-fifties, with a reserved smile and those alert eyes. He wore a sky-blue jumpsuit, a black T-shirt visible beneath. His face was unlined and, for such a small-boned man, his handshake was crushing.

"I can't stay," he replied to Rusty's invitation to join us for dinner. "Got a mountain of paperwork on my desk. Just wanted to say hello, and wish y'all good luck on your fishing adventure. I'll be back in a week to pick you up."

"Carter's the family's legal eagle," John said, patting the small man on the back. "Old and dear friend."

As Mosley made his exit, he gave me one more searching glance. Milligan ushered him out into the twilight, and they had a word on the landing before Mosley left.

The rest of the night sailed by with dishes of hickory-smoked free-range buffalo rib-eye with foie gras yuca cake and soy-lacquered sea bass and three bottles of a tasty red wine that Annette knew a good bit about. She'd visited the vineyard on assignment, met the owner. Told an amusing story about the guy. Everyone joined in the laughter except Mona. She moved the food around on her plate and looked up from time to time to frown at whoever was speaking.

Through most of the main course, Annette took charge, going one by one around the table and shining the spotlight of her attention on each of us. For a while she focused on Rusty and got her to confess that this whole houseboat enterprise had been such a long-deferred dream that she was having trouble believing it was all finally coming true. Plus she was nervous as hell that everything should go smoothly. When she was done, murmurs of reassurance passed around the table.

Then Milligan got his turn and told a brief, self-mocking story about taking up golf, beaning his caddy twice in one week, then buying him a hard hat. When Annette focused on Teeter, he mumbled something about a new recipe for scallops he'd invented, then looked directly at me as if I could save him somehow, and when I made a helpless shrug, Teeter shut his mouth and dropped his head, mortified by the attention he was receiving.

As we waited for dessert, Annette Gordon swung to Sugar.

"I understand you're a private eye."

Annette was half the age of most of us at the table but seemed perfectly at ease directing the show. She had the casual moxie of a big-city girl who thrived in far more sophisticated circles.

"Sam Spade was a private eye," Sugar said. "My world is a little duller."

Annette prodded until Sugar gave in and told them about his latest case.

For several weeks this past fall, he'd trailed Julie Shipman, the runaway daughter of a Delta pilot. Julie was sixteen, had stolen her daddy's Porsche, and made it to Atlanta, where the trail went cold. Sugar shoe-leathered the city for weeks, finally found a strip club where the girl had worked, and got the name of a bouncer who'd seduced Julie and whisked her off to Seattle for the dreamy life of a call girl. It took only two days in Seattle before Sugar located the agency she'd hired on with. He called and requested her by her description. Julie showed up in his hotel in a miniskirt with a bruise on her cheek—ready to perform.

Eight weeks start to finish. The girl despised Sugarman for dragging her home and made nasty claims about him taking sexual advantage in that Seattle motel room. Now the pilot was trying to chisel Sugar out of his fee, saying the shrink bills were eating him alive and his airline had gone into chapter eleven. Then he used his daughter's lies to threaten Sugar with legal action.

Sugar would've done the job for free, but now the thing was a point of honor, so he was heading to court.

Mona leaned forward, planted her elbows on the table, and angled her head to look past me at Sugar.

"So, Mr. Sugarman?" Her voice was low and husky as though these might be the first words she'd spoken in days. "You ever kill anybody?"

In the prickly silence Sugar fetched for an answer.

Then Annette plunged in.

"What I want to know, Mr. Sugarman, are you any good? Do you always get your man? Or lady, as the case may be?"

"I'm okay," Sugar said. "I'm no Sherlock Holmes, but I'm persistent."

"I love those detective shows with the high-tech gadgets, those cool tweezers to pick up hair and tissue samples. Is that what you do?"

"Not really," Sugar said. "I'm old-school. Don't even own a pair of tweezers. Wouldn't know what to do with them if I did."

"But how do you solve your cases?"

"Talk to people, ask a lot of questions. It's not real glamorous."

As Annette was about to press on, mercifully, the dessert tray arrived.

I thought I'd escaped her third degree, but later as Holland was ordering a cognac, Annette said, "So Mr. Thorn, I hear you're our resident curmudgeon."

"Define please," Holland said.

"Killjoy, wet blanket," Annette said. Sounded like a routine they played.

I drew a breath, worked my lips into something of a smile.

"I'm a recovering curmudgeon. Been sociable for the last three days."

"It's the next seven I'm concerned about," Annette said.

While the others chuckled, John Milligan ticked his eyes around the table, landing on each face for a second, then moving on as if he was fine-tuning his assessments of his shipmates.

"And you, Mona?" I said. "What's your story?"

It took a moment for her to surface from the shadowy place in her head.

She gave me a cold glare, then picked up her spoon, stared down at her untouched crème brûlée, and with a series of petulant jabs, broke the hard crust in several places.

"My daughter's suffered a painful loss. Actually we both have."

"I'm sorry to hear that," Annette said. "But this trip should help. All the clean air and sunshine. I always feel refreshed after a stint in the wild."

"That's what I was hoping for," Milligan said. "A little renewal."

"Kumbaya, my Lord." Holland raised his Nikon and snapped three quick shots of my profile.

"You think you could give that a rest, Holland?" I said.

Holland seemed about to make a witty comeback, but Annette sent him a pinched look and he closed his mouth, then made a production of snapping the lens cap back in place and slumping in his seat.

When his performance was done, I turned back to Milligan.

"What kind of loss?"

I knew it was rude to press on, but at that moment I needed to know just what the hell I was getting into. I was about two seconds from wadding my napkin, tossing it on the table, and stalking off. Virgin lakes be damned. Rusty would just have to snag one of her guide buddies as a last-second replacement.

"My mother died," Milligan said. "Mona's grandmother. A few months ago, she drowned in the Peace River. That would be your grandmother, too, Thorn. Abigail Bates."

Annette set her spoon down. The table fell silent. This was a good deal more confession than anyone had bargained for. I felt Rusty's leg pressing against mine, hard as concrete. Holland slurped his cognac, and Sugar absently fondled the stem of his glass. The awkward hush was becoming more awkward by the moment.

To my right, Mona spooned up bite after bite of crème brûlée, then while we watched, scraped out the remains. When she was done, she patted her lips with her napkin, folded it neatly, and set it beside her place mat.

"Grandmother was murdered," she announced.

She stared at me for several seconds, then looked past me at her father.

"No, she wasn't," Milligan said with a weary frown. "Her canoe tipped over and she drowned."

He glanced around the table, and for the first time since I'd met him, he seemed less than certain.

"There was a thorough investigation," he said, looking at each of us in turn. "State, local. All the forensics were done, one of the best pathologists in Florida. There was no evidence of foul play, none whatsoever. She drowned. She was eighty-six and had no business in a canoe by herself without so much as a life jacket or flotation device of any kind."

"She was murdered." Mona's tone was grimly matter-of-fact, as if the two of them had hashed this over so often the bitterness was rung out of it.

Rusty stared down at the tablecloth. Her face was pale. The evening meant to celebrate her maiden voyage was spinning out of control.

Milligan pushed his chair back and stood up. Rusty rose, too. She laid her hand on my shoulder, tightened it, and dug her nails into my flesh.

"Isn't it time we were getting under way, Captain Stabler?" Milligan said. "That is, if we're still planning on fishing tomorrow."

"She was murdered." Mona stood up, stared across at me for a second, then shifted her fierce gaze to Sugarman. "Murdered, goddammit."

"Why do you think that, Mona?"

"Thorn, that's enough," Rusty said.

"I don't think it," Mona said. "I *know* it."

"Based on what?"

"I don't have to justify anything to you."

She blasted me with a scowl and stalked toward the exit. John Milligan crowded up to my shoulder.

"You might as well hear it from me," he said. "Mona thinks I was behind Mother's death. She can't bring herself to say the words aloud, but that's what she believes. That I'm a killer, or that I hired one."

"Did you?"

Milligan allowed himself a faint smile. "What do you think?"

"I just met you," I said. "But so far I wouldn't rule it out."

"Goddammit, Thorn," Rusty said, "back off."

Milligan reached out and gave me a hearty clap on the shoulder.

"That's a good one, Thorn. You're a ballsy son of a bitch. Must be the Milligan in you."

Rusty stood aside and shook her head slowly as though she wasn't sure what she'd just witnessed. She wasn't alone.

On the way out of the restaurant, I caught Sugar's eye. What he saw written in my face caused him to nod twice. In all our years of friendship, I'd never asked for Sugar's professional help. But now, without a word passing between us, I'd just engaged him to investigate my grandmother's death.

CHAPTER SEVEN

The night sky was bristling with stars as I headed the Mother-ship west out the Intracoastal to the intersection with the Yacht Channel, then turned north by northwest and ran outside of Sprigger Bank, Schooner Bank, and Oxford, then past Sandy Key.

I watched our slow progress on the GPS screen, a green arrow plowing through the quiet black sheen. From the galley just below the wheelhouse I could hear the laughter, Milligan amusing Annette, and Annette amusing back. Rusty's coughing chuckles. She was getting a little drunk. The stress of the trip, the unforeseen tension at dinner.

I looked out at the water. The cone of light from the overhead spot shone on the calm seas. On our starboard side a dolphin rolled, basking in the foamy wake. Then another smaller dolphin appeared beside him, two slick shiny creatures hitching a brief ride, tickling their hides in the artificial surf. The twin Mercury outboards were running smooth. Four hundred and fifty horses pushed the big barge at a cruising speed of nine knots, which would make it a ten-hour haul to our anchorage.

It was a journey I'd made countless times, in good weather and foul, outrunning storms and sometimes overtaken and slammed. Many times I'd motored my ancient Chris-Craft up this way, cruising slowly with a variety of friends, male and female. Days of sun and rum and fresh grilled fish, swimming naked in the transparent waters. Nights lying flat on the deck watching constellations wheel across the sky, trying to absorb the magnitude of the heavens, our tiny place in it all. The ache of longing to say the unsayable. Hours touching the flesh of lovers, being touched. The rambling talk, the beer, the wine, the bad jokes. Our laughter echoing across the empty waters. I'd stashed some good memories along nearly every mile of that route.

Beyond Sandy Key, up to Cape Sable, then Middle Cape, Northwest Cape, past Big Sable Creek, into Ponce de Leon Bay, and into the marked channel of the Little Shark River. The Shark was a complicated river system with multiple mouths, several of them dead ends, but I knew every turn. South through Oyster Bay, through Cormorant Pass and into Whitewater Bay where tomorrow around dawn we'd ease into the side bay along the western edge of Whitewater that bordered Joe River.

The unofficial name of the cove was "Cardiac," so christened because years before a tarpon guide friend of mine lost a client there to a heart attack. Among my buddies the name was meant as both respectful and a dark joke. What a perfect place, and a perfect way to go, a giant tarpon jumping three feet in the air. The line tight, the heart seizing up.

Cardiac Bay was a comfortable spot, protected from the wind, with a good rocky bottom that would hold the anchor. By the time we arrived there Teeter would be cooking breakfast.

After the anchor was set, I was planning to head to my cabin for a nap while the others woke and dressed and ate breakfast. I'd sleep for an hour, then when everyone was fed, we'd head out, take the two skiffs and four anglers north into the labyrinth, using our laminated photograph.

Rusty would go her way and I'd already picked the spot I wanted to explore. Three lakes joined by narrow channels. About a half mile of mangroves to fight through, but once inside, if the photograph wasn't lying, we could fish all day in those waters, moving from one lake to another. Could be schools of tarpon back there, snook, redfish, sea trout, or grouper. Since the water was brackish—freshwater coming out of the Everglades mingled with the Gulf's brine—there might even be a few bass. Or there might be nothing at all.

I was going over the day ahead, the fishing. Running through the gear we'd need, how best to load my skiff. Trying to occupy my mind, though now and then as I shifted my feet, swaying with the rock of the Mothership, I could feel the weight of the snapshot in my shirt pocket.

I wasn't ready to examine it yet. I wanted the voices down below to die out—for the party to break up and for everyone to head off to their cabins. When they were all asleep, I'd take another look at the young blond country girl with the strong features and the wide shoulders. At the two older folks sitting on their front porch. I'd study the image and try to extract details I'd missed on my first two looks. I'd try to read my mother's face, my grandmother's. I was girding myself for that.

I gazed out at the darkness, a long narrow path of flickering moonlight on the flat seas. A single vessel glided along the horizon, a slow-going sailboat under power.

The Mothership was handling well, a big lazy vessel, slow and sloppy through the turns, but stable and smooth on a straight heading.

On impulse, I plucked the photograph from my pocket and laid it on the console before me. The low lights provided just enough illumination to read charts without throwing a glare on the windows, enough light to see the photo. But I didn't look. It lay there on the flat dash beside the throttle levers.

I shifted my hands on the wheel, nudged us a few degrees north, heading into a light breeze and a few quartering swells. With the forward motion of the Mothership combined with the freshening breeze, there was probably a fifteen-knot wind out on the decks.

I reached through the side window to check, and the rush of air pushed against my open hand. I was starting to regret asking for Sugar's help. This was none of my business. An old woman's drowning, a granddaughter's fury and grief. These people were strangers. They had nothing to do with the life I'd shaped for myself, or this new course I'd set. Some accident of flesh and blood connected us, perhaps, but that was all. No cause to become entangled in their poisonous affairs.

Without looking at it again, I picked up the photo and held it out the side window. Pinched between thumb and finger, it fluttered in the wind and the rattling noise it made was carried off into the darkness. I held it there for several moments, working up the resolve to let it go.

"You sure about that?" Mona had entered the wheelhouse from the starboard door. She moved across the cabin to stand near me. "Just toss it away like you can't stomach it? Is that who you are? Some chickenshit?"

I looked at her through the dim light, then drew in my arm and set the photo back on the console.

She gave a dry laugh.

"Daniel Oliver Thorn," she said. "My famous cousin."

"My name is Thorn."

"Yeah, yeah. Okay, Thorn. Tough guy extraordinaire."

"What the hell do you know about me?"

"A good deal more than you know about me."

She picked up the photograph and took a long look. Her clothes gave off the scent of sweat-soaked leather with a faint undertone of wood smoke, as though she'd been sitting around a campfire all evening after a hard day on horseback. She shifted her feet and brushed her hip against mine then stepped a few inches out of range. The contact wasn't accidental. As if she was grazing me as cats do to leave their scent, mark their territory.

Mona laid the photo back on the console and stared out the windshield into the cone of light, the slapping seas. The dolphins were gone.

"You think I'm a self-absorbed bitch. That's your first impression."

"Actually, I haven't given it a lot of thought."

She was silent for a while, staring ahead into the darkness.

"That's us, huh? The green arrow." She tapped the GPS screen.

When I didn't reply, she laughed again, though there was no humor in it.

"I guess it should be reassuring. A device to tell you where you are. Never get lost again. A blinking arrow. Blink, blink. Now any idiot can find their way through the wilderness. Just follow the arrow."

"There's more to knowing where you are than that."

"Oh, is there? Are we getting philosophical?"

I reached for the toggle and turned off the GPS. I flicked the main control switch and the instrument panel also went dark.

"You wanted to talk about something?"

I could feel her staring at me, but I didn't turn her way.

"She was murdered. Grandmother was murdered."

"Why?"

"Why do I believe it, or why was she murdered?"

"Your choice."

"Same answer for both," Mona said. "Family business."

"And what's that?"

"What're you, drunk? It came up at dinner. Bates International."

"Never heard of it."

"Yeah, yeah, Thorn, the hermit. No radio, no TV, no Internet. Gets all his news from pressing conch shells to his ear."

"Why don't you go back below? Give your contempt the rest of the night off."

Mona raised her hands to her temples and combed her fingers back through her tangled hair, then lifted the mass off her neck for a moment before letting it drop. The movement released another cloud of scent into the wheelhouse, the sharp musk of her flesh after a long day of travel, wine, and sweat mingled with a quirky blend of spices that must have been her body's aromatic signature. Something like a strong green tea spiked with citrus.

"You have a road map up here?"

I didn't reply.

"A map, a Florida road map."

"We don't have much use for road maps out on the water."

"Where would it be if you had one?"

I flipped on the console lights and drew open the chart drawer.

Mona pawed through the stash and after a minute, to my surprise, came up with a folded Florida map. She opened it on the console, flattened it and refolded it so only the center of the state was exposed. No Panhandle, no South Florida.

"You have a quarter, Thorn?"

"A quarter?"

"Twenty-five cents. A coin."

I checked our position, scanned the darkness for passing vessels. No more lights out there tonight. Everyone safely back on land, watching TV, reading their kid a story, doing what ordinary people do. We were still holding steady on our north-by-northwest course, heading into increasing sets of swells.

I dug a quarter from the change in my pocket and held it out.

Mona plucked the coin from my palm and laid it on the map. She positioned it just east of Sarasota and a few degrees north, then tapped it a fraction farther east and looked at me.

"Bates International," she said. "Or one of its many subsidiaries."

"What are you talking about?"

"Almost every square mile under that coin. The land, the rivers, the streams, the ranches, the pinelands. What Bates doesn't own isn't worth owning."

"So?"

"Abigail Bates, your grandmother, was the second-largest landowner in the state. The sweet hot center of Florida belongs to our family. Put that in your seashell, beach boy."

I stared at the map, the glittering coin, the thousands of square miles it covered. Not as much land as St. Joe Paper Company controlled, or Barron Collier in his prime. Both owned close to a million acres of the state. If Mona was correct, Bates International's property looked to be less than half that. Still, it was a vast chunk.

Over the years I'd driven through the region many times.

Had friends who'd grown up there, most of whom fled as soon as they could. It was tough terrain. Orange groves, cattle ranges, some light farming. Raw and brown and harsh, full of sandspurs and armadillos and vultures. A few gorgeous rivers twisted through the countryside, a little shade here and there, some pastureland.

Mulberry, Pierce, Brewster, Ft. Green, Ona, Wauchula, Bowling Green, Pine Level, Fort Lonesome. The hard-luck towns were usually composed of little more than an aging gas station, a Food Mart, and three or four churches. Mobile homes scattered through the piney woods. Some prefab houses and the occasional rotting remnants of pioneer homesteads with a chimney rising from rubble. Here and there was one of those fifties ranch styles holding sway on a promontory, where the boss man lived. The rough narrow roads that crisscrossed that area shot like bullets straight through the countryside, flat and mostly empty. It was mining country, phosphate. Big ugly pits gouged deep into the Florida prairies.

Not exactly primo real estate, and not the Florida landscape that most stirred my heart, but it had a rugged dignity. And some of the folks I'd met up there had much in common with the dwindling supply of old salts who settled the Keys. Both had cracker toughness and a hard-shell self-reliance. People who'd give you their last crust of bread or could turn mean as a rattler if the occasion required. Hard-eyed men and women without patience for frills or blather.

"So your grandmother was a cattle baron."

"She was your grandmother, too."

"If so," I said, "that's only a technicality."

"She's a blood relation. Nothing technical about it."

Mona handed me my quarter and I dropped it into my pocket. She refolded the map and put it back in the drawer. I flipped off the lights and stared out into the darkness. The Mothership was riding more smoothly through the rollers than I would have imagined. Not rough seas by any means, but rougher than any we'd tested her against.

"Okay, so why are you here?" I said. "What snake oil you selling?"

"Took you a while to get around to that."

"I assume you didn't come for the fishing."

I was quiet, steering the big boat, rocking easily through the weather. Waiting for her to accept my challenge.

Mona took a grip of one of the throttle levers, holding it as though she were trying to sense the power of the engine it controlled.

"Until Grandmother died, no one knew you existed. Not until we opened the lockbox at the Summerland Planters Bank. You had a whole box to yourself. Life and times of Daniel Oliver Thorn. Newspaper clippings, your sordid escapades, some of the shit you've stepped in. That's how we tracked you down. We ran a computer search. A few hits is all we got, but one linked with this houseboat deal. A fishing guide named Thorn, your photo on Rusty's website. There was a family likeness, Dad called Rusty, asked some questions, and bingo, you were the guy. We decided this would be a good way to get to know you. See where you stood on things."

As I spoke the words, I regretted them. "What things?"

"What do you know about phosphate mining?"

In the ghostly glow of the instrument lights I stared at her profile.

You couldn't live in Florida all your life without knowing about phosphate. That it was bigger than citrus, bigger than sugar, nearly as big as Disney. I knew that great, monstrous machines called draglines tore open pits in the Florida earth, scraping away what was referred to as "the overburden" to get down to the strata of gray rock. When they exhausted one cavernous pit, they abandoned the land, leaving it mutilated and useless, and moved on to repeat the process nearby.

I knew that foul and corrosive chemicals were used to turn phosphate into fertilizer and that huge barges loaded with the processed mineral headed off to China every day from the port of Tampa. And other barges headed out into the Gulf to dump millions of gallons of acidic sludge from phosphate production. I knew that phosphate bosses wielded such clout that every politician in the history of Florida had protected the industry from meaningful oversight. That some of the poorest people in the state mined the stuff and made some of the richest people in the world even wealthier.

I also knew that Florida's supply was nearly depleted. The earth was a ruthless bookkeeper and the arithmetic was brutally clear. Millions of years to forge the mineral, a few decades to plunder it, and eons to heal the damage.

"Forget it," I said. "This has nothing to do with me."

"Oh, but it does."

"Listen to me. I'm taking you people fishing. That's all I'm doing. I'm not interested in a family reunion. Some touchy-feely bullshit. Is that clear?"

Mona slid across the wheelhouse, stepped out the starboard door, and stood on the narrow deck. Wind twisted through her hair as she faced into the darkness. After a minute, she leaned back into the stillness of the cabin.

"Like it or not, Thorn, you're a member of this family. Better start getting used to the idea."

CHAPTER EIGHT

For the next hour I steered the vessel through slapping seas. Rusty came up to ask if I was okay. I said I was just fine. She admitted she was a little wobbly and needed to hit the sack, but whenever I was ready for her to relieve me, just come shake her and she'd take the helm.

"And, Thorn, goddammit, don't let this spin out of control."

"I'll do what I can."

She looked at my profile for a while, then said, "You must've had one hell of a past life."

"Why's that?"

"'Cause the karma kickback you're getting this time around is brutal."

I was silent. Nothing to argue with there.

"I don't know how Sugar puts up with your shit."

"He's a saint."

"Well, I'm not."

She stood beside me for several minutes, watching the darkness roll by.

"In fact, I'm toying with the idea of turning this baby around. Refund their money and call it a day. It's got disaster written all over it."

"Your boat, your call."

She stood there a minute more, a little shaky, hands on the console.

"You put a picture of me on your website?"

She patted me on the back. "Guilty as charged."

"Why?"

"What's the problem, I blow your cover? Hey, everybody's face is on the freaking Web. It's no big deal. I thought you looked rugged. It was a business decision. Like it or not, some people are suspicious of women fishing guides. They're so used to the manly-man thing. You fit the bill."

"Manly-man? You're shitting me."

Her hand moved off my back and she gripped my chin, bringing my face around. Without hesitation, she kissed me, her lips going soft, mouth relaxing. I could taste the sharp musk of marijuana on her breath. Out on the walkway she must've snuck a few quick hits to quiet her nerves.

I released the wheel and turned to her. She drew tighter against me and in an instant the years since our last kiss dissolved. Her fingers snaked into my hair, taking hold, and she levered us closer. Then she hooked her right leg around my left and wedged her crotch against mine, crushing hard.

I was staggered for a moment, then just as I began to relax, to sink away into the kiss, she broke the hold with a gasp and stumbled back. Her eyes were red and watering. She rubbed the taste of me off her lips with the back of her hand and looked out at the night and shook her head.

"I made a mistake," she said.

"It's okay," I said. "It never happened."

"Not about this, no." She wouldn't look at me. "About leaving you back then. Walking out. All that Dark Prince bullshit."

"We're going fishing, Rusty. That's what we're doing out here. You're running a business. I'm going to throw some bait into a virgin lake. Anything else, anything personal, we can deal with when we get back. Okay?"

"God," she said. "What next?"

And she tottered off to her cabin.

It shared a wall with mine and was just behind the wheelhouse. We each had our own head, and enough room in the cabin to stretch both arms out without touching the walls. Comfortable single bunks with solid mattresses.

When she was gone, I turned down the console lights and checked the horizon again for boat traffic. Still clear out there.

Five minutes later, maybe ten, when my pulse finally settled, I angled the photo of my mother and her younger brother into the glow of the chart lights.

My mother was no more than eighteen at the time. She wore a simple flowered sundress that was just tight enough to reveal the ample swell of her figure. From the tilt of her head and the angle of her stance, I read that she was pulling away from the touch of her brother, John. Then I noticed the hand on her shoulder had one finger hooked under the strap of her dress. Hard to tell if the gesture was merely teasing or outright invasive. Either way it made my stomach squirm.

Young John had a jaunty look, a man with no respect for boundaries of the flesh, probably any other boundaries. A cocky superiority gleamed in his smile. My mother seemed to be suffering his brashness with a practiced patience.

Perhaps I was simply transferring to this teenage kid from long ago my aversion to the grown-up Milligan. But as I studied the image further, it was hard to miss my mother's stiffness, her tilt away from her kid brother's clinch, that possessive finger. As if neither the photograph nor the embrace had been her idea. She was bullied into it and was doing her best to be a good sport.

For the first time I noticed a bow made of fat ribbons fastened to the hood ornament of the Ford coupe behind them. So the car was probably a gift, a birthday or high school graduation present, and the reason for the photo was to memorialize Elizabeth Milligan's first ride.

I worked the math in my head and, as best as I could figure, shortly after that photo had been taken, that coupe was to become her getaway car. The vehicle she and my father, Quentin, would use to speed away down the dusty roads of central Florida, carting their worldly goods off to the Keys.

For all I knew it was the same car they'd driven that night when they brought their baby son home from the hospital. A dark night, along a narrow stretch where the only escape from the speeding headlights of a drunk driver was for Quentin Thorn to jerk the wheel hard to the right and sail that Ford into Lake Surprise, where the young parents slammed against the dashboard. Knocked unconscious, they drowned in only five feet of water, and I, less than a day old, catapulted from my mother's arms, bounced off the windshield, and wound up in the rear seat wedged atop her suitcase, just high enough above the rising water to survive.

All I could make out of my grandparents in the background of the photograph, sitting on the porch, were their stern profiles and straight-backed postures. They were dressed formally as though for church, he in a stiff white shirt and string tie, she in a high-necked white blouse. She appeared to be speaking and he was listening, his head tipped slightly in her direction. The words that passed between them looked to be weighty. Their dour moods radiated from every detail of dress and posture and facial expression. The photograph had captured a tense moment in a tense household where only one member, young John, seemed either oblivious or indifferent to the strain.

I switched off the chart lights and took a few deep breaths. There was something wrong in this family, something grating and off-center. It had existed in that ancient photograph and it still existed. Maybe tomorrow in daylight when I re-examined the picture that tension would disappear. But I doubted it. More likely in full light there would be even more strain visible. If I had the stomach to study it further.

I stared into the darkness. It was cool and the breeze was growing fresher as we moved farther from the glow of civilization into the dark core of the wilderness. Normally when I made this journey I felt a tingle of exhilaration as we approached the Everglades. It was a homecoming. A return to islands and bays, rookeries and flats and marshes and twisty mangrove channels that had always managed to realign my internal compass no matter how far I'd strayed off course. But not tonight.

I toggled on the GPS to make sure of our position. Without

it, at that moment, even in those familiar waters, I would have been lost.

Sasha Olsen shinnied up the metal pipe all the way to the edge of the roof, snipped the phone line, slid down, walked back to the pickup, and got in.

Griffin came out of the shadows, bent forward to the open window, his breath rattling in his throat. He backhanded his mouth, wiped away the slime.

"Wear your seat belt," he said.

"Hate seat belts. Air bag should be enough."

"Mama, if you get a concussion or break a leg, the whole deal is over. Fasten your seat belt. Don't get all insane on me."

"Screw sane," she said. "What did sane ever do for me?"

Out on the highway, headlights flew past. Then blackness again.

"Shit," he said. "Can't both of us be insane. I got there first."

Sasha had to laugh. Her beautiful son making gallows jokes. She pulled the shoulder harness down, snapped it into place. To keep the faith, the bargain they'd struck. Two righteous avengers off on a road trip.

"Don't make it complicated," Griffin said. "This is a good thing. You know that. You know in your heart. Sacrifice a few for the good of the many. No doubts, no second thoughts. Head of the snake."

"Step back, son. I'm ready to rip."

She sent the window up, fired the engine, sat in the glow of dashboard lights. Griffin stood there a moment, then stooped forward and planted a kiss on the window glass. Left a bloody lip print.

She watched him move into the darkness, then Sasha gunned the V-8, edged the tach toward redline, filling the night with horsepower. She put her hand on the shifter.

Revved the engine higher, then higher still, and racked it into gear. Zero to whatever, screaming for the barred front doors of the gun shop.

Fuck a bunch of concussions.

CHAPTER NINE

Sugarman never called anyone after 10 P.M. unless it was an emergency. He'd been on the receiving end of late-night phone calls and knew how jangling they were.

But after the dinner at Pierre's, he'd gone back to his office, wired by the evening's events, especially that parting look Thorn shot him. "Do this for me," it said. "Just this once."

Sugar had logged onto the Net and for the last hour he'd been reading about Abigail Bates. Starting on the day her body was discovered by a passing kayaker, he'd worked forward, article by article. The early news accounts were thin on detail. An investigation had been conducted by the local sheriff of DeSoto County, someone named Timmy Whalen. The only statement by Whalen that Sugar could locate in his Lexis search was vague at best: "At this time we have no reason to suspect foul play, but we're leaving no stone unturned. Anyone with information concerning the death of Mrs. Bates should contact the office of the sheriff."

Sugarman would've left it there, waited a week till Thorn got back from his Everglades trip, except for a detail in a follow-up story two weeks after Abigail Bates's drowning: "Local canoe outfitter, Charles M. Kipling, Jr., was released from custody after being held for five days as a material witness in the drowning death of Abigail Bates. Mr. Kipling's attorney, Price Hargrove, said his client was cooperating fully with the investigation and had been cleared of any suspicion. Mr. Kipling was taken into custody after two women from nearby Sarasota came forward with claims they had witnessed a violent encounter between Mr. Kipling and Mrs. Bates on the day of her death. Both women, who asked not to be identified, admitted they were surprised and disappointed in the sheriff's decision, but refused further comment on Mr. Kipling's release."

A violent encounter. A suspect let go. Nothing definitive, but it sent a prickle across Sugarman's shoulders. Maybe Mona Milligan knew something after all. Small-town cover-ups happened every day.

When he pushed further back, broadened his search to the months and years before her death, looking for anything on Abigail Bates or Bates International, that's when his heart began to rev and his focus tightened.

Bates International was a Fortune 500 company. Originally based in tiny Summerland, Florida, its corporate headquarters was now in nearby Sarasota, with branch offices in Manhattan, Chicago, Paris, and Beijing, and its 139,000 employees scattered across sixty-three countries. Bates International had hundreds of smaller companies sprouting off the corporate trunk. Companies that manufactured fertilizers and a variety of chemicals: vitamin supplements, biofuels, processed grains, oil seeds, feed ingredients to farmers and livestock producers, corn milling, a range of sweeteners like malitol, sorbitol. Oil and gas leases, mining, drilling. Marketing and trading electricity. Pig farms, dairy farms, cattle ranches, vast corn farms. Poultry- and meat-processing plants. A food giant with its fingers in dozens of lucrative pies.

Estimated earnings of 67 billion the previous year. A personal net worth that put Abigail Bates at number fourteen among the wealthiest Americans.

She was also a member of the Business Round Table, an innocuous-sounding organization that required more Googling. Turned out the Round Table was composed of 120 CEO's of America's most powerful companies. The group met three times a year to discuss governmental policy and put forth recommendations. Position papers that lobbied Congress and the White House for certain business objectives. Though Sugar paid little attention to business affairs or national politics, even he recognized a dozen names on the Round Table list.

This wasn't some old lady in a canoe.

Sugarman would bet there was a smaller round table in some penthouse somewhere. Just three or four people. They didn't put out papers and they didn't do press releases. He knew it was a corny conspiracy view, something left over from reading Ayn Rand at an impressionable age. But it was a lifelong suspicion that at the top of the pyramid three or four people were calling the shots, nudging the world's center of gravity this way or that for reasons only they understood. If that was true, then Abigail Bates was the kind of person who'd be in that penthouse suite. She might even sit at the head of the table.

The prickle became a bloom of belly heat. Thorn's newly discovered grandmother was one of America's elite. The small-town sheriff in charge of the investigation had dismissed the only suspect, a man who'd had a violent encounter with the deceased. Six months later, two members of Abigail Bates's family appeared suddenly, ready to take a voyage on Rusty Stabler's houseboat. As they came aboard, Abigail Bates's son announced to Thorn: I'm your uncle John. Your granny is dead.

Sugar paused a moment and tracked back through the articles. One thing had snagged his attention. Minor point, perhaps.

The different surnames confused him. Abigail Bates's son was named Milligan. It took Sugar another ten minutes combing through databases and websites before he got the answer. In a rare interview with an academic business journal, Abigail explained that she'd held on to her daddy's name out of respect for his legacy. Leopold Witherspoon Bates. A cattle rancher, and the son of Leopold senior, the family patriarch. Leopold senior was a pioneer cattleman who in his ninety years had amassed a vast herd that roamed over thousands of square miles in central Florida, land he'd accumulated when that part of the state went for pennies an acre.

John Milligan and Thorn's mother, Elizabeth, the kids of Abigail Bates and Edwin Andrew Milligan, took their daddy's name. Mother Bates, Daddy Milligan. But it was Bates land and Bates cattle and the Bates ancestry and empire building that was the backbone of the modern-day Milligan family.

At eleven-thirty Sugar dialed the home number for Deputy Rachel Pike of the Monroe County Sheriff's Office. Twenty years earlier they'd both joined the department the same month and had survived their rookie year in large part by sharing their daily trials at breakfast each morning at Craig's Diner. Friends ever since. Even with Sugar spending the last decade freelancing in private law enforcement, and Rachel sticking it out in the public sector, rising slowly but steadily through the ranks, they'd kept the lines open.

Rachel snapped up the phone on the second ring.

"What's up, Sugar?"

Sugarman faltered for a moment. He still wasn't used to caller ID, the edge it gave to the person answering the phone.

"Nothing major," Sugar said. "Well, all right, it might be major. It's a Thorn thing."

"What's the idiot gotten into now?"

"This isn't his fault. Something happened. Asteroid out of the blue."

"It's never his fault. The poor guy."

Sugarman explained the deal, concise but detailed. When he was done, Rachel was silent.

"You don't buy it? Your Geiger's not clicking?"

"Oh, it's clicking," she said. "For one thing, what's a lady that age doing in a canoe by herself?"

"That's a question."

"And what causes a violent confrontation between some young guy and an eighty-six-year-old woman?"

"Another thing I'd like to know."

"A woman with that kind of power and influence, why didn't I hear about it, why wasn't it front-page news?"

"It got coverage in the big papers—*Miami Herald, New*

York Times, Boston, Washington—back in the business section mostly," Sugar said. "Seems Bates International doesn't court publicity."

"And with a VIP like her, Sheriff Timmy is running the show? No big guns from outside?"

"Yeah, I was curious about that. Didn't turn up anything about the Feds being involved, or FDLE, or anybody higher up than DeSoto County Sheriff's Department. That's another thing I'd like to ask in person."

Rachel was quiet for a moment. In the background there was a clinking noise that sounded ceramic, like she was brewing tea.

"And if the Milligans wanted to contact Thorn, why not pick up a phone? Why the surprise attack? Go for a week on a boat out in the Everglades, all isolated. What's that about?"

"Thorn wondered the same thing."

"Okay, granted, something's peculiar. I wouldn't bet my house on it being criminal, but it's worth a sniff. What can I do?"

"Maybe a phone call."

"Sheriff Timmy?"

"Yeah, like prepare the ground. Invoke professional courtesy. Tell him I'm working for a member of the Bates family. Which is true."

"Small-town cop to small-town cop, put the moves on him."

"A little sweet talk. That voice you use on the sheriff when he's pissed."

"You noticed that?"

"Oh, yeah. That's one hell of a soothing purr. You got that down."

"Maybe Timmy's a sexist. He doesn't like lady cops. That happens."

"I got confidence in you. If I could get a look at any evidence reports, prints, fiber, fingerprints, medical examiner's testimony. Those eyewitnesses, their names. You know, the basics."

"You don't want much."

"Whatever you can do, Rachel."

"Calling me this late, why the hurry?"

"I'm thinking I'll drive up tonight, get busy on it first thing tomorrow."

More clinking. Then he heard her sipping and setting down the mug.

"One other thing."

"Let me guess. You want me to run somebody through the National Crime computer?"

"Actually three people."

"Let me get a pencil."

Sugarman gave her the name he'd discovered in his research, the suspect who'd been let go: Charles M. Kipling, Jr. And John Milligan and his daughter, Mona. Priors, DUI's, anything that popped up could be interesting. After a little good-natured resistance, Rachel agreed.

"You settle things with the pilot over his daughter?" she asked. "That legal mess."

"Our lawyers are hashing it out."

"So this is a good time to be out of town. Change of scenery."

"Exactly."

"Plus Thorn is your buddy."

"He is that."

"Even though he's almost got you killed a few times."

"He means well."

"Funny you should call, Sugar. I was thinking about you just today."

"Yeah?"

She laughed. A throaty, full-bodied sound. "Don't get in a sweat. I'm not hitting on you. I was thinking of you in a strictly professional sense."

"You need a private investigator?"

"No, we've got an opening. A couple of grades up from your old job."

Sugar was silent, looking at the walls of his shabby office. Rent due next week. His in-box empty. Out-box the same.

"So, does the silence indicate you're considering it?"

Sugarman sighed.

"I'm kind of used to making my own hours. Coming and going."

"Just thought I'd mention it. Sheriff always liked you. A lot of people around the department think highly of you. Include me on that list."

"Okay, Rachel. I will. I'll think about it."

"So I'll call Timmy tomorrow morning. Purr in the good ol' boy's ear."

"Thanks, Rachel."

"And you think about that job. I looked through the candidate files, and, just between you and me, totally off-the-record, I think you'd have a damn good shot."

After Sugar hung up he sat at his desk and looked around his office for a while, listening to the late-night traffic out on U.S. 1. Somewhere down the highway a siren whooped once—a traffic stop—probably some drunk racing back to Miami, jigged when he should've jogged. He thought of that world—a paycheck every two weeks, the routines, the camaraderie—versus the job he had now, chasing down runaway girls who were pissed off when they were found.

For some reason a poem popped into his head, something from a million years ago in high school English. Two paths diverging in the woods. And he remembered the guy decided to take the one less traveled. Was that the right decision? Going down the weedy path, not the trampled one?

He sat for a while longer thinking about the poem, about paths in the woods, weedy ones and clear ones. Something to talk over with Thorn. Though he knew what Thorn would say: Why the hell take either path? Forge off into the vines and brambles, that's where the cool stuff was.

Sugar locked his office, got in his car, and drove back to his house to pack an overnight bag. It was four or five hours up to Summerland. He could be there by dawn.

CHAPTER TEN

At 3 A.M., without a word, Rusty tapped me on the shoulder and relieved me at the wheel. I went to my cabin, set the photograph face-down on the tiny dresser, and fell into my bunk and into a sleep full of armadillos and leathery crackers on horseback riding through scrubland so gray and desiccated it looked like a desert on some distant moon. There was no story to my dream, nothing I remembered when I woke at 6, just a jittery assortment of disconnected images of harsh people living in an even harsher landscape.

I showered, dressed, slathered sunscreen on my legs and the rest of my exposed flesh, then climbed down the ladder to the main deck.

Teeter was at work in the galley. He wore a tall red chef's hat and white chef's jacket with red piping, white, stiffly pressed pants and a red apron, and a bright red scarf knotted around his throat. He was moving with an unhurried economy, sliding from one dish to another, tending several simmering pans, three bubbling pots, sprinkling, stirring, adding ingredients. Aromas like no breakfast I had ever inhaled. One look, and I knew Teeter had gone overboard. Beyond overboard.

"Where's the roast pig?"

He shook his head several times. Irony wasn't one of his conversational skills. He used a pair of tongs to move a half-dozen kielbasa sausages out of the skillet onto a warming tray.

Every countertop, tabletop, side table, and even the bar was covered with plates of food.

"Did we get some new arrivals last night?" I said. "An army, maybe?"

He shook his head again. The red chef's hat was nearly a foot tall and pleated on the sides. It wobbled as Teeter filled a platter with Belgian waffles and set it beside another plate stacked with Swedish pancakes. There were flaky fruit-filled pastries of every size. Bowls of applesauce and jellies and jams. A dozen beautifully fried crab fritters. Cinnamon rolls, biscuits, a serving dish of oatmeal with blackberries on top, a pot of cheese grits, French toast, lemon bread, strawberry crepes, bacon, Canadian bacon, three different types of sausage, bagels, blueberry muffins, a large iced bowl of shrimp cocktail. The omelet pan was greased, and bowls of diced mushrooms, grated cheese, scallions, and jalapeño peppers stood ready beside the stove. A large warming tray was full of scrambled eggs sprinkled with spices I couldn't identify.

"People get hungry out on the water," Teeter said, when I looked up from taking inventory. "Breakfast is the most important meal."

"There's only seven of us," I said.

"You think I overdid it?" His eyes were misting. He ducked his head with a flash of shame.

"No, it looks great, Teeter. Just great."

"I made everybody's lunch, too," he said, still looking down at the deck. "In the coolers. Sandwiches and cookies. Some fruit tarts with special icing."

"Above and beyond the call, Teeter."

I knew exactly the capacity of our refrigerators and ice chests and was fairly sure without even taking a look that Teeter had depleted the larder by at least a quarter on this one meal alone. We had twenty-odd meals to go before we were scheduled to return to civilization.

Replenishing our provisions would require a two-hour boat ride back to the public ramps at Flamingo; then, assuming I could hitch a ride, it was at least another hour to a decent food market. A six-hour round-trip. It was possible some of the food he'd just prepared would keep for tomorrow's breakfast or a meal later in the day. But even then we would be stretched impossibly thin.

The fishing on this trip was supposed to be catch and release, but now we'd have to reconsider that—possibly do a little meat fishing. Or else cut the whole expedition short by several days.

I was running through the choices when Rusty entered.

She surveyed the feast, walking quietly through the galley, past the bar, circling the long table for eight that was jammed with food. Nodding her head, saying nothing. I saw her swallow a couple of times as she made the same calculations I'd just made.

"Thorn," she said. "Could you blow reveille and get everybody up? I'd like to be on the water by eight."

"And this?"

She gazed around at the food and smiled.

"I'm having a mushroom omelet with cheese grits and bacon," she said. "And those fruit pastries look yummy. Better get our anglers out here before I eat this all up."

But when she looked at me, her eyes were not as nonchalant as her words, silently acknowledging that we'd have to make radical adjustments to our plans, but now was not the time to sort it out. Her concern for her brother's state of mind trumped all practicalities. It was a transaction she must have made a thousand times over the years, and it came so naturally to her, the empathy and forgiveness, the flexibility in the face of disaster, that I felt a rush of admiration for her that stirred some echo of the passion we shared long ago.

I rapped on each cabin door and woke the others, and in twenty minutes they'd assembled in the galley and were digging into the banquet. Fortunately every one of our group was a breakfast eater, and Teeter was right about appetites being stimulated out on the water. Still, even though we did our best, and John Milligan and Holland both had seconds and I managed thirds on the scrambled eggs, we barely put a dent in all that food.

The tensions of the night before had cooled, and everyone, even Mona, complimented Teeter on his extraordinary culinary creations. An unpracticed smile surfaced on Teeter's lips that was touching in its awkwardness. As it was to turn out, that meal would be the last festive occasion we would enjoy.

"Hell's Bay is back that way. Real shallow, but damn good fishing." Sasha waved eastward, then motioned north. "Camp Lonesome's over there. Not really a camp, just a chickee at the end of a little narrow dock."

Griffin nodded, then his eyes followed the flight of a great blue heron, but he said nothing. He'd been quiet for the last hour. Now and then a hacking cough convulsed his emaciated frame, and always there was the wet rattling in his chest. His eyes were the faint gray of rain. They were working the distances like he was searching for some truth hidden in the dawn light or the patches of mist edging the mangroves.

Sasha had been taking it slow, just fast enough to keep the boat on plane, giving Griffin the tour. No reason to hurry. They'd used the ramp at Flamingo, motored up the Wilderness Waterway into Coot Bay, then took Tarpon Creek into Whitewater Bay, that big sprawling expanse with mangrove islands in every direction. The GPS was set, red arrow steering them toward the coordinates.

25 degrees 17' 17" N Latitude
80 degrees 59' 35" W Longitude

About a half hour away.

Their craft was a yellow Skeeter with a 150-horse Merc outboard, twenty-footer, about a ten- to eleven-inch draft, fifteen hundred pounds, maybe as much as seventeen hundred. Brand-new. On open water, a vessel like that would fly, outrun most flats boats and backcountry skiffs. But Sasha knew it wasn't the ideal boat for the super-shallow waters of the Everglades. A backcountry skiff was half the weight of the

Skeeter and could float fine in only four or five inches of water.

But this heavy rig was the best she could find in the boat dealership she'd broken into last night. The Skeeter would have to do.

She had charts and the GPS and a fair recollection of that part of the Glades. Twenty-five years earlier, she and her daddy spent a full week working the creeks and coves out there. Sasha, in her early teens, trying like hell to earn the old man's respect. They'd made the same drive down from Summerland, west across Tamiami Trail, then south on Highway 27 to Florida City, then another hour to the Flamingo ramp, where they put their jon boat in. They'd stayed over in the cabins at the national park. Fished all day, swatted mosquitoes all night. Her father drinking beer, shooting the breeze with the other fishermen, flirting with their wives and girl-friends.

Most memorable moment of that trip was her dad taking her across these same bays up to where the Broad River branched east, then cutting south down a narrow fork into a creek known as the Nightmare, which was navigable only during high tide.

Back then the name was scary to her. Going up a river that could drain away beneath you at low tide and leave you stranded atop a hill of muck and squirming creatures was creepier still. Lose track of time, you could be stuck out there all night, feasted on by mosquitoes, stalked by gators and snakes of every poisonous kind.

"If there ain't no risk," her father liked to say, "can't be no reward."

One afternoon when her dad was reeling fish after fish into the boat, Sasha sat watching the tide ebb, but didn't say a thing for fear of seeming a girly worrywart. Finally her father looked around, threw his rod down, cursed, and grabbed for the crank cord, yanked it half a dozen times, and got only a sputter from the outboard. Sasha felt the terror rise but fought it.

When her old man finally had the motor roaring, the small tributary was turning to solid marsh.

For a half mile they plowed up a trench of mud and dinged the hell out of the propeller, but in the end they made it to the safety of the Broad River. Then sat for a while floating in the deep channel, whooping with relief.

In her mind it was fresh as yesterday. Smell of the salt spray, her father's beer breath, the baloney and mayo in their white bread sandwiches, fish slime on her hands. Sasha learned the ways of men up close, watching him as he decided what risks to take. Her father made no allowances for her being a girl. She knew full well he'd wished for a son, and Sasha tried with all her might to satisfy that desire.

Cruising along in the flashy yellow boat, Sasha could have spent all day picking through the bones of those happy hours, but Grif hauled her back.

"Are those second thoughts I'm seeing in your eyes?"

She shook her head. "Baloney sandwiches," she said. "Me and your grandpa fishing."

"That time on the Nightmare when you nearly got stranded?"

"That time, yeah. How'd you know?"

"Mama, you only got about three stories."

Grif dragged in a gurgling breath and leaned over the side and spat, using his body to block her view of the bloody spume. Trying to spare her.

It was months since the chemo doctor called it quits, but Griffin was hanging on with grim resolve. For weeks, his every inhalation was a gasp. *Stridor* was its medical name. The concluding stages of his cancer. Death clock ticking down.

Since Christmas, his fingers were clubbed, the tips swollen. He fumbled with knife and fork, was ham-fisted in the simplest acts. Worse than any of that, worse even than the ice-pick stabs in chest and spine, was the dyspnea. Air hunger. Her boy was slowly suffocating on his own swelling tissues.

Sasha cut the throttle to neutral, came to his side, but Griffin waved her back. He could handle it. Needed to do this on his own.

He settled his butt against the console, puckered his lips,

drew air through his nose, whistled it out through his crimped mouth the way the Sarasota doctor showed him. He rotated his shoulders. Relaxing his muscles, struggling to loosen the vise crushing his chest.

Sasha stepped back behind the wheel and looked away, giving him what privacy was possible on their small boat.

Rippling across the bay, a dawn breeze stirred an island of mangroves in the east, a breeze as lush as the rising light, as serene and hushed as a lullaby. The oxygen-rich flood teased the bay into ripples and briefly lifted Sasha's heavy black hair from her shoulders.

Fresh crisp air. Though to Griffin, choking and coughing, it might just as well have been the black fumes of burning tires.

"I may need to take a rest," he said.

She cut the engine, unrolled his sleeping bag on the deck, and made a pillow from a flowered bath towel. Griffin eased down. Lately, each time he drifted into a nap, she worried this would be the sleep that lasted.

He smiled at her, blew her a kiss, held her eyes for a second, then settled into a fetal curl.

CHAPTER ELEVEN

At half past eight, Annette and Holland were still loading their bulky gear into Rusty's skiff, when Mona, John, and I pushed off from the Mothership.

I was wearing khaki shorts and my lucky shirt. A blue cotton button-down I'd inherited from Doctor Bill. His initials were embroidered on the cuffs. He'd worn it on Sundays or holidays when his hair was spruced and his face shaved and he intended to make a good impression. The shirt had grown threadbare and mostly hung in my closet, but I wore it that morning as my private nod to the stern old gentleman who raised me. And to Kate, his wife, my adoptive mother—for those two were my real folks, the ones who'd spent the hours and offered caring words to guide my way—not this newfound family whose blood had come to me from some reckless mingling I had no inkling of.

John Milligan took a seat on the bench beside me, and Mona perched on the padded ice chest. Neither had anything to say. They chose their places and looked out at the still water, the lazy drifts of herons and egrets and cormorants, and they waited silently as I cast off the mooring lines and started the engine. Though they'd behaved sociably enough at breakfast, they kept their distance from each other. Now, sitting only an arm's length apart, it was clear there was tension, the clinging afterburn of high emotion.

As I idled to a safe distance from the Mothership before hitting the throttle, Milligan turned to me.

"So where we headed?"

"Those lakes I showed you on the photographic chart."

"What are their names?"

Mona craned around to look at the two of us.

"If it has a name," I said, "I'm not much interested in going there."

He nodded sagely and was about to reply, but I flattened the throttle and the sixty-horse Yamaha thrust us forward, pitched up the bow, and in twenty feet we hopped up on plane and were skimming the flat morning waters that were gray and sleek with a faint mist hanging like ancient smoke around the distant mangroves.

I kept the gas full open, going faster than I would ordinarily, faster than would be considered polite. Too fast to talk above the roar of the wind and the flapping clothes.

We had nearly an hour's ride back out the Shark River into Ponce de Leon Bay, then north along the coast past Harney River and the Broad. And I'd decided the best way to handle that long stretch of time alone with my newfound family was to proceed in flat-out silence.

The aged mangroves along the western shore had grown as tall as twenty-year oaks, and all of them along the waterline were solidly brown, dead or dying, blasted by Lance, last summer's category 4 hurricane, which had churned into the Gulf of Mexico and sat for a day over this shallow portion of the Florida Bay. They were tough, resilient plants, and sometimes hurricanes brought new life to mangrove forests by supplying them with a large dose of freshwater. But it wasn't clear yet if these mangroves and the buttonwoods scattered among them would survive the blow, or if it would take years for the new growth to spread from within the marshes to push their dead elders out of the way and reclaim this area with the green and vibrant look it usually had. It might stay brown forever as far as anyone knew.

For miles the devastation stretched along the shoreline until we reached the wide mouth of the Broad River and turned east into its ample expanse. Inside the river channel the mangroves were still green and flourishing, for this area had been considerably less exposed to the hundred-mile-an-hour lashing of that storm.

Mangrove leaves were the cornerstone of the food chain for the region. An acre of mangrove forest shed around four tons of leaves per year. Because the tree is an evergreen, its leaves fell steadily through the twelve-month cycle. That constant supply of decomposing vegetation was broken down by protozoan and bacteria in the brackish water, and the nutrients released became an organic stew of minerals, carbon dioxide, and nitrogenous waste, which in turn provided the food source for worms, snails, crabs, and finger mullet. Those creatures were born and developed to adolescence back in the safe nursery within the mangrove mangle. When they left the protection of the forest, they became the prey for the larger game fish we were seeking that day—tarpon, snook and redfish, sea trout. Ospreys, bald eagles, sharks, and even dolphins also depended on those same crabs and schools of mullet that were a step up the food chain from mangrove leaves.

Mangrove roots acted as filters. Without them skimming out the sediment runoff created by heavy rains inland, the turbidity of the water in the Gulf and around the coral reefs of the Keys would grow so milky that marine life of various kinds, including the reefs themselves, would be in even greater peril than they already were.

Those simple trees, with salt-filtering roots and salt-excreting leaves, were a crucial resource, buffering the land from storms, year by year setting out new roots and expanding the boundaries of the islands and coastlines they protected. To the untrained eye they seemed humble, barely more than weeds, no bright flowers, no towering branches. Simply a dense tangle of slick brown limbs and shiny green leaves.

Mangroves were the forests of my youth. They were my sequoias and my hemlocks and my giant sugar maples. Scrubby vegetation, unlovely, nothing awe-inspiring about them, mangrove forests were frequently thought to be dismal wastelands, mosquito-breeding habitats with no useful purpose. As with much of the Everglades, a sensitive eye was required. Any fool could stand at the rim of the Grand Canyon and experience awe. But the majesty of those low-lying, unvarying mangrove-lined estuaries and bays was far quieter and harder to grasp, which was one of the many reasons why the ever-growing legions of newcomers to the state were so dangerous.

To have an unobstructed view of blue waters, those idiots were eager to raze the lowly mangroves, to call in the bulldozers and dredges and hack them away. Though it was illegal to destroy those crucial trees, in the rare instances a developer was actually caught and fined a few thousand dollars, most of them considered the penalty simply part of the cost of providing their clients a million-dollar vista.

As we entered the Broad River, pelicans and great blue herons broke loose from their perches and circled away from our unnatural racket. When we were safely past, they floated back to their watchtowers in the highest branches of that primordial forest. Our wake sloshed into the warren of roots, agitating the alluvial silt and the rich brew of decomposing vegetation, no doubt jostling whole communities of organisms into radical readjustments, exposing some, hiding others, initiating some new challenge in their never-ending struggle for survival.

The sky was still polished to a faultless blue from the recent cold front, and the air blasting into my face was so oxygen-rich I felt light-headed.

Inside the console, the laminated photographic chart was tucked into the webbed pocket, but I doubted I'd need to consult it. I'd spent so many hours tracing the intricate maze of bays and tributaries, creeks and snaking waterways, each twist and jog of the journey was imprinted into my long-term memory banks.

We were heading directly toward the southernmost tip of mainland Florida, but it was our intention to push as far northward as the winding waterways would allow. Where the water dropped from two feet to one foot, then inch by inch gave way to the muck, then the hard-packed marl and limestone of terra firma.

Just as the Broad River was narrowing to a few dozen feet across, I swung the wheel and carved a sharp path through the tranquil morning water southward, then swung east into the Wood River. The lakes I'd chosen to explore were a few miles east up the Wood. There were no markers back there, no dramatic turns I could use to measure off the distance to the hidden creek that appeared on the photographic chart to be the only possible entry point. So from this moment on, I had to count down each kink in the river's path and measure them against the image in my head, because I suspected that at water level the creek mouth would be all but obscured by mangrove branches.

John Milligan was gazing around at the scenery, his expression set in a solemn pose, as though even he, a man not easily impressed, could not help being stirred by the primal vibrations of the wilds we were passing through.

Mona, dressed in jeans and a long-sleeve white T-shirt, stared forward, her hair whipping around her face. She made no effort to rein it in, seemingly content to take the full blast of our forty-mile-an-hour clip.

That brush she gave my hip last night came back to mind. A gesture more intimate and bold than the rest of her self-absorbed behavior, as though she'd been seeking a connection with me, an alliance she couldn't bring herself to admit any other way. I watched her hair twist and snarl in the wind and wondered for the dozenth time what the hell I'd gotten myself into by leaving the safety of my house and my quiet routines.

For months I had been hankering for this day. In all my debates and calculations about making this foray into uncharted waters, I'd tried to weigh the effect of sharing such a rousing experience with complete strangers. I knew that having others aboard would be, at the very least, a distraction—that it might even blunt the pleasure in some major way, just as it might also, given a lucky break and the right companions, give the whole experience an added dimension. But I had not factored in the possibility that I would be escorting members of my own newly discovered family—people whose motives for joining this expedition seemed to lie somewhere between murky and treacherous.

I counted down the twists in the river's path, and studied the northern shoreline of the Wood for any break in the density of the mangroves. With my head turned, my left ear out of the wind, I heard an unnatural rumble behind us. I cut the engine back to idle, and as we lurched to a halt, I turned to peer back down the river.

"What is it?" Milligan followed my gaze.

At the last turn we'd rounded, through the dense screen of roots and branches, there was a flash of yellow. Then the low, sleek hull shot past the jutting mangrove roots and around the sharp bend.

"We have company."

As the boat came into our stretch of river, it dropped off plane and its huge wake died away behind it, the waves overtaking the boat and crashing into the mangroves we'd just passed.

A tall woman was at the wheel. Dark black hair braided and tucked down the front of her clothes. White-skinned and lean, she wore black wraparound shades and a green camouflage hunting jacket and jeans and sported a red baseball cap.

Running across other anglers this far back in the Glades was rare but not unheard of. A woman alone, however, was another thing. I'd seen it only once—a cast-iron cracker from Chokoloskee or Everglades City making the long run into the vast national park, intent on packing her ice chest beyond the legal limit with snook and reds. Later on she'd be selling her illicit catch out of the back of her pickup on the shoulder of Tamiami Trail.

Any encounter in such isolated spots generated heightened suspicion. The chance for menace was greater, and the vigilance was more acute than it would be closer to civilization. This far into nowhere, when two strangers met, a rank, animal tension always filled the air.

And because I was so near the turn into our fishing hide-away, I had an even greater desire to make no lingering contact with this woman. A polite nod would do.

As she approached, I made that nod, but the stranger did not return it. She continued idling in our direction without a break in her posture.

I recognized the brand of boat as a cheaply made fiberglass craft used to chase bass and corral them in the back bays of freshwater lakes. It was fitted out with an electric trolling motor mounted on the bow and a flip-up seat for the lazy beer-drinking crowd. The boat appeared to be brand-new, and I saw there were no Florida registration numbers affixed to its hull. A second after that I noted that the rod holders were empty.

I turned the wheel and nudged the throttle to give her more room to pass. The raven-haired woman took off her sunglasses and set them on the console, then fixed her gaze on us, moving her eyes from my face to John Milligan's then on to Mona's. Studying each of us, then returning to me.

She kept her focus on my face as she coasted not five feet off our starboard rail. During the instant she passed abreast, I felt something like the crackle of current, black and invisible, arc across the narrow gap between us. My neck hair bristled and something in my chest rotated off-center. Our skiff seemed to rock out of all proportion to the wake that swelled under it, as though this woman had momentarily disrupted the force field that governed our small corner of the planet.

In silence the Milligans and I stared back at her, and when she'd passed ten feet beyond our boat, the woman fitted her sunglasses back in place and mashed her throttle. The heavy boat shot forward and lifted her up onto the slick steel-gray surface. She traveled not more than fifty feet before she veered the bass boat close to the right side of the mangrove-lined waterway and executed a tight U-turn, then came roaring back toward us.

There were only a few seconds to react. I swung the wheel sharply to the right and gunned forward, but there was no way

I could dodge her speeding craft if her intent was to ram us head-on.

But she did not. She skimmed past our port side not more than an arm's length away and her wake splashed high and doused us all. She kept her eyes trained on the river before her until the boat fishtailed around the bend and was gone.

"What the hell was that?" Milligan brushed water from his face.

"Who knows," I said. "Maybe a warning, something territorial. People in these parts can be very protective of their fishing holes."

Mona stood up and came around the console. Her shirt and jeans were sopping and ribbons of seawater seeped from her hairline and ran down her face like steam-room sweat.

In the confusion, I'd failed to monitor our position and the skiff had swung around and the bow was stabbing into the mangroves. Branches scraped the hull and swatted at the console, and one poked Mona in the back and made her yelp.

I reversed the prop and backed us on a hard angle toward the center of the waterway. Ten feet out, as we swung around, I saw it—the opening in the dense growth I'd been looking for—that elusive entrance to the ancient stream that led back to the three joined lakes.

At the mouth, just as the aerial photo had shown, there was a slight indentation in the undergrowth. Oddly, the opening had been more discernible from a speeding plane several hundred feet in the air than from where I stood, twenty yards away at water level.

"What kind of weapon do you carry?" Milligan asked.

I pulled a clean towel from my waterproof duffel and handed it to Mona. A smile crinkled the corners of her lips. Good humor getting the better of her for the moment. Then she turned away to scrub the water from her hair.

"Don't tell me you come out here in the boondocks unarmed?"

"This is a national park," I said. "No firearms allowed."

"Not even on the houseboat? Nothing?"

I held his fuming gaze for a moment, then stepped back to the wheel.

"A woman in a passing boat has you spooked? She splashes you and you're ready to start shooting?"

"There was more going on back there than being splashed."

He was probably right. Up close she looked more culti-vated and well-maintained than some roadside fishmonger. The whole encounter had the feel of a reconnaissance. Test-ing our reactions, getting a closer look.

I dug through the duffel and pulled out the cell phone Rusty had given me. I flipped it open, but no bars showed on the screen, zero reception. Lance, the same hurricane that last August had ravaged the shoreline mangroves, also wrecked the cell towers on the mainland that once served this region. Five months later, only a couple were back in service, but we were just beyond their range. The satellite phone Rusty car-ried for emergencies was locked up back on the Mother-ship.

Though I knew it was useless, I switched on the handheld VHF radio, tuned it to our agreed-upon channel 67, and tried to hail Rusty. By now she was probably on the far side of Whitewater Bay, beyond the reach of my meager wattage and stubby aerial. The Mothership had two twenty-foot an-tennae with boosters, so there was a chance that Teeter might hear my voice, but after three tries and no response, I set the radio back in its holster.

There was something quaint and pleasing about passing beyond the range of modern electronics. Even the map on my global positioning screen was wildly inaccurate, show-ing the Wood River to have dwindled away to nothing a half mile back. According to the GPS indicator map, the spot where we were floating was a half mile inland on the solid ground of Florida's southern tip.

That seemed a pretty fair definition for a wilderness zone—a place where none of the gadgets worked, and if you were going to save your ass you better have a command of the basics.

I couldn't remember the last time I felt so relaxed.

I slipped behind the wheel. Milligan was still staring at me and shaking his head.

"Let's go fishing, why don't we?"

I eased the skiff forward a few feet so the bow brushed the outer branches of the creek mouth. I bent forward to peer down the corridor to see if there was any hope we could penetrate the snarl.

The good news was that there was a line of sight for about two hundred yards. The bad news was the line was crosshatched by branches at intervals of about every yard or so. If we were to penetrate that overgrown stream, we'd have to claw and cram and scrape the skiff ahead for a good part of the morning.

I tilted the engine up so high the propeller was barely below the waterline. That way we could muscle ahead through as little as five or six inches. If it got any shallower back there we'd have to kill the engine, tilt the prop all the way up, and drag the boat ahead by hand.

"You sure about this?" Mona said.

"I'll need you up front, John." I drew the loppers from beneath the console. "You keep us in the center of the channel, clip as few branches as possible. Be on the lookout for any submerged logs. And don't fall overboard. This is gator country. And a few crocs show up back here, too."

"We're going in there?" Milligan said.

"That's the idea."

I flipped open the rear hatch and drew out the two net bags that held the foul-weather gear.

"Put the jackets on, hoods up."

"It's not going to rain," Mona said. "Skies are perfectly clear."

"Spiders," I said. "It's going to be raining spiders."

They put on their slickers, and I inched forward into the thicket.

"Spiders?" Mona said. "The biting kind?"

"I don't know. Let's not find out."

* * *

Sasha killed the engine and let the boat drift a mile beyond the perimeter of Ponce de Leon Bay, out in five feet of water in the quiet gulf. They had a straight-on view of the mouth of the Broad River, with empty miles of silver-blue in every direction squirming like a pan of mercury.

On the deck beside her, Griffin lay still on the bedroll with his eyes closed. Sasha knelt down, looked for the rise and fall of his chest, and when she couldn't detect it, touched a fingertip to his throat.

Griffin opened his eyes. Smiled at her.

"Not yet," he said.

He struggled to sit up, then extended an arm and Sasha hauled him to his feet. He coughed, spit a gob over the side.

"What was the fuss back there, all that roaring around?"

"Milligan and his daughter and another man. I made a pass at them to make sure."

"Was it Thorn?"

"I don't know. Didn't seem as big and bad as advertised."

"Middle of nowhere. Why didn't you go ahead and take them down? You're not losing your nerve?"

"I was only scouting. Making sure. We want to get this right."

Sasha sat on the flip-up seat on the bow and looked back at her son. Her mind was flashing with ravenous blackbirds, dark bursts of beak and feather, a whirlwind flock feeding on a cloud of fat lazy insects. A vision she could neither eradicate nor decode.

"What kind of fish you and Granddad catch out here anyway?"

Sensitive Grif saw her strain and was fetching for a pleasant memory.

"Reds, cobia, some snook. Lot of trash, ladyfish and cats."

Griffin nodded and closed his eyes on a smile as if he was picturing that kind of paradise. Lost to him now, lost to both of them. All they had was this yellow boat, stolen, and the rifle and the pistol in the duffel beside the console. A day of killing ahead.

"Damn," Griffin said. "We forgot the rods and reels."

"Not to mention the bait," Sasha said.

"Next time we come out here, it'll be for pleasure."

The only answer she could muster was a nod.

"What's in the cooler?" He settled into the swivel seat behind the wheel.

"Sodas, turkey wraps, some pork rinds. You hungry, need a sip?"

Griffin didn't answer, his gaze drifting off toward the wavering horizon, the gray listless bay, staring at the mudflats and the sandy banks where herons stood a mile offshore, the air quaking with heat as the sun gained its place.

"Wonder what Dad would say about this mayhem we're into?"

"He wouldn't like it a damn bit."

"Hell, if he was alive, he'd still be out knocking on doors, getting names on one petition or another, making posters, lobbying his congressman, playing by the rules. Thinking everyone else was, too."

"He was a good man."

"Turns out being good doesn't get you far."

"He did what he thought was right."

"That why you married him, 'cause he was good?"

They'd been having these conversations. A kind of fast-forward courtship. Her boy trying to plumb his mother's depths in his final moments.

"I married him because he was smart and handsome and had a good heart. He was the best man I ever met."

"Until I came along, you mean."

"Until you came along."

"Give me the truth on something, Mama."

"I don't lie to you, Grif."

"Is this a kamikaze mission? Coming out here, this killing? You plan on getting out of this alive?"

She couldn't answer that. From the first moment she'd returned fire in Iraq, the old definitions of survival no longer ruled. Trying to stay alive wasn't part of it anymore. Good death, noble death, useful death, taking as many of the enemy with you. That's another thing she brought back from that wretched place, a different way of seeing death.

"You're a beautiful woman. You shouldn't let this be the end. Just because of me and Dad. You should get out of this alive, go somewhere. Live. Your looks, you could get a rich husband, enjoy some luxury."

"You hitting on me, Griffin?"

"I would if it were allowed. I would indeed. You're beautiful. Anybody can see it."

"You're a sweet boy."

"There's things you could do, places to see. You could do it for my sake, be my eyes. Go see Spain, Switzerland, the Alps. Florence, Berlin, Tokyo, California. Travel and take me along. You know. China, that'd be cool. Hell, I never even seen Atlanta."

She couldn't speak. She couldn't let herself breathe. The blackbirds, ravens, vultures were whirling inside her eyes.

Her boy, her bright shining star. Somewhere in the last month Griffin finished being her son. Now he was something else, some other designation. Sasha had witnessed the same thing happen in the war. Kids transforming overnight. One day they've got a sappy grin, next day it's gone. Everything hardened up inside. Eyes still and distant.

The boy retrieved his blue backpack from a storage locker, hauled it out and dug through it.

"What're you doing, Grif?"

He came out with a couple of old white T-shirts, then a red metal can.

"Grif, what's going on?"

He held up the red can. Lighter fluid for a charcoal barbecue.

"You know what a Viking funeral is, Mama?"

Griffin was gazing out at the diffused grays and blues, the ragged shoreline of mangroves. Breath rasping in his throat.

"Boat on fire," Sasha said. "Corpse put out to sea."

"Make my reservation." He smiled her way, his cheeks burnished with sun, a smear of dark spittle on his chin. "Could you do that for me when the time comes?"

"Why, Griffin?"

"If the color of the fire matches the color of the sunset, that means I led a good life and I'm going to Valhalla."

"You've led a good life, Griffin. A damn good life."

"Valhalla is where warriors go. Their private heaven. They feast on roasted boar and get drunk every night on grog or beer."

"This is something from a book?"

"Dad read it to me when you were off fighting in Iraq. We talked about it, how it would be a good way to go. He wanted it for himself, but that didn't happen. The goddamn hospital and all that bullshit."

He set the lighter fluid on the deck beside him, bundled the white rags back around it, and tucked it away into his backpack.

She managed a nod, then looked off at that wilderness of water, off toward where that houseboat was anchored up, only a few minutes away.

CHAPTER TWELVE

It took more than an hour to reach the final snarl of branches, with the secret lake shimmering just a few feet beyond.

By then John Milligan had become adept at snipping with the loppers, making only the cuts necessary and trying not to open the lane so wide another passerby might notice it was accessible.

I'd mastered a technique for maneuvering the skiff through nearly impassable gaps, reversing the prop, then slamming us forward, cutting the wheel in short choppy strokes from side to side to wriggle past obstructions. The bottom paint on my wood hull would be nicked and scored by the half-dozen logs and rocks we'd rammed, and the deck itself was blanketed by hundreds of tiny agitated spiders and the crumbled white crusts of barnacles and a thick coating of mangrove leaves. But otherwise the three of us seemed unscathed.

As we'd worked down the narrow channel, I was pleased to see no signs of other explorers preceding us. If the woman on the bass boat was trying to scare us away from her private fishing hole, this nameless lake was not it. Either no one had ever passed this way before, or their passage had occurred so long ago that no mark of it remained. I could sense a high, thrilling whistle in my veins that had gradually risen to a pitch I had not known since I was a boy basking in my first ecstasies.

Once we entered the still waters of the first lake, we spent a while whisking the spiders away and swept the deck as best we could with hand towels and scrub brushes. We worked in silence, part reverence, part exhaustion.

While John and Mona finished swiping at the remaining cobwebs and shook the spiders off their foul-weather gear, I knotted orange bucktails onto the leaders, then set their spinning rods in the holders. Afterward, I tilted up the motor and examined the prop. Along the route, I'd dinged two or three solid objects, and the stainless-steel blades showed some minor scarring, but nothing that would substantially alter their performance.

Mona took her seat on the padded ice chest while John finished cleaning the deck. I slipped the fiberglass push pole out of its clips and climbed up on the rear platform to propel us deeper into the lake.

John shook out his towel, folded it, and set it on the deck, then gave me a quick questioning look and I nodded my assent. He took a rod from one of the holders, set his feet, and after a practice motion he cast his lure toward the mangrove roots. Though his technique was capable enough, he was clearly rusty and his bait plinked into the water well short of the tangle of roots.

Using short jigs he retrieved his bucktail and after only two or three jerks of his rod and cranks of the reel, his road bent sharply. One cast, one strike. The tarpon was smallish, ten, twelve pounds, but it jumped a half-dozen times. A bright silver projectile launching several feet into the air, twisting and splashing on its side. Back in the water it made sizzling runs toward the roots before John managed to turn it each time and angle it back toward the boat. Finally he brought it up to the side, and I netted it and held it up for them both to admire. Smiles more genuine than I'd seen on their faces before.

I slid the fish back into the water and it shot back toward the roots.

On her first cast, Mona hooked a redfish and nailed a sizeable snook on her second. We'd been in the lake for less than ten minutes and we already had a backcountry grand slam. For the next half hour it was another fish at every cast, the closer the bait landed to the mangrove roots, the bigger the catch.

I gave only minimal directions. "Keep your rod tip down; cast side-armed." Other than that all three of us were reduced to yelps and whoops of wonderment. To my surprise, I was starting to warm to these two—not for anything they'd done or said, but for their silence and restraint, their understanding of the rare good fortune of such fishing and such isolation, and for succumbing to what I took to be the same wonder and awe I was feeling.

Fifty yards to the west, I spotted the narrow channel that connected the first lake with the second and I began poling us quietly in that direction. The wind was light, the water brilliantly clear, and the circling egrets and cormorants seemed to be eyeing us with lazy indifference. We were one of them. We'd earned the right to be there.

Songbirds reveled in the dense branches, and the breeze was as plush and bracing as a swallow of aged whiskey. The fish we'd caught were not even close to the largest of their kind I'd landed, and I'd fished other remote backwaters where they were more abundant, lagoons where schools of giant tarpons rolled, their big scales flashing in the sun like rows of silver badges. But this nameless lake, in its utter isolation, had a purity I'd never known. So far removed from the squalor and jangle of urban streets, the jackhammer racket of brute machines, the bellow of fourteen-wheelers rolling by on the overseas highway, that for a moment it was possible to believe that all was not lost, that scattered here and there relics of the original Florida lived on, still with the power to absolve and restore.

"Want to take a shot, Thorn?" Mona held up her rod.

I nodded my thanks and set about stabbing the push pole into the muddy bottom, then lashing it to the platform to anchor us in place. But as I came down from the platform, John snatched the rod from Mona's hand and slid it into one of the rod holders on the console.

"It's time we talked."

I stared at him for a moment, then let it go. I didn't want

to lose my high in some petty squabble. As I took a seat behind the wheel, a great blue heron watched us from a perch atop the clicking branches of a mangrove, taking a break from its ceaseless forage to study these curious creatures.

"So talk."

"And I was so relaxed," Mona said with a sigh. "This place is magical."

"Give it a rest, Mona," her father said.

She opened her mouth, then shut it and took a seat on the bow.

Milligan drew a breath and held me with his hard gray eyes. He rubbed a finger back and forth against his lips, pushing aside the black bristles of his mustache. I could see the clench in his neck and the swell of bulky muscles in his chest and shoulders. A man priming himself for hand-to-hand combat.

"I grew up on a cattle ranch," John said.

"Oh, here we go," said Mona.

"My daughter has no respect for family history, but I'm deeply proud of my heritage. My father and mother worked long, grueling hours, as did their parents. And when I was a boy, I joined them, side by side, mending fences, moving the herds, feeding, branding, watering, slaughtering. Exhausting days, harsh work. From the time I was five, I was riding horseback and was expected to keep up with the adults. We raised cattle. A good portion of the herd was descended from Andalusian stock. Cracker cattle. Forty years I busted my ass working that land. No vacations, no breaks. While you were being a beach bum or playboy or whatever the hell you did, I was a cattleman, shoulder to shoulder with the laborers we hired. A cowboy pure and simple."

"Don't forget the wolves," Mona said, "and the mosquitoes."

Milligan looked away and shook his head. When he turned back to me, his eyes had hardened. Nostalgia time was over.

"When Mother passed away last summer, she left us quite a surprise."

"The lockbox, you mean."

Milligan glared at Mona.

"I told him that much," she said. "I left the good part for you."

Milligan swung back to me.

"Yes, the lockbox. It seems Mother had taken a keen interest in following your . . ." He searched for the word.

"My career?"

"If you want to call it that," Milligan said. "In any case, she collected a good bit of information about you. For a woman of such hard-bitten temperament, such a tough old bird, she had a sentimental streak she kept hidden. Somehow she kept track of her daughter's son. Her only grandchild."

I looked over at Mona.

"Only?"

"I'm adopted. Milligan in name only. None of their blood. Lucky me." She faked a smile then let it go.

"It's a legal matter now," Milligan said. "Mother left a will that none of us knew about. She went behind our backs. Our corporate legal office was unaware of the second will, one that superseded the estate plan they helped her draw up. She wrote it up herself, in her own handwriting, created an entirely new structure to her estate."

"Did a damn fine job, too," Mona said. "Dad and Carter tried to tear holes in it for months but couldn't find a judge who'd turn a trick."

Milligan stabbed a finger in her direction. "Shut up, Mona. Just shut the hell up for once."

She smiled back at him but complied.

He fumed for a moment more, then turned to me. I was struck again by his hard-muscled build. Rangy and limber, with long arms, meaty hands. The sinews and tendons rippled beneath his flesh like restive snakes. I shared just enough of that physique to sense the strength he had at his command. Even at his age, he was not a man I wanted to test myself against.

"She divided her estate into three portions: corporate, cash, and land."

"I get cash," Mona said. "Lots and lots of cash."

Once again Milligan's face darkened, and I thought I might have to seize him before he attacked his daughter. But he caught himself and looked off at the lagoon as though seeking solace in that isolated spot, and in a few seconds the blood seeped from his face and he stepped closer to me.

"I'll be running Bates International," he said. "Chairman of the Board, CEO. The business is a vast and complex enterprise, and I'm grateful Mother saw fit to bestow that kind of trust on me."

"But the land is yours, Thorn. That's the kicker." Mona gave her father a gloating smile.

"What land?"

"What I showed you last night," said Mona. "The quarter on the map. The land where Daddy played cowboy."

"It's a great deal of property," Milligan said. "An enormous responsibility. Parcels of immense value and variety. It would present a challenge for even an accomplished businessman to manage competently."

"And completely impossible for a fuck-up like you, Thorn."

"So that's why you're here. Why you booked a trip on the houseboat. To negotiate with me, convince me to give up the land. What? You're going to dangle a few million dollars in front of me? Is that what's coming next?"

"I told you, Daddy-O. He wouldn't be a pushover. He's one tough nut. Must be channeling Abigail."

Milligan gritted his jaw, smiled out at nothing.

Mona said, "A good chunk of your land, Thorn, has already been mined. There are problems. Lawsuits. Environmental issues. It's a mess."

I was silent, waiting for this to end.

"Know what a gyp stack is?"

"I've heard of them."

"Well," she said, "you're the proud owner of two dozen gypsum stacks. Mountains twenty stories high, their bases covering a few hundred acres, each one full of toxic leftovers from the strip mines. They emit radon gas, leach sulfuric acid into the aquifer. Now and then they collapse and spill millions of gallons of contaminated sludge. Nobody knows what the hell to do with them long term. You own two dozen of them, Thorn."

I watched a school of tarpon flash past, biggest tarpon I'd seen in years.

"This is why Abigail Bates was killed?"

"Could be," Mona said. "She had lots of enemies. One bunch hated her for what she'd already done, like putting gyp stacks in their backyards, and the other bunch despised her for what she was planning to do: strip-mine the watershed. Some hated her for both."

"That's enough, Mona," Milligan snapped. "Quite enough."

He aimed a finger at his daughter, but she stared him down, and after a moment, he folded the finger back into a fist. Clearly he was a man bedeviled by strong women. A mother who had set an unmatchable standard. A daughter who dismissed his gruff bluster. A sister who long ago abandoned him to live alone in the shadow of his colossal parents.

And now a final treachery. His own mother had betrayed him. Passed on the land that was the foundation of the family wealth and status to an outsider. A man who had done nothing to deserve the gift.

"No, it's not enough," Mona said. "Thorn needs an education, and he needs it quick. And you're sure as hell not going to give it to him."

Milligan was about to bark at her again when the VHF radio squawked.

"Mayday, Mayday, Mayday."

Teeter's voice came in a rush, quivering with fright.

"Mayday, Mayday, Mayday, Mayday."

I snatched up the mike, punched the button

"Teeter? Teeter, what's going on?"

"Mayday," he said. Then chanted again, with a forlorn pause between each word. "Mayday . . . Mayday . . . Mayday."

A second later I heard the electronic snap of his radio going dead.

CHAPTER THIRTEEN

"Sheriff's on a call. Won't be back till this afternoon."

Nine A.M., Sugarman stood in the front office of the De-Soto County Sheriff's Department. He was wearing black jeans and a blue oxford shirt and his best boat shoes. Picking the wardrobe carefully, he'd tried to split the difference between city slicker and shit kicker. Even in a supposedly broadminded age, a black man in rural Florida had to be prudent.

Sheriff Timmy Whalen's gatekeeper was a plump woman in her seventies named Nina, who wore a purple blouse that clashed with the valentine red of her froth of hair. And the heavy slash of crimson on her lips clashed with both. On the metal file cabinet beside her was a vase of plastic flowers and a collection of gift-shop figurines, mostly brightly colored tropical fish, but none as gaudy as Nina.

She eyed Sugarman from his boat shoes to his courteous smile, then picked up her notepad, studied it for a few seconds, and set it down.

"You're the one from Key Largo. Rachel's friend."

"You know Rachel?"

"I do now. Talked to her for most of an hour. Got the goods on you, that's for sure." She picked up an emery board that lay beside her ancient Selectric typewriter and took one pass across a nail. "The sheriff's supervising a crime-scene investigation. Says to send you over when you arrive."

Nina tapped her emery board against her desktop, lifting her nose as though trying to catch a whiff of him.

"Rachel tells me you're a private eye."

Sugarman nodded.

"And you're poking around into Abigail Bates's death?"

"*Poking* isn't the word I'd use."

"The granddaughter," Nina said. "Mona Milligan. She hired you."

"I really can't say," Sugar said.

"That girl made a lot of noise after her granny died. Nearly every day she was in here huffing and puffing at the sheriff. Calling us bunglers, a bunch of backwater idiots. A little snot, if you ask me."

"I can't disclose my client," Sugarman said.

"Yeah, yeah, I know the drill. Got to keep it hush-hush."

"That's right."

"Well, good luck on keeping anything hush-hush in this town."

Nina was a gabber. No doubt she had tried to wheedle juicy bits from Rachel, but he trusted his friend's savvy. She would've spotted Nina as a gossip and given her just enough to chum the waters, prime her for Sugar.

"I take it the sheriff officially closed the Bates investigation?"

"Drowning," Nina said. "Medical examiner ruled on it, not a shred of doubt. The way her lungs were, I forget all that scientific mumbo jumbo."

"And what became of the young man who had the violent encounter with Ms. Bates, this guy Kipling?"

She waved the thought away.

"A wuss," Nina said. "Charlie Kipling couldn't swat a mosquito. He's still renting canoes just where he's been for years. Out on Highway 70. I marked his place on the map."

Nina picked up a sheet of paper from her desk and held it out for Sugar. He took it, thanked her, and looked it over.

It was a hand-drawn diagram. The sheriff's department on East Cypress was marked with a star, the crime scene the sheriff was working was marked with an X, and the canoe-rental place was assigned a C. All the streets had been rulered out, their names printed alongside each one. Compulsive Nina.

"And were there any other suspects? Anyone might've had a grudge against Abigail Bates?"

Nina laughed. "Suspects?" She set her emery board aside and straightened a stack of papers that lay on her ink blotter. She chortled again, then looked up at him with the grin still in her eyes. "Mr. Sugarman, there's more than thirty-five thousand residents in unincorporated DeSoto County. The county covers six hundred and eighty-four square miles, and I guarantee you there's only a handful of folks in all that area who didn't celebrate Abigail Bates's death."

"The wicked witch?"

"You got it," Nina said. "When I was a girl, this was God's green acre. Clean air, pure water, rivers flowing, birds and trees and possums and people all getting along. Then that Bates woman inherits her daddy's empire and, Lord have mercy, single-handed she spends the last forty years trying to trash every square mile from here all the way up to Tampa. And if that wasn't enough, she decided to work her way down to the Gulf, where all the rich folks dock their yachts. That's when her unfortunate drowning occurred."

"Phosphate mining, that's what you're talking about?"

"Yes, sir. Gray gold. It's making somebody rich, but nobody I know. And next to coal it's the dirtiest business there is."

"Hires a lot of people, though. Must affect the local economy."

"Hires a few, and even some of those are celebrating her death. You want suspects, I'd take a gander at the school videos. Cast of thousands."

"School videos?"

"Protest speeches. Tearing into Abigail Bates and her gang. They stood there at the podium, said the awfulest things right to the faces of Bates people. I think there were four meetings. All of them recorded."

"Maybe I'll check it out."

Nina cut a glance toward the sheriff's office door. "Maybe you should."

Sugar took his leave and drove his Honda through Summerland's historical district: a brick courthouse, a mom-and-pop drugstore, a hardware store, a diner, a dress shop, lawyers' offices, then a main-street stretch of antebellum mansions with big generous wraparound porches. He worked his way down a few potholed backstreets until he found the intersection for Highway 70, then turned north and followed Nina's drawing, passing the canoe-rental shop along the way.

A few minutes later he pulled into the lot of a small cement-block building seven miles from downtown Summerland. The crime scene.

The shop was squat and unpainted with a Confederate flag fluttering from a pole on its roof. Sugar heard the tune echo in some sound chamber of memory. The land of cotton, old times there are not forgotten.

The billboard out front identified the business as Hankinson's Army Surplus and Gun Shop. Parked in the gravel lot were two police cruisers, white with green accents, and a white DeSoto County crime-scene van.

Rammed through the security bars and double front doors was a blue Ford pickup truck. The entire length of the truck's hood was lodged inside the store, its windshield shattered, a corner of the air bag hanging out of the driver's window. Must've been rolling at least forty miles an hour to crash that far inside those reinforced doors. Hell of a collision.

Kneeling down beside the deflated flap of air bag, a black woman in khaki trousers and a dark blue shirt was clipping part of the material free. Only African American on the scene.

Sugarman came up behind her and watched for a moment over her shoulder. The section of material she was snipping loose was smeared with red. She wore latex gloves, and when the fabric was free, she pinched an edge of it and dropped it into a plastic evidence bag.

"Nice scissors," he said.

The woman rose and turned to face him. She was a few inches shorter than he, slender, with none of the Caucasian ancestry Sugarman had inherited. Dark-skinned, with large lips, widely spaced eyes that were caramel-colored with a hint of gold, she had a fine, high forehead and wore her short hair in a finger wave. A couple of curly strands dangled across her forehead.

"Buck ninety-five at Wal-Mart. Nothing special, but they do the job."

"Somebody had a sudden urge for guns."

"Ten years in law enforcement, I'm still waiting for my first criminal mastermind."

"Truck was stolen, I suppose."

She squinted at him, hesitating a moment. He tried for a harmless smile.

"Stolen, yes," she said. "Dealership in Sarasota. They didn't know it was missing till we called."

"Well, you got the bad guy's DNA, that's a start. You been an ID tech long?"

She shook her head and held up the plastic bag.

"That look like blood to you?"

He was leaning close to see the specimen when a man came huffing up. Five-six, five-seven, close to three hundred pounds. Ratty jeans, grease-stained white T-shirt with a Harley logo on it, a melon-belly. His face was red and bloated, and he'd braided his chin hair into a three-inch pigtail.

"I got the inventory," he said. "Sheriff Whalen."

He spoke her title with such blatant scorn that Sugar felt his hands curl into fists at his sides. But the sheriff just smiled, apparently used to these peckerheads. Probably took this level of shit every day. Sugar looked at her again. Sheriff Timmy.

"So what'd our brazen bandit make off with, Mr. Hankinson?"

"M-fourteen with the Kevlar stock, uses the three-oh-eight rounds. Took the one with the high-capacity magazine. Thing just came in last week. Asshole must be a vet, served in Nam or Iraq. Knew to skip the M-sixteens. Fuckers jam all the time. Only niggers and morons steal those."

"The clip is high-capacity?"

"That's right. But it's preban, it's legal."

"How high is the capacity?"

"Holds twenty rounds."

"Anything else missing, Mr. Hankinson?"

He gave her a lazy sneer that seemed to say, "Don't push me, I'm getting there."

Sugarman forced his hands back open, spread his fingers, took a breath.

"An HK forty-five handgun, five boxes of shells, one camouflage jacket."

"That's it?"

"I know my stock, and that's what he got. Asshole wasted a brand-new fucking pickup truck to rip off a rifle, a handgun, and a jacket. Oh, yeah, and two cheap walkie-talkies."

"Somebody's going hunting," Sugarman said.

Hankinson gave him a sour look, then turned back to the sheriff.

"You got twenty-four hours, Whalen. You don't slap the cuffs on the fucker, me and the boys kick it into gear. Twenty-four hours."

She nodded wearily. Heard it all before. Didn't bother with a civics lecture, like she knew the guy was all bluster and bullshit.

"I hear a bass boat got stolen last night, too," Hankinson said. "Off the lot at Fisherman's Paradise."

The sheriff nodded.

"This fucking town been going to the dogs ever since you took over."

She let Hankinson get halfway across the lot before she called his name. He halted but didn't turn. Not only was the sheriff a female, but black to boot. The very idea must have tormented his lizard brain.

"You behave yourself, John. Don't let me hear about you and your boys harassing our good citizens. Last time I checked you chalked up two strikes. Third fall's the charm, baby. So you take care now."

He turned his head and gave her a red-eyed withering look and stalked back to his gun shop.

"And you must be Mr. Sugarman of Key Largo."

She peeled off her gloves, then held out her right hand. She had a firm, no-bullshit grip.

"Welcome to Florida's heartland, where the glorious Southern traditions live on."

"Those guys are everywhere," Sugar said. "You don't have a corner on the bubba market."

She gave Sugar a brisk look of appraisal as if he might be gaming her. Probably happened a lot to her. This town, these people. A constant struggle to find the proper balance between authority and deference, goodwill and suspicion. Sugar couldn't tell by the slight softening of her gaze if he'd passed the test or was still on probation. Probably the latter.

"So you've been employed by the Bates family to second-guess my police work. And out of the generosity of my heart and professional courtesy I'm supposed to throw open my books."

Sugarman sighed, watched the deputies who were milling around the front of the store trying to look busy. A tow truck pulled into the lot, and a twenty-year-old kid with long hair jumped down, paced around a little, keeping to himself, sizing up the mechanics of the job.

"For eleven years I was a deputy for the Monroe County sheriff in the Upper Keys. I have nothing but respect for the position. The professionalism required, hard work, the whole deal. Nothing but respect. If you're inclined to share some information with me, that would be generous, but if you're not so inclined, I'd certainly understand."

"A speechmaker."

"I polished it a little on the drive up."

She fought off a small smile.

"You used to be a deputy, but you quit. Went private."

"I was bumping against the good-ol'-boy ceiling," he said. "It was either spend the next twenty years running in place or take a risk on my own."

"Has it worked out?"

"Less paperwork," he said, "but I sure miss my dental plan."

That got a full smile. Good teeth. Very white and straight.

"You didn't know I was the sheriff, did you? You walked

up, decided to hit on the black woman. Play the race card. Afro to Afro. See what you could trick out of the poor dumb colored girl."

Sugarman was silent.

"True or false?"

"Somewhere in between," he said. "Not the 'poor dumb colored girl' thing. Just trying to do my job. Same as you."

After a few seconds of watching her deputies, she held up the plastic bag and gave him another look at the fabric.

"Look like blood to you?"

It came across as part challenge, part something else. Sugarman couldn't put a finger on the second thing, why she'd engage him like this. Intrigued, he noted it, printing it in bold letters for later consideration.

"When did the break-in go down?"

"I put it at around midnight," she said. "Cut the phone line to disable the alarm, then rammed. Two hours ago a passing cruiser spotted it."

"Well, that's too bright, too red to be blood nine hours old."

"So what do you think? What's your professional analysis?"

"What it looks like is lipstick."

Timmy Whalen smiled again, but the test continued.

"That's kind of a stretch, don't you think? A woman puts on her lipstick before she goes off to steal a truck, heist some guns."

"Force of habit," Sugar said. "Ritual. She's not thinking about it, just going through her routine to keep her nerves steady."

Timmy Whalen watched the tow-truck guy amble over to one of the deputies. Both of them lit up smokes, started talking.

"Not bad. For most guys, trying to decipher the female mind is right up there with cracking the atom."

"That's what you think?" he said. "Person who rammed the truck into the gun shop was a woman?"

"Either that," she said, "or one hell of a kinky guy."

Sugarman smiled, then took another look at the truck. One of the CSI guys in jeans and a police T-shirt was taking photos.

"Something I'm wondering."

"Yeah?"

"Why doesn't she throw it in reverse, use the rear bumper to crash the doors? A lot less damage to the truck and to her. If things go right, she drives off after it's done. This way she's got to walk away loaded down with her loot. Or she's had to stash her own vehicle somewhere nearby. Or I guess she could have a partner, and he drives her away."

"This one's a hard-ass," the sheriff said. "Going in backward? No, I don't think it ever crossed her mind."

"No?"

"First, if things don't go right, she's stuck just the same, so there's uncertainty. Plus, backing a truck in the dark at thirty miles an hour, I don't see it. Too tricky. Too many ifs."

Sugarman rubbed the back of his hand across the stubble on his cheek.

"Still, it's weird," he said. "The whole deal, headfirst or not. It has desperation written all over it."

Sheriff Whalen watched her deputies work.

"What're you doing, interviewing for a job?"

"Just trying to be helpful," Sugarman said. "Maybe bond a little."

She smiled again, meeting his eyes. "Candid, aren't we?"

"It's the only way to go."

"All right, Mr. Detective. Anything else pop out?"

"Not really. Just what the owner said. She goes to all this trouble, steals a truck, rams it into the front, then only steals four or five things, including a camouflage jacket? It's a weird list. Very short. Very precise."

She took a deliberate breath and her eyes blurred again. When she spoke, her voice was flat, a long way from banter.

"It's what you said. She took what she needed. She's going hunting."

The solemn tone, her eyes bouncing off his, then fixing

on a blue scrap of sky, gave Sugar another thing to jot down on his memory pad.

Sheriff Timmy was confiding in him. But what and why, he had no idea.

CHAPTER FOURTEEN

John and Mona Milligan pressed flat against the deck while I crashed back through the snarl of the overgrown creek. Branches swatted and clawed at my face and bare arms, drew blood more than once, but I wasn't feeling anything. The second time the engine stalled, I had to tilt it out of the water to clear the tangle of roots and weeds from the prop before I could forge on.

Finally in the main channel, I flattened the throttle and milked every RPM from the Yamaha, screaming back down the Wood River, knifing around dozens of sharp bends and switchbacks on the Broad and then back into Ponce de Leon Bay. I yelled for the Milligans to stay down, as streamlined as possible, then I huddled behind the console out of the rip and scream of the wind and tried to hail Rusty or Teeter on the VHF.

But no one was answering.

As I rounded the last bend and entered Cardiac Bay, I caught sight of the Mothership about a mile off, still anchored in the same position. A light easterly breeze was riffling the bay, pushing silvery scallops out toward the horizon like the pulses of sound waves. The last fumes of elation from our fishing expedition had burned off, and at that moment the landscape looked stark and harsh, its austere beauty a cruel hoax.

I gave the VHF another try but got no response, then I

fixed on the straightest heading to the houseboat, though I knew that course would take us across some risky oyster beds and rocky shoals. I believed the tide was just high enough for us to skim safely across them if I kept us in the narrow trench that cut across the flats.

Running that fast across such skinny water was always an act of faith and denial. A hypnotic state takes over, as if you were skating across an unbroken layer of solid ice. You tell yourself it'll all be fine if you stay in the blue water, or settle for the green, avoid the brown and the white. But the sun and clouds can scatter the colors into wildly different tones, producing a devious camouflage that can fool the eye and send even the most experienced boater slamming aground. I'd made my share of errors over the years, failed to see a shoal or coral head, and crashed the lower unit into unyielding boulders. Had to limp home or call for help or spend the night at sea until rescued by a passing boater. But at that moment, skimming the sleek skin of the bay, the skiff seemed to be airborne, riding a slippery cushion of air so insubstantial that I felt for a moment that we were about to break contact entirely with gravity and lift off into the clear atmosphere.

Halfway into the bay, just as I saw the dark outer rim of the oyster beds twenty yards ahead, something caught my attention in the distance. I rubbed the focus back into my eyes and craned around the console. From behind the Mothership, the yellow bass boat was slowly emerging. It seemed to be nosing around the mangroves that formed the sheltered cove of our anchorage.

Distracted by the distant boat, I angled out of the head of the channel, and the skeg clipped a rock, knocking the skiff hard to port. Mona yelped, and John was thrown against the bulkhead.

I tugged the wheel too hard, overcorrecting, and veered beyond the other side of the groove. The props banged another rock and the engine sputtered and died.

We lurched to a stop, and in the sudden silence, as I was reaching for the ignition key, faint pops of gunfire echoed across the water. Six shots, then six more after that, and a last group of six or seven, like the methodical hammer whacks of a master carpenter.

John Milligan rose to his feet.

"Get down, goddammit! I'm not saying it again."

Milligan dropped to his knees and I got the engine started, revved it hard, plowing up a furrow of mud and silt behind us, ramming ahead until I had us back up to speed. I steered back into the narrow channel, once again racing flat out, but this time holding precisely to the twisty course.

I was just exiting the far end of the rocky shoal when the woman in the camouflage jacket turned her head and saw our skiff approaching.

Without another look our way, she gunned her sluggish boat up onto the gray sheen of the bay, made a wide loop around the mangroves, and roared west toward the maze of channels that led out to the Gulf.

There was something in the leisurely manner of her getaway that suggested she was trying to lure me into chasing her. But I didn't bite.

I streaked across the remaining half mile, my cousin and uncle lying side by side on the deck. A hundred yards from the Mothership I spotted a red object floating near the mangroves. It didn't belong there, wasn't right, but I kept my heading straight on the houseboat for those last hundred yards.

As I was backing down the RPMs, preparing to sweep alongside the rear platform and make fast to the cleats, the red object came into focus.

Teeter's chef hat.

It was waterlogged and about to disappear below the surface, bobbing on the dying wake of the bass boat.

I swung us in that direction, carved a tight turn around the stern of the Mothership, and tugged the throttle lever back to neutral. The skiff wallowed to a stop, and I cut the engine off.

"Teeter!"

I yelled his name twice more but heard nothing.

The Milligans rose, Mona dusting the last clinging spiders off her T-shirt, John climbing up onto the bow deck, peering ahead into the tangle of limbs and roots that rimmed our mooring spot.

"Over there," he said. "Up on the bank."

He pointed toward a hump of marl and muck that jutted out of the stand of mangroves. The water thinned out quickly in that direction, going from three feet where we were to only inches near the bank. So I tilted up the engine, unclipped the fiberglass pole, and climbed onto the engine platform.

"Stay forward," I told them. "Both of you. Up front."

Mona stepped up onto the bow beside her dad, and when the boat leveled out, I got us gliding toward the bulge of mud and sand and rotting vegetation.

I saw Teeter's shoes first, old black basketball high-tops that he must have owned for thirty years. Then his white chef's pants, spattered with mud and debris. He was lying on the marl, propped up on his elbows, watching us approach. Chest heaving, mouth open, eyes dazed.

"Oh, shit," Milligan said.

"How the hell did that happen?" said Mona.

I shushed them both.

A crocodile was sunning, half submerged in the mud of the bank. Teeter's back was propped against its midsection. The only scenario I could imagine was that in some panicked state he'd scooted backward out of the water and pushed himself atop the creature, then went rigid when he realized what he was pressed against.

The croc's hide was a dark olive green, and he had a row of horny plates running down his back and tail like the jagged peaks of a mountain range. Long narrow snout, fourth tooth on the bottom jaw overlapping the upper lip, giving the creature a toothy smirk. His outer eyelids were drawn closed. He was around fourteen feet long, large for an American croc. Probably weighed four hundred pounds—most of it muscle and teeth.

It was long past mating season, well into the dry months of the year, when the few crocodiles that inhabited this area slept through the day and plied the silty waters at night. They were far less fierce than gators, shy creatures, rarely seen. Usually only aggressive in protecting their nest or their hatchlings. Late summer, when the water was at its highest, that was nesting and hatching time. So, in that regard, at least, things were tipped slightly in our favor.

I drew the pole out silently and slipped it forward, planted it in the soft mud, and leaned my weight against it, nudging us ahead another few yards.

"No noise," I whispered.

Teeter was gagging on his sobs, stopping every few seconds to draw a ragged breath, then giving out a husky groan of doom.

I kept my voice low and called to him to quiet down. It was going to be all right. No sweat.

He turned his head, his right cheek just inches from the left eye of the croc. He raised his hands in helpless pleading. What was he to do?

"Don't move. Just stay cool."

Mona turned to me and rolled her eyes. Yeah, right.

In the distance I heard the drone of an outboard engine. Whether it was approaching our position or passing by was impossible to tell. I poled into shallower water, coasting forward till we were only ten feet off the bank where Teeter lay paralyzed. I was so focused on him and the sleeping croc, I didn't notice the submerged log in our path. When the chunk of timber scraped the starboard hull, the screech it made was as piercing as a startled parrot.

And that's what woke the croc.

The eyelids slid open, the creature's eyes reflecting an orange light. It lifted its snout a few inches.

I reset the push pole and shoved us forward till the bow was only a yard offshore. The crunch of the sandy bottom grinding against the keel turned the croc's head in our direction. Crocs, like gators, have a limited area of high-resolution vision. I just didn't know exactly how limited.

"Don't move, Teeter. It doesn't know you're there."

I wasn't sure of that either. The croc's eyes were impossible to read. It might be looking directly at the approaching boat, or in its peripheral vision, it might have noticed the large human lying against its back.

I tried to work out the reptile's age. He could be a young buck full of reckless energy, or might be sixty years old, a seasoned veteran whose long survival had depended on avoidance not confrontation. The only certain way to know the age of a croc was to study a cross-section of its teeth, which had growth rings like trees. But from my limited vantage point, I was pretty sure this one had to be fully mature. Based on his size and a couple of dings and broken plates on his tail, I judged him to be on the downhill side of middle-age. An aging warrior. Even less likely to attack.

With the bow now touching the shore only a couple of feet from Teeter's outstretched shoes, we were in the red zone. Whatever happened was going down in seconds.

I drew the tip of the eighteen-foot push pole from the suck of mud behind me and swiveled it around slowly from the opposite side of the skiff, keeping it level to the water and out of the view of the croc.

"John, Mona, kneel down. Flat on the deck. Slow."

As they lowered themselves, the croc huffed and arched its back, which jolted Teeter upright into a sitting position. Then it slapped its snout twice against the muddy bank in warning.

The geometry of the situation was delicate. The direction the creature faced led off toward a narrow break in the mangroves, maybe a creek, definitely a tempting getaway. Behind him along the shoreline was more sand and marl and a deep burrow that looked like the remnants of the croc's nest. Best outcome: The croc shoots forward, Teeter rolls away behind him. Worst case: The creature makes a U-turn and flees back toward the familiarity of his burrow, sending Teeter sprawling right into his path.

I brought the tip of the push pole down to the water's edge, inching it slowly toward the croc's snout. A poke in the neck was what I had in mind. Startle it into motion and direct it, as much as possible, forward, away from the prodding pole.

It didn't work that way.

I had the pole positioned for my first jab when the

outboard engine I'd heard earlier roared around the Mothership and headed straight into our cove.

I took a quick look over my shoulder. Rusty was at the wheel, Annette and Holland standing beside her at the edge of the console. When she was twenty yards off our stern, she cut the engine back and coasted up fast.

"Thorn! What the hell's going on? Teeter was calling Mayday."

Her arrival sent the croc into action. It lunged at the pole, a move so quick and crushing, I was hurled backward against the engine and poling platform. Before I could draw the pole away, his jaw clamped three feet up its length and he gave it a vicious shake, wrenching it from my grip.

As the croc shook his head, he bucked Teeter off his perch and threw him several feet. He landed hard and lay spread-eagled on his back, motionless, staring up at the empty sky.

Rusty had seen enough. She revved her engine and blew past my skiff, crashing ashore between the croc and Teeter. As her bow slammed the hump of marl, Annette pitched toward the bow deck, Holland onto his side, shooting pictures the whole way down.

The croc shot straight ahead toward the overhanging branches and splashed into the shadowy waters of the narrow creek, swishing away into the thicket. I jumped overboard and slogged through the deep mud to the beach. I was hauling Teeter to his feet when Rusty arrived beside me.

Teeter blubbered, trying and failing to shape words.

Embracing him, Rusty smoothed her hand across his wet hair and cooed to him: "Hush, hush, it's all right. The alligator's gone, it's gone now, Teeter. Everything's fine."

"It was a crocodile," Mona called.

Rusty pulled away from Teeter and turned on Mona. I'd known Rusty for more than twenty years and had seen her in more taxing situations than nearly anyone I'd ever met, but I'd never seen her lose her cool, much less witnessed the look that hardened on her face just then—both stricken and dark with fury.

Mona recognized it as well and turned away under its glare.

"I told her a lie," Teeter said.

"Hush, hush, sweetheart. Everything's okay."

Teeter pried himself out of Rusty's embrace. He dragged in a breath and looked at his sister, then at me.

"She asked my name, and I lied."

"Who?" Rusty took Teeter's hand in hers. "Who, Teeter?"

"The woman in the yellow bass boat," I said.

Teeter nodded.

"Bass boat?" Rusty dropped Teeter's hand and closed in on me. "What happened here, Thorn?"

"I don't know. This morning, about a mile up the Wood, we had a brush with a woman in a bass boat. She came at us head-on, missed by a few inches. Few hours later I heard Teeter's Mayday, and came running. Halfway across the bay I spotted the same yellow boat near the Mothership. When she saw us, she ran."

Teeter clenched his eyes tight, determined to stop crying.

"I lied to her. I don't know why."

"Enough," Rusty said. "Let's get back to the ship. We can talk about this inside."

"No," Teeter said. "I have to tell you. It's important." He was fetching for breath. A wet gargle in his throat.

With a gentle finger Rusty steered a loop of hair out of Teeter's eyes.

"All right, honey. So tell us."

Teeter drew a swallow of air, his eyes tilted toward the water's edge.

"She asked me if I was Daniel Oliver Thorn."

"What?" I grabbed hold of his shoulder. "Daniel Oliver Thorn? She said that?"

Rusty peeled my fingers off her brother, and I stepped back and raised both hands in apology. I looked over at Milligan. He and Mona had heard the exchange. John was moving to the rear of the skiff with Mona dogging him, speaking under her breath.

When I looked back at Rusty, her stare was fixed on me as she spoke to her brother. "All right, Teeter. What did you say when she asked you this?"

"I said yes, I was. I don't know why I said it."

"You told this woman you were Thorn, Daniel Oliver Thorn?"

"Yes."

"And then?"

Rusty was still glowering at me. Thorn, the poisonous black cloud. The man with toxic karma.

"Then she asked me . . ." Teeter shivered and gazed off at the horizon. "She asked me how long I could hold my breath."

CHAPTER FIFTEEN

"The presence of aqueous liquid in the paranasal sinuses in conjunction with other findings—a plume of froth around the mouth and nostrils, *emphysema aquosum*, Paltauf's spots, increased hemolysis, and so on—is regarded as clear and definite signs of drowning. You following this, Mr. Sugarman?"

"So far."

Dr. Dennis Dillard sniffed and shook out his white handkerchief and blew his nose into it for the third time in as many minutes. He was a small, thin man with a carefully knotted red tie, a starched white shirt, and black trousers. He wore black off-the-rack reading glasses low on his nose. His whitish blond hair had thinned away to a transparent layer combed across his oily scalp. He was in his mid-forties. The walls of his office were crammed with plaques, framed diplomas, and other credentials.

"So you're in law enforcement, Mr. Sugarman?"

"I am."

"With the state?"

Sugarman shrugged, noncommittal. Let him believe what he would.

There was a fist-sized ceramic skull on the desk, a gag gift with a springy hinge on its jaw. The only sign of levity in the room. Sugar reached out and jiggled the jaw into motion, watching it flutter up and down like the silent prattling of the dead.

"FDLE?"

Sugarman said nothing. He was not a practiced liar and wasn't about to begin practicing today.

"Maybe you could show me some ID."

"Would you like me to call Sheriff Whalen, have her ask you again to cooperate with me?"

"Well, at least tell me this: Are you here in response to my emails?"

Sugarman kept his face blank. This peevish little man was a snitch, tattling on the sheriff about something. Probably disgruntled about petty department politics. It was none of Sugarman's business, but he saw no reason to set the medical examiner straight.

"Just give me some kind of sign so I know who I'm talking to," the doctor said.

"I'm here to get to the bottom of Ms. Bates's death."

"Does Sheriff Whalen know your mission? Why you're here?"

"To this point, the sheriff has acted very professionally with me."

Dillard huffed. Still not sure how deferential he should be.

Sugarman had seen it before, feuds between the lab coats and badges. Desk jockeys and street cops battling for the bureaucratic table scraps.

"So you ruled it an accidental drowning. You're a hundred percent certain of that?"

Dillard looked down at his notes inside the open folder and smiled to himself. A smug man, probably the most educated person on the county payroll. The type of guy who thrived on that fact, having found the ideal venue to browbeat his inferiors.

Outside his single window, a team of brown-skinned workers mowed the grass and clipped the hedges while two white guys stood watch in the shade and chatted.

"As you may or may not know, Mr. Sugarman, the sphenoid sinus is easily accessible at autopsy; and its content can be aspirated from the base of the skull with a cannula. In the scientific literature, the valency of the liquid content in the sphenoid sinuses has been consecutively investigated in deaths by drowning and compared with deaths of other causes. The results showed that in ninety-two percent of the deaths by drowning between one milliliter and four milliliters of aqueous fluid is found in the sphenoid sinuses. Ms. Bates's sinus contained three milliliters."

"So she drowned," Sugar said.

"Without a doubt."

The doctor's office was only big enough to fit two people comfortably, and Dillard had arranged his large desk crosswise, hogging two-thirds of the space for himself, leaving any interloper with a cramped third. A single chair was wedged into a corner. Sugarman stayed on his feet and prowled his tiny area. He touched the corner of a framed diploma, a B.A. degree from some college he didn't recognize, a medical degree from a state university in Iowa. Sugar straightened that frame a couple of degrees.

"No second thoughts about your ruling?" Sugar said. "Not a heart attack, some other incident prior to the drowning?"

"She went into the water alive, inhaled, and drowned."

"So she lost her balance, tumbled out? That's how you see it?"

"That's one scenario. Strictly speaking, it's not my job to hypothesize. Florida State Statute four-oh-six-eleven puts any accidental death under my jurisdiction. Maintaining liaison with the sheriff's office, as you know, is my role. To pass along my findings. However, let's be clear: In some departments, medical examiners are a crucial part of the investigative team; however, in this particular setting, I'm treated as a subordinate, merely an advisor. Sheriff Whalen, and she alone, determines the direction of the investigation."

Sugarman waited for a moment, letting Dillard's pissy tone die away.

"Tell me about the Peace River. I floated down it once a long time ago. We're not talking white water. Right?"

"It's a calm waterway, yes, but as the sheriff likes to point out, the victim was eighty-six years old. People of that age frequently lose their balance."

"No other signs of trauma?"

Dillard settled his elbows on the desk, steepled his fingers, fingertip to fingertip.

"Sheriff Whalen didn't seem to think so."

"I take it you're not a fan of the sheriff?"

"I need to see some ID, Mr. Sugarman, before we go any further."

Sugar was tempted to play on Dillard's wishful thinking and impersonate a Florida Department of Law Enforcement agent. It was probably the most direct way to get the truth out of this weasel. But if Sugar was going to lower his standards, this wasn't the day and this wasn't the man.

"I'm a private investigator. I'm working for a member of the Bates family. Not Mona and not John."

"Who else is there?"

"I'm not at liberty to disclose that."

"Well, well, well," he said. "That puts a new light on things."

"Whatever findings I make, Dr. Dillard, will be exposed. If someone has been concealing facts or manipulating the investigation, it's my duty and privilege to set the record straight."

Dillard tucked his chin and spent a few seconds appraising Sugarman over the brim of his glasses. Not the white knight he'd been hoping for, but better than nothing. After a moment more, a thin smile formed on his lips and his eyes brightened a degree. Sugar was in.

"The body had no bruises?" Sugar said. "Contusions, bumps, fractures, anything consistent with a struggle before drowning? Or maybe something odd in her bloodstream— prescription drugs or alcohol? I assume you did a full toxicology workup."

Dillard ran a long finger along his neck as if checking his morning shave.

"And I need to see the photos," Sugarman said. "The autopsy."

He knew he was pushing it. But this little man in his cramped office with his framed degrees and his pallor and transparent skin and haughty style had pushed some button deep in Sugarman. Or maybe it was the accumulated effects of the day: Hankinson and his nigger remark. The white boys outside in the grass, supervising their Mexican slave labor. The Old South motoring on into the twenty-first century as if Lincoln had never freed anybody, as if Dr. King had never had a dream. Such a spike of rage was new for him, surprising. It twisted the muscles in his cheeks, felt like it was distorting his face into a teeth-baring growl. Not like him. Not at all.

Dillard must've caught a whiff of Sugar's anger. His eyes dropped to his desk and for a moment he seemed to be having a silent debate with himself. Weighing the risk of extending his hand to a stranger against his fear that his long-hoped-for savior would abandon him and never reappear. The fear won out, for when he snapped his eyes up at Sugar again, the brittle light of defiance had dimmed.

"I want you to know I've acquainted myself with Human Rights Provision one-twenty-nine, July seventh, nineteen-ninety-one, the Florida Whistleblower's Act. The sheriff has absolutely no legal authority to retaliate against me."

"Lay it out for me, Dillard, top to bottom. Stop wasting my time."

The doctor swallowed once and looked out his window. A fine gloss of sweat shone on his forehead. He closed the folder, slid it to the edge of the desk, and offered it up with averted eyes.

It wasn't Sugar's way to bully. But maybe he'd have to reconsider that, seeing how quickly Dillard caved.

In the file there were eighteen black-and-white photos. Fairly good quality for a small-town medical examiner, clear focus, good lighting. Abigail Bates was a tall woman who had carried no extra fat. She looked tough and defiant, even flat on her back, naked under the glare of operating room lights.

Despite the flattening effects of death, Sugar could see from her strong Roman nose and the wide flare of cheekbones a family resemblance to Thorn. There were five close-ups of her white flesh. Two showed her left upper arm and shoulder. On her triceps were four small but distinct bruises.

Dillard had isolated them, taken two shots of the same four bruises. Sugarman set those photos next to the ceramic skull. He fanned out the others on the desk and examined them one by one. Another bruise on her thigh, as large as a pinecone, just above the right knee. A small laceration on her throat, a jagged cut that looked like something a submerged branch might do as Abigail Bates's body was dragged downstream by the current.

"And all this was included in your written report? These four bruises?"

He nodded, his eyes on his wall of honors.

"That's a handprint, isn't it?"

"That was my professional analysis." Muscles clenched in the doctor's face.

"Fingerprints, anything under her fingernails?"

"One would've hoped, but no, nothing like that. Just those bruises and another set of slight discolorations on the edges of her hands which would be consistent with the victim striking at an object, hammering."

"Looks to me like someone looped an arm across the old lady's chest and gripped her upper arm."

With his eyes on his wall, Dillard spoke in a pinched voice.

"The sheriff thought otherwise. She said there could be any number of explanations for those bruises."

Sugarman took the file over to the chair and sat. Double-spaced, it was three pages long. Dry and clinical. No embellishments or ornament. A passing couple in a canoe spotted the body on the riverbank two miles short of the takeout. Sometime before that, Abigail Bates was last seen alive by a young woman in a kayak. The woman, a Ms. Featherstone, estimated the encounter to have taken place four miles short of the takeout.

So somewhere within that two-mile stretch Abigail Bates had drowned. Included in the file was a map of the river, neatly drawn on graph paper, that sketched that two-mile section. Within that portion of the waterway were three lazy turns and one sharp one, but other than that the river took a straight shot to the southwest.

"Someone took her under," Sugar said. "Held her till she drowned."

Dillard was silent, staring at his hands lying on his desk.

"You showed Sheriff Whalen these bruises, and she discounted them?"

Dillard pushed his chair back and rose to his feet. He took his reading glasses off and set them on his ink blotter. Then he drew a sharp breath and held Sugarman's gaze.

"Abigail Bates was the object of loathing in this community. There was no political outcry when the investigation ended without a suspect. The sheriff knew full well she was under no pressure to produce one."

"You made your case to the sheriff that it wasn't an accident, but she blew you off."

Dillard touched a finger to the corner of his mouth as if freeing a crumb.

"Precisely."

"Why would she do that?" Sugarman said. "Why would Sheriff Whalen ignore such compelling evidence of foul play?"

That won a bitter smile from Dr. Dillard. Misogynist to misogynist.

"You'd have to ask the sheriff that. Personally, I never saw anyone work so hard to *ignore* evidence."

"You think she's covering for somebody? She knows who did it, and she's giving them a pass?"

The smile on Dillard's lips was almost too loathsome to behold. A pompous ass who'd been humbled by a black woman and was still stinging.

That Sheriff Whalen might be guilty of protecting a murderer seemed to be of far less importance to Dillard. He'd been sitting in his tiny office stewing about the personal injustice of being treated as hired help, the injury to his ego, composing emails, trying to stir up the higher powers. He'd been plotting his revenge when Sugarman stumbled into the picture.

"Covering for someone is one possibility, I suppose." Dillard lifted his eyebrows. Letting Sugarman fill in the blanks.

"But you think it's more than that."

"I have my suspicions."

"What? Whalen is in on the crime? She's an accomplice?"

Dillard sat back down in his chair with a quiet sigh as though elated to finally hear the words uttered aloud. After a moment his shoulders lifted and he washed his dry white hands against each other. Now, on to business.

"I heard something about videos," Sugar said. "Protest speeches."

Dillard cocked an eyebrow.

"Well, well, someone's been a busy boy."

"You know about them?"

"Of course. They were made by C.C. Olsen at Pine Tree School, his folkloric record of the ills of the community."

"Bates International, the big bad corporate villain?"

"Oh, my yes, a lot of anger seething around these parts. Misdirected, I must say."

Sugarman looked down at the ceramic skull. Its jaw had stopped moving. Quiet now, said its piece.

"So," Dillard said. "I presume you'll be needing copies of everything. The autopsy report, photos. I'll have my girl reproduce them for you."

"Yes," Sugarman said. "Have her do that."

CHAPTER SIXTEEN

Rusty took teeter to his cabin to help him get washed up, and I ordered Mona and John Milligan to have a seat at the galley table.

"I need a whiskey," John said.

I stepped to the right, blocking his path to the bar.

"Sit down. We're going to talk."

We stood face-to-face, an arm's length apart. His face was ruddy from our hours in the hard, unfiltered sun, but there was a darker shade simmering beneath the surface, the unmistakable burn of rage. I readied myself to duck and sidestep the right cross he seemed to be measuring.

Then he closed his eyes, sucked a noisy breath through his nose, and blew it out in disgust. He turned away and slid into the leather booth. A man unfamiliar with backing down.

Annette wedged in at the other end of the booth while near the bar Holland bebopped to some tune in his head and tinkered with the settings on his Nikon. He was wearing black trousers today, a black open-collar shirt, and a white watch cap that he'd rolled down over his ears. Some kind of punk-ass fashion statement. Across the galley Mona had begun to wander about, carrying dirty plates to the sink and rinsing them, straightening the countertops, storing leftover food from our breakfast in Tupperware containers.

"Now talk to me, John. This complete stranger comes out of nowhere and terrorizes Teeter. She knows my full name.

That's two people in two days. You and her. So, talk. What the hell's going on?"

"It's about the river," Mona said. "The watershed, phosphate mining. It has to be."

"All right, Mona. Go on."

"My grandmother was drowned in the Peace River. That was no coincidence. It was a warning, clear and simple." She studied the backs of her hands pressed against the countertop and nodded to herself as if lost in a long calculation.

"Come on, let's hear it."

She sighed and raised her head, then finger-combed some snarls out of her hair and glanced around the galley at nothing in particular.

"I'm a biologist. A Ph.D. from Florida State."

"Relevance," Holland said from the bar. He had Mona in the sights of his Nikon, adjusting the focus.

"I run the mitigation program for Bates."

"Define 'mitigation,' " Holland said.

Annette said, "Mona is a problem solver. Her job is to find ways to ease tensions between the company's interests and the interests of the community."

"Use the word in a sentence," Holland said.

I swung around and put myself in the center of his frame.

"Here's a sentence for you, Holland. Either cut the shit, or I'll mitigate your ass overboard."

From four feet away he snicked a picture of me, then another. Then switched to his motor drive and machine-gunned me with a dozen more.

"He's like that," Annette said. "He's just playing. Don't get in a huff."

Mona's eyes were muddy as though her emotions had burned down to a hard nub of grief.

Mood swings all around. John's bullyboy gleam had dulled, and Annette, our poised social director from the night before, seemed shrunken and a little lost. I'd seen that happen before with urban hotshots out for their first tour of the Everglades. All their jaded world-weariness struck a hollow note in that vast, trackless place. The best of them were humbled into silence. The worst, like Holland, buzzed along with callow disregard for their surroundings as if nothing short of a gunshot to the brain could break the grip of their narcissism.

"Last summer I worked out a deal." Mona met my eyes, searching them for a long moment, then resuming her speech. "I proposed a solution to the Horse Creek issue. Bates had applied for permits to strip-mine land in the Horse Creek basin, twenty-one thousand acres of virgin forest and grassland. There was fierce resistance, meetings, DEP hearings. Lots of protests. It looked like the deal was tanking. So I talked Grandmother into cutting the acreage in half, donating ten thousand to the county for a wildlife refuge, and that swung it. Protestors backed off, the project revived. Permits on the verge of approval. It pissed off extremists on both sides of the issue. That's when she drowned."

Holland continued to slink around the galley shooting more film.

"Annette," I said. "You and Holland go to your cabins."

"No, way, dickweed," Holland said. "No tinhorn fish guide is sending me to my room. We're under attack. We got a right to know what the fuck's going on."

"Nobody's under attack," I said.

Annette said, "I'm with Holland. Given the uncertain circumstances, it's vital we're all on the same page." She thrust out her jaw at a plucky angle.

"All right," I said. "But keep camera boy on a tighter leash or he'll be swimming with the crocs."

Annette wrinkled her nose at my crudity.

Standing at the kitchen counter, Mona finished her pitch on Horse Creek, how some of the land I'd inherited surrounded the headwaters of that pristine stream, which supplied a vital fifteen percent of the freshwater supply of the Peace River. If that land was ripped open and mined, it would ruin the natural groundwater flow, and if Horse Creek died, the Peace River would follow. Then downstream, Charlotte Harbor, on the Gulf, would lose its crucial dose of freshwater, and the snook and redfish that depended on that would die, the region's fishing industry and tourism would lose millions, and the whole fragile ecosystem of the region would be in peril. A grim cascade of small disasters leading to a full-scale crisis, until a lot of people lost their jobs and a lot of creatures would die off, fly off, or disappear.

It was a story I'd heard a hundred times. Some version or another. Florida's story. Knee bone connected to the thigh bone. The wobbly dominoes clicking against one another until the whole structure collapsed.

I'd watched it happen since I was a kid. People with cash and power who respected nothing except more cash and power were busy poking their drinking straws into the juicy earth and sucking out the marrow. Grave robbers with giant shovels or derricks and mile-long drills, tapping into the black veins of coal, underground oceans of crude, exhuming those formations of white fossilized bones that were hidden beneath the crust of Florida.

At fifteen my high school biology teacher showed us maps of Pangea, the supercontinent. North and South America fused with Africa. I was frozen at my desk. Two hundred million years ago when the tectonic split happened, great plates buckling against each other, mountains erupting from the sea, Florida was dragged off into the northern hemisphere where it promptly sank beneath the ocean onto the continental platform.

For most of earth's history, Florida remained underwater. Limestone deposits built up, fine-grained shale, mudstone, sandy strips, and a few rare layers of phosphate. For brief intervals it rose above the sea, but every time the polar ice caps melted, Florida was submerged, and more sediments were deposited over the peninsula. The biology guy was passionate, and that afternoon I caught a touch of his fever because it all made wonderful sense. Florida was a land with its roots in three continents, and its taproot in the sea itself.

All that dunking in the sea had turned our state into a vast plain of corpses, layer upon layer. The remains of marine creatures drifted to the ocean floor and combined with sand and marl, hardening over the ages into rich gray mineral.

Century after century more carcasses floated down on top of those, and more and more and more.

Now we were harvesting them, the fossils of unimaginable fish that had turned to stone in their million-year sleep. We were feeding off the dead to maintain our insatiable cravings. To grow lusher crops, faster and taller, more fruitful. To keep the cities bright and throbbing. The cars running at full bore. Maintain the delirious drumbeat of what passed for civilization.

There was a sharp silence in the galley. All four of them were waiting for me to rejoin. Mona cleared her throat, brushed some crumbs from the countertop.

I went over to the galley windows that looked out at the bay. The perfect blue sky from earlier in the day was thickening with clouds as the next front approached. Cardiac Bay was turning to lead, and the sky was dull brushed silver. Egrets and herons scattered south in a hurry.

Out the starboard window I watched the V of a wake spread across the surface, probably a big tarpon sweeping past or a bull shark chasing a school of mullet. The cove was quiet again. No doubt the croc was lurking nearby, half submerged, spying on us with its high-set eyes.

I felt a faint shift in the Mothership, heard a creak I didn't recognize. I moved to the window and peered out but saw nothing. Water flat and gray, a great blue heron standing knee-deep just off the crocodile's nesting spot.

"So Abigail Bates was murdered because of this mitigation thing. Somebody thought she didn't go far enough, or somebody from the other side believed she went too far."

"Exactly," Mona said. "She dies. Her killer thinks the problem's solved, then out of nowhere, you pop up."

I turned around. "That makes it pretty simple. Who else knows about the lockbox? Who else knows my full name? I assume it wasn't public knowledge."

With a bitter smile, John shook his head.

"Come on, John. Who else? Lawyers? People at Bates International?"

He pushed himself out of the booth and came over to stand

beside me. Holland snapped the two of us together. Trigger-happy for an action shot.

"My lawyer, Carter Mosley. He's the only one. And he's well aware of the sensitivity of the issue. Under no circumstances would Mosley spread your name or any other private family matters."

"Well, good. That narrows it some. So if I'm dead, who gets that land?"

John turned his back on the question.

"Uncle John, that's who," Holland said. "Yeah, yeah, bingo."

John's shoulders tightened, but he said nothing.

"Holy shit," Holland said. "Look who's walking among us. Uncle Johnny is Colonel Mustard with the dagger in the parlor."

Milligan growled and heaved toward Holland, took a swipe at the camera, but the kid shimmied away, all the while snapping shot after shot. I clapped a hand on John's meaty shoulder and spun him around. Milligan froze.

"The woman in the boat is the backup plan," Holland jeered while watching through his viewfinder. "If Uncle Johnny can't convince big-dog fishing guide to sign away his land, then whammo, he switches to Plan B: Mystery woman takes out fishing guide. Badda-bing."

"Holland watches a lot of crime trash on TV," Annette said.

Holland flicked his camera, eager as a rat in heat.

"Is that true, John?" I asked. "If I'm dead, you control the land?"

"That's outrageous. I have nothing to do with this."

"Answer the question, John. What happens to the land if I die?"

"I have no idea. Carter and I never discussed that possibility."

"Never came up, not once?"

Milligan backhanded the thought away. Nothing more to say.

"And you, Mona? What do you want from me? You and your dad in this together? If I sign away the land, does that make you happy?"

Milligan snorted and stalked past me toward the bar.

"Dad and I are on opposing sides. I was pushing Grandmother to move in an entirely different direction when she died."

"And what direction is that?"

"Mitigation isn't enough. The only solution is to stop all mining, shut down everything. Just stop. Let the Chinese find their fertilizer somewhere else. Bates cleans up their mess, restores the wetlands, and pays restitution to citizens whose health has been compromised by the gyp stacks or the air quality around the mines of the fertilizer factories. We cancel all future proposals in the Horse Creek watershed and put things right, including Pine Tree School."

"What's that?"

"There's a school, a county school, built near a gyp stack. There's been some health issues among the kids and teachers there."

"So shut everything down. That's your plan?"

"Sure," Mona said. "The company would take a short-term hit, but in the long run, it'd be a huge PR boost. And it's the right thing to do. Bates would survive. Phosphate is a tiny fraction of the corporation."

Milligan stared at the carpet, shaking his head in disdain.

"Tiny fraction?" He indulged in a small chuckle. "Thirty years of minerals left in the ground? That's the big B. Billions of dollars."

"And your grandmother was seriously considering this option?"

"She went on that canoe trip because I kept pestering her to take a firsthand look at what was at stake. I think she was about to do the right thing, though I can't prove it."

"How'd you feel about that, John? Mona's plan?"

"It's ridiculous." John settled on a stool at the bar. "Mona was exercising an undue influence over Mother. She was manipulating the woman, insinuating herself into corporate affairs. Her actions bordered on the illegal."

"Boy, oh, boy," Holland said. "There's your freaking motive. That's as good as a confession, Uncle Johnny. Whack

Granny 'cause she's turned tree-hugger and gonna cost you some major bucks."

"How about you, Mona?" I said. "You bring anything for me to sign?"

She smiled dryly.

Since we'd returned to the Mothership, she'd fastened her auburn hair into a ponytail, which made her eyes seem larger, cheeks more sharply defined. The stubborn glower she'd worn yesterday had softened. In her quiet manner there was still a lingering tragic air, which I took to be the long-term effects of Abigail's death, a condition her father clearly did not share.

If love could be described as undue influence, I could see how Mona might be guilty of exercising it, and how even a tough old broad like Abigail Bates might succumb to this young woman's earnest zeal.

I'd always been a sucker for certain true believers and the infectious tug of their idealism. As sappy as they sometimes were, so easy to mock, the genuine ones like Mona, whose passion was still pure, who trusted that generations of bad choices could be undone, and fervently believed the world was still worth saving, those were the ones who stirred something in me, and could even inspire a rare upwelling of optimism.

"If that's what you want, Thorn, papers to sign," she said, testing out a slender smile, "I could draw something up for you, a week, two weeks."

I looked out at the hard silver light bouncing off the bay. Something old and familiar was swimming through my chest, and I felt a flush heat my skin, a stumbling pulse that left me slack and unsure. I closed my eyes and willed it to cease. Wrong time, wrong place, wrong person. I could feel her eyes on me and knew that Mona Milligan in some way sensed my condition.

I sighed and stalled a moment more, looking out at the riffling bay. Then I turned back to the others and shifted my gaze across each of their faces.

"Okay, listen up," I said. "Here's what's going to happen.

This trip is officially over. We're heading back as soon as I pull anchor. Until then, no more arguments, no discussions. Just sit there and watch the scenery go by till we're back in Islamorada."

Annette checked her watch, then hunched over her laptop and began to tap beneath the table, probably noting the latest disastrous turn.

For a long moment the cabin was quiet except for the click of her keys.

And then the shriek.

The houseboat's walls were crammed with high-density soundproofing. It had been Rusty's last-minute decision when she realized she could hear the jabber of the TV from the crew cabins on the upper deck. I'd overseen its installation and Rusty's financial backers shelled out an extra five grand for the fix.

But Rusty's scream penetrated all that easily, an agonized wail that sent me flying out the back door, scrambling up the ladder toward the crew deck.

As I was clearing the last rung, over my shoulder I spotted movement in the water below and came to a halt.

The woman in the bass boat was twenty feet off our stern. Perched in the casting seat in the bow, she was using the silent electric motor to glide away to the east. Behind her were our two skiffs, tethered to her stern cleat.

"Thorn! Help me, God, help me."

Rusty stumbled through the crew quarters doorway. Her hands were outstretched, dark with blood.

CHAPTER SEVENTEEN

Teeter's face was ghastly white. His butt was planted on the deck, back against the side of his bunk. He was naked, his hands folded modestly over his genitals.

As I entered the cabin, with Rusty a step behind, Teeter's eyes tracked lazily across my face as if he were trying to recall my name. His mouth was open, his face loose, and he was breathing in ragged intervals.

"What is this? What's happened?"

"I took a bullet." Teeter's mouth twisted into a tortured grin.

He bent halfway around to display a ragged wound a few inches to the right of his spine. An ooze of blood, dark and oily, escaped. The carpet was stained beneath him.

"Teeter, leave it alone."

Rusty dragged a blanket from his bunk and dropped to his side. She draped it across his shoulders, wrapped it around him, and tucked it tight.

Teeter's legs glistened with water. A smear of blood stretched across the carpet between the tiny bathroom and the place where he slumped.

"He collapsed in the shower. I dragged him out and discovered this. She must have shot him while he was swimming away. The mud from the shoreline concealed it."

"That woman shot me." Teeter's voice was airy, drifting. "I called Mayday on the radio then jumped overboard and she shot me. The water slowed the bullet, that's why it's still inside me. Happened before I got tangled up with the croc. It doesn't hurt. Not much. I'm okay."

"I'll hail the park rangers, get a helicopter." I started for the door.

Teeter called out for me to wait. The sharp authority in his voice brought me to a halt. He worked his blue eyes across my face with such intensity, it was clear a fierce resolve had risen through the layers of his suffering and taken possession of him.

"You need to know this," he said. "When the woman came on the boat, she pointed her pistol at me and asked where our guns were."

"She was looking for guns?"

"I didn't tell her a thing. Didn't say a damn word to her. She started tearing through the closets and drawers. But she didn't get a chance to finish looking 'cause I jumped over the side."

"Hush, sweetie. Thorn's going to call for help. You just relax."

"See what I'm saying, Thorn? She doesn't know what we got, whether we're armed or not. So she can't just come flying back. You need to know, Thorn. That's why I stayed alive, so I could tell you."

It was important information and I told him so.

"I did good," he said, staring up at me.

"You did great, Teeter. Now relax, just relax. I'm getting help."

He smiled, then without a flinch or flutter, his face firmed up, his eyes closed, and he passed beyond our reach.

Rusty groaned and grabbed him around the shoulders, cradling his head against her chest, hugging him hard.

I went over and kneeled beside her, put my arm around her. Rusty's flesh was icy and she was shivering. Tears streaked her cheeks, but she was biting back the sobs. Years of training had switched on. It was a survival skill in her profession— staying cool around the other guides, the tough, stoic gang on the dock.

She lifted her head, her face empty. She seemed entranced by a slash of light angling through the starboard window.

"Listen to me, Rusty. She came back. She's out there off our stern."

"Who?"

"The one who did this. She's towing our skiffs away."

Rusty tugged away from me.

"And you let her?"

"Wasn't anything I could do."

She eased Teeter onto the deck, covered him with the blanket, and rose.

I followed her outside to the narrow walkaround deck. The bass boat was two hundred yards east. The woman had switched off her trolling motor, and she'd moved behind the wheel and was using the outboard, idling away toward the mouth of a distant creek. A large bundle lay beside her on the deck. It might have been a body, but I couldn't imagine whose.

Rusty ducked into the bridge and grabbed the mike for the VHF to hail the park rangers. They monitored channel 18 and there was a remote chance our power-boosted antenna could deliver a signal to their station back at Flamingo. But when she held the mike to her mouth, we both saw the spiral radio cord dangling loose beneath it.

"Pull the anchor, Thorn. We're getting out of here."

Rusty reached for the ignition, but the keys were gone. I'd already seen they were missing and moved to the drawer where we kept the backups. I rifled through the jumble of tools and notepads and pens, but couldn't find the other set of keys. Then I saw the ignition wires hanging below the console. The intruder had slashed the wiring harness. I knelt down and flipped open the circuit box that controlled the twin outboards. She'd smashed the fuses, stolen the box of replacements, hacked up the contacts. With that much damage, a hot-wire would be a major challenge.

Together, Rusty and I headed for the wall locker where the Sat phone was stowed. She reached it first and whipped the door open. Gone. Black zippered case and all. Two spare handheld VHF's were missing as well. Even our Zeiss binoculars were gone.

"She stripped us bare."

Rusty wheeled on me and grabbed a handful of my shirt and bulled me backward against the console. I didn't resist.

"What the hell is this, Thorn? You did something. This is about you."

I said nothing.

She twisted her fist, grinding her knuckles against my sternum, straining the fabric of my shirt. Then little by little her rage smoldered out and she forced down a breath and relaxed her grip. She stepped away and turned her back to me. When a moment or two of silence had passed, I laid a hand on her shoulder and she didn't shrug it off.

"I need to know something, Rusty."

She bent forward and planted both hands on the console and leaned her weight against them, staring out at the distant creek where the bass boat had disappeared. She looked dizzy and faint.

"Why did Teeter lie? Why did he tell the woman he was me?"

"What difference does it make?"

"I'm trying to understand."

"It's not important." She stared out at the empty bay.

"Tell me, Rusty. Why?"

Rusty swallowed and turned her head just enough to bring me into view.

"Teeter worshipped you. He worshipped your fucking sweat."

"What?"

"He idolized you. Thorn, man of action. It's why he quit his job at Ballyhoo's. When he heard you signed up as my first mate, he gave them notice that same day. It was his big chance to be near you, watch you, learn how to be more like you. It makes perfect sense he pretended he was you. Maybe at the end he was even trying to protect you, take the hit instead of you. Who knows? But whatever he was doing, he was trying to earn your respect."

I had to blink hard to clear the burn in my eyes.

"Well, he did that," I said and turned away. "He damn well did that."

We placed Teeter on his bunk and covered him with the blanket. We stood there for several moments in silence, then Rusty mumbled under her breath, a few phrases with the solemn cadence of a Catholic prayer. I tried to find some parting words for this man who very possibly had given his life for mine. But nothing rose from the dark hollow in my chest.

Rusty kneeled down and kissed him on his broad forehead and swept a hand across his cheek. She pressed the side of her face against his still chest for several moments. Then she rose and headed for the cabin door.

For the next half hour the two of us took an inventory of the vessel, looking for anything we might use in our defense. At one point Milligan tracked us down and informed us that our skiffs were missing. Rusty told him we were aware of that. He demanded an explanation, but neither of us responded. He'd had a few drinks by then, and his eyes were glassed over and his tongue sloppy. His bristling arrogance had subsided, and an awkward whine had crept into his bullyboy bravado like some deposed tyrant who was starting to comprehend his fallen circumstance.

Milligan tagged along for a while longer, badgering half-heartedly, then recognized it was useless and marched back to the salon to join the others.

"We're going to have to level with them," I said.

"When we've sorted it out."

Rusty and I were standing on the roof of the ship. Overhead the gray sky seemed within arm's reach, and the wind had swung around and was coming out of the northwest, churning patches of the bay to froth. Up on that top deck there were plastic chairs for sunset viewing and a small table where we had intended to serve happy-hour cocktails. Fastened to the rear railings with bungee cords were a pair of kayaks. I was staring at them when Rusty stepped in front of me.

"Forget it, Thorn."

I checked the angle of the sun. It was midafternoon, two, two-thirty.

"If I started now, I could make it back to the docks by eight tonight, nine at the latest. With a little wind at my back, maybe sooner."

She shook her head.

"No way. The bitch would pick you off in a heartbeat."

I looked out at the empty bay, the half-dozen coves, the sweep of mangroves. The creek mouth where the bass boat had disappeared was about a half mile off the port quarter.

"Here we are," I said. "Easy targets. No one's shooting."

Rusty swallowed, eyes scanning the distance.

"Relax," I said. "She thinks she killed her man, her job's done. She's gone."

"Why come back and steal the skiffs?"

"To keep us from chasing. Give her more of a head start."

"I think she's still out there," Rusty said. "I think this is just beginning."

"Look, if this woman wanted to murder everybody aboard, she could've started this morning back in the Broad River. She had the drop on us. It was totally isolated. We were defenseless."

Even as I spoke the words, they sounded hollow. All three of us could have been armed and ready to return fire for all she knew.

"I've been thinking about that line she gave Teeter," Rusty said. " 'How long can you hold your breath?' What the hell is that about?"

I told Rusty I didn't know. True enough, though I had a growing suspicion. Since Mona's outburst at the restaurant the night before, I'd been brooding about Abigail Bates's death, imagining the horror of her last seconds, the grisly act itself. Face-to-face, hand to hand, an intimate murder.

In some echo chamber of my heart, I could even hear the killer's taunt.

While I hold you under, I will suffer what you suffer, because I know I can outlast you. I've bet my life you will succumb before I do, because my will is stronger than your will, my readiness to endure pain greater than yours. I am risking everything to watch you die. All so I might be touching your flesh when it happens.

Standing at the starboard rail, Rusty shivered and lowered her head, and I thought she was finally going to surrender to a long heaving cry. But after a moment more, she straightened, drew a deliberate breath, and her eyes followed the flight of a white pelican as it coasted past us on an oblique angle to the wind. She watched the bird sail across the sky until it dipped below the next stand of mangroves a half mile off.

"We should get back inside," I said.

Rusty led the way. As we backed down the stern ladder, I heard an osprey make three sharp cries, then three more.

Once in the past, I'd felt the wispy prickle of a telescopic lens pass over my flesh just before a slug exploded nearby. But this time I had no premonition, no signal beyond that osprey's insistent cry.

Rusty stepped onto the deck, and just as I jumped down beside her I heard the dry crack of a rifle. Above us, a section of the rooftop railing blew apart and a foot-long section twirled past our heads into the bay. I'd been holding on to that chrome handrail moments before.

At the mouth of the distant creek dozens of egrets and herons exploded from their roosts and sailed in a white thrashing cloud toward the west.

CHAPTER EIGHTEEN

Rusty ducked inside the crew cabin and I slipped in behind her and shut the door. The tinted windows were dark enough to conceal our movements from a distance. Just the same, both of us stepped away from the glass.

She took a careful breath, then turned back to the door and reached for the handle, but I grabbed her and pulled her away.

"Got to warn the others," she said. "They're my responsibility."

"In a minute," I said. "Just hold on."

"What?"

"The shooter's stopped. That wasn't about killing anybody."

"You're sure about that?"

"She's not still firing, is she? The woman's not in any hurry."

"What, she's toying with us?"

"Could be calibrating her rifle, or just trying to scare us."

"Well, she accomplished that."

"Or maybe it's what Teeter said. She doesn't know for certain if we're defenseless. She can't be sure she didn't miss our weapons stash. We could have our own rifle with a sight. So she takes a shot, then waits to see how we respond. She's probing."

"Fine, except we *are* defenseless."

"Not really."

"What?"

"The flares," I said. "And there's the Makita, for starters."

"The reciprocating saw? Christ, Thorn. She's got a rifle, and we're going to defend ourselves with a handsaw?"

"It's something."

I'd decided to cart along the saw in case we had plumbing issues and needed to plunge-cut into the drywall to access the pipes. It had happened once in the master stateroom head, an L joint coming unglued. The Makita had a six-inch serrated blade and trigger-controlled speed and was a tough piece of hardware.

But Rusty was right. Saw versus rifle, shitty odds.

Without further discussion, we exited the west door onto the deck shielded from the creek mouth and circled the cabins to the stern. With Rusty at my shoulder, I opened the transom tool chest. The killer had missed it. Everything was intact. The battery-powered saw, a crowbar, boxed sets of screwdrivers and socket wrenches, all the Coast Guard safety equipment, including a half-dozen flares, a plastic whistle, an air horn, life jackets for ten.

"Time to lay it out for the others."

"I'll do the talking, Thorn. This is my show."

"Tell me something, Rusty. When you were describing the trip to John and Mona, did either of them ask you exactly where we'd be anchoring up? The name of the bay, anything specific?"

"No."

"You're sure?"

"Absolutely."

I looked off at that distant creek.

"But Carter Mosley did," Rusty said. "He wanted the GPS coordinates."

"Carter Mosley."

"He said he might fly in, join us for a day or two if he could shake loose from work."

The rest of our group was assembled in the salon. Hushed, calm. Apparently they hadn't heard the rifle shot. Behind the bar, Milligan was pouring a Scotch over rocks. A glass of red wine sat on the table before Mona, and she was skimming her finger around its rim squeaking out a high whine. Cross-legged on the couch in front of the TV, Annette was hunched over her keyboard, fingers flying. Luxury Vacation from Hell, by Annette Gordon. In the galley area, Holland had rolled his white watch cap up off his ears, and it sat high on his head like a hip-hop crown. He stood guard over a plate of muffins and was tearing off the crusty lids one by one, taking wolfish bites, then setting the rest of the muffin aside. His camera hung around his neck, dusted with crumbs.

I placed the saw and crowbar and half the flares on the coffee table. Beside them Rusty lay the air horn, whistle, and the rest of the flares.

No one spoke, but there was a collective stiffness in the group, no eye contact, as if the four of them had been hashing out the situation and had reached a decision. A budding mutiny.

"For the record," Mona said, "I'm totally against this."

"Against what?" Rusty moved in front of the TV. Someone had turned it on. CNN was covering a snowstorm in Colorado, airports closed, highways clogged with abandoned cars. Rusty picked up the remote and snapped it off.

Holland tore the lid off a blueberry muffin and crammed it in his mouth.

John reached under the bar and came up with a yellow walkie-talkie. Earlier in the fall when I'd shopped for equipment I'd noticed similar models on the shelves of marine-supply stores for about sixty bucks. Its runty aerial and cheap electronics gave it a range of about a mile—a half step up from a kid's toy. It wasn't on the Mothership's equipment list.

"It warbled," Mona said. "Kept warbling, the call signal it makes."

"I tracked it down." Holland took his lens cap off. "It was on the shelf behind the TV, up there with the Audubon books."

Milligan set it on the bar beside his drink.

"It's her," he said. "She wants to make a deal."

"The woman?" Rusty edged over to the bar. "You talked to

her without giving me a heads-up. Is that what you're saying?"

"Uncle Johnny is pissed," Holland said. "Mr. Big Shot's used to running the show, and you guys blew him off. He's royally pissed, aren't you, Uncle Johnny?"

Milligan touched the walkie-talkie with a fingertip. He glanced at his watch, a gaudy Rolex encrusted with tiny diamonds.

"A couple of minutes she's going to call back for our response."

"What kind of deal?" I said.

"She wants to talk to you, Thorn." Milligan picked up his drink and tossed it back.

"Then she lets us go," Holland said, and snapped two quick shots of my reaction. "You two talk, whatever happens happens, then the party's over, we get a free pass home."

Rusty stepped closer to Milligan.

"She thought my brother was Thorn. How did she learn different?"

Milligan's gaze was trained on his empty glass.

"Uncle Johnny spilled the frijoles. Blab, blab, blab."

Holland snapped a shot of Rusty's stunned face.

"Okay, I slipped," Milligan said. "She wanted to talk to Thorn. I spoke without thinking. I told her you weren't here. You were up on the roof."

"You idiot." Rusty cocked her fist and came for him, but I seized her arm and hauled her to a stop.

"I blew it," Milligan said. "I had a couple of drinks, I wasn't thinking straight. But that's her deal."

"Bullshit," Rusty said. "No way in hell is that going to happen."

"Sounds like a bargain," Holland said. "Swap *muy macho* fishing guide for the rest of us. I call that a fucking steal."

"Holland, you're a weasel."

"Hey, Annette, write that down. Lesbo houseboat captain insults internationally esteemed photojournalist."

"When this is over, kid," I said to Holland. "When this trip is done . . ."

"Ooooh, my knees are quaking. I'm having palpitations."

Rusty swung to me. "Like I said, Thorn. It's just beginning."

She stepped over to the rear door and peered out toward the creek.

A second later the walkie-talkie trilled, then trilled again.

I picked it up and held it out to Rusty. She snapped it from my hand, gripped it while it made another electronic cheep. She held it to her mouth, but before she could utter a word, the shooter spoke.

"Who am I talking to?" Nothing pushy in her tone, almost deferential.

Rusty extended the walkie-talkie to arm's length and stared at it as if it were something poisonous. For a moment she seemed ready to fling it across the room. Then she swung around and thrust it toward me.

"Take it," she said. "I can't do this."

I took the unit and pressed the answer button.

"I'm here," I said.

"Is this Daniel Oliver Thorn?"

I drew a slow breath.

"The name is Thorn."

Holland was inching his lens closer to my face. Clicking, clicking.

"Get in one of the kayaks," she said. "Paddle three hundred yards east of the houseboat and wait."

Mona was staring at me from across the room, something flickering in her eyes, a squint that might have been recognition.

"No," I said.

"Yes. Fifteen minutes. Paddle out and wait."

"You want to talk, go ahead. I'm listening."

I pointed at Mona and waved her over. She got up from the couch and was by my side as the woman spoke again. I tipped the walkie-talkie so she could hear the voice more clearly.

"You paddle out and meet me. Or the others go down, too."

I mouthed the words to Mona, "You know her?"

She shook her head, paused, then shrugged. Not sure. Maybe.

"Why're you doing this?" I said. "What's this about?"

It took several seconds for her to reply.

"How long can you hold your breath, Daniel Oliver Thorn?"

Annette slammed her notebook onto the coffee table and stalked over to my side. Without a word, she snatched the radio from me.

"Listen, whoever you are," Annette said. "This isn't funny. This game you're playing, it's not going to work. You don't know who you're dealing with. There are important people on this boat. I happen to write for a national magazine with a circulation of over two million. Lots of people know exactly where I am. So you stop this prank. Do you hear me? Right now."

"Give me back to Thorn." Her tone was impassive, almost bored.

Annette held the radio to her mouth again, about to resume her lecture, then thought better of it and thrust it back at me.

"I'm here," I said.

"Fifteen minutes to get that kayak into the water. Paddle due east three hundred yards and wait."

"I'll give it some thought," I said. "Get back to you later."

Before she could reply, I switched the walkie-talkie to OFF and dropped the unit into my pocket.

"Think about it?" Holland said. "You're going to think about it?"

I took two quick steps and shoved Holland against the dining table. He reached out to stiff-arm me, but I waded in closer and got chest to chest with him, breathing in his face.

Annette may have screamed. Milligan may have made some stern remark. There was such swelling in my ears I wasn't sure. I unlooped the camera strap from Holland's neck, swatted his hands away, and went to the rear doorway, pushed it open, and started to lob the bulky camera out into the bay.

Holland yelled at me to stop.

I turned around, shut the door behind me, still holding the camera.

"Holland, let's get this clear. Next time your asshole alter ego opens his mouth, this thing goes in the drink. Got it?"

"All right, all right. I got it, I got it."

"Not even a joke. Not even a lighthearted jest. Clear?"

He nodded morosely.

I held up his camera to examine it. "You have other lenses for this thing?"

"What? I'm a professional. You think I have only one lens?"

"What about a telephoto?"

"What're you talking about?"

"You heard me."

"I got one, yeah. In my case."

"Put it on. Stand right here at the salon door and keep looking through the telephoto at that creek mouth over to the southeast. You see it?"

Holland came over and looked.

"Where those birds are in the branches?"

"Just to the left of the egrets, yeah. Twenty, thirty yards left."

"Why?"

I turned back to the group.

"Teeter's dead," I said. "The woman out there shot him in the back when he was swimming away, trying to escape."

Mona groaned and closed her eyes.

Even Holland shut his mouth. He cradled his camera with both hands as though he might drop it otherwise.

"What's going on here?" Annette said. "What the hell is this about?"

"All we know for sure," I said, "is that the woman's got a rifle, probably with a telescopic sight. She's a good shot. She's got a handgun, too. But she doesn't know what weapons we have. That's why she's being cautious."

Annette was standing up now, an uncertain smile playing on her lips.

"What weapons *do* we have?" Milligan said.

"What you see on the coffee table. Some flares, a saw. The tools."

"You're shitting me," Holland said. "A saw?"

"So there it is," Milligan said to the others. "She can do anything she wants. She could sit out there and plink away, fill the houseboat full of lead, cut us down one by one."

"Not if we play this right," I said. "She's been careful so far. We can use that to our advantage."

"Use it how?" Holland said.

"If we don't give her a clear target, we might steal enough time to get the motors up and running."

"And what then?" Milligan said. "Outrun her in this barge?"

"When we get closer to land, our cell phones should work."

Milligan snorted. "That's it? That's the plan?"

No one would look at me. Not even Rusty.

"Hell, if that's all you've got," Milligan said, "I'll have to fix this myself."

"And your fix is what, John?"

Milligan stood his ground behind the bar, staring at me with a look he must have acquired from Abigail, a mingling of disgust and triumph—the human race once again confirming his low opinion. The luster in his eyes was dulled by the booze, and his tone had taken on a bleak, stony edge. Through the starboard windows the harsh sunlight illuminated his face and the dark sweep of hair, revealing every enlarged pore in his cheek, the glossy welts of scar tissue on the bridge of his nose and another seam at the edge of his eye probably from a hard right hand he hadn't seen coming. The slant of light also exposed the reddish shimmer of dye he used to darken his roots.

With his eyes hard on mine, he said, "What the hell are you staring at?"

My uncle stepped away from the glare of sunlight, and picked up his glass and swigged the remains.

Mona said, "When we were coming back across the bay, I heard at least a dozen shots. Is that the sign of a good marksman?"

A valid point, though I had no answer. I'd seen no evidence of gunfire anywhere on the houseboat. And Teeter had only the single wound.

"Holland," I said. "Put on your telephoto, keep it working across those mangroves. First move you see, sing out. John and Annette can take the west and north windows. Head on a swivel. You see any sign of her, yell."

"Teeter's not dead," Annette said. "You're kidding us. This is all staged, a big production for my benefit. The crocodile gag, all that stuff. The woman taking our boats, she's an actor. It's a practical joke so I'll write up this fantastic, exciting story, and people will be flocking to go out with you guys."

I looked over at Rusty. Her tanned face had gone pale.

"Tell the truth," Annette said. "Teeter's not dead."

"Annette." There was an ache in Rusty's voice. "You and Holland come with me, have a look at my brother. Just so you know."

Annette flattened her lips and gave her head a bratty shake.

"It's true," Holland said. "We're all going to fucking die out here."

"Not if we're smart," I said.

"We got a fucking saw, a bunch of fucking flares."

Annette was staring out the salon windows into the bleak distances of the bay. In less than a day, she'd lost the poise of the seasoned traveler. The brash city girl's eyes were dissolving into haze.

"Rusty," I said. "I'm going to the wheelhouse, see what I can do with those ignition wires. You okay with that?"

She nodded.

"Let's go, you two." Rusty's voice was hoarse with stifled fury. "Pay your respects to Teeter, then you're pulling some guard duty."

"And you." I pointed to Mona. "You come with me."

CHAPTER NINETEEN

Sugarman parked his Accord along the shoulder of Highway
70 a mile upstream from the pullout ramp, then cut through
the woods to the Peace River. With the map Dr. Dillard provided, he backtracked one mile along the riverbank between
the spot where Abigail's body washed up and where she was
last seen alive by Carla Featherstone, the woman kayaker.

The shoreline was mostly open, but there were spots where
he had to squirm through vines and thick stands of palmetto,
and a couple of barbed-wire fences to cross.

He walked slowly and paid attention, looking down at the
ground, surveying the river and the surrounding brush, but not
expecting much.

He came across a pair of ancient sunglasses in some tall
grass halfway along his hike. Aviators. He found a single
white athletic sock, five soda cans, and a kid's red plastic pail
half buried in the mud beside a cow pasture.

He paced alongside three gentle curves in the river, finding nothing along the shore. At the first hard-angled turn he
came to, he halted. It was a narrow spot about half a mile
downstream from where the kayaker passed Abigail Bates.
He climbed atop one of the boulders that loomed over the
turn, then he worked his gaze foot by foot along the bank
and shoreline, seeing nothing but mud and grass and a narrow sandy edge.

He changed his angle, shaded his eyes, and caught sight

of a piece of black cloth peeking from the riverbank mud. He climbed down the boulder, stooped over, and tugged the cloth out of the glop. It was the brim of a cap.

After rinsing the grime off in the river, he held it up. Marlins baseball hat.

He climbed back onto the large smooth rock that seemed to watch over that narrowed crook in the river. It was early afternoon, sky free of clouds, a warm day for January in central Florida. He tipped the hat toward the sun and squinted at it. There was a long hair snagged in the metal clasp. It was dark, either brown or black. Hard to tell. His eyes weren't as sharp as they'd been a few years earlier. But it was a long hair, which meant it was probably a woman's.

The drowning had occurred six months earlier, but human hair degraded at different rates depending on exposure to the elements and its own structure, depending on whether the person it came from was healthy or sick, a smoker or anemic, a drunk or a teetotaler, or any number of other factors. Sugarman had logged a weekend forensics refresher course a couple of years earlier at Baptist Hospital in Miami. From what he could recall, hair cuticle scale pattern survived even if the internal structure collapsed. Which meant that even in degraded condition, certain microscopic and DNA analysis was still possible.

And this hair seemed to have a putrid root at its proximal end, which was a feature of decomposition. Nothing strange there. Hair was tough. Some hair had survived in thousand-year-old tombs. Microbes were the problem, and a hair left out in the elements on the edge of a river was about as exposed to microscopic critters as anywhere Sugar could imagine. But there were freakish situations. He remembered from the training session—hair that survived for years because it was trapped in clay, or isolated from air or sunlight. But no real ID could be made without the proper lab work. Postmortem banding, a microscopic strip near the root of the hair, was a clear signal that the hair had been pulled out of a decomposing body. If the hair was alive at the moment of its plucking, it wouldn't show any banding. That was probably something his buddy Dr. Dillard could answer with one quick peek through the lens.

If it was Abigail Bates's hat, it might have come loose in a struggle, or it might have been knocked off when she fell overboard. So the banding wouldn't prove for certain she'd been the victim of an attack. But if the hair was black or brown as he thought, then probably it wasn't Ms. Bates's hair at all. Perhaps it belonged to the attacker, snagged during the melee.

He had to be careful not to jump to conclusions, but also had to treat the hat as evidence. He realized he should have brought along some surgical gloves and a plastic bag for such a situation. But the truth was, he hadn't expected to find anything. He was just going through the motions, killing time before his three o'clock at the Pine Tree School. Sheriff Timmy had agreed to walk him through the four video-tapes shot during county-sponsored meetings, where local citizens faced off with bosses from Bates International.

Sugarman wasn't expecting much from that either. He had no idea what Nina and the medical examiner were trying to steer him toward. Even though he felt like he was wasting his time, it was his duty to follow the lead. It's what Thorn would've wanted, what Thorn himself would've done.

As he was setting the Marlins hat on the rock beside him, a young couple in a red canoe came ripping around the bend.

Sugarman waved hello and watched them work to swing the craft around the turn. It was a sharper angle than he'd noticed at first. The kids seemed proficient enough at paddling, but they struggled a bit to make that corner without drifting to the side where he sat.

"Nice day," the boy called, when they'd straightened the canoe and were back in the middle of the river.

Sugar gave them a half wave, half salute as they slid away downstream.

He rose to his feet and looked down the river, then turned and walked inland from his position. There were no clearly marked paths through the brambles, but he found a few bro-ken branches about ten feet in, maybe an infrequently used trail, and when he pushed through an oleander shrub that blocked his view, he saw a narrow paved road about fifty yards off. Easy access from the road to the spot where he stood. Shorter distance between road and river than most places he'd noted.

He walked back to the rock. He studied the angles again as another kayaker shot past. This guy was an expert. Had the headgear, a nifty aluminum paddle, some kind of high-tech gloves, but even he had to take an extra dip of his paddle to fend off the current that thrust him toward the rock where Sugarman stood.

When the guy was gone, Sugarman climbed back down the boulder to the narrow band of mud at its base. This time the place he jumped onto wasn't solid, and he sunk to his ankles in the glop. By the time he made it to firmer ground, his shoes were waterlogged.

He leaned out and peered into the water to check the depth. Some roots protruded from the bank directly beneath him, and there were some fairly large fish hanging steady in the current, waiting for bait to come tumbling into their faces. The river was at least twenty feet deep, with steep sides, a hard place to climb ashore if you went overboard.

He was turning to climb back up the rock when he spotted an odd color off to one edge of the crook in the river. Something was lodged about ten feet below the surface in a crevice or shelf of rock.

Something pink. Beyond that, he couldn't say.

Probably another soda can.

He climbed back upon the rock and sat in the sun for a few minutes. Another two canoes passed. The woman waved, but the guy was clearly suspicious of Sugarman and made a few extra strokes to get by faster.

Sugar took off his boat shoes and laid them on the rock beside him to dry. Pink soda can? Had he ever seen a pink soda can before?

After visiting Dr. Dillard, he'd swung by the sheriff's office, and Timmy Whalen told him that he was welcome to poke around the Peace River all he wanted, though she assured him that she and her deputies had searched every inch of river-bank from the canoe rental place to the location where the body was found and beyond. They'd done it a half-dozen times in teams of two, looking for any sign that somebody might have lain in wait for Abigail Bates. They found a few camping spots where overnighters had illegally pitched tents. They found some used condoms, some whiskey bottles, and a pair of swim goggles, but nothing suspicious.

Sugarman took off his shirt, folded it, and placed it on the rock beside his shoes. He leaned forward and squinted at the pink thing ten feet down. Hell if he could bring it into focus. Was it worth getting his jeans soaked, diving down to re-trieve a pair of panties or some old swim cap from twenty years ago?

But this spot intrigued him. It was the only piece of ter-rain in the entire two miles he'd tramped through that seemed like it might work as an ambush point. Most of the river was forty or fifty feet across. Hard to imagine anyone diving from the bank and being able to outswim a canoe going down-stream. Even if the paddler was eighty-six.

But this spot, no, it was a bottleneck that required a little backpaddling and quick maneuvering. Not a lot, nothing that could be deemed dangerous. But it was a kink in an other-wise smooth course.

If someone had taken a position where Sugarman was sit-ting, then as the paddler came around the bend just twenty feet upstream, she'd have only a few seconds to react before she was alongside the rock. The boy and his girlfriend had been surprised to see him there and had faltered for a heart-beat. Even the high-tech kayaker who'd sailed on by was carefully focused on his stroke. So it was plainly a spot that gave the advantage to the rock-sitter.

Sugarman unbuckled his belt and skinned it out of the loops and set it beside his shirt. He'd brought a change of clothes and some overnight shaving stuff, but that was back in his car parked a couple of miles downstream. If he stripped to his Jockeys, would that qualify as indecent exposure? A black man in underwear in this backwoods spot? Probably would. With the right eyewitness and the wrong judge, Sugar might be looking at thirty days in jail.

In his jeans, he hopped down to the mud bank again and squatted as close to the water as he could get. But the pink thing wasn't any clearer.

What the hell. It was a hot day.

He hopped forward and dropped feetfirst into the river and was immediately swept forward by the current, banging a knee into the rock wall. He found a hold on the ledge and positioned himself directly above the pink object, then took a long breath and pushed himself straight down.

He opened his eyes for a few seconds and glimpsed the object, but his buoyancy was drawing him away from it. He snatched at a root and held on. Nice thick wood, bowed out from the riverbank ledge like a handle for stand-up riders on a bus. He gripped the root with one hand and bent lower and plucked the pink thing from its cranny. Then he stayed there a moment more, feeling the cool current wash over him. When he let go, he bobbed back to the surface, let the river carry him toward the bend, then kicked his feet and swam a few strokes to a small muddy ledge. He dragged himself out, his jeans weighing about fifty pounds.

The pink thing was a shoe. A Keds tennis shoe.

He climbed back to his rock, then lay down in the sun and examined the shoe. Torn at the toe, some scraping in the rubber rim. Shoelaces were green-and-red plaid. Nice identifier. Sugar set the shoe beside the hat.

He lay in the sun for fifteen minutes until his jeans were a little drier. Then he put on his damp boat shoes, picked up his loot, pinching the sneaker and cap by the edges, and hiked back through the brush to his car.

A little scene was playing in his head. An old woman wearing pink Keds, held by someone beneath the water. Maybe her attacker used that convenient root to stay stationary while the old lady drowned. While the old lady, Thorn's grandmother, kicked and fought, and in the process wedged the toe of her tennis shoe into a crevice in the rock.

Goose chills washed across his back. Then another wave.

The chills were probably triggered by his wet jeans. Yeah, probably that.

He'd never been one to trust gut reactions or telepathic prickles on the skin. Most of the cases he'd solved over the years were accomplished through thoughtful consideration. Boring but effective logical steps and rational, orderly reasoning. Goose chills weren't evidence. Goose chills were just the body's attempt at raising its hairs to increase their loft. Some evolutionary leftover from when man was covered in monkey fur and fluffing it could keep him warm and make him appear larger and more threatening. That's all it was. Invisible monkey fur trying to fluff.

Sasha unfolded the Bimini top to put Griffin in the shade. He lay on top of the bedroll, staring up at the canvas straps and aluminum poles. She wet a cloth and brought it to his forehead, but he pushed her hand away.

Though it was hard to imagine his breathing could grow worse, it had. More mud-sucking gasps. Spasms in his throat, airways rattling. But he brought his eyes to hers, bearing down on her like she was the one suffering.

"You still strong? You still stone cold, Mama?"

"I'm fine."

"When I get well, you know what I want? I want to get a tattoo. *Mom* inside a heart. Put it on my forearm."

"With flowers," Sasha said.

"No, keep it simple, just *Mom* and a heart." He drew a breath and let it out. "And you know what else? I want to learn to play the electric guitar. And something else. Maybe I'll write a book. Tell our complete story. Start to finish."

"You could do that. You're smart enough."

"Sure I could. How hard could it be? Just tell one thing, then the next. Keep it simple, stay out of your own way. Everything that's happened. That'd make a hell of a story. Play up the biblical angle."

"Biblical?"

"Family of Davids versus the Goliath clan. Smooth stones from the stream, barefoot shepherd with no armor standing in a field with his sling and rock. The giant laughing, mocking, saying he'll cut off all our heads with a single swipe, feed our flesh to the birds and wild animals. Our boy lets loose his stone, and down comes that monster. Puts their army on the run, saves our people. That's a story. That's a great story. Archetypal is what that is."

Sasha was quiet, looking out at the cove.

"You don't think that's a great story?"

"The Lord was on David's side. The side of the Israelites."

"What? You don't think he's on ours?"

"I hope so."

"You hope so?"

"I think we're about to find out."

"Hell, if God's on Goliath's side, I'd just as soon be dead. Isn't any reason to go on clawing and scratching in that kind of world."

After a moment, Griffin levered himself to his feet, looked out at the bay Sasha had chosen as their home base.

A narrow creek had carved a deep inlet into the mangrove forest; it was out of the wind, a mile east of the houseboat. Griffin drew a guarded breath, trying not to agitate the inflamed tissues. Turning his head from side to side, taking in the cove, the comings and goings of egrets and pelicans, the sharp squeals of an osprey, the slap and jostle of water in the maze of mangrove roots.

"This is a pretty place you brought us. A wild, beautiful Eden."

"Yes, it is."

"Hard to believe there's places like this left."

Sasha was silent. Let him have his say.

"Actually," he said, "it's breathtaking."

She looked at him closely.

He turned a faint smile her way. "Word of the day," he said. *"Breathtaking."*

His laugh started out fine, then turned into a deep, rattling cough. She moved to his side and pressed the damp cloth to his forehead and hugged his wasted frame to hers.

CHAPTER TWENTY

Walking across the gravel lot toward the canoe rental shop, Sugar spotted a thirtysomething guy down by the riverbank, sitting in an unpainted cane-back chair, smoking what looked like a hand-rolled cigarette. Sugar walked over and stood in a cloud of smoke that reeked of cloves.

"You Sugarman?" Charlie kept his eyes on the river.

"Yep."

Charlie reached out and patted the seat of the chair beside him. The young man had dirty-blond hair, hippie length, and a wispy goatee. He wore a single pearl in his right earlobe.

Sugarman sat. His damp jeans had begun to chafe his thighs, and his boat shoes were slippery with mud. Not his finest hour.

"Sheriff Whalen called, said you'd be by. Told me to co-operate."

Sugarman thought about that. Had she massaged Charlie somehow? Was she being helpful or trying to control the situation? Sugar thought again of the look she'd shown him at the gun shop. A sign that she knew more than she was willing to say. He let that go for now and settled back into the chair.

"Pretty river," Sugar said. "Nice spot to work."

"You want to know what happened. That's why you're here, right?"

"Anytime you're ready."

"She came to rent a canoe. I recognized her, then got on her case about what Bates International was doing."

"All right."

"I made some crack about wishing I'd brought a gun to work that day."

"That was fairly hostile."

"I was pissed off. It just came out."

"You own a gun?"

"Hell, no. I hate guns."

"Okay."

"So I make this crack, and right away she pulled out this automatic. I found out later it was a Beretta nine millimeter. Serious-ass pistol. And she handed it to me."

"She handed it to you?"

"She was like that. Put-your-money-where-your-mouth-is kind of lady. She was testing me. Held it by the barrel, offered me the grip."

"And you did what?"

"I took it, pointed it at her. Man, just thinking about it now makes my asshole pucker. Right over there's where it happened." He waved at the shoreline about ten yards away. "I was putting her canoe in the water and we got to arguing, and out comes this gun and next thing I'm pointing it at her. First gun I've had in my hand, ever. No shit. I hate guns."

"Yeah," Sugarman said. "There's not much to love about them."

"And right then a van came rolling up."

"Two women from Sarasota," Sugar said. "I read the newspaper story."

"Yeah, they had kids with them. They saw me aiming the gun at Ms. Bates and jumped back in and got the hell out of here. Used their cell phone to call nine-one-one, because Sheriff Whalen shows up like ten minutes later. She wanted to know what I'd done. I showed her the gun. And, man, she was pissed."

"You kept the gun?"

"When Ms. Bates was sitting in the canoe, daring me to do something, I fired it into the water. I don't know why. I was freaking out. I just fired it and fired it till it was empty and dropped it in the river. Shallow water at the bank."

"Okay, you dumped the pistol."

"When Sheriff Whalen showed up, I dug it out of the mud and gave it to her. She bad-mouthed me for a while, called me every kind of fool, then left. A few hours later she comes screaming back, her along with the whole police department, lights blazing. They'd found Ms. Bates's body, and bang, there I was in the backseat of the sheriff's car and on the way to jail. Five days I spent in a cell. Never been arrested before. Now that was bad."

Sugarman looked out at the river rolling by. The young man sounded sincere. The story he told had a well-worn feel, but not the kind of rehearsed quality of someone who'd worked out a lie to repeat over and over. This guy wasn't complicated. Wasn't cynical or two-faced.

Sugarman had a fairly dependable feel for people. Usually he could hear a story and tell if some of it was phony. If the false note was there, most of the time Sugar could detect it. He guessed it was something irrational, some gift. He didn't try to overanalyze how he accomplished it. It worked and he used it, and mostly it helped. But there could be false positives, too. Sometimes when he was sure he'd heard a lie, it turned out the guy was telling a true story but thought no one would believe it, so his voice got squeaky and it all came out sounding like a lie. That confused the issue and kept Sugar on his toes.

"The sheriff didn't really believe you drowned her."

"She acted like she did."

"But then later on she let you go."

"Yeah."

"She tell you why?"

"Not really. She just said the medical examiner's report called it a drowning, and she was ruling it accidental, and I was free."

"You didn't drive downriver and jump in and drown Ms. Bates."

"Hell, no. After the sheriff left, I just sat around shaking.

Mad and worked up. My hand hurt like hell from firing the pistol." He shook his right hand at the memory.

"You said the first time the sheriff came by and you told her what happened she was pissed."

"Royally."

"She tell you why?"

"What do you mean? 'Cause I was such a doofus, threatening the old lady, shooting off a pistol."

"I saw the sheriff earlier today. She was dealing with a guy named Hankinson. You know him?"

"Christ, yeah. White-power Nazi guy. Spent half his life in jail."

"He was a little more than a doofus, and the sheriff seemed pretty patient with him."

"Oh, yeah. She's easygoing for law enforcement."

"So it doesn't strike you as strange she was so pissed about the gun incident? That wasn't out of character for her?"

"I don't know. Maybe a little. What're you saying?"

"Maybe you stepped into something. You were a monkey wrench."

"I don't get it," he said.

Sugarman shut up. Airing his suspicions in front of Charlie Kipling wasn't smart. What he was starting to see was two Timmy Whalens. The cool, unruffled lady he'd met earlier with Hankinson. And the Timmy on that July day last summer. Jittery, stressed-out, pinballing around town.

"What do you think happened to Ms. Bates after she left here? Everybody seems to think she fell out of her canoe and drowned."

Charlie turned his head and stared at Sugar. His eyes were sad, tired, dark circles and pouches underneath, and the whites were spiderwebbed with red veins. His eyes seemed a couple of decades older than the rest of him.

"You're the first person to ask me that."

"Really?"

"The sheriff doesn't care what I think. None of my friends wants to talk about it. They're worried I did it and they don't want to get involved."

"You didn't do it."

"Damn right, I didn't. I was getting ready to drive my truck down to the pullout and wait for Ms. Bates to show up to bring her back to her car when Timmy came back the second time and arrested me."

"You think somebody waylaid her."

Charlie Kipling was quiet for a while. He tugged on his blond chin whiskers and dug a toe in the loose soil.

"Who you working for?"

"Can't talk about that."

"It's Mona, isn't it?"

"I can't go there, sorry."

"Well, it sure as hell isn't John Milligan."

"Why do you say that?"

" 'Cause he's gotta be happy as a pig in shit how it's turning out. This way he inherits the whole deal. The Horse Creek plan cranks up again."

"I see."

"So John Milligan, he's the one I'd be looking at. He's the natural suspect. He's a badass. Barroom brawler, likes throwing his weight around."

"He'd kill his own mother?"

He shrugged.

"Ms. Bates was eighty-six. All Milligan had to do is wait a little and it's his."

"Word going around is Ms. Bates was considering shutting down the entire mining operation, just pull the plug, walk away. Mona was working on her to do that. So maybe Milligan got worried the old lady was about to cave and do the right thing, and he whacks her."

Sugarman was silent, looking out at the river, its dark sparkle.

"I'd put my chips on Milligan. Every chip I had."

"Let me ask you something, Charlie." He watched as a couple of kids on inner tubes floated past. "You remember how Abigail Bates was dressed that day?"

"Dressed?"

"Any details? Her clothes."

"Fly-fishing shirt, all the vents," Charlie said. "Baseball hat, tennis shoes, I think. Old beat-up jeans."

"Color of the tennis shoes, you remember that?"

He shook his head.

"How about the baseball hat? Any logo on it?"

"Marlins," he said. "I hate the Marlins, so I remember that."

"You're sure?"

"Goddamn Marlins. Win the World Series, very next year that owner breaks up the team, trades everyone away. What kind of scumbag does that?"

"Thanks, Charlie. Appreciate your time."

He nodded as Sugarman rose.

"You know I can't sleep worth a shit anymore," Charlie said. "All these months later, I had maybe one, two good nights' sleep that whole time."

"Why's that?"

"The goddamn guilt," he said.

"About what?"

"Taking that old lady's gun, dropping it in the water. If I hadn't done that, she'd be alive today. She could've defended herself. That was my fault. Just at the exact moment she needed her gun, she didn't have it."

Sugarman patted the young man on the shoulder.

"You were a small piece of the action, Charlie. Don't take that weight."

"Can't help it. It's how I'm put together."

Sugar gave his shoulder another pat.

"Thanks for your help. You take care."

Sugar was behind the wheel of the Honda, about to slam the door, when Charlie turned in his chair and called something. Sugar leaned out the door.

"Didn't hear you, Charlie."

"Pink!" he yelled. "Tennis shoes she was wearing were pink. Like some teenage kid."

CHAPTER TWENTY-ONE

It should have been simple. All I had to do was find the ignition wire, which was yellow with a red stripe, then locate the solid-red power-feed wire, then the kill-switch wire, which was tan and blue. Three wires. Strip the plastic covering back about three-quarters of an inch and twist the three together, voilà. After the engines started, I'd remove the red wire.

It would've been that easy, except for one thing: The electrician Rusty had hired to wire the Mothership was Millard Slattery of Tavernier.

I'd warned her about him. A sly drunk. Kept his flask hidden, always had his mouth full of Juicy Fruit to cover the reek of booze, never garbled his speech. Nice fellow, sharp wit, good stories.

Since Millard's last day on the job, I'd spent maybe a hundred hours rewiring switches, tearing out light fixtures, and redoing every plug in the staterooms and heads, grounding them, reversing the feeds, tightening loose connections. And then I spent another hundred hours tracking down a dozen other fire hazards Millard left behind.

Rusty had hired him because Millard was cheap and she was cutting every corner she could find to hit her budget. She knew he was a lush, and had given him a stern warning to stay sober on the job. It hadn't worked.

As the trip got under way, I'd been pretty sure I'd located all his screwups, and corrected them, but I still found myself constantly sniffing for the telltale tang of shorting-out circuitry.

I'd never thought to check the wiring harness. There was no outward sign of trouble. The ignition system functioned perfectly, all the instruments in the wheelhouse operated fine. If the woman in the bass boat hadn't slashed the harness, Millard's shortcuts probably would have gone undetected for years.

Instead of the standard color-coded wires, Millard had decided, God knows why, to use a random mix of red, green, white, blue, and black. No apparent rhyme or reason to his choices. Probably a two-flask afternoon.

I had the electrical blueprint open on the chart table and was looking back and forth between its orderly diagram and the tangled clutter spilling out of the wiring harness, trying to figure out which wires were connected to the relay that would turn over the Mercury outboards without shorting out the rest of the system.

So far the Westerbeke generators had been running fine, the air-conditioning still pumping, the lights and appliances powered up. But I could wreck all that with one wrong move. Blow the entire panel.

The Mothership's keyed ignition used a multiple-position switch, same as most cars. A quarter turn of the key lit up the accessory circuit that powered the radios and interior lights. Click two was the instrument cluster and spark-control computer, and click three engaged the starter motors. With three positions, times two engines, times six batteries, the number of wires running to the ignition switch was in the mid-double-digits. Even on a lazy day moored safely at the docks under no pressure, I would've had a hard time concentrating on finding the right combination.

Mona shifted at the edge of my vision.

"You wanted to talk to me?"

I kept my focus on the schematic for a moment, trying to bring some order to my thoughts and let my pulse cool. I wasn't sure what triggered my arousal. Maybe it was the flush that came to Mona's face out in that nameless lake, a woman lit up by that place, those fish, savoring that stillness. A kindred spirit. Her hair, her face, some trick of light. Or the briny scent she secreted like some lush flower releasing its spores into the wind. Maybe watching Teeter die on the floor of his cabin had quickened my needs. That weird catalyzing effect the dead have on the living. Thanatos stimulating Eros.

I ran a finger along the blueprint, tracing the intricate path of the ignition wire, from the batteries in their hatch on the stern deck through the aluminum tubing that crisscrossed the inner walls and eventually led to the wheelhouse. The task was to choose the right wire and trace it back to the fuse box, jumping over the busted-up circuit breaker to draw juice directly from the twelve volts and send it to the Mercury outboards.

"Okay, then, I'm leaving. I'm going back below."

"You recognized her voice, Mona. The woman in the boat. You know who she is."

Mona sighed and settled into the swivel seat beside the wheel. She looked out at the darkening sky, the whitecaps kicking up on the bay.

"I did and I didn't," she said.

"Let's hear the 'did' part."

"Her voice is familiar. I believe she's someone I've met."

"You're sure of that?"

She waffled her hand. Somewhat sure.

"And her face? When you saw her this morning, did you recognize her?"

"I don't know. She came at us so fast, I didn't get that clear a look." Mona drew her shoulders back from the slump she'd settled into. "It's somebody from home. Summerland, Wauchula, Ona. Somebody from that world. But I don't know. Familiar features, familiar voice, but no name, nothing specific. I can't place the context. Some store or office around town, she's a clerk, maybe works at the school. I'm almost certain it's somebody from up there, but beyond that, I'm drawing a blank."

"Okay."

"Not that it would matter much if we knew her name."

"It would," I said. "It'd give us more than we have. Some leverage."

"If she knew we recognized her, we'd all be targets. She couldn't let any of us go."

"We're all targets now."

"You believe that?"

"It's crazy to think otherwise."

She gazed out at the white suds kicking up on the bay as if that potent landscape could fortify herself, help her summon the words.

"Dad lied," she said.

I waited, saying nothing, held by the burn in her eyes.

"Last week before we left home, we met with Carter Mosley."

"So he could give you the papers for me to sign."

"Yeah, but there's more. We went over different scenarios. If you refused to sign. If you wanted to bargain, what changes might be acceptable. Carter needed to free up some cash in case you wanted to make a deal."

"That's all?"

"No," she said. "Dad brought up the other thing. If you were to die."

"That didn't strike you as odd?"

"Of course it did. But Carter's very analytical. He seemed to think it was a perfectly appropriate question."

"Okay, so what is it? If I die, what happens?"

"You have next of kin? Wife, children?"

"No."

"You have a will?"

I shook my head.

"Holland had it right. The land would revert to the corporation, which means it would fall into the lap of the board of directors."

"And who is that?"

"Dad, me, Carter."

"That's it, just three people? That's a board of directors?"

"It's a family business. And it was four people until Grandmother died."

"Where does Mosley stand on things?"

"You mean Horse Creek? My big plan to save the world?"

"Yeah, start there. Was he on board with that?"

"He never took a stand. I was arguing for it, fleshing it out, making the case for what a good PR move it would be, how it was the ethical thing to do. We're sitting around a big table, and Dad is mocking me, Grandmother asked a question now and then, Carter Mosley just listened. That's his role. Advisory."

"But he has a vote."

"Yes. There were four votes, Carter, Dad, me, and Grandmother."

"Four equal votes?"

"Theoretically. But whatever Grandmother wanted, game over."

"So with Abigail dead, Carter Mosley's got the swing vote."

"True."

"Do I get a place at the table? Is that part of the will?"

"Yes."

"So there it is. Mystery man comes out of left field, throws the cozy arrangement out of whack."

She nodded, looking out at the ashen bay.

"Tell me, Mona. When you discovered you had a cousin, this guy Daniel Oliver Thorn, and you read through Abigail's clippings, what'd you think? That I'd be for you or against you?"

"I didn't know."

"What was your guess?"

"All right," she said. "You want the truth? From the stuff in Grandmother's lockbox, you looked like a loser, some small-time fuck-up."

"Not too far off."

"But I've changed my mind." Mona rubbed a finger across her lower lip, scraped off a dry flake. "I think you're a reasonable guy. I think you'd do the right thing, given the chance."

"But when you arrived yesterday, you saw it differently. I was some asshole who'd take one look at this big gooey pie and demand my slice. That's why you were pissed. You'd made up your mind about me."

"It's how you seemed from a distance. A guy who didn't have two nickels to rub together. Looking for a score."

"The two nickels part is right. I like it that way."

Her eyes held mine for a moment, then drifted toward the open water.

"You trust Mosley?"

"You saw him," she said. "He's okay, board-certified straight arrow."

"What I saw was a small man with a vise-grip for a hand-shake and a strong curiosity about me."

"What's that supposed to mean?"

"He was taking my measure," I said. "Trying to read me."

"Carter's fine. He can't admit it publicly, but he's on my side."

"Billions of dollars? The legal advisor of a major corpo-ration is going to throw away billions of dollars so a river doesn't dry up? Doesn't sound like any lawyer I ever met."

"I think I know Carter a little better than you."

"Why did John lie?"

She shook her head. Not going there.

"Would John go this far, hire somebody to kill me? Erase a swing vote that just might go against him?"

She clenched her jaw and closed her eyes briefly. It was all the answer I was going to get.

"Maybe this woman's a lone wolf," Mona said. "She's got her own agenda. Maybe Dad has nothing to do with any of this."

"No way she followed us from Islamorada last night with-out me noticing. Which means she had our location and came from another direction. Then there's my name. I haven't heard that in forty years. Now it's twice in two days. She's con-nected with John and you."

I settled back in front of the harness, the wild nest of wires. It could take hours to test every combination, this red with that red, this blue with that blue. A roulette wheel's chance in hell I'd get it right before sunset.

I turned back to Mona and watched her face carefully. "Rusty gave Mosley our GPS coordinates. He asked her for them."

"What?" She was squinting at me.

"He said he might fly down and join us for a day or two at the end."

Her eyes cleared by slow degrees as if she were resurfacing from a long nap. A bite of anger tightened her face. If it was a display for my benefit, she was a better actress than she'd shown before. I didn't trust her completely, but I was a few steps further along that path.

"So Mosley knows precisely where we're anchored. That leaves only a few choices: He could have told you or John and one of you passed on the information to the shooter, or Carter could have passed it on directly. Or some combination."

"Why would I want to kill you, a complete stranger?"

"I might vote against something you're passionate about."

"Passionate, yeah. But passionate enough to murder somebody? Come on."

I showed her the blandest face I could muster.

"Wow." She stared at the wires beneath the console. "Is this where you read me my Miranda rights?"

"Out here, we're a little beyond the reach of legal technicalities."

"And you honestly think Dad and I could be in cahoots?"

"I don't think the two of you could agree which way was up."

"But in your mind I'm still a suspect."

I said no, not really, and it must have sounded convincing, for there was relief in her sigh. She stared out the window at the rising weather. Wind was beginning to moan around the sharp corners of the wheelhouse.

I fiddled with the wires and tried a couple of combinations. Got nothing. I tried to focus on the snarl, but I could feel her watching me.

I tried another grouping, then another. I was already losing count of which I'd tried and which remained untested.

To do the job right, I'd need to tag them, label each combination, scribble down a record, to do more than this flailing.

"Your mother," she said, then halted, eyes roving the empty bay.

"My mother what?"

I tried another combination. Red with green with black. Nothing.

She drew a deep breath and blew it out through puckered lips.

"You ready to hear about her?"

I made an effort to keep my eyes on the wires. Tried to sound indifferent. "Why? What do you know about her?"

"Only what Grandmother told me."

I used the pliers to clear the tips of two more wires.

"Why was Abigail Bates talking to you about my mother?"

"I suppose she knew one day we'd meet. She wanted me to pass it on."

"And how would she know that?"

"The will with your name in it, and the news clippings in the lockbox kind of guaranteed it. Like she's out there somewhere, still running the show."

I wasn't certain of Mona's motives for choosing that moment to tell me the tale of my past. To distract me, to reward me, or just to unburden herself. But after a moment or two, I no longer cared why.

While I stripped the wire tips clean and twisted three more of them together, Mona told me about my mother, and eventually about my father, Quentin Thorn. Whatever chance I'd had of hot-wiring the ignition was gone.

Gradually my hands sank into my lap, and I sat staring at the nest of wires as I listened to Mona. She told the story expertly as if she'd spent a long time honing it, filtering out the trivia, all the tempting digressions that any story offers. Her voice warmed and grew heavier than I'd heard it before, a husky directness that gave the tale a melancholy hue.

CHAPTER TWENTY-TWO

My mother, Elizabeth Milligan, was known as Liz. She was a quiet, withdrawn kid, a reader of books. In her early childhood, during the darkest years of the Depression, she began disappearing for hours in the woods and far-flung fields near her family's ranch house. She wrote plays and poems and stories. She drew elaborate sketches of imaginary kingdoms with dragons and fairies and knights. While her father indulged these diversions, Abigail grew ever more impatient with her daughter's flightiness, and when the girl turned ten, her mother started to impose strict rules on Liz's daily routines. Abigail came up with a list of chores that grew ever longer, meant to ground the girl in the fundamentals of farm life, force her to confront the hard facts of subsistence living.

By any standard the Milligan family was the wealthiest in the county, probably among the most affluent in that part of Florida. But they lived with sober simplicity, forgoing modern appliances, making their own clothes, and running their cattle operation with the minimum of hired help. Abigail was the driving force behind this rigorous ascetic life.

In what became the last year of her life, Abigail confessed to Mona that she'd fought a lifelong battle with anxiety and despair, a condition that now might be moderated by medications. But back then, with the shadow of the stock market crash still hovering over the shaky economy, gas rationing, food shortages, troops massing across Europe, and

America lapsing into sterile isolationism, Abigail's despondency seemed a reasonable reaction.

Within the family she imposed a ruthless campaign of self-denial. Work and more work. Grinding days, a strict focus on thrift. Sweets and books and fairy-tale frivolity were outlawed, shows of affection were restrained. A quick cold kiss good-night. Now and then a lifeless pat on the back.

Though Liz's father was more tolerant and open, he remained loyal to his wife's regime and never challenged her in front of the children. Maybe on the sly there was a hug or kiss for Liz. Abigail suspected there were hours when she was working with the herd or immersed in bookkeeping when Charles indulged Liz with a session of pleasure reading or drawing. But when Abigail was present, the rules were enforced.

Though she had every reason to be one, Liz was no rebel. She was diligent and reliable and an excellent student in school. Yet Abigail forever found fault with her performance. No job she completed, from washing dishes to cleaning the stalls, was without defect.

When Liz was twelve, the Thorn family arrived from south Georgia and settled in an abandoned farmhouse a mile down the road. They kept to themselves, stayed indoors with the windows shuttered up through most of the daylight hours. None of the children attended school. Broken couches crowded their porch. Oil drums, piles of scrap metal, the rusty hulks of cars, and old bathtubs, sinks, and assorted plumbing fixtures soon littered their yard. Two thick-necked dogs were chained to the trees, one that howled all night like a famished wolf. The Thorn family, by Abigail's gauge, was a cut below white trash.

The eldest son was named Quentin, and he quickly earned a reputation as a gifted shade-tree mechanic. Ineligible for the military because of two missing fingers on his right hand, he was his family's sole breadwinner. His skill with machinery was so notable that Abigail eventually yielded to temptation and engaged him to repair their tractors, keep their tillers up and running, and tune their cars and trucks on the cheap.

There was talk that Quentin's father was running from a federal beef. A bank holdup, or counterfeiting. From time to time, Quentin's old man would vanish for a week or two, and those occasions always coincided with the arrival of some man with a fresh haircut, a dark suit, and polished shoes who rode up and down the back roads in a new Ford. A few days after the agent left, Quentin's father would reappear. That's how the law worked in those parts. No love lost between backwoods sheriffs and federal outsiders.

Then the A-bomb leveled Hiroshima. Confetti snowed from the American sky. Liz turned eighteen and graduated high school. First in her class, valedictorian. Abigail's view was that Liz's schooling was now complete and she would assume more responsibility for the family's growing business. The war had been good to the Bates family. Cattle prices soared. Bates Inc. branched into fertilizer production, and Abigail began acquiring adjacent citrus groves. What land she could not purchase outright, she secured the mineral rights to. Amid this flurry, Liz was expected to assume responsibility for the day-to-day operations of the ranch to free her parents to concentrate on their expanding enterprise.

"The photograph," Mona said. "Your mother and my dad standing in front of that new car. That was her graduation day."

I nodded. The wires before me had turned to mist.

"Her daddy bought Liz the car without Grandmother's knowledge and she was pissed. Very pissed. It was an outrageous extravagance by her measure."

"And the next day Liz was gone," I said.

"How did you know?"

"I knew."

"What? You read that in the photo? In your mother's face?"

"Go on," I said. "Finish your story."

Liz and Quentin had become lovers a year before that photo was taken. Though Abigail had no suspicion of the affair, she later assumed that her husband must have known, and maybe even John. And it was likely the two of them conspired in Liz's escape, each for his own reason.

Hours after that photo was taken, the lovers disappeared. Years would pass before Abigail uttered her daughter's name. She never wasted a tear, never permitted a mention of her, and never forgave her husband for buying that car.

She would have drawn her last breath without knowing what became of Liz were it not for Charles preceding her in death. When he passed away, a half-dozen notes and postcards tied up in red ribbon were discovered hidden inside his shotgun case. Liz had addressed the letters to her father's office in downtown Summerland.

Liz and Quentin had landed in Key Largo. Quentin had found work repairing marine engines. They rented a tiny house with a view of Tarpon Basin, and within a year Liz was pregnant. She loved the place, the water, the light, the fresh ocean scents. They were saving for a boat.

The tone of the letters was restrained, apologetic, almost formal. They seemed to be written with the knowledge that one day Abigail would read them and grade them by her severe standards. Then abruptly the letters ceased.

"They died in a car crash," I told Mona. "Quentin and Liz."

She nodded solemnly as if that was one option she'd considered.

"I'd just been born and they were hurrying back from the hospital to Key Largo. Drunk driver ran them off the road. Somehow I survived."

She was silent for a few moments, her nails against the console tapping out some grim Morse code.

"You remind me of her."

"Abigail?"

She nodded.

"There's something going on inside—hard, stubborn parts grinding against each other. Sand in your gears. I don't know. Gruff on the outside, but something else underneath. Something you work hard to keep hidden."

"You got a license to do this kind of thing?"

She kneeled down beside me, reached out, and ran a fingertip along the line of my jaw, from hinge to tip.

"The bone structure, too. You're one of them."

"And luckily you're not."

She smiled.

"Luckily I'm not." Then the smile weakened. "An interloper, that's me. A stray brought in from the rain."

"What do you know about your own parents?"

"Not a damn thing. Five foster families, Tampa, St. Pete, Bradenton. I was nine when Christine Milligan showed up and took me away. Two years after I had moved in with John and her, I'd just turned eleven, Christine decided she couldn't hack the parent thing. One night she tucked me in, pecked me on the forehead, wished me luck, and flew. From that point, Dad went through the motions, but it was Grandmother who raised me."

"She treat you any better than Liz?"

"Yeah, I got a long leash. She let me screw up. Just stood back and gave me something she hadn't been able to give your mother."

"Got to love her for that."

Her eyes muddied and she blinked them clear, then straightened her shoulders, sniffed, and backhanded her nose.

"She wasn't a bad woman. She had her own demons. Grew up in the shadow of domineering men. Those old pioneer roughnecks. Badasses."

"Lots of demons in this family," I said.

"I think that's why your grandfather never got in touch with the couple who raised you. He didn't want Abigail to botch another generation."

She eased down and settled onto the deck beside me. She brought her hip flush with mine. I inhaled her aroma again, fresh plums, wood smoke, leather baking in the sun, a jasmine bloom breaking open. She turned her face to me.

I reached up and ran a finger around the rim of her right ear, tucked away a strand of hair that had fallen across her cheek. My touch closed her eyes.

When I kissed her, Mona held back. Lips so indifferent I

almost drew away. But a second or two later, her mouth warmed and softened and I felt her rise from somewhere distant and wintry, as though she'd been hibernating and was shaking free of that slumber, coming into my arms with a slow, drowsy need and a ravenous hunger.

She planted her hand flat against my chest as if feeling for my heartbeat or else preparing to shove me away.

As our kiss deepened, the hand coasted down my shirt, button by button. At my waist, she wormed a finger inside the fabric and circled in on my navel. She broke away from the kiss, drew a long gasp, smiled at my bewilderment, then brought her lips to mine again with new frankness. Her fingertip still skimmed the edges of my navel.

It felt like more than simple physical exploration. Something instinctive. As if driven by impulse, Mona was harkening back to the primal situation. Invoking the umbilical, the broken cord. The scar that marked the severed union between mother and child, one generation and the next, the closest bond two people ever have, and the endless exile that follows.

As I was easing her back onto the deck, Holland cleared his throat and broke us apart.

He was in the doorway of the wheelhouse, camera in hand. But he managed, with some new show of restraint, not to snap us in our intimacy.

"Sorry, kids," he said. "But Uncle Fuck-up is trying to fix things. You better see this. He's pretty trashed."

Before I stood, I looked into Mona's eyes. Neither Bates nor Milligan, but more than their match in certain ways. A woman who easily could have surrendered long ago to the poisonous rivalries, the lessons in isolation at the core of that family, but somewhere she'd overcome, and had even managed to win for herself the childhood Abigail had not granted my mother.

When we made it outside and saw what was unfolding, I cursed and hammered a fist against the rail. Milligan was in one of the kayaks and was paddling at a leisurely clip, heading east into the open bay, closing in on the spot where the killer had instructed me to go.

Mona called out to him, then called again and another time, her voice lost in the wind. Milligan continued to paddle.

We hustled down to the lower deck. Rusty was there, hands cupped to her mouth, bellowing his name, commanding him to turn around. Holland took a picture of John, focusing his long lens.

Only Annette stayed inside, typing away on her laptop.

"Here we go," Holland said. "Party time."

He offered me the telephoto lens, but I waved it off. I could already make out the yellow bass boat idling from the mouth of the distant creek.

CHAPTER TWENTY-THREE

I ducked back into the salon, found the walkie-talkie on the bar, thumbed the call button, then thumbed it again.

Annette looked up from her typing, saw what I was doing, and hastily settled her fingers on the keys to get it all down as it was unfolding.

In my hand, the radio crackled and the woman spoke.

"Yes." Same dispassionate tone. Neither question nor statement, just a dead one-syllable word floating through the ether.

"Leave him alone. He's not the one you want."

"This is Thorn I'm talking to?"

"That's right. Turn your boat around and wait. When he's safely back on board, I'll meet you out there."

Rusty had opened the door and was listening to my speech. She shook her head firmly. No way was she going to allow me to put myself in that kind of jeopardy, not on her watch.

"I give you my word," I said into the mike, staring hard at Rusty. "I'll be there. Let him turn around and come back, I'll give you what you want."

"How good is your word?" It was more challenge than question.

"You'll have to trust me."

There was a long silence. I could hear the light swells sloshing against the hull, the purr of the generator turning gasoline into fluorescent light and chilly air.

When she came back, her voice was sharp.

"Your word any better than Abigail Bates's?"

"You drowned her, didn't you? You killed that old woman."

Rusty's shoulders slumped. She stared down at the carpet, shaking her head in helpless disbelief.

"Why'd you do it? Who hired you? What's your name, goddammit?" I didn't expect answers. I wanted to goad her, get that anger to foam up again. I wanted her, most of all, to focus on me. "What's wrong? You afraid to talk? What're you worried about? You're not too smart, are you? Afraid to engage with me, afraid I'll confuse you, manipulate you?"

"You got it wrong," she said, resuming her patient tone.

"I don't think so. I think you're the one who's got it wrong. You've lost your way. Nobody drowns an eighty-six-year-old woman. Nobody with a soul. Nobody human."

"There," she said. "Now you're getting it."

A flash of chilly sweat lit up my skin, and in the next moment my cotton shirt was glued to my back.

This woman was no wild-eyed maniac. That's what she was telling me. No emotional zombie, no flailing crazy. She was like me, like Rusty and the rest of us, except for one small defect: Somewhere along the way she'd stopped giving a shit. And she recognized the fact, knew how far she'd drifted. There was discipline in her actions, self-control. She wasn't the kind to be rattled or misdirected. This wasn't the brash and reckless adversary I'd been imagining and secretly hoping for.

Through the back window I watched the bass boat cruising slowly toward John Milligan's kayak. Maybe a hundred yards separated them.

Mona pushed through the door and saw me holding the walkie-talkie.

"Can she hear?" Mona whispered.

"No."

"Dad's got a gun."

"What?"

"He takes it with him everywhere. A Beretta automatic, like Abigail's."

"You're sure?"

"He was carrying it today when we were fishing. Holster under his arm. That's why he kept his Windbreaker on the whole day."

"Oh, great," Rusty said. "Fucking wonderful."

"Why didn't you tell me that before? You didn't think it was relevant?"

"It honestly slipped my mind."

"So is there anything else you haven't shared?"

Mona flinched, then glanced back out the window at her father paddling steadily toward the approaching boat.

"He's an excellent marksman," she said. "Goes to the range every weekend. He's trying to save us. I didn't know he had it in him. Risking his life to save us."

I wasn't so sure that's what was happening, but I let it slide. I wasn't certain of anyone's motives anymore. Not even my own.

In the stiff silence, Mona's gaze drifted back to me for a moment, and the hurt I'd given her was clear. The flush in her cheeks radiated upward into her hairline, and her ears were glowing with warmth as if she'd been bitch-slapped by some charmer who'd lured her close with sweet talk just to get a clear crack at her.

I told her I was sorry, and after a moment she nodded.

I pressed the call button again. When the woman didn't respond, I spoke in a loud, unmistakable voice: "Let him go and I'll be there in ten minutes."

There was no response for several moments. The bass boat continued to close in on the kayak. They were about fifty yards apart. A good marksman would have had a high-percentage shot by then.

"Maybe I'll take all of you down," the woman said. "Just to be sure."

"Sure of what?"

There was no response.

"Sure of what?"

The radio clicked on, then a second or two of static ended with another click, as if the woman had been about to reply but caught herself.

I smacked the walkie-talkie onto the bar and headed to the door.

Rusty blocked me, lifted both hands.

"No, Thorn. Absolutely not."

I drew a breath, tried for a coherent sentence, though the whistle shrieking in my head made that nearly impossible.

"I'm getting the other kayak and paddling out there."

"Why? Are you suicidal?"

"I have to, Rusty."

"Thorn, goddammit. For once in your life think it through."

I reached for the doorknob and she steered my arm away.

"John put himself in the middle of this. Going off half-cocked apparently runs in your family, Thorn. But here's how it is. For some reason she wants you, which makes you our bargaining chip. Think about it. You rush out there, she shoots you, the rest of us are out of options."

I brushed past her, went through the doorway and into a hard gust. As the wind direction changed, it had repositioned the Mothership on the axis of our anchor line, swinging our stern closer by thirty yards to John's kayak.

Out in the bay the bass boat revved, then the woman slammed it into gear, gunned it, and steered straight for John. I grabbed the camera from Holland's grasp and focused the lens tight on the action. Ten yards away from Milligan, she swung to the right and cut the motor, slewing sideways toward the bow of his kayak.

I saw the black flicker of the automatic in John's right hand, and the wake from her boat swelling under him, jostling his aim.

"Why the fuck doesn't he shoot?" Holland said.

I watched as the woman lifted her own weapon, what looked like a bulky .45, and held it steady on John. She was shielded by the boat's console, exposing only her head above that pulpit of fiberglass. They were twenty feet apart, the choppy water dying out around them.

Then her lips moved. She was speaking to John, and I watched as he replied. I couldn't read their expressions, could not decode the tension in their stances. The lens flattened all that. They could be negotiating, or arguing, or greeting each other with the warmth of lovers after a long separation. They held their pistols in place and conversed, a back-and-forth that lasted half a minute. In the middle of their conversation a cormorant sailed into the frame and flopped onto the water between them and began to paddle toward the kayak. Glossy black bird, a notorious moocher looking for scraps.

Whatever passed between John and the woman caused Milligan to lower his aim, take hold of his paddle, and ease alongside the bass boat.

"Give me that." Mona reached for the camera.

I released it into her grasp, leaned forward, and squinted at the scene. John rose unsteadily to stand on the seat of the kayak. The woman set her pistol on the console and bent over the starboard gunwale and held out her hand. Milligan took hold of it, and she boosted him on board.

They exchanged words, then she returned to the wheel, cut it sharply, and accelerated back toward the creek.

"What the hell just happened?" Rusty said.

"Didn't look like he was forced," said Holland. "That fucker was on the dark side the whole time."

Mona lowered the camera and stared down at the water slapping against the transom. I watched the bass boat carve a sweeping turn into the creek mouth, then disappear behind the veil of mangroves.

All I could be sure of was that Milligan knew exactly how defenseless we were, and if he'd teamed up with the woman, as it appeared, we were now outgunned, and we'd been seriously outsmarted. If massacring us was their mission, they had no reason to wait. Once Milligan filled her in about our lack of defense, they could simply return within range and circle the Mothership with guns blasting.

I scanned the restless bay, watched the drifts of foam gathering at the shoreline. The cormorant nosed around the bobbing kayak for a few more minutes then flailed its wings and executed a clumsy takeoff. Around us the wind hummed through the railings and set off a chorus of clangs and tinkles as it rushed across the open decks.

"That slime weasel," Holland said. "That lying cocksucker."

Mona's eyes were blurred. Her shoulders were hunched forward, and for a moment I thought she might be about to hurl herself overboard.

"It doesn't make sense. Dad and her. It makes no sense at all."

"Who is she, Mona?"

She shook her head, her lips sealed tight against the words muscling into her throat.

"Inside," I said. "Everybody inside."

Rusty moved to the door and Holland followed, but Mona kept her grip on the rail, squinting against the gray sunlight that pulsed off the surface of the bay. She was focused on the trail of white froth, the dying wake of the bass boat.

Wrapping an arm around her shoulder, I drew her from the edge and steered her toward the doorway. Rusty waited there, her gaze alert to my arm cradling Mona. As I approached, her lungs emptied in a slow, silent heave, and her shoulders sagged. The recognition settled on her face, grew firm and final.

As I passed, I dodged her gaze and guided Mona into the salon and eased her onto the couch. She slumped back against the cushions and stared through the starboard bank of windows toward the distant creek mouth.

"What's going on, Mona? You saw something. You recognized her."

Before she could answer an electronic ring tone sounded, then it played again. The first dozen notes of some chuga-chuga rap song.

Annette extracted the cell phone from the holster fixed to her belt. She flicked it open with a practiced snap and huddled forward, pressing it to her ear.

In unison Holland and Rusty went for their own phones, but after they'd fiddled with them for half a minute, it was clear that neither had reception.

Annette glared up at me as I positioned myself in front of her and held out my hand.

"Tell her this trip's a total bust," Annette said into the phone. "There won't be any article. I'm not about to give these people one word of promo. They're a bunch of world-class losers."

She got out one more bit of juvenile complaint before I bent down and pried the phone from her hand and snapped it shut.

"You fool," Annette said. "That was my editor."

"You didn't say we were in trouble. You didn't ask her to send help."

"What difference would that make? She's in New York."

Holland groaned.

I opened the phone. In the small screen's bottom right corner the signal-strength indicator was showing a single bar.

It was instinct that made me dial Sugar's cell. I pressed the phone to my ear and walked to the rear door as the wavering ring faded and returned.

Apparently when the wind swung us around on the anchor, it pushed us thirty or forty yards farther east toward the distant mainland, just enough to bring us into the fringes of the nearest cell tower's coverage.

I heard Sugarman answer. Down a well full of static.

"Listen, Sugar, it's me."

I heard him say my name, then his voice broke off.

I pulled the phone from my ear and checked the reception. Nothing. I opened the salon door and stepped outside, extended the phone toward the east, feeling like some Stone Age fool presenting a sacred stone to the sun. Still nothing.

I went back into the salon, grabbed a pair of scissors from a kitchen drawer, located one of the laminated aerial photographs Rusty had made, and snipped out the section I wanted and tucked it inside my shirt.

I went back onto the deck, climbed the starboard ladder to the roof. Keeping my profile low, I held the phone up to the sky. Still no bars, still feeling like an idiot.

Maybe it was some electromagnetic fluke that brought us

fleetingly into range, something totally unrelated to the houseboat's shift closer to the mainland. But there was only one way to find out for sure.

A moment later when Rusty appeared on the roof, I had the green kayak loose from the bungee cords and was angling it over the edge of the upper deck.

"What the hell're you doing?"

"Stay low," I said. "Down, Rusty."

She glanced back at the creek mouth, then settled to her knees.

"Thorn, talk to me."

"I'll stay in the mangroves." I held up Annette's phone. "Just go far enough to get a signal."

"You're a crazy man."

"Roger that."

She helped me get the kayak down to the water, bringing it alongside. She held it steady while I climbed into the cockpit.

I wriggled a hand into my shirt and came out with the section of the laminated map. An overhead view of Cardiac Bay's eastern edge, our mooring spot, and the creeks and channels just to the east. I got my bearings, ruled out a half-dozen dead-end creeks, and studied the maze of wider canals that penetrated the solid forest of mangroves. I was looking for some waterway that carried me as far east toward the civilized mainland as I could get.

Then I looked out at the water, sighting across almost a mile of open bay, and located what appeared from the photograph to be the veiled opening of a narrow canal that led maybe a hundred yards almost due east. A canal I would never have noticed without Rusty's aerial image. Only trouble was, the canal dead-ended on the fringes of the inlet where the shooter was.

"Pretty funny," said Rusty. "You, of all people, depending on modern technology."

I peered at the horizon as if I could catch a glimpse of the wispy beams of electrons showering down from distant towers.

"Yeah," I said. "Funny as hell."

I pushed away and dipped a paddle into the choppy water. Bobbing ten feet off the stern, I brought it around to face her.

"Tell me something, Rusty."

"Yeah."

"Why'd the shooter leave the walkie-talkie?"

"What?"

"If she thought she'd killed me already, why leave the radio behind? And more than that, why bring the damn thing along in the first place?"

She gave me a bewildered shrug.

"I left it on the bar," I said. "Keep an eye on it."

And I dug the paddle in deep.

CHAPTER TWENTY-FOUR

A few minutes before his three o'clock at the Pine Tree School, Sugarman made a quick detour by Dillard's office. The good doctor was at lunch, so Sugar took a run at his secretary, Mary Suarez, a brisk woman of about fifty, with close-cropped hair, orange lipstick, and a pugnacious squint.

As Sugar inquired about the clothing Abigail Bates was wearing when her body was found, Mary stared down at her telephone, and her right hand inched toward it as if she was considering summoning security.

Sugarman waited, staring at the top of Mary Suarez's head. He was trying his damnedest to give the woman the benefit of the doubt. Maybe she was weak on social skills. Bashful, tongue-tied.

"May I assume your office returned Ms. Bates's property to the next of kin?"

She flicked her eyes up and took him in. No, not bashful—something else entirely. She studied the baseball cap he was holding. She probably assumed he'd doffed it in a display of servitude.

Sugarman bulled ahead.

"So I'm asking if you kept any record of those articles in your evidence package? Photos of her clothes, jewelry, things of that nature."

The woman clucked her tongue three times. "Are you insinuating this office is less than professional?"

"No, ma'am. I'm not doing that."

"Well, of course we keep records of the deceased's possessions."

Sugarman shrugged.

"I need to take a look."

Before she could refuse, Sugar said, "As Dillard told you, I'm here to double-check the sheriff's work. Something doesn't smell right."

"Well, it's about time someone double-checked that woman."

Mary Suarez pushed back her chair, got up, and tramped into an adjoining office. In half a minute she returned with a red file folder. She slapped it down on the edge of the desk and stepped back out of Sugarman's range as if sharing his breathing space might pose a health risk.

Carefully, Sugarman set the Marlins cap on her desk, picked up the folder, and leafed through the documents and photos. Same autopsy shots he'd viewed earlier. And there were pictures of Abigail Bates's clothes laid out flat on what looked like a surgical table. A vented fishing shirt, frayed jeans, white lacy underwear, and one pink tennis shoe with plaid laces.

"Nobody asked me," Mary said, "but it's obvious there was foul play."

"So you agree with Dr. Dillard."

She weighed her response with an evasive light playing in her eyes. Not about to be conned by some outsider.

"Based on what I've seen so far, I'm not so sure," Sugar said. "The sheriff's decision might be right. This whole thing could be nothing more than an accidental drowning. I'd have to see something a good deal more convincing than some bruises on the woman's arms."

"Oh, my," she said, her voice tightening. "I didn't realize I was in the presence of a forensic pathologist."

Sugar touched the bill of the cap.

"There's a hair snagged on the snap of this ball cap," he said, keeping his voice as quiet as he could manage. "Please treat this item with the same care you'd use on any crime-scene evidence. And when he returns, have Dr. Dillard check that strand of hair for postmortem banding. Pay special attention to the proximal root."

She narrowed her eyes.

"DNA analysis will be critical. That strand of hair might belong to Ms. Bates, or it might belong to the killer. You want to write that down, Mary, or can you remember it?"

She gave him a freeze-dried smile.

These people were starting to seriously piss him off, but somehow Sugar managed to bid the woman good-day and get out of the office without strangling her.

It had been such a long time since he'd felt the death-ray of bigotry aimed in his direction, he wasn't sure if he was reading it right. Maybe he was just being thin-skinned. Yeah, he'd have to work on believing that.

He was getting into his car when his cell phone chirped. He dug it out, snapped it open, and Thorn spoke his name.

"Hey, Thorn? How's it going?"

But the connection broke. Sugar sat for a minute waiting for Thorn to call back, but he didn't, which didn't surprise Sugar. He could count on one hand the times Thorn had used a cell phone. Had to be something pretty special to make him do it now. Probably wanted to brag about a fish they'd caught, some hundred-pound tarpon. Sugarman got the cell number off his ID screen and returned the call, but was forwarded to the automatic voice-mail system. The party he was calling was unavailable.

Sugarman tried to hear again the tenor of Thorn's voice. A little strained, hurried. Not surprising that he might be getting cranky after twenty-four hours crammed together with so many people. Sugar let it go.

Sasha cut the engine and the boat coasted deeper into the narrow inlet. Griffin was propped up against the transom, eyeing Milligan, who stood on the other side of the console. The big man would have to take two or three steps to be in arm's length of Sasha, time enough for her to put three rounds in him.

"I can deliver Thorn," Milligan said again. "No risk to you. End this whole thing. You take him down, we get out of here, nobody has to know who you are or why you did it. You just disappear."

"We're past that point," Sasha said.

"Mona put you up to this. My daughter's paying you."

"Sit down and shut up."

"Then it was Carter. Carter Mosley. That bastard wants control. He's behind this whole thing. Tell me, goddammit. It's Mosley, right?"

Sasha cut her gaze to Griffin. He had his eyes open and he was sitting up, his breath noisy, but he was still alive. His skin had taken on a waxy gleam.

"Get over the side," Sasha said.

"What?"

"Over the side. Into the water."

"I'm offering you a deal. I'll give you Thorn. That's who you want."

"Over the side," she said. "I'm not saying it again."

"Look, I'm an ally. I can make anything happen you want. Name it, it's yours. We'll find your son the best damn doctors in the world. A new home, cash. You tell me what you want. A million dollars, two. Give me a number."

"Your mother said the same thing, just about those exact words. Right before I drowned her."

"What does it accomplish, killing me, killing the others?"

"Head of the snake," Griffin said.

Milligan stared at the boy.

"I know who you are," Milligan said. "I recognized you this morning. You're the Olsen woman. Your husband was the one who died. An activist, worked at Pine Tree School. Taught science or something. Got the natives all riled up."

"Died of lung cancer," Sasha said. "Same as my boy."

"Same as me," Griffin said.

"Whoever you're dealing with, I'll double whatever they're paying you. Hell, I'll triple it. We'll cease the mining operation. We'll cap that gyp stack next to the school. What do you want? Name it, make me a list."

"I want you to get overboard, Mr. Milligan, into the water."
She gave him a good view of the .45.

"Why?"

"We're going to find out how long you can hold your breath."

He was a big man, wide shoulders. Early sixties but without paunch or jowl. Good head of hair, clear pitiless eyes like his mother's. Sasha had seen him a few times before, strutting around Summerland like he owned the world and simply out of the kindness of his heart was allowing a few others to share it with him.

A bullet in the leg or shoulder, something to weaken him, to even up the odds, that would have been the wise thing.

"Nice and easy, slip in the water. I'll be with you shortly."

Milligan seemed to be making the calculation most men his size and strength would make. He didn't smile outright, but she could see the cunning play on his lips.

"Shoot him, Mama. Don't risk it."

Milligan sat down on the starboard gunwale.

"You and me in the water? That's what you're saying? Hand to hand."

"That's what I'm saying."

"I'm not an eighty-six-year-old woman."

"Go on, Mr. Milligan."

"Shoot him, Mama."

"No, son. She thinks she can drown me. Your mama's a certified loony."

"I don't want to shoot you, Mr. Milligan. But I will if you don't get in that water. Right now."

He swiveled on the gunwale, brought his legs over the side. He looked down between his knees into the shallow creek. Pushed off and splashed.

He treaded water five feet away, stirring up the muddy bottom.

"Come on in, gal, the water's fine."

"Mama, goddammit, use the pistol. He's too damn big."

She set the .45 on the console.

"At least leave me the gun."

"No need for that."

"Mama, don't."

"I'll be fine, son. It's not the size of the muscles, it's what you're willing to do with them."

Sasha climbed onto the gunwale, winked at her boy, and hopped into the water. It was nice and warm. Much warmer than the Peace River.

CHAPTER TWENTY-FIVE

The Pine Tree School was two miles north of Summerland at the end of a gravel lane that was lined with a dozen wooden signs. On each sign a one-line saying had been carved into it, the grooves filled in with bright red paint. Every ten feet there was another one.

> Any fool can make a rule, and any fool will mind it.
> Aim above morality. Be not simply good; Be good for something.
> In wildness is the preservation of the world.
> Our life is frittered away by detail. Simplify, simplify.

Each of them was a quote by Henry David Thoreau.

Halfway down the entrance road, Sugarman stopped and scribbled down a couple of the quotations. Something he could trot out later, amuse Thorn.

At the end of the lane, he rolled into a large gravel parking lot. To his right was a one-story cinder-block building with covered walkways and lots of picture windows and a flat roof covered with aluminum ductwork. Apparently air-conditioning had been added as an afterthought: It was an architectural style Sugar had noticed several times since arriving in the region. Built back in the sixties, the school looked like a cheap motel of that era, or a child's creation built of Legos. Military-barracks motif. A stark concrete block that no one had bothered to stucco or beautify in any way. In the relentless Florida sun, the yellow paint job had blistered and faded almost to white.

On that Friday afternoon the parking lot was swarming with kids. A handful of teenagers skulking among the grade-schoolers. The yelps and squeals of several girls playing tag, darting through the crowd. Backpacks bulging with books, bright lunch boxes, a few kids clamped inside headphones, a couple on cells. Most of them in old jeans, T-shirts, a few plain dresses, some overalls. Lots of baseball caps. Off in the shadows, a few of the big kids were sneaking smokes.

But what drew Sugar's attention was what loomed behind the school. Rising above a stand of pines was the treeless slope of a solitary mountain. Sugarman had seen a half-dozen of them earlier in the day. Steep, grassy berms that funneled upward a couple of hundred feet. From a distance they resembled the unnatural humps of abandoned landfills. This one was even more massive than the others he'd spotted in the distance as he drove down the back roads of DeSoto and Manatee counties.

Its shadow enveloped the school building and most of the parking lot. As Sugarman pushed open the car door and stepped onto the gravel, some harsh scent carried by the breeze stung his nostrils and thickened in his lungs. The odor had an industrial density, a scent blend in the same family as roofing tar, with a bitter edge of ammonia. After two breaths the compound nearly triggered his gag reflex.

He was halfway across the parking lot, wading through a throng of chattering kids, when he spotted Sheriff Timmy Whalen's patrol car rounding the last turn and idling up to park beside his Honda.

He stopped and waved hello, but either Timmy didn't see him, or else he'd been demoted to her shit list. She was all business, cranking her shifter into park, pushing her door open, and stepping out with no eye contact, no acknowledgment of any kind. Some of the moms and dads parked nearby watched her warily as she bent back into her car to adjust something in the backseat.

While Sugarman waited, he noted that the chemical smell

had subsided. After only a minute or two, his olfactory nerves were nearing exhaustion, same as it happened upon entering a bakery, when that initial burst of yeast, cinnamon, and warm dough wore off, passing swiftly into forgetfulness.

Sugar looked back at the school building, at the shadow lengthening across the parking lot. Kids racing to waiting pickup trucks and vans and dinged-up cars, and a couple of half-sized yellow school buses with DESOTO COUNTY printed on their sides. Mothers and a few fathers, most dressed in jeans and shabby shirts, were standing around chatting, with an eye out for their kids and an occasional glance in the sheriff's direction.

Although the odor had died away, there was now a metallic film growing in Sugar's mouth, a tingle on his tongue like the afterburn of spicy food.

He walked over to the cruiser as Timmy Whalen was snapping off the two-way radio fixed to the epaulet on her left shoulder.

"Alone at last," Sugar said and smiled.

Timmy took a step back and studied him with cool neutrality.

"I understand you've been turning over a few rocks." She moved past him, heading at a good pace toward the school. Sugar put it in gear and caught up.

"Don't tell me you've been spying on me."

"In this town, you kick over a rock, I choke on the dust."

Sugar chuckled. "What's the deal? Now I get the sheriff's official-politeness routine."

She stopped and gave him another careful look.

"You're a tricky bastard, aren't you? All your straight-shooter bullshit, that's an act. You're just trying to wheedle whatever you can out of me."

"Not really."

"Yes, you are, Sugarman. You may not be conscious of it, but you're a cagey guy."

"Does it count if I'm not conscious of it?"

"There," she said, pointing at him. "That's what I'm talking about."

Sugar raised both hands in helpless surrender.

Timmy sighed and waded on through the swarm of children. He saw her touch a finger to a wave of hair that had fallen low on her forehead and nudge it back in place. A gesture Sugarman found pleasantly feminine.

He assumed that in the hours since he'd seen her last, Whalen had taken time to reassess the threat of Sugarman's investigation. That easy rapport they'd had from the get-go was over. Still, it was better she was treating him with blatant distrust than to be coming on with the smiley-face act she used on her other constituents.

Not that it changed anything for Sugarman. He had only one gear. Straight on, no bank shots, no subtle spins.

He waited till she was almost to the entrance to the school, then said, "I found a couple of items. A pink tennis shoe, for one. With plaid laces."

She halted, kept her gaze fixed on the school's front door.

"It's in my car. Want to see it?"

"Where'd you find this shoe?" She swiveled her head slowly and stared at him, one eyebrow arched as if she'd caught him in a lie.

"Seven feet down in the Peace River, wedged into a crack in the rock."

He plucked at the leg of his black jeans.

"See?" he said. "I'm still damp."

She pursed her lips and blew out a shot of air.

"While I was underwater, pulling it out of the crevice, I saw a root—cypress, pine, or something. It was bowed out from the bank. Probably make a good handhold if you wanted to keep from bobbing back to the top. You know, while you drowned somebody."

"A root," she said.

"Found a Marlins baseball cap, too. It was buried in the mud along the bank, same location, about two miles upstream from the takeout. Big boulders on the north shoreline, a sharp easterly crook in the river. Pretty convenient location to lie in wait, get the jump on somebody passing by. I left the cap with Dr. Dillard because it had a hair snagged to it.

Thought he might want to look at it under one of his polarized-light microscopes."

"We searched every inch of the riverbank. Searched it several times, hundreds of man-hours devoted to that."

"I got lucky," Sugar said. "Nobody's criticizing your effort."

"Wedged in a crack of a rock?"

"Yeah," he said. "Consistent with a struggle. Like maybe Ms. Bates was kicking, trying to break free. It gets stuck."

Timmy was silent for a moment. Probably seeing the same ugly scene that was playing in Sugarman's head.

"Thing I'm curious about," Sugar said. "How's the assailant know Abigail Bates is going canoeing at that particular time? Killer's got to get to the ambush spot, set up shop, which had to take some advance planning. Somebody had to pass the word, somebody who knew Ms. Bates's schedule that morning. Which suggests an insider. Someone on her staff, maybe. Friend, relative."

The sheriff stepped aside for three squealing boys rushing out the entrance. She watched them merge with the larger group of kids in the parking lot. Sugarman was no expert on body language, but Timmy seemed to be drawing deeper breaths than earlier, as though working to stay calm.

"Way I see it," Sugar said, "you find out who knew Abigail was going on that canoe trip, you're a giant step closer to your suspect."

"No one knew."

"No one?"

"I questioned all her staff, associates, family members, and no one knew she was planning that trip. Mona had been campaigning for her to do it for months, trying to soften her up about stopping the mining. But Mona didn't know Ms. Bates had chosen that particular day. In fact, she was surprised Ms. Bates decided to do it, and felt responsible for putting her up to it."

"She was telling the truth?"

"I have no reason to doubt her."

"I met her yesterday," Sugarman said. "She seemed pretty

broken up about the death. Months later she's still mourning. Unless that's an act."

"Mona's straight up. No acting there."

Her tone seemed a shade too offhand.

The flow of children coming out the door had slowed. Timmy drew it open, smiling at the kids and saying hi, calling some by name.

"And Dr. Dillard," she said, "I suppose he was helpful."

"Your medical examiner is not a contented worker bee."

"No shit."

A mother heading out the front door flinched at the word, gave the sheriff a sharp look, and snatched the hand of her red-haired daughter. The scrawny tot coughed, wet and deep.

"Sorry, Ms. Metcalf," Timmy said.

"There's children," the woman said. "Watch your language, please."

"Yes, ma'am, sorry."

With an unforgiving scowl, Ms. Metcalf marched onward as if filing away this latest grievance for later distribution.

"Man, you're walking on some serious eggshells around here," he said.

"Yeah, and you're turning into one of them."

"How the hell did you ever get elected, an African-American woman?"

"I won ninety percent of the black vote, plus ten percent of the uninformed white vote. That won't happen again. The word's out."

She had a nice smile when she wasn't scowling.

"Why do I keep getting this same weird feeling from you?"

"And which weird feeling is that?"

"Actually it's several feelings. Hot-cold, plus-minus, yes-no. I think it's called ambivalence."

She looked him over again with those sleepy gold-flecked eyes, then shook her head with something like disgust, though Sugar thought it looked more like disgust with herself than him.

"Who'd you say you're working for?"

"At this point," Sugar said, "I believe I'm working for myself."

CHAPTER TWENTY-SIX

Goddamn cell phones.

I settled the paddle across my lap and flipped open the small silver phone. Still no bars. I had crossed a mile of open bay east of the Mothership. I withdrew the aerial photo from inside my shirt. Based on the photograph I had to go another twenty yards east, then there was a narrow opening that angled off to the south and slightly east. That narrow creek was bordered by a skinny mangrove island that formed the western border of the inlet where I'd seen the woman in the bass boat disappear.

Which put me a lot damn closer to the shooter than I wanted to be. Even if I got a signal, I'd have to whisper.

I guided the kayak down the last few yards of the creek. All around me the water was moving, part tidal, part river flow.

In the Everglades it was easy to forget you were navigating a river, a great wide swath of water seeping steadily down the hundred miles from Lake Okeechobee toward the open Gulf. Intersected by highways and drainage canals, it found its way south nonetheless, in some places no more than a thin sheet of water, in others deepening to sloughs and marshes, bays and lakes, but always moving. Not the mournful stagnant swamp that outsiders imagined, but an ever-freshening flood.

I backwatered on the port side, careful to keep the aluminum paddle from knocking against the edge, as I made the sharp-angled swing into the narrow gap that led south and east.

Two yards to my right a six-foot gator slid from the bank and slipped below the surface, and ahead of me in the lower branches of a mangrove a little green heron marveled at my intrusion into its sanctuary. With the canopy so dense overhead, the light had dimmed to a vague olive, and the surface of the water was a shifting mosaic of midafternoon sunlight. In a few sunny spots bromeliads had taken hold. Insects whirred past my face, and in the branches dozens of spiderwebs quivered in the breeze. Orb weavers mostly, with their thoughtful little white tags placed prominently in each web to steer birds and mammals clear, like a warning decal affixed to a sliding glass door.

I made two hard strokes, then let the kayak coast the final few yards toward the terminus of the canal. I was floating within an oblong swimming hole, banked on all four sides by dense growth.

I opened the phone and saw with some surprise that two bars had appeared in the lower corner.

As I was punching in Sugar's cell number, the bow bumped hard and the kayak jolted to a halt.

I leaned to the right as far as I dared to see what I'd rammed. It was a tippy vessel, and this was not water I wanted to be swimming in.

Up ahead there was no sign of a submerged log, but the kayak seemed to be lodged firmly. Either it was a mud bank I hadn't seen, or the gator and I had crossed paths and he was stubbornly refusing to move.

I punched in the last few numbers and a second later heard the faint ringing. To the east through the warren of branches I caught a glimpse of color. The object was low and sleek. Its pale icy blue was an alien hue in the drab color scheme of the Everglades.

I bent forward, twisting for a better angle, and saw it, bobbing high on the choppy water—Rusty's skiff. Empty, it was drifting not more than twenty feet away on the other side of the stand of mangroves.

I took a closer survey of my surroundings and saw a few yards ahead a wide break in the growth that hadn't shown up on the aerial photograph. The gap was about the size and shape of the doorway to a hobbit's house, but from at least a couple of angles, it would make my green kayak visible from the inlet where Rusty's skiff was floating and where I suspected the shooter was harbored.

"Thorn?"

Sugar's voice was faint. He spoke my name again, but I could not answer. The air was clenched tight in my lungs.

"Thorn?"

Just ahead of the kayak's bow, near the hobbit door, I'd caught a silver flicker of metal and felt a stab of recognition.

"Hold on."

Sugarman said, "Thorn? What's going on, man?"

I set the open phone on my lap, picked up the paddle, and sculled a figure-eight pattern over the starboard side. I could hear Sugarman speaking, repeating my name as the kayak swung a foot to the right, then another foot, the bow tip still locked in place.

I leaned as far as I could.

The shiny object hovered a few inches below the surface and came into view as the kayak reached the end of its arc. It was a watch. A flashy Rolex.

The man whose wrist it was fastened to was floating face-down. He'd sunk a few inches beneath the waterline, but as the kayak swung closer, I could see his outstretched arm was hairy and muscled. Then I made out Milligan's white polo shirt waffling with the tidal flow. I stared at the body for several moments, my ears humming with a crazy throb. My eyes stung and the breath in my throat had turned scratchy and hot.

The tide must've carried the body from the inlet on the other side of the mangroves through that hobbit door and stranded it in this small pool.

What I did then was reflex, some ancient wink of synapse, a self-protective impulse sent down the chain of blood from Quentin Thorn. That man, my father, had lost two fingers somehow, though maybe he would have lost the whole hand, or even his arm, if he'd not been so split-second quick.

Without knowing why, I jerked backward a microsecond before the shark exploded in a wave of water and chomped at the blade of the paddle. He missed, but his snout slammed broadside against the kayak, and I managed only one sharp jab with the paddle between his eyes.

It didn't register.

Bull shark, *Carcharhinus leucas*. Chunky body, small eyes, blunt round snout, dark gray, around seven feet long, which meant more than likely it was a female. Very aggressive, they'd eat anything, anywhere. They were ever-present in the Keys and the Everglades, flourishing in brackish water or saltwater. Far as I was concerned, bulls were as menacing as great whites, especially when disturbed while feeding.

I craned forward to track the bull's path, and a wasp chose that instant to dive-bomb my ear. While I swatted it away, the shark heaved again.

It tore into the kayak's stern, jarred the phone from my lap, and sent it skittering overboard. Then a third angry crash tipped the kayak and spilled me against a cage of mangrove roots.

I scrabbled for a hold, gashed my palm on a row of barnacles as nasty as broken glass. I managed to get a lucky lock on a main limb and boosted myself from the water. The bull shark circled halfway between me and Milligan, pausing for several seconds as if deciding with slow prehistoric logic which of the delicious items on her buffet table would be her starter.

I watched as she made her choice, turning away from me and gliding across the pool toward my uncle.

But it wasn't over. The limb I was clinging to was coated with algae slime as oily and slick as lard, and inch by inevitable inch I slid back toward the capsized kayak. I tried to keep my feet still as my boat shoes eased into the water, then my ankles disappeared and my knees. The kayak was a foot away.

Before the bull shark's attack churned the water to an opaque brown, I'd noted the bottom was only few feet down. But it was not solid earth I could trust. Like all the Everglades it was a false bottom, an airy froth of mud and silt, as yielding as warm pudding, probably several feet of it, neither earth nor water but a blind mix of both where the shark was perfectly at home.

I stretched out my right leg, curled my toe, hooked it into the seat compartment. The shark hovered just a foot from Milligan's extended arm, as if transfixed by the abundance that had dropped into her watery domain.

I lifted the edge of the kayak and drew it to me and slowly righted it. The sunken seat compartment was full of leaves and twigs and brown slush, but the craft was designed to float despite being waterlogged.

Then I lost my grip entirely and splashed. I kicked back to the surface, wiped my eyes and saw the boil of water as the bull shark swerved from Milligan's arm and flashed across the twenty-foot span, homing in on the stink of fear.

I lunged upward, swiped at a branch directly overhead, missed by an inch, then heaved again and got both hands around it and chinned myself out of the water, swung my ankles up to meet the branch, until there I was, hanging upside down. My lowest point, closest to the water, was my head.

As I listened to the splash behind me, I shot a look aloft to judge my prospects for climbing higher into that maze of limbs. More bad news. The plant I was holding had been battered by wind or disease and was scabby and withered. It wouldn't have supported a child for long. Already I could hear the faint crackling of its fibers straining under my weight.

I looked backward at the bull shark's approach.

She slowed. She came to a stop. Her small eyes were as inert as shards of moon rock. Maybe her vision could penetrate beyond the waterline, maybe not. I know I felt the touch of her stare. If it was true and she could see me, surely she was mystified. What I was, and what I was doing hanging from a tree upside down like some giant bat, must have baffled her radish brain.

For she floated there a few seconds longer, then abandoned me and swung once again to John Milligan.

While the shark closed in on my uncle's body, I eased into the kayak, plucked my paddle from the water, and pushed off. Backpaddling down the narrow corridor from which I'd come, backing and backing, while in that shadowy bower, the bull shark writhed and thrashed and the water foamed red.

I had not cared for the man. In less than a day I'd made a long list of grievances against him. Moral failings, sins against my mother, an arrogant disregard for honesty. I'd pegged him as a greedy bastard with little respect for the natural world. I'd found little to like and nothing to admire in this, my last blood relative. But no man deserved such an end, such a feral dismantling of his remains.

Five minutes later, I was in the main channel, paddling smoothly with deep rhythmic strokes, when I heard the warble of a two-way radio.

I drew the paddle from the water, held still.

The warble came again. I U-turned and tracked the sound, angling across the channel, peering ahead to catch any movement through the barrier of limbs and leaves. Then she spoke. My grandmother's killer, Teeter's killer, John Milligan's killer.

"I'm here. What do you want?" It was the same detached tone I'd heard from her earlier.

She was only a few yards south of me, screened by a hammock of white mangroves and buttonwoods. I drew out the photographic image and found my location. If I kept paddling west for a few more minutes, I'd be in the open bay well to the south of her and out of her sight line. I lifted up the paddle and slid it into the water, dipping to the right side, then the left side, smooth stroke, smooth stroke.

I was ten feet farther west when I heard the voice reply to the killer.

"This is Mona. Listen to me, Sasha. The job's done. It's over. You can go home now."

I exhaled long and slow, which seemed to ease the stabbing ache behind my eyes. I must have been holding my breath for several minutes.

CHAPTER TWENTY-SEVEN

Sheriff Timmy Whalen led Sugarman into the school, down a long stuffy corridor, to a room in the rear wing. The sign above the door said MEDIA CENTER. The room was full of chrome-and-pressed-wood school desks. A television set was perched atop a rolling stand, and a padded chair was positioned a yard in front of the screen. One large window looked out at the steep grassy slope.

"Those plaques out front, along the entrance drive," Sugar said. "What's that about? Somebody a Thoreau fan?"

"A former teacher here, C.C. Olsen, was an admirer of Thoreau. They're a memorial to Olsen."

"Memorial."

"You'll be seeing Olsen in the videos. He passed away a year ago. Not quite fifty. Had lots of admirers in this community."

"How'd he die?"

"Small-cell broncogenic malignancy."

"That's lung cancer?"

"As aggressive as it gets."

Sheriff Whalen cleared her throat. She walked to the TV cart and switched on the DVD player on the shelf below the television. All brisk and bustle, keeping her distance.

"The video is a collection of the four public meetings. They began two years ago after much urging from Mr. Olsen, and took place in the gymnasium, which seats about two hundred. It was over capacity every time. Bates International was kind enough to send reps to try to assuage the community's concerns. Lots of charts and smooth talk. Not much assuaging."

"Concerns about what?"

Timmy switched on the TV, then turned to face him.

"Oh, come on, don't be coy. You know what."

"Concerns about what?" Sugarman said again.

"About that." Whalen stepped from the TV stand and pointed toward the window, at the steep green hillside beyond. "It's a gypsum stack, where they dump the leftovers of phosphate mining. About seventy million tons of acidic, radioactive sludge. The one you're looking at happens to be twelve times the mass of the Great Pyramid at Giza."

"Whoa."

"You're telling me you didn't know about this?"

"I still don't know."

She looked at him suspiciously.

"I heard about the Peace River and Horse Creek, the flap about the watershed. A lot of people are pissed off about Bates strip-mining sensitive land, the impact it's going to have downstream. I know a little about gypsum stacks, but nothing about that one in particular."

Timmy Whalen walked over to the window, stared out at the grassy mountain. It wasn't exactly an invitation, but Sugarman walked over and stood beside her, within the aura of her perfume. Something flowery. Jasmine maybe. Not strong, but noticeable enough to suggest she'd spritzed herself in the last hour or so. More mixed signals.

She turned her head and burned him with a reproachful look as if she'd read his thoughts. Sugarman took a step back.

"Okay," she said. "Here's the deal. Bates wants to increase the size of that gypsum stack by a third so they can dump more tailings. It's a cost-cutting measure. They own the land that borders school property, and evidently it's a lot cheaper to increase the size of one stack than start fresh with another.

"After a lot of back and forth, Mona Milligan worked out

a compromise, a list of concessions: restore native habitat on some acreage they own near here, do odor testing and try to find a solution to what's causing the bad smell, all kinds of sleight-of-hand mitigation bullshit. Finally Bates wore everyone down, or paid them off, and county, state, even the Environmental Protection Agency signed off. Everybody but the folks with kids in Pine Tree School. There was a great hue and cry. C.C. was the point man. He claimed the stack was already a serious health hazard. Increasing its size would only make matters worse."

"Health hazard how?"

The sheriff glanced around the room, then marched over to the window and unhooked a small box that hung from a nail on the wall.

She brought it to him and Sugarman looked it over. It was the size of a cell phone, and 23.4 flickered in red LED lights on the small screen.

"There's a meter in every corner of the school. C.C. Olsen paid for most of them out of his own pocket."

"Radon detector?"

"That's right," she said. "Measures units of radioactivity per volume of air. Picocuries per liter. According to the EPA, a four is cause for alarm. You get an indoor reading above that, you're supposed to have your building ventilated. You probably didn't notice those air ducts on the roof of the school."

"I noticed."

"Well, that's what they're about. Cost the county forty-eight thousand bucks and only lowered the average readings from a thirty-six to what you see there. Some help, but it didn't fix the problem. A reading of twenty is about a hundred times the average outdoor level. Or, in down-and-dirty terms, breathing the air inside this building is equal to smoking two packs of Marlboros a day."

Sugarman looked around at the walls of the bare room.

"Kids are still going to school here. How does that happen if the building is contaminated?"

"For one thing, there's conflicting science. Two sides to every coin. You know that old game."

"Experts contradicting each other."

"Yeah, and for another thing, this isn't Miami or Sarasota. The county's dirt poor. We're talking tens of millions for a new school, land, construction costs, which means a major bump in property taxes unless the state kicks in, which it refuses to do. A couple of years back, Olsen did a petition drive and got a bond issue on the ballot, but the good citizens of the county said no thanks. Fixing something like this, it's not as easy as snapping your damn fingers."

"Hey, calm down. I'm not the enemy."

She gave him a long look like she wasn't so sure.

"Watch the video," she said. "Get an education. You want some suspects, you'll see a few hundred of them."

The sheriff handed him the TV remote and walked to the door.

"One more thing," he said. "You got a time line? How Abigail Bates spent the hours before she went canoeing?"

Her jaw muscled up, then relaxed. She traced a finger along the curve of her right eyebrow as if buying a moment to get her face under control.

"She drove from her condo on Longboat Key to the canoe rental place."

"No stops along the way?"

She heaved a sigh. A woman not used to being cross-examined.

Sugarman waited while her eyes roamed the wall above the window.

"You know I'll find out," he said. "One way or the other."

"Oh, yeah. I'm beginning to see how you work."

"Where'd she stop, Sheriff?"

She shook her head and showed him a rueful smile.

"According to Ms. Bates's secretary, she was scheduled to swing by her lawyer's office in downtown Sarasota. Drop off some papers."

"Carter Mosley?"

Her lips parted a fraction, then she caught herself and closed her mouth.

"My, my, you're such a sharpie. Hard to believe you've only been here since breakfast."

"I met Mosley last night in Islamorada. He flew the Milligans down."

She was silent, looking out the window at the steep green hill.

"So Ms. Bates stopped by Mosley's office," Sugar said, "which means he may have known she was headed off on her canoe adventure."

"Apparently she changed her mind. She never made it to Mosley's."

"That's what he said?"

"That's what he said."

"You double-check his story? Interview his secretary, his staff?"

Sheriff Whalen stared at him, her eyes flickering with shadows and her lips moving distractedly.

"Listen, Timmy, I'm sorry, maybe I'm out of line."

"More than likely."

"But I have this sense you need somebody to open up to. That's how you're coming across."

"And I bet you're volunteering."

"I'm a fairly good listener."

She chuckled at his audacity. Reaching out to the window, she ran a finger down the edge of the pane as if checking its seal.

"Let me ask you something, Sugarman. Philosophical question."

"Shoot."

"Is everything always black and white to you? Justice, I mean. You ever find yourself puzzled, struggling to sort out right from wrong?"

"It's happened, sure. More than I'd like."

"For instance?"

"Okay. I have this friend down in the Keys, he's a good guy, but shades of gray are his specialty. He's spent his life slogging through one moral muddle after another. So, yeah, from all the bullshit Thorn dragged me into over the years, I know things aren't always as clear-cut as we'd like them to be."

Her body hardened, head lifting.

"Your friend's name is what?"

"Thorn."

She blinked. All the shadows were gone from her eyes.

"He's a longtime buddy. Why, you've heard of him?"

"The name came up recently. Long-lost relative of the Milligans."

"I didn't realize it was public knowledge."

"Not public, no," she said. "But I'm a cop. We have our sources."

She looked out at the green slope blazing with sunlight.

"Look, I've got some rounds to make," she said. "Watch the videos. I'll be interested in your take on things."

When she was out the door, Sugarman stared out the window for a while. The woman was gaming him, but he still couldn't decide just how. He shook his head, then pulled out his phone and redialed the cell number Thorn had been using but got the same woman's robotic voice: "This number is not available . . ."

Sasha knew it was down to minutes. The invisible filaments joining her heart with Griffin's told her that his hour had come around at last. His breath was slow and smooth. Beyond the reach of pain, he was smiling quietly, the way she'd seen them on the battlefield. Bodies torn open, limbs blown away, yet the dying soldier flushed with an eerie exhilaration.

She held him in her arms and savored his scent, his warmth. Imprinting it all, storing it deep. From time to time he opened his eyes and looked at her. He had nothing to say and neither did she. So she cooed to him, a wordless song she'd invented when he was born, half hum, half hymn.

For years it put him to sleep and it seemed to ease him now, as they lay in the shade, the water rocking the boat in rhythm with Griffin's departing breath.

A wind from the north had begun to drive thunderheads

before it, the northwest sky turning into a curdle of darkness. Tree limbs flexed, the foliage swelling and heaving as the wind prowled the nearby island.

She fingered away the bubbles from his lips and looked down into his half-open eyes. It was nearly done.

So goddamned unjust. She'd never asked for much. Just the simple things. Nothing extravagant, no wild dreams of riches or knights on white horses. All she wanted was the husband she had and the son that came to her.

That was more than sufficient. Her cup overflowed.

For years she lived her dream—the uncomplicated routines with C.C. and Griffin. Cooking, doing laundry, a garden out back, a view of the woods, one close friend she loved like a sister, classes at the junior college. Seeing the boy flourish. Watching him become a man, become more than Sasha ever was, smarter, funnier, happier. Watching him embrace his rural life while quietly yearning as his father once had for challenges beyond. An orderly rotation of the planets and the seasons and the moon and all things natural. It was more than Sasha ever expected, more than she believed she deserved. A gentle man who loved her. A boy who made her proud.

Griffin tapped her on the hand.

"What, baby? You need water?"

He motioned behind her, a drowsy wave.

She swung around, drawing the .45 from her hip holster, bringing the pistol up with both hands, panning back and forth across the empty inlet. Spooked by her own spookiness.

Griffin patted the deck. She came back around, lowering the weapon.

He pointed at his blue knapsack. Five feet away near the console.

She got up, retrieved it, brought it over. The sound of his breath was the rattle of seedpods in a parched desert breeze.

She held the backpack close and he tucked his hand inside and came out with a can of lighter fluid. Sasha set the backpack aside, feeling the weight of other cans inside.

She had a vision, a quick gut-kicking memory of C.C.

and Griffin lighting up the charcoal for weekend burgers. A pyramid of briquettes, the flicker beginning to take hold, and the two of them, being silly, flaunting good sense, standing side by side taking turns squeezing from a can just like that, trying to outdo the other by shooting streams of fluid at the grill and laughing at the blue-yellow whoosh of flames.

Griffin pulled himself up against the transom. He drew the can to his chest, and looked past her eyes. His head wavered from side to side like a man drifting off at the wheel. He flicked the red button top loose, raised the can, tipped it on its side and closed one eye as if aiming down the sights of a sniper rifle.

He squirted a stream onto his sneakers, coated them good.

Sasha moved aside. The boy knew what he wanted, always had, and it wasn't her place to manage this. He'd known with some certainty that he wasn't coming home from this journey and had hauled along the cans. Who was she to say he couldn't have the end he'd pictured?

She kept away from the splash of fluid till he'd wet both legs of his jeans and settled the can on his lap. Tired now, breathing heavy, wincing with the effort, his shoulders squeezing forward as if he meant to fold his wings closed across his body.

She took the can from his shaky hands and set it on the deck and kneeled to him.

"There's two more," he said. "In the bag."

"Okay."

"Do the rest," he said.

"I will."

"You promise me. Say it."

"I promise you."

He held her eyes and she saw their withering light, and behind her own eyes was the flapping and swirling of dark wings, the caws of angry crows.

"Thank you," he said and got another breath. "Thank you, Mama."

He closed his brown eyes on that thought, his cracked lips smiling. She watched the air torture him. His spindly chest rose and fell, and he managed it again, using all his concentration, and yet again another breath filled him and let him go.

Sasha Olsen was no more. Whatever she'd been was lost. She was out of body, out of mind, out of humanity.

She rocked her boy in her arms and looked out at the gray paradise of the Everglades. Her mission now was simple. Good death, noble death, useful death, taking as many with her as possible. Find out whose side God was on.

She crooned the song she'd made up long ago. A hum, a hymn, and now a dirge.

CHAPTER TWENTY-EIGHT

Sugar clicked off, and then tried Deputy Rachel Pike. Got her, first ring.

"So what's my new assignment?"

"I realize this is a lot to ask," Sugar said.

"Ask it."

"Pull some phone records."

"You got a warrant or subpoena by any chance? Know a federal judge?"

Sugarman was silent. He knew the law and knew what could be done to get around it.

"No, I didn't think so. Good God, Sugar, this isn't Homeland Security; we can't go data-mining when the mood strikes."

After a moment more, Rachel sighed and said, "Just out of curiosity, where're these phone records from?"

"Sarasota. Law office of Carter Mosley, Esquire. Got a particular day. July eighteenth, anytime between nine and noon. Either incoming or outgoing. Or if he's got a cell, it could be that."

"I have a full-time job, honey. I can't put that at risk. There's some strings I just can't pull. Even for you."

"I understand."

The line went quiet long enough for Sugar to ask if she was still there. When she came back, the last of the teasing tone was gone.

"You give any thought to that job offer? We're interviewing some applicants, nobody in your league, but I can't hold it open forever."

Sugar looked out at the grassy berm. Not really debating it, just trying to find some polite words.

"I take it that's a no?"

"Sorry, Rachel. I've gotten used to the footloose thing."

She was quiet for a long moment.

"Maybe it's not my place, Sugar."

"Go ahead."

She sighed another time. He knew what was coming and suspected it had been brewing for a while. It wouldn't be the first time someone had given him the advice.

"I care about you, Sugar. As a friend. It's just that I think you'd be a lot further along in your career, and maybe in your personal life, too, if you stopped letting Thorn drag you into these shit-storms he's so fond of."

"Thorn's my friend. He'd do the same for me."

"Think about it, Sugar. Think what that friendship costs you."

Sugar was silent, collecting himself, his face growing warm.

"You're right, Rachel," he said. "Maybe it isn't your place."

They listened to each other breathe for a few seconds, then Rachel clicked off without a good-bye and Sugar slipped his cell into his pocket. Another bridge burned. Shit, shit, shit.

He fumbled with the remote for a while before he had the DVD synched with the TV and got the video running.

It didn't take him long to get the idea. Over the years he'd attended more public meetings than he cared to recall. Most involved the latest brainstorm of some real-estate scammer. The meetings were usually hopeless displays of earnest citizens failing miserably to stand firm against the hustlers and their bulldozers.

After watching a few minutes of the general public of DeSoto County, Sugar felt the same sense of doom.

Fast-forwarding over several rambling rants, he was about to shut the whole thing down when C.C. Olsen climbed on-stage. Olsen was a rangy man with long swept-back hair, a hawk nose, and a Pancho Villa mustache, like some renegade biker from the 1960s.

His voice was subdued, almost shy as he introduced himself to any who might not know him. The hubbub died away and the room stayed silent until he finished his talk. In the dozen rows the camera captured, nearly every person was leaning forward to catch Olsen's words.

First, he roll-called the names of eighteen locals who'd died of various diseases within the last few years, mostly cancer, a few respiratory ailments Sugar had never heard of. After Olsen pronounced each person's name, their age at death, he gave the number of years they'd spent in the classrooms and hallways of Pine Tree School.

Only two of the eighteen were cigarette smokers.

In his calm, deep voice C.C. Olsen said, "If these eighteen folks, all of them friends and neighbors of people in this room, if these eighteen human beings don't count as a cancer cluster, then I don't know what would."

Then he read off the EPA's official report on radon in that region. How government investigators found that concentrations of uranium and radium in gypsum samples taken locally were ten times the average background levels in soil for uranium and sixty times the background levels in soil for naturally occurring radium-238.

Radium-238 decayed into radon gas, which was colorless and odorless. In about four days radon decayed into polonium-218, which gave off alpha particles. These high-energy specks could penetrate to the nucleus of a cell and permanently change DNA. So if radon gas was inhaled into the sensitive tissues of the airways and lungs, over time the cells could be permanently damaged and the chances of contracting lung cancer or other respiratory ailments were greatly increased.

Sugarman saw how challenging it was to make the science clear to such ordinary folks. But C.C. was patient and slow and kept things mostly to one and two syllables. A teacher teaching.

Radium showed up in high strengths in the waste of phosphate mining. And when that radioactive clay and sludge was stacked two hundred feet high, it didn't take a genius to see how easy it was for particles to be kicked up by prevailing winds. Those particles settled onto nearby ponds and trees and agricultural areas, and got trapped inside buildings, where they built up the way grease will film the walls of a restaurant from years of deep-fat frying.

On the upper crust of the gypsum stacks the radioactive clay collected rainwater that grew into scummy ponds. That standing water evaporated and the fumes spilled down the sides of the harmless-looking mountain same as fog descended hillsides and gathered in valleys. But you couldn't see radon like you could see fog. The only means to measure the stuff was with detection meters that monitored exposure over extended periods.

And in the first video, that's all C.C. was asking for. Funding from Bates International to pay for a few dozen radon detectors. Sounded like a no-brainer to Sugarman.

When C.C. Olsen was done, Carter Mosley stepped to the podium amid scattered catcalls. With a half-smile, he waited till the noise died away. Though Sugarman had met him the night before, he hadn't paid much attention. He took him to be a quiet, unassuming man.

The Mosley he saw on the TV screen was something else. In denim shirt, khakis, and scruffy moccasins, he'd dressed the part of some disheveled poet just back from a ramble through a fairy-tale forest. But his expression was anything but blithe.

Sugarman froze the video, then advanced frame by frame till he got a focused image of Mosley's face.

Black reading glasses were perched on the tip of his nose and Mosley's sharp blue eyes squinted above them at the audience. White Scandinavian skin, expertly barbered silver hair, eyes a deep blue. On first glance his smile had a bemused air, but the longer Sugar looked, the more it resembled a sneer.

Sugarman punched the PLAY button and watched Mosley continue to smile as the hoots and grumbling subsided. When the room was completely hushed, Mosley seemed to count off a whole minute before he began, as if letting the air clear of the fumes of their childishness.

When he spoke, he echoed Olsen's slow delivery and folksy manner and seemed perfectly at ease before the crowd. After only a sentence or two, though, Sugarman's bullshit-detector was jiggling full-tilt.

"I want to compliment Mr. Olsen on his skillful presentation. I can certainly see where he came by his fine reputation as a teacher. I'm sorry to admit I'm not in the same league as C.C. when it comes to eloquence. So bear with me, please.

"He paints a gloomy picture, and to be honest it gives me the shivers. I'd be terrified for us all if what Olsen claims turns out to be true. That's why Bates International has decided to commit substantial resources to examine these accusations of Mr. Olsen.

"Starting this week we're bringing to Summerland the best scientific minds available, men and women from all over the United States, and they'll be setting up their monitors around the perimeter of the gypsum stack, examining the data and statistics these devices capture. Bates International, and in particular Abigail Bates, is fully committed to tracking the source of any airborne migration of radon gas. Absolutely committed to being good citizens in this community where we live."

Sugarman fast-forwarded. Listening to Mosley's patronizing twaddle was giving him a headache. It was a typical gimmick, letting some corporate-sponsored lackeys handle the scientific investigation. Fox and the henhouse. Amazing that citizens still fell for it.

He rolled past a couple of minutes, then froze another frame. Worked it forward till he had another focused image. And there it was again, that smile that was not a smile, but a smug grimace, faintly predatory.

It was an expression Sugar associated with grown men who'd once been victimized by school yard bullies and never got over it. Such men rarely openly confronted their adult antagonists. They were wilier than that, using their smarts and fake charm to gain advantage. But the anger and hurt and vengefulness born of long-ago humiliations were still burning hot, just below the surface. He knew that was a lot to pin on a half-second facial expression, but somehow Sugarman knew this guy. He was sure of it. A mean-spirited little shit.

He zipped to Mosley's exit line.

As to the radon monitors C.C. was asking Bates to purchase, well, that sounded like a reasonable request, so Carter Mosley promised, right then and there, to take the appeal directly to Abigail herself and report back to the assembly promptly.

Most of the folks in the audience knew a dodge when they heard it. The rustling grew to a growl and somebody started stomping on the gymnasium floor, and soon the stomping spread to the bleachers and grew in volume until Mosley had no choice but to step away from the microphone. As the noise increased, he waved a stiff good-bye and ambled away.

The next two videos were more of Olsen's unhurried, common-sense science, including a list of readings from the radon monitors newly installed in the classrooms, and a progress report on the ventilation system the county had grudgingly agreed to install. Then more of Mosley's pie charts and mealy-mouthed arguments, the preliminary results of the various scientific studies that Bates International was funding.

Abigail Bates made an appearance at the end of the third meeting. She was booed for a full minute before she began to speak. During the razzing, she stood impassively, scanning the audience row by row as though taking names.

When the heckles finally died away, she cleared her throat and gripped the edges of the podium and spoke in a voice that brooked no contradiction.

"I'm older than dirt. Older than anybody in this room. Eighty-five, about to be eighty-six. And nearly every one of those years I lived within two spits of phosphate mines and gypsum stacks. So if you folks want to see what radon does to someone, take a good long gander at me.

"I've already spent more money on your complaints than I consider reasonable. That's money I worked hard for. Money I earned from my own sweat, and the backbreaking labor of my daddy and his daddy. I'm nearing the end of what I'm willing to pay. So right here and now, you've got fair warning. If these attacks on Bates International continue, I'll just have to start looking elsewhere for employees.

"I'll fight this nonsense till my last breath. And that's a long way off."

She proceeded to suck down a huge lungful of air, then puckered her lips and let it go like a dope smoker treasuring the last of her joint. She meant it as a taunt, of course, but watching this old dame who would soon die of drowning, Sugarman couldn't shake a creepy sense of foreboding. With that public display of scorn, it was very possible Abigail Bates, Thorn's feisty grandmother, had just sealed her death sentence.

CHAPTER TWENTY-NINE

When I emerged from the sheltered creek mouth into the open bay, I wasn't ready for the north wind. It slammed me from the starboard and tipped the kayak halfway over. I wind-milled for a second, fought the wild dip and rise of swells until I finally found my balance, and thought for half a moment I was under control, then got jostled sideways by another wave and almost capsized a second time.

There was no yielding to such wind, no answer for it but to quarter into it, paddle hard, stay low, cut into the belly of the waves, make my way forward with a zigzag tack, and hold on tight to the paddle's rubber handgrips.

I hunched down and dug my way toward the Mothership, a mile of open water that looked like a hundred leagues of wind-ripped sea.

My sixty-horse skiff would have skimmed that sloppy bay easily, maybe slamming now and then in a trough and taking some dousing spray, though nothing it couldn't handle. But settled low in the kayak's seat, riding with only the thin plastic skin separating my butt from the bay, that chop felt like the mother of all tempests. Before I'd gone twenty feet, my arms and back and shoulders were aching and my nicked and bleeding hands were sending jolts to the base of my skull.

The slate sky started to spit rain as the fringes of the front collided with the warm, moist atmosphere we'd been enjoying.

I'd been neglecting my first mate's duties and hadn't monitored the weather channel, so I had no idea of the strength or duration of the system that was slamming us. It could be an all-night event, or might be only a small cell and last a few intense minutes.

In my defense, I'd been somewhat distracted.

Half blind from spray, I ducked my head and tried to find a rhythm. But that proved nearly impossible. All I could manage was to react to each new thump, moving ahead in spurts of a foot or two, then pitched sideways, clipped from behind by another breaker, hammered by two more. Soaked and dripping, I recovered and corrected my heading as best I could. Two strokes forward, then one slam cockeyed.

I kept my bearings by focusing on the rooftop of the Mothership, which was the only section of her I could make out above the whitecaps and spray. Even that was blurry, and no amount of blinking could clear my vision. The Mothership seemed to be riding badly in the seas, pitching more than I would have expected.

At least the squall was providing me cover as I passed into the section of bay that left me most exposed to the inlet where the shooter was. Mona had called the woman *Sasha*. Even through the radio's distortion, Mona's tone was chilling, one accomplice speaking to another.

For the moment, I had to put that aside. This next mile was about focus, endurance, and balance, about tipping points and reaction time, about staying loose but not too loose, and it was about digging one stroke after another into water that was pitching and bucking like some hell-bent rodeo ride.

By the time I'd progressed several hundred yards closer to the Mothership's stern, the wind had dropped by half. Though the bay was still choppy, it had smoothed enough for me to take a breather without fear of tipping over. It was entirely possible that the black squall that brushed by was an outer band of something larger still on its way, so I couldn't dally long.

I took two deep strokes and drew my paddle out and lay it across my lap to shake the cramps out of my arms. My legs were numb, and my spine felt like it might be locked into a permanent hunch.

After a minute's stretching, I picked up the paddle to get going again and it was then I noticed at my right elbow that part of the plastic kayak was missing, a ragged chunk roughly matching the bull shark's bite print. I checked my sleeve on that side and found a five-inch rip. Beneath the ragged tear my skin was untouched. No blood, not even a scrape.

Which suggested that in some shadowy corner of the bull shark's brain, she'd mistaken the kayak for my flesh and found that first swallow too dry and bloodless for her taste. I felt my pulse throb in my throat and a fist opened and shut in my bowels. If the shark had taken slightly better aim, or had one more inch of thrust in the swish of her tail, my body would still be back in that lagoon, reduced to morsels only minnows would find appealing.

I straightened up and peered across the sloppy bay. The Mothership was no longer rocking, but she didn't look right. Worse than that, she looked stricken. Maybe I was delusional. Circuits overloaded by surge after surge of adrenaline. Buddhists claim the world springs from the mind and sinks again into the mind. Perhaps that's all it was, a topsy-turvy hallucination I was projecting outward.

It took me several seconds to absorb the situation, put it into an orderly sequence my mind would agree to. What I was seeing was impossible, yet it was happening. The Mothership had sunk.

Or more precisely, she had half sunk. All that tonnage, all that splendid engineering and design, intricate mesh of aluminum and fiberglass and oak veneer, custom cabinetry and high-tech instrumentation, all of it was slanted to port by around forty-five degrees. The starboard pontoon was cocked ten feet in the air; the other side was submerged. Which could mean only one thing: The entire port pontoon had filled with water and was resting on the bay floor.

Our pontoon hulls had eleven airtight sections, each one about six feet long. A total of thirty-three separate airtight compartments for the whole vessel. The sections overlapped and had been ferruled and welded for strength, designed and built so no single puncture could bring her down.

I dug the paddle in and found a rush of energy I thought was beyond me. The kayak sliced ahead, no tacking this time, plowing straight on.

As I muscled ahead, I replayed those gunshots I'd heard when racing back to answer Teeter's Mayday. Fifteen, sixteen, maybe as many as twenty. They'd nagged at me at the time, but I let it go. Now I understood it was very likely the woman named Sasha hadn't been firing at Teeter at all.

In fact, she'd proved herself to be more disciplined than that. Not one to spray lead indiscriminately. Instead, it was likely she'd been blasting methodical holes in the port pontoon below the waterline. Creating a set of slow, persistent leaks that hour by hour had brought the Mothership to her knees.

Even at high tide our anchorage was only six feet deep, so the houseboat wasn't going to be disappearing to the bottom of the deep blue sea. But it was cocked so severely, life aboard the ship was going to be very messy from this point on. The generators were now underwater, so there'd be no power, no air-conditioning, no lights, and what food and other essentials survived would depend on what Rusty and the others managed to rescue from the lower deck when they first realized the water was rising. Then there was the challenge of simply moving around on a ship tipping at such an angle.

Rusty, Mona, and our guests would be flushed out of their staterooms and the salon by the flood, and more than likely would be huddled on the second deck, in the cramped crew quarters and the wheelhouse. All the furniture would have shifted, glasses and wine and whiskey bottles tumbled from shelves, the television, the paintings, the gewgaws, the pots, pans, charts, anything not battened down.

But worse than that, much worse, was the fact that hot-wiring the engines was no longer an option. The Mothership was not going anywhere for a good long while.

CHAPTER THIRTY

The final video had a time stamp running in the lower right corner. October of last year, three months after Abigail Bates went canoeing and drowned.

This one only ran ten minutes. Same gymnasium, same camera angle, capturing the first dozen rows of folding chairs, an edge of the bleachers, and the small raised platform used as a stage.

Only this time the podium and backdrop were draped with black banners and cluttering the stage were hundreds of flowers. Flowers in vases, flowers still in their plastic wraps, clusters of wildflowers, armloads of roses and daisies and gladiolus.

At the microphone a teenage boy stood shakily and peered into the glare. He was sweating and his face was gaunt, his scalp gleaming white, eyes full of fever. A few feet to his right, a lanky woman kept an eye on the boy. She wore black slacks and a dark long-sleeved blouse and was tilted ever-so-slightly in the boy's direction as though poised to catch him if he toppled.

He looked like he might. There was such a wobble in his stance, such a rattle and rasp in his throat as he brought his mouth close to the microphone, it sounded like his next breath could easily be his last. Sugarman winced and had to force himself to keep watching.

The resemblance was clear. The boy split the difference

almost exactly between C.C. Olsen and the rawboned woman standing nearby. He'd inherited her cheekbones, strong mouth, swan's neck, and milky skin, along with C.C.'s wide shoulders, sunken eyes, and hawk-bill nose.

"I'm Griffin Olsen, in case there's anybody doesn't know. Son of Sasha"—he nodded at the woman hovering nearby— "and the late C.C. Olsen."

A smattering of applause, then shushing, and the gym grew still.

"The air in the school is poisoned," Griffin said, "and we damn well know whose fault it is."

He swallowed a couple of times, then dragged a red handkerchief from his back pocket and hacked into it. He closed his eyes and seemed to be concentrating on getting his breath. His mother took a step his way, but the boy turned and waved her off, then tucked the kerchief away.

"We've heard the science say one thing when it comes out of Mr. Mosley's mouth and another thing when it came out of my dad's. What's clear to me is that science can be made to lie."

He got some more applause.

"But everybody in this room knows in their gut what's happening. Whether science agrees or not, you know, I know, everyone knows."

He waited till the next clamor died away to a murmur.

"I'm a goner." With that, the quiet room got even quieter. "They say I'm down to weeks. Which is no big deal. I'm tired out, sick of being sick. I'm just plain ready. Except I got one last thing I want to say."

Sasha had bowed her head and was staring down at her feet.

"If the Bates family were storm troopers goose-stepping down Main Street, you all wouldn't think twice. You wouldn't let them spew mustard gas over this town. You'd risk your lives, do anything to protect your families. Pick up your shotguns, your pistols, you'd fight back." Griffin worked his focus around the big room. "You wouldn't let them murder your children. You wouldn't let them steal your water, poison your air.

"Just because they're Americans, just because they're running a business, paying piss-poor wages to a few people around these parts, that doesn't change a thing. These people are goose-stepping down Main Street and nobody's doing a damn thing. Look at you. You're hiding in the back room, hoping they won't come for you or your little girl or little boy. You're cowering in the dark, hoping it'll all go away."

Griffin's voice was thickening. Each breath sounded like the rasping gasps of a gut-shot dog, as though more blood than air was filling his lungs.

"Well, it isn't going away. Not till you people stand up and fight."

He looked out at the silent crowd and could not bring himself to say more. Nearly half a minute went by with him simply standing there, then his mother came over and put her arm around the boy's frail shoulder and turned him from the podium. But Griffin leaned back to the microphone.

"Somebody worked up the guts to cut off the head of the snake. But a few months later, look what happened. That snake grew a new head. This time somebody needs to chop up the whole damn thing and be done with it for good."

The TV screen turned to white static. Sugarman stood watching it.

After a while he walked over and had another look at the radon detector. It said 27.4 in red LED lights.

He glanced around at the bare walls, listened to the squeal of a few schoolkids still in the parking lot, a car starting its engine.

The hallways were empty as Sugarman walked out of Pine Tree School. The last bus kicked up a white cloud of dust as it rolled down the narrow lane.

Sugarman opened his car and let it air out a couple of minutes before sitting behind the wheel. The harsh odor that gagged him an hour earlier was no longer apparent. Maybe the wind had shifted, or maybe his body was adjusting. Neither possibility particularly cheered him.

He replayed what he'd just witnessed in the video, then went over it a second time. If Timmy Whalen had steered him to the video to bewilder him with an abundance of suspects, it hadn't worked. He'd seen only one. A woman with a dead husband and a failing son.

Door open, sitting behind the wheel, Sugar waited for the sheriff to return. Half hour, forty minutes. The last of the parents left, the final straggling teachers pulled away for the weekend.

It was closing in on happy hour, and still no sheriff, when Sugar slammed the door and cranked up the Honda. He'd have to find a motel for the night, track down a decent restaurant. He was just making a U-turn to head out the gravel road when his cell phone chirped. He pulled over into the shade of a loblolly pine.

Rachel Pike's name appeared in the glowing box.

"Hey."

"Hey," she said.

While he waited for her to speak, he watched a hawk catch the updrafts above the gypsum stack. Beautiful bird riding the radon.

"Look, I want to apologize," she said. "That crack about Thorn, that wasn't fair. You were right to be peeved. Truth is, it's one of many things I admire about you, Sugar. Your loyalty."

"Thanks, Rachel. Apology accepted."

"Whew, I was afraid I'd lost your friendship for good," she said.

"You didn't."

She was quiet for a moment, then said, "So anyway, I pulled Mosley's phone records."

"You did? Jesus, well, thanks."

"I got a source at AT&T. He owes me a couple."

"Add me to that list."

"You probably thought you'd never hear from me again."

"That seemed like a possibility," he said. "So did anything pop out?"

"Not much. Maybe it will for you. For that date, between

nine and noon there was considerable traffic from the law office. I made you a printout. Mostly calls back and forth to other law firms, a couple overseas, one to a restaurant in Sarasota, an airline, somebody paying an electric bill. That kind of thing."

"Maybe you can fax the list. I'll find a machine somewhere, call you back with the number."

"I ran Mosley's cell, too. Two calls that morning, both outbound. First was at nine-twelve, and two minutes later he made a second call."

"That would be about the right time."

"You want the numbers, addresses, the names, what?"

"Let me take a wild guess," Sugar said. "One of the numbers he called was listed to C.C. and Sasha Olsen."

"Hey, you're good."

"And the other one?"

"DeSoto County Sheriff's Office. Timmy Whalen's direct line."

Sugarman watched the hawk bank hard and dive at a steep angle toward the west, talons out as it vanished into the late-afternoon shadows. Maybe it got its dinner, maybe not. In the long run, Sugar's money was on the hawk.

"You there?"

"Barely," he said.

Rachel said, "Those three people you asked me to run through the NCI computer—John Milligan, Mona Milligan, and Charles M. Kipling, Jr. Nothing much there. The Kipling guy, you already know about. In jail a few days, then released. The other two, the Milligans, they came up empty. Not even a speeding ticket."

"Figures."

"I felt so guilty, I even ran the other two."

"Which two?"

"The Olsens, C.C. and Sasha. Mosley called them, so I was curious who they were."

"Guilt is a beautiful thing."

"Yeah, well, I got squat on C.C. A drunk-and-disorderly charge when he was eighteen. But the other one, this woman,

Sasha, now there's a special lady."

"How's that?"

"You know what the Silver Star is?"

"Sasha Olsen? Get out."

"Only the second woman since World War Two. Sergeant Sasha Lane Olsen. Florida National Guard, one-forty-third military police unit. Want to hear what she did?"

"I'll make the time."

"She was ten months into her first rotation, her squad shadowing a supply convoy, Hundred-and-first Airborne riding shotgun. Convoy is ambushed. Guys with RPG's pop up out of trenches at one end of the street, bunch of snipers block their escape. Olsen manages to break away from the convoy and flanks the insurgent snipers. She and her guys kill three, mortally wound two more. Then things go bad up ahead, two squads of Screaming Eagles taking major fire, serious casualties, so Sergeant Olsen leads her guys, these weekend warriors from Podunk, Florida, directly into the kill zone. They assault one trench line with grenades and rifle fire, and then on her own, Sergeant Sasha Olsen jumps down in this ditch and cleared the second trench, killed four insurgents, one of them hand to hand."

Sugarman was silent.

"You know this woman?" Rachel asked.

"Not yet."

"Thorn's mixed up with her?"

"I'm not sure. Maybe."

"So are we good? I can stop feeling guilty now?"

"Oh, yeah, we're good, we're very good. Thanks, Rachel."

CHAPTER THIRTY-ONE

Rusty met me at the rear deck and tied off the kayak to the only cleat still above water. She didn't ask me why I was drenched, or about the gash in the side of the plastic craft. She didn't ask me about John Milligan or if I'd gotten through to Sugar or anyone else on the cell phone.

She looked me over and seemed to know everything she needed.

"We've got a problem," she said.

"I noticed."

We were both gripping the spiral stairway that led up to the wheelhouse like a couple of commuters hanging onto subway straps while the train careened around a bend. The tilt of the ship was even more severe than it appeared from a distance. Navigating the roof of an A-frame would have been easier. I peered into the salon and it too was worse than I'd imagined. The TV was facedown, surrounded by the glitter of its smashed screen. All the furniture had broken loose and was piled against the port wall. Water three feet deep, the remains of Teeter's breakfast mingled with the flotsam.

"It's more than the ship," she said. "We'll right the ship. It'll require some time and money, but it'll be okay."

"You're taking it well."

"Not much choice."

"And the other problem?"

"That would be Mona."

"Yeah," I said. "I overheard her talking to the shooter."

"You did?"

"Other side of the mangroves, twenty feet away. I caught a snatch."

"Well, I heard the whole thing," Rusty said. "Both sides. Then Mona and I had a little talk afterward."

"Let's hear it."

"She remembered the woman. Name's Sasha Olsen. Her husband died a few months back, and now her son's at death's door. Sasha blames it on radon gas, uranium, some bullshit. I didn't follow that. But it's related to phosphate mining and your damn family. So that's what Mona thinks. Sasha's playing avenging angel. Payback for her husband dying and her kid being sick. Wiping out the Bates family and anybody else who gets in her way—like my brother."

We watched a squadron of pelicans skimming the bay.

"From the bit I heard," I said, "it sounded like Mona was pulling the woman's strings."

"I heard what you heard," Rusty said. "No question Mona's trying to call her off. Flip her switch. But I can't tell if she's running things or not, and at this point, frankly, I don't give a shit. If Sasha's taking orders from her, then fine. It's over, Sasha's gone. We'll watch our backs with Mona, get the hell out of here, sort it out later. Is that a plan?"

"And if Mona's not running the show, then what we heard was her pleading, not giving an order."

"Yeah," Rusty said. "I like the first choice better."

"You believe she's dirty?"

"I honestly can't tell."

"Maybe I'll give it a shot."

"Yeah." Rusty cut a look my way, then shifted her gaze back to the water. "You two seem to have such a nice rapport."

"Where's she now?"

"Last I saw she was up on the roof, off by herself."

"The walkie-talkie?"

Rusty patted her hip pocket.

"And our other passengers? How're they faring?"

She shook her head and sighed, then took a minute to fill me in.

When it became clear the Mothership was sinking, there'd been panic, shouting, name-calling. Apparently there'd been a slap, Rusty on Annette. Then even louder name-calling and threats. Holland sticking his camera in Rusty's face until she snatched it away and slammed it into the wall.

"Wish I'd had a ticket for that."

"It got worse," said Rusty.

Holland, by God, was going to sue her for damages, pain, suffering. He'd take Rusty Stabler's last goddamn nickel. His father happened to be a personal-injury attorney, best in Philly. He'd make it his life's work to destroy her. And Annette chimed in. Her magazine had a shark pool full of lawyers who'd salivate at the thought of dismantling Rusty's operation, selling that stupid boat to the junk man piece by piece.

That's when Rusty ordered Annette and Holland to go cool off. They refused. Rusty gave them one more chance, but they refused even more snottily, so she grabbed their collars, hauled them to her cabin, and pitched them in and slammed the door.

"Both at once?"

"Both at once."

"You're some kind of strong."

"I'm running on nitroglycerin, Thorn. Best not to fuck with me."

Then I told her about finding Milligan's body, leaving out the part about the shark.

She groaned, took a thin, whistling breath, and closed her eyes.

"I think he'd been drowned. I had a good look at his body floating in the water and I didn't see blood or bullet wounds."

"This drowning thing," Rusty said.

"Yeah?"

"Mona says it has to do with how Sasha's husband died, and the way her kid's suffering. Lung cancer. Gasping for breath, suffocating."

I looked off at the horizon. It was darkening in the north,

some pink ribbons of sunlight in the west, sprays of gold and green shooting through the gaps. Not much daylight left.

Rusty said, "Like Sasha's doing some kind of fucked-up poetic justice. 'How long can you hold your breath?' Tit-for-tat bullshit. Make us suffer what her loved ones suffered."

"Sink the houseboat. Get us in the water, take us under one by one."

"Be a lot easier to shoot us. Like she did Teeter. Get it done and go."

I shook my head.

"This woman's not into easy. I think what she did to Teeter was only to slow him down. She probably meant to finish him in the water, drown him like she did Abigail Bates and John, but I showed up before she could do it."

She looked at me for a long black moment.

"You got something in mind, Rusty? Some plan?"

"I want to get my hands on her," she said. "Beyond that, no."

"She's strong. Milligan was no weakling. We have to do this smart."

"You got a smart idea?"

"How's your night vision?"

"What? Wait till dark?" Rusty said. "You think we have that long?"

"Twilight would be better."

"To do what?"

"Fake her out."

"Talk to me, Thorn."

"You paddle out in the kayak, like you're offering yourself up."

"And where are you?"

"You're towing me with a rope. I'm in the snorkel, mask, fins, I've got the dive knife. I'm a few inches below the surface. When you get close enough, you tug, I go down a few feet, circle past you, flank Sasha, and while you keep her busy, I pop over her stern."

"Twilight," she said. "Gotta be at least twilight. Otherwise she sees what's coming."

"Twilight, but not full dark. I'd never find my way."

"It should be you in the kayak, Thorn. Me in the water. She knows you're part of the Milligan clan. She's not interested in me."

"My way confuses her. You distract her long enough, it could work."

"I'm going to have to roll that around."

She reached out and poked a fingertip to my elbow.

"What happened to your shirt?"

"A brush with the wild kingdom."

"Hell, I always liked that shirt. That was the doc's, right?"

"You knew this shirt?"

She nodded. "Like losing an old friend."

"I think it can be saved," I said.

"Yeah?" She slipped a fingertip through the rip and touched my arm. "You think so, huh?"

"A little patching up can work miracles."

She tilted her head, giving me a skeptical look. "What're we talking about?"

"Shirts," I said. "Mending things."

Rusty worked her eyes across my face for a moment, then tried and failed to conceal a swallow. Her short sandy hair was riffling in the wind. Sweat had darkened her shirt, revealing the sharp outline of her breasts.

"All I wanted," she said, "the only goddamn thing I was trying to do was take some people out here, explore some spots nobody'd ever seen. Sit up on that deck at night with those damn stars, a glass of red, shoot the shit after a great day of fishing. That's all I wanted." The words were thickening in her throat.

"We'll get it back on track."

"Oh, the ship can be salvaged. But when all this gets out, this disaster, my backers will run for cover, insurance canceled. Coast Guard'll pull my ticket. This is the end, Thorn. Scratch one off the dream list."

I was never very good at fake solace. She was probably right.

"Shit, I could end up like you, Thorn. Hermit in a cave."

"It's not so bad. You could try it for a while. Might grow on you."

Her eyes clicked to mine, squinting to be sure she'd heard right. Like I'd uttered a proposal of marriage.

"It might come to that," she said. "The mother of all last resorts."

"Go ahead insult me, but you're always welcome at Club Thorn."

She blinked away the haze in her eyes.

"Christ, listen to the self-pity bullshit. Teeter's in there with a blanket over his face, and I'm whining about the goddamn houseboat and my freaking captain's license."

We stood in silence, looking out at the bay, listening to the wind hiss around the hard edges of the ship like the whispery voice of evil.

I watched the next blue-black mass thickening in the northwest, clouds piling on the backs of other clouds, rising up.

"We've got to keep our focus, Rusty."

"Yeah? On what?"

I reached out with my right hand and cradled her cheek.

"On the good fight."

Her hands rose slowly and she gripped my wrist and seemed to debate it for a moment before letting her cheek settle against my palm. Her body softened, then a moment later she caught herself and drew back.

"Not now, Thorn. Take your famous charm upstairs, use it on your kissing cousin. And while you're at it, find out whose team she's on."

CHAPTER THIRTY-TWO

Sugarman got Dr. Dillard's home address from the Summerland phone book. His house was a boxy two-story, several blocks from the downtown historic district. The charm factor dropped off drastically in those few blocks. Second-tier Summerland was treeless and stark, and the air smelled of fried food and motor oil. Battered pickups in driveways, spavined couches and recliners parked on porches, the grass patchy and brown. A pack of skinny mutts were foraging along the garbage cans left out by the street.

When no one answered Sugar's knock, an old lady who was smoking on the front steps next door called out that Dillard was probably out back.

"With his brand-new choo-choo," she said when Sugar thanked her. The old lady pointed her cigarette to the side of her head and made a crazy twirl.

The door to Dillard's workshop was ajar, so he stepped inside without knocking. Banks of fluorescent lights glared from overhead, sun poured in from two large windows, and a couple of halogens were aimed toward the center of the room. The good doctor was wearing bib overalls, a blue work shirt, a red-and-white-striped engineer's cap, and some kind of magnifying spectacles. He was stooped over a plywood table, using a pair of tweezers and a long needle to make adjustments to the tiniest model railroad set Sugarman had ever seen.

"All aboard," Sugar said.

Dillard straightened and frowned when he saw who it was. He pulled off the jeweler's eyeglasses and set them and his tools carefully on the plywood sheet, just beyond the border of his imaginary world.

The track looped and twisted through green hills with cows standing beneath one-inch trees, past ponds and cascading waterfalls, then the locomotive and its cars and red caboose descended into a valley and clickety-clacked through a charming American village somewhere in New England. Church steeples and storybook main street, kids on bikes, teenagers in convertibles, a firehouse with its dalmatian. Sugarman bent close to make out some of the finer detail.

"That's awful tiny," he said. "But I guess even fleas need to travel."

"You dropped by to make jokes?"

The two of them watched the train pass through the little town. A crossing guard lowered, the tiny whistle whooped, but all the people and dogs and cows and a herd of horses galloping through a meadow stayed frozen.

"In case you're interested," Dillard said. "That strand of hair is not the victim's. But that doesn't mean it's the killer's. It could be anybody's. It's like you found a random fingerprint or drop of blood. It's meaningless without having another hair to associate it with. Do you happen to have one of those?"

"I'm working on it."

"Oh, are you?"

"Actually, I didn't stop by about the hair."

"I'm sorry, is this a game? I'm supposed to guess what you want?"

"Something you said earlier. At the time it seemed weird, but now that I've seen the videos and I'm up to speed on this, it seems even weirder."

"Well, well. What in the world did I say?"

"You said *misdirected*. That was the word you used. *Misdirected*."

Dillard turned back to the hills and valleys and rivers and waterfalls.

"We were talking about the public meetings," Sugarman said. " 'A lot of anger seething around these parts.' Those were your exact words. Then you said, 'Misdirected, I must say.' Referring to the anger, like you knew something all those other people didn't."

"You have a remarkable memory."

"It was just a few hours ago. I'm not dotty yet."

"All right, so what do you want to know?"

"Just that. What did you mean when you said their anger is misdirected? They're mad at Bates, they're mad at the gypsum stack, at the high readings of radon. How's that misdirected?"

Dillard shot a longing gaze at his train. Still on its tracks, still circling, the dalmatian still asleep in the shade of the fire truck.

"Well, it's complicated. It involves scientific matters."

"Try me. If I don't understand something, I'll raise my hand."

He sighed and reached out to the transformer box and switched off the power. The train halted on its downward swing through Happy Valley.

"Are the radon detectors accurate? The measurements really that high?"

"Those electronic gadgets Olsen bought are nothing but cheap toys." Dillard stepped past Sugarman to the door. He hooked his hat on a nail and went outside.

Sugar followed the doctor into the shade of the neighbor's house—a box as characterless as his own.

"Toys, meaning they're inaccurate?"

"Oh, they're probably accurate within a few points, I suppose. But to be taken seriously by the scientific community, a true study of ambient radon levels would have to be done by exposing a charcoal canister for several days and performing gamma spectroscopy for absorbed decay products."

Dillard fingered some of the fine gold threads of his remaining hair into place. His pale scalp glowed beneath.

"Let's put the science aside for a second," Sugar said. "How's the community's anger misdirected? What do you know that they don't know?"

Dillard shook his head and firmed his lips so not even a peep could escape. Sugar stepped closer to the man, inside his comfort zone. Dillard took a step backward, bumped into the trunk of a scrawny tree. Sugarman took another step, closing into body-odor range. Dillard's was as moldy and rank as mushrooms left too long in the fridge.

Sugarman whispered the words: "Who should the citizens be mad at?"

Dillard swallowed.

Another whisper: "Unburden yourself, Doctor. Let it out."

"I want immunity."

Sugarman had just been poking for rotten places, weak spots in the story line. He hadn't held out much hope for Dillard and the whole "misdirected" thing, but after the sticky trail of sweat appeared on the doctor's cheek and he blurted out the magic word *immunity,* Sugarman felt the decayed place give way, as if he were about to plunge his hand down into the moist underbelly of this whole rotten mess.

Sugar made a gun of his right hand, then brought his pointing finger slowly into Dillard's sight and touched the muzzle to the underside of the doctor's jaw, the soft bristly flesh yielding.

"This is just between you and me, Doc. No immunity. No need."

Dillard swallowed again and drew a breath.

"What do I get out of it?"

"Out of telling the truth?" Sugar said. "You get to go back in your workshop and play with your train. I walk away. You never see me again."

"You promise me that?"

"Cross my heart."

He took a long breath as if it might be his last.

"It's in the building materials," he said. "The cement, the wallboard, the plaster."

"What is?" Sugarman dug his finger in a little deeper.

"Phosphogypsum."

"The radioactive stuff that's dumped inside the gyp stack?"

"Exactly. The building contractor was cutting corners."

"Using phosphate mining waste for cement and drywall?"

"The practice wasn't illegal when the school was built."

Sugarman withdrew his finger and stepped back. Dillard was panting.

"And you learned this how?"

Dillard shot a look back at his workshop, his perfect world.

"I did some scrapings at the school, bored a few holes and analyzed them. I was curious. A big ruckus is going on in town. Scientists from all over the country are coming into my backyard to present position papers. No one thought to ask me to be involved. So I took it on myself. I did some sampling at the school, and, yes, that's what happened. The contractor used mining waste to build the structure."

"So it's not the gyp stack causing all the cancer?"

"Oh, no. That's a ridiculous claim. C.C. Olsen was grasping for straws. Of course that's the obvious target to attack. That giant mountain of waste so close by, but it's not the stack. The science doesn't support that."

"Did you tell anybody about this?"

The doctor hesitated.

"Who'd you tell, Dillard?"

Dillard's eyes flitted to Sugarman's and dodged away. "I told the parties responsible."

"Who, the contractor?"

Dillard stared out at nothing.

"Why'd you do that?" But as soon as he spoke the words Sugarman knew the answer.

"That's all I'm saying." Dillard tried to move forward, but Sugar put a hand on his bony chest and held him in place.

"Bates International, or some subsidiary thereof. That's who built the school. In the long long ago. That's right, isn't it?"

Dillard thought about it for a moment, then nodded faintly.

"So you went and told John Milligan, Abigail Bates, Carter Mosley. Look what I found. Look at the bad thing you did. If this goes public it's going to cost you millions. Liability suits, health costs, penalties, not to mention tearing down the school, building a new one. This is going to be huge. This could destroy you. At least put a big dent in your bottom line."

"I thought they should know," Dillard said with a burst of huffiness.

But even he could see how pathetic it sounded, for he closed his eyes and bent his head down as if offering a plea of forgiveness to whatever god held sway in his puny universe.

"I bet they were thrilled to find out," Sugar said. "I bet they were so happy you passed this on, they wrote you a check. Maybe a couple of checks. And you went out and bought yourself a brand-new miniature New England village. A little world where you could toot-toot your horn every day. God smiling down on his creations."

"You're twisting things."

"So all those meetings, focusing on that mountain out back of the school, that's diversionary."

He nodded.

"They must have loved C.C. Olsen. He kept the spotlight on the gyp stack. Nothing they did was illegal. But once the cancer deaths started cropping up, they started lying. Down that slippery slope, like the tobacco companies did, the asbestos people, and that cost them hundreds of millions in fines."

"Yes, that worried them."

"Why isn't the state involved? Why don't they send their own researchers in?"

"Out of respect for Bates International."

"Respect? No, you mean political pressure. Stay out of my business, or else."

"Well, those are the realities in Florida. Phosphate is king."

"Sooner or later," Sugar said, "somebody's bound to do what you did, right? It's so obvious. Take some samples, figure out the real cause. Look up the building records."

"Every day it goes undiscovered is a good day for Bates."

"But not for the kids going to school inside that building.

You ever think about them when you're counting your blood money?"

"Look, you don't know what it's like," Dillard said. "Living in a place like this. After all my years of training and education, being treated like some hack, some illiterate file clerk. The lack of respect. You don't know."

Sugarman had to chuckle.

"Oh, I think by now I've got a pretty good idea."

CHAPTER THIRTY-THREE

Mona was on the rooftop deck reclining in a plastic chair that was propped against a stanchion. I staggered along the canted deck using the rail partly as banister, partly as crutch, like negotiating the lopsided floor of a fun house.

I stood beside her for a moment and together we watched the busy sky.

The scattered droves of terns and snowy egrets, herons and gallinules, were taking hasty shortcuts back to the safety of their roosts before the next wave of weather set in. A single great blue heron cranked by, as gawky and improbable as some wired-together grade-school project.

In the west the sun was a silver halo muffled behind gloomy clouds. Maybe two hours left before twilight.

Mona registered my presence with a sigh.

"We're a little exposed up here, don't you think?" I said.

"Who cares? We're sunk anyway." She flashed a mock smile at the sky.

"Oh, I think there's still hope."

"None," she said. "Any way you look at it. We're sunk."

"That's pretty dark for a mitigation person. I thought you guys were famous for finding the middle way."

"Doesn't always work that way," she said.

"Yeah?"

"Plenty of times the parties get crazy, harden their position.

Then it's win or lose. One side gets the trophy, the other gets screwed."

I fingered the torn cotton of my shirt.

"Tell me something, Mona. How long have you known what was going on?"

"I still don't."

"Give me some reason to believe that."

"Don't believe it. I don't care. You're not the sheriff."

She watched a single roseate spoonbill flaunt its pink across the sky.

"Sasha Olsen," I said. "She a friend of yours?"

"Never met her."

"But you've seen her around Summerland. You know who she is."

"Her husband was an activist. Pretty hard to miss, especially in my line of work. I never sat down with him one-on-one, but I went to some of his rallies at Pine Tree School. He was good. Had an appealing manner, very understated, smart. I wouldn't call him charismatic, but for a backwater town, he was impressive."

"He died, the son's sick. The Olsen woman blames it on phosphate mining. Now she's killing off the Bates family as revenge? That's what this is?"

"Apparently."

"You knew who it was from the start, Mona. I saw it in your eyes the first time you heard her voice on the walkie-talkie."

"My cousin the clairvoyant."

"You're lying, Mona. You're in this up to your chin. That's why you can sit up here on the roof, exposed. You know she won't shoot you."

I wasn't sure of that. Wasn't sure of anything. I was only trying to provoke her, see if she'd stumble.

She turned her head just enough to rake me with a look. In the breeze her auburn hair looped and twisted and I remembered my first impression—hair whipping like a warning flag, a warning I'd ignored. Swayed instead by the scent of her, the sulky way she moved, her shape, her smart-ass cutting tone.

"Jesus, Thorn, how does anybody put up with your shit?"

"Not many do."

My polygraph was registering nothing. I couldn't tell if Mona was for real or if I just wanted her to be.

While she continued to admire the sky, I shaped the words to tell her about her dad.

"So, I take it you didn't get through on the cell phone?"

"It went overboard before I got the chance."

"I'm surrounded by fuck-ups," she said. "Total, complete fuck-ups."

She tipped forward and stood up. The plastic chair tumbled over and the wind took it for a ride up the railing.

"And Dad? Any sign of him?"

I was silent, staring out at the choppy bay.

"You hear me, Thorn? Dad, any sign of him?"

"Tell me something, Mona."

I could feel her eyes on my face.

"Do you have an image in your head, someplace you go back to over and over? When you're feeling shitty I mean, need something to balance you out. Something from your past."

"Of course I do."

"You've been back a hundred times to that same place, and squeezed more and more juice out of the moment, but it's still ripe, still has the power."

"They're called memories, I believe."

"Okay, memories then. But special ones."

"I have a few of those. A few that hold their heat."

"Are there any of those that include your dad?"

"Sure," she said faintly. "One or two."

"Good. You're going to need them."

I turned to her. The wind kicked her hair across her face. She drew the straggling strands out of her eyes and changed her angle, bearing down on me.

"He's dead. That's what you're saying. Dad's dead?"

She read the answer in my eyes.

"You're guessing. You didn't actually see his body."

"I'm not guessing."

She looked up at the sky and inhaled through gritted teeth. "Goddammit. Goddamn this whole twisted fucked-up mess."

She looked me in the eye and drew back a fist and punched my chest, knocked enough breath from my lungs to make the light waver.

She squeezed her eyes tight and was about to let go of a wail when Rusty called out from below a single "No!" that lasted longer than a word ever should.

From my angle I couldn't see the span of bay, so I pitched headlong up the sharply inclined deck, scaling the pebbled surface on all fours like a chimp up the side of a pyramid. I made it to the top, took hold of the rail, and pulled upright.

About forty yards north the yellow bass boat was idling toward us. The tall black-haired woman was at the wheel. Thirty feet or so behind her boat, at the end of a taut red line, my wooden skiff was bouncing along in tow. Someone was hunched behind the wheel. A boy, a teenage boy.

Mona struggled up beside me.

"Oh fucking Jesus," she said. "He's on fire."

Her eyes were better than mine, for it took me several seconds to catch the blue waffling flame on the boy's clothes.

"That's the son," Mona said. "Sasha's kid."

As the procession closed in on us, I saw the boy's hands were lashed to the wheel, and his body was bound by ropes to the seat. His jeans and shirt were aflame, and his bare arms were black and blistered, his face becoming a charred ruin.

Then I noticed a shiny object thumping against the starboard hull, close to the waterline. I craned forward and squinted until I made out the aluminum gas cap bouncing on the end of its safety chain.

The fuel spout where the cap belonged was plugged instead with a white fluttering length of cloth. Its tip end was scorched, the bluish yellow flame snaking up that makeshift fuse.

I turned and dropped to my butt and slid down the slope

of deck. Got to the spiral stairway, thudded to the main deck. Rusty was there.

"She's some kind of fucking lunatic," she said. "That's a Norse funeral. Lighting the dead on fire, setting them adrift."

"Our funeral," I said and pushed past her and jumped down to the loading dock. "She's towing a goddamn bomb."

I unlashed the kayak, got the paddle out, and pushed off.

"Thorn? What're you doing?"

"Fuck if I know."

And I didn't. But I dug the paddle in and drove forward, floundering in the rough water. The one crude idea forming in my head was to lure her away from the Mothership, offer her the next dance.

I swung around the stern of the houseboat and sliced the paddle in as deep as I could go, then dug it in on the other side. The clotted gouges on my palms came open and the blood formed an oily slick on the grip.

Sasha Olsen had closed to a few hundred feet, the wind muscling her along and whipping at the flames.

I knew the tank on my skiff was at least half full, maybe twenty gallons left, and the rag could ignite the fumes at any second and the bloom of fire would turn everything inside its span to brimstone.

She eyed me with disinterest as I paddled toward her. She put her engine in reverse and turned the wheel to hold her position against the wind. The helpless skiff swung out around her.

Moving dreamily, she went to her stern cleat and unfastened the knot and flicked the tow line off. She watched the boy's death barge separate from her boat, drifting past her on the open water.

My old fishing craft was gripped by the wind and turned, then driven toward me at such a clip that I had only a handful of seconds to cut the kayak left, then swing back to the skiff as it bore down. The wind pushed the stench ahead of it, a gagging cocktail of charred flesh and gasoline.

Back on the Mothership voices were shouting. I kept my

focus on that T-shirt, the raveling flame. I made two hard digs of the paddle forward, then swung my boat parallel to the skiff as it came surfing closer. Paddling one-handed to hold position, I managed a single snatch at the white cloth, but the wind whipped it past me a foot beyond my reach.

As it scooted by, I saw she'd knotted the cloth at intervals to keep the fuse from burning too fast. Only two knots left before a quick spurt to the finish.

More voices came from the houseboat: Rusty's commanding shout, and a bleat from Holland that sounded like some cheap threat.

I churned hard, chasing the skiff into the shadow of the Mothership. Three hard pulls brought me alongside. I was putting myself in the eye of the fireball, but not out of any selfless valor. I was pissed off to my core, blind with cold fury to have lost so much so quickly and for nothing that mattered.

I drove on, eyes fixed on the burnt tail of the T-shirt flirting close to the sloppy bay, the final knot turning black, flakes of crisp cloth sailing past me. I could never recall being suicidal, but I suppose at that moment I was close. Not seeking death, but not trying to duck it.

Pulling alongside, I set my butt at a hard angle to the seat, took aim, then pitched toward the white cotton. It grazed my fingertips, but at that instant I was thumped by a roller, tossed up and out of the kayak, taken under, then instantly spit back out.

From the left another wave battered me. I lifted over it, coughed out a slug of the bay, and swung left and right till I located the skiff.

Chin above the water, I began to crawl toward the boat, but a sloggy weight dragged my arm to a stop. Wrapped around my right hand I found the tattered remains of the white cloth, a half-burnt T-shirt. I'd hooked it somehow in my flailing, disarming the bomb with blind luck.

I shook it off and let it sink. I treaded water and rode up one side of a swell and down its back and when the next one lifted me, I shot a glance back to where the yellow bass boat hovered. So close I could read the lifeless look on Sasha Olsen's face. Her eyes were aimed above me and behind.

Nestled deep beneath the Mothership, my wooden skiff banged against her uplifted hull, jarred by every gust. The ropes holding the corpse in place had burned through and as I watched, the body spilled onto the deck. Smoldering, it sent its foul whorls of smoke spinning off. The boy's face was a black and shriveled mess, his mouth open wide like some raving ghoul.

Above me on the Mothership, the clamor of voices rose. Working my way toward the kayak, staying low and keeping the green boat between me and Sasha, I got hold of its stern, swung it alongside, and heaved myself aboard.

On the lower deck of the Mothership, Holland aimed the 12-gauge flare pistol out to sea. A few feet away Rusty barked at him to drop it, but Annette blocked her passage down the narrow walkway.

"Somebody's got to stand up to the bitch," Holland yelled. "Nobody on this motherfucking boat has the guts."

"Do it, Holland. Let her have it." Annette thumped him on the shoulder. "Do it. What're you waiting for?"

Holland sighted along the stumpy barrel of the flare gun and let one go.

The plug of spewing magnesium lofted high above the bay and trailed behind a shower of red sparks. On a windless day it had a range of 250 feet, but in such heavy weather it made less than half that. It was a bad shot all around, thirty yards to the right, with the wind pushing it even farther off course. Not that it mattered much, but the meteor was going to fall well short of the bass boat.

I tracked each of the dozen trails that sputtered behind the rocketing canister. Like flaming skeins of yarn they drizzled down around me. Red-hot slag and ash. Two or three landed dangerously close to the skiff. I didn't know how much flammable material was still coating the decks of my small boat, or if the fumes rising from the open gas spout were sufficient for an explosion. I'd smelled gasoline earlier, or something in the same family. For all I knew the wooden decks were already smoldering and the boat was about to blow.

Above me Rusty made a lunge for the flare gun, but Annette put her shoulder down and butted into her, flashing her crimson claws at Rusty's face. A full-fledged mutiny. Holland had reloaded and was taking aim.

I swung the kayak toward the skiff and paddled hard enough to ram its stern and knock it ahead two or three feet. Best hope was to thrust it out of range of the next set of fiery trails. Get it around the front edge of the Mothership and let the wind grab it and take it for a ride.

If the skiff was destined to explode, it was my only chance to spare us. That sixteen-footer had been mine since I was ten. My first, best boat. On its poling platform and behind its wheel, I'd learned my way around those waters. Studying the fish, their habits, the mysteries of tides, how to spot treacherous coral heads and shoals. On her deck, I'd learned to read the clouds, the fickle winds, acquired what water skills I had. It was the vessel I'd used to stalk fish from one stunning end of the Everglades to the other. Over the years it had proved more faithful than half my friends or lovers, and if it was doomed, then some part of me was doomed as well.

The rushing sea and north wind jammed the skiff hard against the underside of the Mothership. I butted the kayak's bow into the skiff's stern again, struck off-center against the engine casing. I plunged another stroke deep, pushing forward, then again, using what leverage I could rouse from arms, shoulders, and back, milking the maximum from each paddle stroke.

I'd driven the skiff ahead until it was five feet from the bow when Holland fired his second round and dozens more twisting threads of slag showered around me. I watched two streams of glowing sparks spiral down and separate from the others, then catch some malevolent gust that sent them corkscrewing toward the skiff.

One glowing shard landed on the poling platform and winked out, while the second hit the gunwale on the starboard side and began to dance and sizzle not more than a foot from the open gas spout.

I kept an eye on the red-gold sputter and banged the nose of the kayak hard against the port rear-quarter, dug in another paddle stroke and one more after that and sent the skiff around the bow of the Mothership, where the wind was ripping the tips of foam off the whitecaps. A gust caught the skiff, turned it on its fulcrum, and it went skidding away.

Breathing hard, I lingered in the shelter of the Mothership's underbelly. Five seconds, ten seconds, then realized my mistake. The houseboat might be more precariously settled in the muddy bottom than she'd seemed, not able to withstand what was likely to happen. If she dropped even a few feet from her present perch, I'd be crushed beneath her keel.

Just as I began my backpaddle the blast sent a rush of scalding air around the corner of the bow. The concussion was short and deep, and its shock waves thumped me backward in the kayak. Overhead the big ship shuddered, rocked, and began to dip. I sat up, paddled two quick strokes, and scooted past the upraised pontoon, out of range, into the open bay.

The Mothership quivered but somehow held her lock on the bottom and absorbed the punishment without so much as a broken pane. In only a second or two the trembling died away and the big ship was still again.

I set the paddle across my lap and looked off at the rich blue smoke tearing south toward the Keys. I didn't need a further look to know the skiff's condition.

I took a breath and let it go, picked up the paddle, and swung the kayak back beneath the uplifted pontoon. Out in the yellow bass boat I watched Sasha Olsen bend down for a moment and come up with a rifle. She flicked its bolt and checked its readiness with practiced efficiency.

I was around the stern, about to tie up, when the first shot came. Then the second and the third, and from above, the bodies began to drop.

Sasha watched the blue smoke ripping south. Griffin flying off.

His atoms scattered toward the Gulf. Mingling already with the rest of what was out there. Becoming other. At last her boy was breathing easy, running loose in the wider world just as he'd wanted.

She aimed again and held her aim as she'd been instructed. Held her breath and fired.

CHAPTER THIRTY-FOUR

Sheriff Whalen would be back first thing Monday morning. And no, her phone was unlisted, her address not public information. That's what gaudy Nina, the sheriff's secretary, informed Sugar as she was locking up her desk and file drawers.

"You guys close up shop for the weekend? Down my way, things just start to get interesting on Friday afternoon."

"It's the sheriff's down time. There's three deputies on this shift. Use nine-one-one if you have a legitimate emergency."

"I only need a word with her. I promise not to pester."

"I said no. No's no. Got it?"

"I'll have to find another way."

"If she wants to talk to you, she'll find you. You don't need to find her."

Sugarman tried to untangle the illogic of that, but stalled.

Nina shooed him out of the office and locked the door behind her.

By the time he found his way to the Olsen house on Prairie Avenue on the eastern fringes of Summerland, his belly was rumbling and he could feel the first contractions of a headache. It was almost six. He'd skipped lunch, and his only breakfast had been a greasy bag of road food from Burger King. The hunger was throwing him off, making him uneasy in the gut.

Or maybe the cause was worry. In particular that second phone call from Thorn, the strain in his voice, the splashing in the background, and the odd, gurgling disconnection. Was it a distress call interrupted by an act of violence, or simply Thorn fumbling with that unfamiliar device? Sugarman decided it must be the latter. Thorn's manual dexterity was impressive, but it didn't seem to extend to objects containing silicon chips.

The Olsen place was a one-story redbrick shingled in gray. Brick was a sufficiently uncommon building material in Florida to make the house stand apart from all the others on the block. Children were playing down the street, a game involving two soccer balls and lots of screaming. In a couple of front yards there were mud-caked four-wheelers, and parked in the driveway beside the Olsen house were three Camaros in various states of rehab.

A single sabal palm shaded the Olsens' front walk, and a hibiscus bush with scattered yellow blooms and a scraggly bougainvillea inhabited the planter beneath the picture window. Efforts to beautify had lately gone unattended.

Sugar rapped on the door, then used the knocker and heard nothing. Down the street, a mother called a couple of kids to supper, and a bulky yellow dog with tiny seashell ears and a smashed-in pit-bull face came stumping up the walkway to give Sugar's pants a sniff, then moved on, unimpressed.

He pressed the doorbell but heard no sound.

He tried the handle and it was open. Small-town customs still hanging on. He looked up and down the street and saw no one monitoring his presence. Maybe someone was peeking from behind a curtain across the way. It didn't matter. If someone called the cops about a black man breaking and entering, at least he was likely to get another word with Timmy Whalen.

He opened the door and stepped inside.

Called out "Hello" and got back only a hollow echo.

From the video, the impression Sugarman formed of Sasha Olsen was one of a stalwart mother. Raw anguish had pinched her face—natural enough, given the situation of her boy using his dying breath to summon the citizens to arms. It had been hard for Sugar to watch, for he'd naturally thought of his own twin girls, the obvious what-ifs.

On the drive over, he'd started to consider this visit to the Olsen house as his last stop in Summerland. Meet Sasha one-on-one, take her measure, that's all. If he got one more crack at the sheriff, fine, if not, he could live with that. Forget the motel, just drive home tonight with what he had. He'd need to talk things over with Thorn, lay it out, get his buddy's approval before Sugar went public with what he knew and what he suspected. A sheriff who had either bungled a murder investigation or was intentionally concealing criminal activity. An international corporation knowingly poisoning children, and using all means necessary to avoid detection.

He called out "Hello" again and made another step into the room. A gold couch ran along one wall, a painting of a mountain stream with a deer drinking from its edge hung above it. A cheap breakfront full of china and tarnished silver. The wall-to-wall carpet was burgundy and a worn trail led across it toward the kitchen. The air was warm and smelled of fried onions and dust and moldering laundry.

He went to the kitchen and stood at the sink and looked out at the woods that bordered their property. Pines and scrub oaks, a few palmettos, then the land beyond this neighborhood turned again to cattle country and citrus groves.

There were large crows working the field out back. Cawing and hopping. Big-shouldered birds, glossy black, making the kind of persistent and eerie noise that could infect your daydreams.

The kitchen was clean and orderly. On the counter was a wicker bowl of yellow apples going bad, a single milk glass in the sink. Silverware and plates filled the plastic drying rack.

To the left of the phone was a notepad from a local motorcycle shop. Sugarman held it up to the light from the kitchen window and angled it back and forth till he saw the impressions. Two lines of writing, a carefully printed series of numbers and letters. He looked through the drawers till he found a yellow wood pencil, then lightly shaded the page till the print emerged.

25 degrees 17' 17" N
80 degrees 59' 35" W

GPS coordinates. Some intersection of latitude and longitude. He knew the Upper Keys were at latitude 25, and that 80 degrees longitude could be anywhere from the middle of the state to the east coast. But the finer fractions weren't in his memory banks. Weird to find such a thing on a notepad in a kitchen in Summerland, Florida. Actually a good deal more than weird. He tore off the sheet and put it in his shirt pocket.

He made the rounds of the three-bedroom house. The boy, Griffin, had covered his walls with posters. Einstein with his white electric hair, two rock groups Sugar didn't know and one he vaguely recognized as rappers. An M. C. Escher black-and-white. One of those Sugar had always liked. The more you stared at it, the more your eyes lost focus.

There was a guest room full of cardboard boxes and a computer set up on a small desk. Books were piled on the floor beside the desk, and more books were crammed in a metal bookcase that looked like army surplus. A stack of papers with red-ink scribbles in the margins. C.C.'s office. Where he'd done his grading, planned his speeches. Where he'd studied the science, written his letters of appeal to politicians and state agencies and all the others whose job it was to protect people like C.C., but rarely found the time.

The parents' bedroom was cramped. They'd chosen the smallest of the three for themselves, given the master to Griffin. The bed itself was only a double, a black-and-white quilt for a cover, a single painting on the wall of a slightly sexy portrait of a naked lady sitting in a rocking chair. It wasn't Sasha and wasn't even close to her body type. But it hung directly across from the bed like some aphrodisiac that both of them found arousing.

He went into the blue-and-white-tiled bathroom. One toothbrush, the usual soaps and lotions and shampoos. Hanging on the back of the bathroom door was a green one-piece bathing suit. Sugarman touched its silky fabric and wondered about it hanging there so long out of season.

The tour told him nothing except these were ordinary people. A family of modest means. A couple of splashes of color in an otherwise unexceptional home. He stood in the living room awhile and scanned the furniture and walls to see if there was anything he'd missed, to pick up any stray vibrations.

On the big screen at the multiplex, homicidal monsters inhabited rooms with obscene scrawls on the walls, notebooks full of depraved drawings. Violated Barbie dolls hung by strings from their ceilings, jelly jars full of eyeballs and minced-up body parts, all the sick, bizzaro stuff that scared audiences silly. But Sugarman had been in enough killers' houses to know that most were indistinguishable from their neighbors'. Peanut butter on white bread and cable TV.

He went back to the kitchen, opened the fridge. The usual OJ, butter, head of iceberg lettuce turning brown, jelly, skim milk, and a white paper sack.

Sugar looked back toward the living room. No one kicking the door down to take him off to prison. Not yet anyway.

He took out the paper sack and rolled it open and peeked in at half a bagel. Exciting stuff.

There was something he hadn't come across in his cruise through the house. Something almost every family had and that usually told more about them than any other item.

After a few minutes going through closets and drawers, he found it in the bedside table that stood by Sasha's side. He deduced that it was her side because a jar of hand cream sat by the base of the lamp. Call him Sherlock.

In the second drawer was a fat red leather photo album.

Sugar sat down on the black-and-white quilt and flipped it open. He was feeling no sense of urgency, no reason to hurry except for the churn of hunger in his belly. He paged through the baby pictures, the first bike, the football phase. Griffin had been a wide receiver, it seemed, won a varsity letter. A scholar athlete. And there were report cards, all A's, an SAT printout with the boy's scores. Missed a perfect 2400 by five points. Slipped on the verbal part, must've flubbed an analogy. There were photos of fishing trips, some of C.C. and Griffin barbecuing out back. Father and son shooting lighter fluid into the Weber grill and ducking back from the flames.

Love. Fun. Pride. One shot after another of those same three things. Then there was Sasha in camouflage uniform and boots—standing awkwardly for the occasion, a hokey salute and grin. A page later was another of Sasha wearing jeans and a white T-shirt and sitting at a picnic table beside a black woman. Griffin was in the background tossing a Frisbee to a kid about his age. A family outing at some park. The black woman mugging for the picture, a toothy smile, her arm slung over Sasha's shoulder, giving her a girl-pal hug.

Of course.

Sasha and Timmy Whalen. Same age. Small town. Maybe former classmates. Two strong women, outcasts who'd found each other.

Sugarman flipped to the last pages.

A black-and-white photo was fixed cockeyed to the page. Sasha Olsen standing with some army buddies. Behind them was the famous square, Saddam's statue broken off its pedestal and dragged into the dirt. Sasha was the only soldier not smiling. "Love you, miss you, be home soon, Mom" was scrawled at the bottom of the shot.

And that was it. The rest of the pages were blank.

Sugar put the album back in the nightstand.

He sat for a while looking at the naked woman in the rocker. Big nipples, a fringe of pubic hair peeking above her crossed thighs. Not smutty in any way. Just a natural pose. A naked woman in a rocking chair. Sugarman was still staring at that, trying to imagine what it signified to Sasha and C.C., when he heard the front door shut hard.

He got up and walked to the bedroom door.

Whoever had come inside was standing out of view in the living room.

There were times when Sugar wished he carried a concealed weapon. This was one. But he'd driven to Summerland to sniff around, not shoot anyone, and still, even now, even caught in the act of burglarizing a house, he considered civility to be his best defense.

Going toe-to-toe with a war hero was not an inviting prospect. He kept in shape and still had a few take-down moves from his cop days, but he couldn't recall when he'd last used one.

He looked around the room for something to defend himself with. A fireplace poker would've been nice. But all he saw were lamps.

So he did the only thing he knew to do. He called out hello.

CHAPTER THIRTY-FIVE

The person in the living room didn't answer.

"My name is Sugarman. I'm not armed. I'm not here to steal anything. I came on a social call. Door was open, I just walked in."

He heard the crack of a floorboard, maybe out front, maybe beneath his own feet. His pulse was chunking so loud in his ears he couldn't be sure.

"I'm in the back bedroom, and I'm stepping into the hallway now. I've got my hands up. No weapon. No gun, no knife, nothing. I'm stepping through the living room door now. Don't get nervous on me."

She was sitting in the fake leather recliner. Changed from her uniform of khaki trousers and blue shirt into scruffy jeans and a black top. Her nine millimeter lay in her lap, a Glock, her hand around the grip, finger resting against the edge of the trigger guard.

"Come here often?" Sugarman took a step into the room.

"Let's drop the wiseass thing, what do you say? It's such a strain."

"Fair enough."

Sugarman edged to the center of the room. Being in close quarters with a cop whose weapon was drawn was like coming upon a hammerhead while snorkeling. Look away, go about your business. If he wanted you, he could have you.

"Mind if I get an apple? I'm starving."

Sugarman moved to the kitchen before Timmy could answer.

"Get back in here."

He was at the sink, a quick pass of his left hand across the silverware in the drying rack, while he reached out with his right for an apple. He managed to palm a table knife and turned to Timmy, holding out an apple.

"Care for one?"

"Put it back."

"I'm starving," Sugarman said.

"Put it back in the bowl, turn around, and walk slowly into the living room. Do it now."

Sugarman got the knife up his shirt cuff, pinching it in place with one finger.

Timmy followed him back into the living room.

"Don't turn around," she said. "Raise your hands straight up. You know the drill."

Sugarman lifted his hands and waited. Knife pinched against his wrist.

She tapped her pistol barrel once against his spine, then frisked him one-handed, sliding up and down his jeans, to his crotch, then around his waist. Up and down his rib cage. Patting his pockets, front and back. Slower than seemed strictly professional, or maybe that was wishful thinking. Then another tap against the spine to let him know she was done.

He stepped forward, lowered his hands and sat in a blue wingback chair. She took a seat across the room, ten feet.

"Houses this close together," Sugar said, "lots of people would hear the gunshot."

"A black man burglarizing a house," she said.

"Yeah," he said. "You'd probably get a raise."

"I wish you hadn't come to my town," she said. "And I wish I'd kept my mouth shut a whole lot tighter."

"But I did. And you didn't."

"Yeah."

"I'm curious why. I don't think I tricked anything out of you."

"Give yourself more credit. You noticed what a lot of men wouldn't."

"You know what?" he said. "I think you've been waiting for me. You knew it was coming. You had to. A person like Abigail Bates, no way that's just going to blow over."

"Okay," she said. "There's some of that. Counting off the seconds. Looking up when the door opened. Sure, I expected someone to come."

"And yet you weren't all that prepared to fake it."

"You're better than you think, Sugarman. Disarming, is what you are."

"Oh, come on. I'm not that good. I think this has been burning a hole in your gut. You've been waiting for somebody to confess to."

She forced a smile.

"It usually works the other way," she said. "The person the gun's pointed at does the confessing."

"So where do we go from here?"

"Why don't you tell me what you know, or what you think you know. And then you tell me what you think you're going to do about it."

"Okay," he said. "That's fair."

He could feel the knife cold against his wrist.

"So go."

"You and Sasha were friends. Best friends."

"And you know that how?"

"Photo album, back bedroom."

She gave him a quiet look and shook her head.

Sugarman glanced out the front window. In the yard across the street two couples were having a neighborly chat. A handful of kids taking turns on a slippery slide rolled out on the front lawn in front of them.

"So C.C. Olsen dies. It's ugly. It tears her up. Sasha's been in Iraq, seen terrible shit, but losing her husband like that, no, that's worse. Especially because it looks like the cancer didn't just pop out of his genetic code. In some way or another it was Bates cancer. Milligan cancer."

Timmy Whalen shifted her eyes to the floor between them.

One of the girls across the street, seven, maybe eight, was sprinting too fast and throwing herself headfirst onto the slippery slide, a reckless dive. The parents weren't really watching, and Sugar felt like going to the door and shouting at them to be more goddamn vigilant. Then he remembered the Glock in Timmy's lap and eased back against the cushions.

"Then there's Carter Mosley," Sugar said. "Your phone buddy."

Timmy flinched and released a breath. He'd crossed a line with that one. This was the watershed moment for Timmy Whalen. One way or the other, it was the beginning of a new way of life for her.

"Here's how it went," Sugar said. "Mosley calls you on the morning of July eighteenth, right after Abigail Bates left his office. He informed you of her destination, that she was going canoeing on the Peace River. For some time she'd been suggesting she might do this, so you've all been waiting for this day. As soon as Mosley hangs up, you call Sasha, pass it on. He calls you, you call her. Like laundering money. You don't deposit your ill-gotten gains directly in a bank, just like you don't call the hit man's home phone. You dial the hit man's friend, the sheriff, of all people, leave it for her to do.

"So there. You call, Sasha gets into a bathing suit. Maybe the green one hanging back there in her bathroom. She jumps in her truck and off she goes to the highway Ms. Bates would have to use to get to the canoe place. She spots Abigail's car, follows her till she turns off, just to be sure, then goes up the river to where she knows Ms. Bates will pass by. Sasha knows the river. Everybody around here knows the river and where the tough turns are. So she goes there and waits."

"Why does she do that? The sheriff."

"Why does the sheriff get her hands dirty?"

"Yes. Why would she do that? Something that extreme."

"Oh, I think anybody who's been a cop could sympathize. It's because of that oath she's taken. She's come to believe Abigail Bates is the biggest threat to the people of the community she's sworn to protect and defend. So when the opportunity arises, she aids her friend in removing that threat."

Timmy Whalen was holding his eyes.

"And you, Mr. Sugarman? You approve of that kind of behavior?"

"I wish I did."

"You don't. You don't see how that would serve justice? More than standing by and letting kids sit all day long inside a poisoned schoolhouse."

"I can see the temptation. I'll give you that."

He studied the bright pinpoints in the center of her caramel eyes. If she was about to kill him she wasn't giving it away. If anything, her eyes looked sad. Worn out. But it was not an observation he'd bet his life on. So he kept his legs taut, ready to spring.

"Let me get this straight, Sugarman. If you'd been in my place, you would have resisted the temptation. You would've been strong. Knowingly sacrifice more young people to the great god of capitalism and the Boy Scout honor code. Is that it?"

"A sheriff doesn't get to decide those things. I wish I could lie and say otherwise, but, no, you did wrong."

She licked her upper lip, swallowed, then reset her hand on the Glock.

"Well, I appreciate your candor."

Sugarman checked on the kids across the street. The parents had dispersed and the children were bored with the slippery slide and had moved on to their skateboards. No broken necks yet. Once again his anxieties had flared over nothing. Been happening a lot lately. Ever since his own girls got so damn exploratory, Sugar found himself worrying about threats the rest of the world didn't seem to notice.

"If you'd done your job a little differently," Sugar said, "if you'd gone looking into the problem itself instead of joining this conspiracy and sanctioning the killing of people you thought responsible, you might've found out those children are being poisoned by the school itself, not the gyp stack."

"What?"

"The radioactive waste, the gypsum, it's in the walls, the plasterboard, the cement."

"Where'd you hear that?"

"Your disgruntled doctor Dillard filled me in. Long time ago when that school was built, Bates International owned the construction company that did the work. Penny-pinching bastard. He used gypsum throughout the school. All that free mining waste he had access to, he used that, and that's where the high readings come from. They've known it for a while and they're sitting on it. Carter Mosley knows, Milligan knows. That school's got to be torn down. No choice. Not one more Monday morning can those kids walk into that building."

"In one day you found this out."

"The day's still young."

"What do you want?"

"To know the rest."

"And then you'll go away and leave us alone?"

"You know I can't do that."

"Which of the rest do you want to know?"

"The details, like did you and Mosley and Sasha sit down and plan this out?"

"It didn't happen like that. Not like that at all."

"Mosley recruited Sasha?"

"You're missing it," she said.

"Mona? Mona was driving the bus?"

Timmy Whalen studied his eyes as if trying to do to him what he'd tried with her—read past the surface, evaluate his threat.

"Goddamn Mona," she said. "She took advantage. She knew how vulnerable Sasha was. Home from the war, lost her husband, son sick. Mona came over one night, sat right where you're sitting, and propositioned her."

"I could've sworn Mona was the grieving granddaughter."

"Well, she fooled you."

"Yeah, fooled me good."

"She's a sly one. She and Mosley worked out some kind of deal. A way to sideline John. Mona gets the environmental stuff she wants, and for Mosley, it's what it always is with business guys."

"A bigger bite of the apple."

"So Mona meets with Sasha, makes her pitch. She offers money, fifty thousand to take down Abigail. Sasha needs the cash for medical debts, but it's not just that. It's the chance to fix the problem, do something for the greater good. You ever heard of that concept?"

"Once or twice. A lot of bad shit happens in its name."

"You're not going to cut me any slack."

"I'm listening. I'm trying to see your side."

"Oh, yeah, my own Mr. Empathy."

She lifted the pistol, adjusted its fit in her hand, and laid it back in her lap.

"Sasha confided in me," Timmy said. "Told me about Mona's scheme, basically asked my permission. How'm I going to refuse? Her husband died, she's losing her son. Abigail Bates was a coldhearted bitch. You saw her in action. Thumbing her nose at the town. She was eighty-six years old, for godsakes."

"So there's a cutoff age for murder? Pass eighty-five, you're fair game?"

"You're not even trying to see the other side."

Sugarman was silent. Working to translate her tone. Did her confession mean she was about to hand the pistol over, or use it on him? Sugar was guessing that Timmy Whalen probably didn't know the answer to that herself.

"So Milligan wasn't part of the cabal?"

"That's right. Just Mona and Carter Mosley."

"They recruited Sasha, then she recruited you."

"Yeah."

"That was a clever move."

"Clever?"

"You should be honored, Timmy."

She stared at him and said nothing.

"Mona and Mosley have a lot of respect for your abilities. They could've brought in anybody to murder Abigail. Some out-of-town contractor. But they were worried about you.

Worried you'd figure it out. So they draw in your friend. Make sure you're on board before they put the plan in motion. They used Sasha to neutralize you. Once your hands are dirty, they're home free."

She closed her eyes briefly, fingers tightening on the Glock.

"But before the plan could work, Thorn pops up. Fly in the ointment."

"Where is he now, your friend?"

"Fishing somewhere in the Everglades. Why?"

She dropped her eyes, stared down at the burgundy rug. Sighed.

"Why, Timmy?"

"The gun-shop break-in this morning. The rifle, handgun, all that."

"Yeah?"

"I think it was Sasha. I believe she hit that boatyard, too, stole a twenty-footer on its trailer."

Sugarman shot to his feet, and she came to hers.

"Easy, now. Easy."

"That goddamn houseboat. That's what this is about. Take Thorn out in the Everglades and kill him. That's what you're telling me?"

"Down in the chair. When you sit, we talk."

The pistol's aim was fixed on a spot a few inches above his navel. Her hand was steady, her body tensed to unload. A trained shooter with a trusty hand. He could see that in the easy way she leveled the weapon, in the neutral focus of her eyes.

Sugarman sat. He touched his shirt pocket and felt the folded paper. Thorn's exact address in the middle of nowhere.

After Sugarman was settled in the chair, Timmy took her seat again.

"When you mentioned Thorn's name earlier, I realized what might be going down. I didn't know they were targeting him. No one told me."

"They didn't need your permission this time," he said. "It's out of your jurisdiction. Nothing for you to cover up."

Sugar was perched on the edge of the cushion. Ready to

cut left or right, or rush the woman head-on. Whatever made itself available.

"Take a minute, Sugarman. Stand back, see the big picture. Bates is huge, a global force, thousands of enterprises all around the world, a hell of a lot more than phosphate mining. Having the right people call the shots, someone like Mona, that could mean more than just doing right by Summerland, Florida. It could mean moving the world in a better direction. Fix a hundred Pine Tree Schools, a thousand creeks and rivers."

"That's the speech, is it?"

"Yes, that's the speech."

"My friend has to die," Sugar said, "so there'll be peace on earth."

She gave him a bruised look.

"I'm sorry about your friend. I had nothing to do with that."

"Not true, Timmy. Chain of cause and effect. You were a crucial link. You still are. Whatever's happening down in the Glades is because you gave your friend a pass."

Out in the street a white Lincoln Navigator pulled to the curb. A little man got out and started up the Olsens' walkway. Carter Mosley in his poet's uniform. Blue denim shirt, khakis, moccasins.

"What's Mosley doing here? He coming to confess, turn himself in?"

"No," Timmy said. "He's here to help me dispose of your body."

CHAPTER THIRTY-SIX

She fired a round every other second, as if timing the trigger pulls to her unhurried pulse. The wind was dying down. Her boat held steady about thirty yards off the Mothership, suspended in some perfect stasis between the incoming tide and the northerly breeze, as if God himself was collaborating with her.

There was something dreamlike about the cadence of her firing. Like a drumbeat that gave an orderly rhythm to the wild confusion of shattering glass and screams.

In the first few minutes of the fusillade, I managed to slip into the water on the submerged port side, then duck about three feet below the surface and frog-kick twenty feet north. I came up quickly for a breath and dove back as a spurt of water erupted two feet to the right of my face.

I grabbed Holland's left ankle and sidestroked back to the loading platform, tugging him along. Twice the water dimpled close beside me.

I wasn't sure if he was still alive. His eyes were open, but if he was breathing I couldn't detect it.

While Rusty helped boost him aboard, slugs blasted golf-ball holes in the fiberglass behind us. One of the Mercury outboards took a hit that tore open the cover; another round ricocheted off its props, snapped one blade, and set the others spinning. The bob and dip of Sasha Olsen's boat was probably all that was keeping us alive.

As we positioned Holland on his back, he grunted once and drooled a shot glass of spume. One round had scraped his throat, another had winged his right arm. Ugly flesh wounds. He swallowed and gritted his teeth and seemed to be trying to speak.

I tilted down to hear him.

"Fuck-er."

It could've been one word, or it could've been two.

Then he shut his eyes and began to moan some off-key song.

Thirty feet out, Annette floated faceup, the upper portion of her skull gone. The tide had her in its grip and was dragging her body south faster than I could swim. The city girl whose been-there-done-that smugness never gave the Everglades a chance. Usually the jaded scoffers were converted by a few hours in that wilderness. Maybe it would've happened eventually with Annette. Then again, she might have been one of those rare ones who were constitutionally unable to yield to forces larger than themselves. Their self-importance was so deeply rooted, so habitual, they were immune to the grace that nature can confer and found endless ways to scorn its power.

"Why's she staying out there? Why not come finish the job? She has to know we're helpless."

"Maybe she's having too much fun," I said.

I slung Holland over my shoulder and Rusty waved me ahead. I lugged him up the four-rung ladder and rolled him onto his back in front of the salon door. I was slumped low, as another slug shattered the tinted window three feet overhead, and a moment later the window beside it blew apart. Holland winced and grumbled a feeble complaint.

At the top of the ladder, Rusty faltered and lost her footing, then I saw her face go out of focus, and I lunged for her right hand.

She huffed deep and long as if she'd lifted too much weight.

Her eyes fixed on mine for half a second, then her mouth went slack. I grabbed the front of her shirt and slung her on top of me and fell backward, a double body-slam, and spun us down the slope of the tilted deck out of Sasha's sights.

Rusty was groaning softly in my arms. "Aw, Jesus . . . aw, Jesus."

I skimmed my hands across her body until I found it. Rusty's left knee was blown open. A single fragment of bone poked through her tattered trousers. Her head lolled in my arms. Aw, Jesus. The gunfire kept time to its demented metronome, opening hole after hole in the thin skin of the Mothership.

I hooked an arm around her chest and, flat on my belly, wormed our bodies across the deck to the salon door and into the cabin that was half full of bay water.

And still they came, one and-a two and-a three and-a four. The thousand-feet-per-second chunks of lead cartwheeled through the walls and windows, Sasha squeezing off another round and another, following the beat of the mad conductor's baton.

Mona was huddled in the passageway to the staterooms, knee-deep in water. She stared at me with such blind detachment I was staggered for a moment, thinking she might be dead.

"Mona?"

"She's crazy," Mona said. "Sasha's gone insane."

I settled Rusty in the high, dry corner, went back for Holland, and stretched him out nearby. Then I slopped down into the pool of oily water and sorted through the jumble of furniture and pots and pans and toaster and coffee maker until I found the heavy oak dining table. I dragged it on its side up the steep incline and pressed the thick tabletop flat against the wall, then eased Rusty and Holland behind its screen. It wasn't much, but it was better than relying on the three-inch wafer of fiberglass.

Sasha Olsen ceased firing.

Maybe taking a moment to snap in another clip. That she might have run out of ammunition was too much to hope for. I hadn't been counting, but it seemed like close to two dozen rounds since she started. High-capacity magazines could hold twenty, sometimes slightly more. When she began firing again it would be worth noting the number. Use the reload interval to make a move. If I could still count at all by then.

No doubt when she'd blown open the pontoon, she'd emptied a full clip. From a half mile away I'd counted roughly eighteen shots. How many clips could she have brought on such a mission? If her original intent had been to knock me off, more than forty rounds seemed excessive.

Rusty groaned and closed her eyes. I took her hand and squeezed it and she gripped back. She wasn't going gently into that goddamn night. No need to cheerlead, urge her to hang on, stay with me. All that bullshit didn't need saying with Rusty. Hanging on was what she did. What she'd always done and always would.

Holland was chanting a string of curses and seemed to be drifting in some twilight of consciousness.

Stooped low, I hiked across the salon, wedged past Mona, went down the passageway by the staterooms and out the door onto the bow. Since I'd last looked, Sasha had changed her position, and when my head emerged, a slug blew the door from my hand and knocked me forward on the deck.

A hornet was stinging my neck and wouldn't stop. I blinked my vision clear, reached up, and fingered the spot. Red strobes blazed inside my eyes. I bit down hard, used thumb and first finger to pinch at the protruding nub, and plucked the splinter free.

A jagged one-inch needle of fiberglass. Blood seeped down my neck, soaking the collar of my shirt. A trickle or a flood, it was hard to tell. If I'd lanced an artery I'd bleed out in minutes. Not much I could do. I'd get that verdict soon enough.

I stuck my finger into the ripped opening at the elbow of my lucky shirt and tore off the bottom of the sleeve. Then I wrapped the fabric once around my throat and knotted it like an ascot.

On all fours I circled to the submerged port side, out of Sasha's sight. With water to my chest, I held to the top rail and half swam the length of the ship to the wheelhouse spiral stairs. I'd given up hope of finding the medical supplies we stored in the galley. Even if I could've located the kit, it would've been unusable, since the storage cabinet was four feet beneath the waterline. Worthless wet bandages. The only other first-aid box was in the wheelhouse where I was headed.

For the seconds it took me to climb the spiral stairs and duck into the cabin, I'd be fully exposed. But I needed to close Rusty's wound, and if she was going to survive the next few hours without going into shock, she'd do well to gobble a handful of the codeine tablets we carried in the kit.

Assuming we had a few more hours.

The sky was overcast and dusk was nearly done. Bad light for shooting. Though it was small comfort to consider the night ahead.

At the base of the metal stairs, I gathered my breath and touched an experimental finger to the wound on my neck. I shouldn't have. Teeter's waffles rose up an acid column at the back of my throat. I turned and heaved them overboard along with another plateful of food. A pretty target I made for several seconds. But she wasn't shooting anymore.

I made it up the stairway, found the medical pack, and got down again in half a minute. I slogged back to the bow, peeked around the corner, and found she'd disappeared. I ducked inside, then jogged down the passageway into the salon.

It was all exactly as I'd left it: Mona still crouched in the passageway, the half-swamped cabin, Rusty breathing unsteadily behind the cocked-up dining table, Holland auditioning for some punk-ass band.

I unscrewed the hydrogen peroxide and took aim. When it met the open wound, it frothed like beer into a frosty mug. Rusty rocked her head back, shut her eyes, and endured my clumsy field dressing in silence. She couldn't straighten the leg, and I didn't see any point in trying to splint it. I used an entire roll of gauze, wrapping it as tight as I dared to staunch the bleeding, bandaging her from ankle to thigh and adding three more wraps around the knee itself. She passed out once but came to a few seconds later. I retrieved a plastic bottle of water floating with the rest of the debris and fed her three codeine tabs.

When I was done with Rusty, I sterilized Holland's wounds. The one on his arm was a ragged groove just above the elbow. The welt on his neck was more like a burn, as though he'd been touched with a branding iron. I used the last of the roll of gauze to wrap both of those.

I spotted his broken camera stranded at the edge of the debris on the salon deck. I retrieved it and set it on his belly. Holland looked at it, then looked at me. He cradled the camera to his chest and nodded his thanks.

The sun had set and the last silver flush was draining from the clouds. We had about fifteen minutes till night settled around us.

I gathered all the flashlights I could find and handed them out. For Mona, the big bruiser: eighteen million candlepower, brighter than the tungsten floods that indoor photographers use. Visible more than eight miles away. Sixty-watt H4 halogen bulb, using a battery that could go half an hour without a recharge.

I laid the black police Maglite next to Rusty. Four D batteries in the long heavy cylinder. Could be used as a baton to club drunks and other assorted idiots. Fresh batteries, weighed four pounds.

I took the Mini Maglite for myself. It was the size of a half-smoked stogie and fit in my shirt pocket. Three triple-A's powered the circle of tiny halogen bulbs. Its beam was narrow. Using it in the dark was like looking around a room through a hole in a sheet of paper.

"Will they survive?" Mona had come over and was squatting beside me.

"Damn right they will."

Rusty's eyes were closed and every few seconds she puckered her lips and blew out a sharp breath as if she were in the last moments of labor. Holland seemed to be sleeping, his chest rising and falling like a sprinter at the finish line.

"What now?"

"Now it gets dark," I said. "Very dark."

"And then what?"

"We'll have to see."

"Maybe she's gone."

"No."

"Maybe out of ammunition. Maybe she's had a change of heart."

"She just set her son on fire and murdered several people. That's not a mind I can read."

We sat on either side of Rusty and watched the darkness invade the cabin. The wind lay down and the Mothership grew still. I heard a hundred thumps of wings passing overhead, and some squeal and creak of metal, the ship's structure straining from the unnatural position.

"Don't use the flashlights," I said. "Only as a last resort. If she's out there, it could draw fire. So keep them off. Do you hear me, Rusty? Only in the worst-case emergency."

She nodded that she understood.

I slipped my hand into her hip pocket and drew out the walkie-talkie, then held it out to Mona.

"What?"

"Take it," I said.

"You want me to call her? Now?"

"No."

"What then?"

"Is your wristwatch still working?"

She shot her cuff and nodded that it was.

"Illuminated dial?"

"Yes."

"Now this is the big question, Mona. Can I trust you?"

She had to consider that longer than I would've liked.

"What're you doing, Thorn?"

"I'm going to get her."

"How?"

"It'll take me about thirty minutes to reach the inlet. It took longer this morning, but the seas were rough. Thirty minutes max."

"In the dark?"

"In the dark."

"And you're sure she'll be in the same place?"

"No," I said. "I'm not sure of anything."

"What's with the radio?"

"Thirty minutes, then call her. Keep calling her, keep talking to her. That's how I'll home in on her position."

"If she has her radio on, you mean."

"She'll have it on."

"Why me? Why don't you take it with you? You press the call button when you're set."

"Then if she presses hers, I'm exposed. No, you've got to do it. Thirty minutes from the time I leave."

"How do you find your way, Thorn? There are no lights, no stars."

"I'll make it."

I leaned close to Rusty's ear. She was focused inward, working on each breath, in and out and in again.

"I've got to go," I told her. "I'm going after her. Will you be all right?"

She made a noise in her throat. It had already grown so dark, I could barely see her face. I found her hand and squeezed it and her grip was as strong as it ever was, maybe stronger.

I slipped the Mini Maglite into my pocket, got up, and located the reciprocating saw balanced on the backside of the television. I took it out of its case and flicked it on and pressed the trigger. She was still alive and well.

"You're taking a saw? Why?" Mona asked.

"If I get a chance, I'm going to cut her in half."

"I think you should stay, Thorn. I think it'd be safer for all of us."

"Thirty minutes," I said to Mona. "Starting now."

CHAPTER THIRTY-SEVEN

"Buckle up," Mosley said. "It's the law. Right, Sheriff?"

Carter Mosley pulled away from the Olsen house and headed down Prairie Avenue. Lights were coming on in living rooms, children winding down their lawn games. All along the Florida coast, all through the Keys, wineglasses were being lifted to the flashy horizon, conch shells blown. Toasts all around, ice in the blenders. Let the serious drinking begin.

As Mosley slowed for a four-way stop, Sugar inched the table knife from his cuff, tested the blade with his thumb. Dull, very dull.

He worked the knife into his pants pocket. Timmy noticed the squirm of his shoulders and leaned forward to nudge him with the Glock.

"There's about a dozen different stories that could account for why I had to shoot you, Mr. Sugarman."

"In the front seat of Mosley's car?"

"Don't let's argue," Mosley said. "Let's keep this civil and businesslike, what do you say, people?"

"Mind if I ask where we're going?"

"Don't mind at all," Mosley said. "Sheriff, you mind if he asks?"

"Don't be a smart-ass, Carter."

"We're taking a little plane ride," Mosley said, giving Sugarman a cordial smile. "Swing out fifty miles or so over the Gulf of Mexico, see if we can spot any illegal activity on the waters below, or maybe catch sight of one of those alien spacecraft."

"Carter. Knock it off."

"The sheriff's a serious person," Sugarman said. "Dropping innocent citizens out of airplanes—that's not something she takes lightly."

"Both of you," Timmy said. "Shut the hell up."

"I don't know how innocent you are, sir. From what I gather you've made rather a nuisance of yourself around these parts in a very short time."

Carter cut east on a narrow state road, into the heart of cattle country, the houses dropping away and with them the lights and road signs and billboards. Nothing to advertise, no one to buy it.

"Covering up for Milligan must've pissed you off something fierce."

"I don't know what you're talking about."

"Just a guess," Sugarman said. "Some screwup Milligan pulled when he was a kid. A kid with all the advantages. He builds that school with radioactive waste product and forgets to mention it when people start getting sick. Makes you wonder how long he might've known before Dillard brought it to your attention. But he never said shit, did he? Old John just let it slide. He's the rightful heir to Bates International, so why should he care? He's got Abigail to defend his ass. But it's you standing up on that stage, taking all that razzing. You're the scapegoat. That couldn't have been easy. A man like you, so dignified, so polished. So goddamned short."

Mosley shrugged it off and drove in silence for a while. Sugarman cut a look at Timmy in the backseat, and she shook her head at him. Something in her eyes he couldn't make out. Maybe she was dazzled by his in-your-face style. That take-no-prisoners honesty that Sugarman was becoming famous for. Or maybe she was just telling him to shut the hell up before Carter Mosley decided to pull off on one of these side roads and finish him off right there.

Another silent mile went by, then Mosley slowed the big

SUV for a turn down a narrow lane, blacktopped, but only wide enough for a single car.

"A man like you, Mr. Sugarman, a common working man, a man with limited knowledge of the world of business affairs, might be surprised to learn that emotion plays a very limited role in most decisions."

"Like hell it does."

"I don't know where you come by this view, but you're wrong, sir. John Milligan did what any good businessman would've done forty years ago when he built that school in the most efficient and cost-effective manner possible, and he's continued to behave in the most forthright way ever since. He's merely been protecting his investment."

"Covering his ass," Sugarman said. "Or having you do it for him."

Branches swatted at the passenger side of the Lincoln and the high beams seemed to be barely making a dent in the darkness up ahead.

"Almost there," Mosley said.

"Do you have children, Mr. Mosley?"

"No, sir. I've not experienced that pleasure."

"I didn't think so."

"What's that supposed to mean?"

"I don't know if I can explain this. It's kind of abstract."

"Oh, my. Well, then it's probably way over my head," Mosley said. He took a look at Sugar, then glanced over the seat at the sheriff.

"And you, Timmy?" Sugar said. "I take it you don't have kids."

She was silent.

"Okay, I'll take a shot," Sugar said. "Seems to me this whole deal comes down to those with children and those without."

"A philosopher," Mosley said. "How special."

"Abigail protects John at your expense, Mosley. And Sasha Olsen defends Griffin at Timmy's. It's that blood-and-water thing. When it comes right down to it, family wins. You guys catch the shit."

"You're not very smart, are you, Sugarman?" Mosley was slowing the SUV as they came into a glen. The headlights lit up an old stone birdbath toppled over, a wide lawn of shaggy grass, a rotting bench.

"It's the way I work," Sugar said. "Say the obvious, see how it sounds."

"It sounds like bullshit," Mosley said. "Don't you agree, Timmy? Wipe a baby's butt, burp it on your shoulder, that makes you superior. Gives you some favored status. I don't think so."

She said nothing. And it was then Sugarman had his first faint hope that he might make it out of this alive.

"I think you're missing my point, Mosley."

"Fuck your point," he said.

Through the halo of suspended dust, the lights of the Lincoln showed an old two-story house with a wraparound porch and a swing suspended from the overhang. Sugar had seen the place before, but it took a few seconds to recall where. It was the house from the photo Thorn laid before him last night at Morada Bay. The couple sitting stiff on that swing were Thorn's grandparents, and the two youngsters who'd posed next to the car were his mother and his uncle. Mosley parked the Lincoln in nearly the precise location where that old Ford coupe had been sitting all those years ago. The dizzy swirl of déjà vu passed through him.

"Come on, everyone, let's go flying." Mosley opened his door and got out. "Sheriff, can you do your duty? Or do you require my help?"

Timmy stepped out of the door behind Sugarman's seat. "I'm fine," she said.

"Don't let me down, girl. Can't take any chances. Either one of us."

He angled off toward the side of the house. In the dark somewhere he flipped a switch that lit up a pathway of lights. There was a landing strip back there, Sugarman was sure of that. And a Cessna, and his one-way ticket to the lovely Gulf of Mexico. At least his body was scheduled to make that flight.

He got out and stood facing Timmy Whalen.

"May I?" he said to her, pointing to his shirt pocket.

"May you what?"

"Show you something."

Carter called from the other side of the house, "You coming, Sheriff? Everything all right?"

"Make it quick," Timmy said quietly.

He drew the paper from his pocket, unfolded it, and tipped it toward the light from the pathway.

She looked at it for a while and said nothing.

"You recognize that?" Sugar said.

"GPS coordinates."

"Yeah. It's Thorn's current address. I found it in your friend's house. Sasha. You know, the one who didn't tell you she was going to rob a gun shop, steal a boat, take her son off to the Everglades to kill an innocent guy named Thorn. Sasha Olsen, same lady who drowned an eighty-six-year-old woman because she blamed her for her husband dying and her son getting sick. Of course, she was mistaken. It wasn't Abigail's fault. It was her son's, and a bunch of people deciding that making their quarterly targets was more important than a bunch of kids' lives."

"You can stop right there, Sugarman."

She stepped back, put two yards between them. She had the pistol tipped toward his shoes. Not good procedure from a cop. A little slack. But not so slack Sugarman was ready to risk a lunge.

"You make a good case," she said. "You're a smart, thoughtful man. And your moral certainty is inspirational. I wish the situation were otherwise."

"You have the power to make it otherwise. You've had that power all along."

"Sheriff!" Carter Mosley was coming back around the house. In his hand he held a chrome .45. "You having a problem? Don't tell me you're getting attached to that boy. I sure hope this hasn't become a racial issue."

In the same motion, Sugarman swung on Mosley and drew the blade from his pocket. A pistol behind him, a pistol in front, Sugarman with a dull table knife. Not since he was a kid had he tossed a knife. Mumble-de-peg or something. Bury the blade in the sandy soil, stretch your opponent's legs wide. He was good at it, but that was forty years ago. Been a long time since he did any knife throwing. None at all to save his life.

It wasn't bravery or some wild impulse. That was Thorn's realm. Sugarman made the only logical, reasonable choice. A tactical decision. Present his back to an officer of the law who should have had an ingrained reluctance to fire on defenseless targets. A woman who an hour earlier had run her hands across his body with something other than professional briskness. It's not that he trusted Timmy Whalen, but that he distrusted her some fraction less than the small man with the gaudy pistol in front of him.

Sugar took a small step toward Mosley.

"Sheriff," Mosley said. "Sheriff, take him down."

Carter Mosley raised the .45 and aimed it in Sugarman's direction, though his hand bobbed an inch up then an inch down. Twenty feet of shadows between them, the width of a master bedroom. Even practiced shooters missed at such close range and with such bad light, though Sugarman had also seen the damage a .45 could do and felt the jelly in his stomach quiver.

"Sheriff!" Mosley took a step backward.

"The sheriff is a public servant, Carter," Sugar said, "not your butler. She's not shucking and jiving to your tune anymore."

"Stand back, Sugarman. Last chance." Mosley brought his left hand up to steady the pistol, and that's when Sugarman wrist-flicked the knife, watched its end-over-end flight for a split second until it thumped hard against Mosley's chest. Not enough to do damage, but it distracted the hell out of him. He yelped and staggered to the side, not knowing what struck him.

Sugar came straight on, diving low at Mosley's legs.

And that kid who'd been bullied on the playground, the teased and taunted runt that Carter Mosley had worked so hard to rise above, grunted and fired and fired again. Blasts to wake the dead.

For a second Sugar didn't know if he'd been hit or not—the concussion so startled him, so numbed his senses.

His arms tangled around Mosley's thighs, and he gripped and twisted and slung the man sideways, the two of them tumbling together into a groaning heap. Not his finest tackle. Sugarman landed on his back, while Carter Mosley, a gristly little fuck, scrambled to his knees, bent forward, and rammed the barrel against Sugar's chest. It should have been over then. The logical, orderly sequence Sugarman had mapped out had whirled into chaos. Stretching before him was that dark highway leading off to nowhere.

Mosley's hand quivered, his face full of grim elation. He'd won a rare physical victory, and crossing into that unfamiliar territory must have made him dizzy with delight. He fumbled his grip on the pistol.

Sugarman lashed out, seized the barrel, twisted it to the side, and tore it from the man's hand.

He scrambled up, yanked Mosley to his feet, and turned to face Timmy Whalen. But she wasn't there.

Sugarman dragged Mosley into the shadows of the lawn where she'd been standing, and after a minute's search, he found her lying on her back in the weeds. One arm was extended out to her side as if she meant to flag down a passerby, the left hand cradling her lower gut where one of Mosley's slugs had torn into her. She was drawing deep humming breaths.

Sugar kneeled beside her and found an angle that put her face in light.

Her eyes held his. Those pretty eyes, looking sleepier than ever.

"Go," she said. "Save your friend."

"No, I've got to get you to a hospital."

"My phone." She closed her eyes, got another breath. "Give it."

Sugarman drew her cell from the holster on her belt. Laid it in her open hand.

"Go on, hurry," she said. "Your friend."

"I can't leave you," Sugarman said.

"I'm okay now. I'm good. I'll make it."

Sugarman couldn't speak.

"I'll call it in," she said. "Go, goddammit. Do what's right."

CHAPTER THIRTY-EIGHT

Sick of weapons, sick of their noise, the jarring kicks, and of what they did, the percussions and repercussions, Sasha slid the rifle overboard. She dropped the .45 and the remaining rounds. She stripped off the camouflage jacket. Stood there for a moment thinking. Then she peeled out of her jeans and shirt, her bra and panties. She reached behind her, peeled the band off the end of her braid, unraveled it, and shook her hair loose.

She took her time, smoothing her hands across her hips, breasts, nipples, her soft white belly, the black coarse triangle of hair. Gliding palms across her flesh to wake herself, revive her senses. For a moment something sexual stirred, then was gone.

She bent at the waist, ran her hands up and down her legs. Bristly, untended. She felt a bruise near her knee. Felt an ache and puffiness in her left ankle. Arthritis she'd inherited from her dad, that man who'd hungered for a son and got only her. She thought of him and saw once again that afternoon on Nightmare Creek, stranded as the tide ran out. How good the fishing was, how scared she'd been, and how well she'd hidden it from her father.

Here she was, stranded again. Stranded worse than ever. No one left to hide her feelings from.

Griffin urged her to flee. He called her beautiful, said she still had a chance at life. Go to California, Spain, Switzerland, the Alps, someplace distant. Be his eyes, see the far-off lands. Travel, take him with her.

She could start over. Find a man who'd sweep her into his arms. Marry him, cook his food, eat, watch sunsets, talk and listen. She was still young enough, just barely, to have more children. That's what Griffin wanted for her, and it's what C.C. would've said, too.

Disappear from this and reappear somewhere else.

Like getting new orders. Open them, read them through. Where she was being sent next. Her mission, her destination. Put on her uniform, pack, and go. Protect her buddies. Kill those trying to kill her. Good death, useful death.

She'd done it all before. Done it once as well as it could be done.

Sasha Olsen stood naked in the night. She looked out at the dark bay. A mile due west was the houseboat. Close enough that she could swim.

She didn't know who was still alive. She'd killed Milligan, held him under like his mother; she'd killed the retarded guy, the one claiming he was Thorn. She'd shot two others, a young man and young woman. Shot them down and watched them tumble. She'd fired so many rounds her body ached. She was half deaf from the noise.

But the others could still be alive. They could be hurt and dying. Or if she left them, they might survive and someday they'd resume what they'd been doing. Pine Tree School, the Peace River. Nothing would have changed.

From the first she'd had her doubts. Head of the snake.

She was never a true believer, though she'd hidden it from Griffin. She knew enough of the world to have those doubts. She could kill every Bates and every Milligan, and the corporation would survive. The draglines would still be carving giant pits, stacking up the waste. Some other group of men with different names would arrive and fill the offices and chairs and sit behind the desks. Some faceless people in rooms off in big cities. There were always more snakes to replace the snakes, and more snakes to replace those. Where they came from she didn't know, but they came and they came.

The breeze from the north ran its hands across her flesh. Sexy.

A ghost of what C.C. could do to her. Those whispery things that never got routine or lost their flame.

That joy—could she ever have anything close to that again?

Did she want to try?

California? What was there? What was anywhere?

The night was darker than dark could be, and the breeze was steady across her flesh. There were night sounds, twitters and squawks and splishes in the mangroves she couldn't identify. Creatures prowling, reptiles on the move.

Who was Sasha now? Stripped of everything. What nub of self was left that might sprout and grow into a new thing?

She inhaled the Everglades and let it go. What she'd had and lost was more than she could imagine regaining. Her emptiness had no bottom. Timmy was another loss. Sasha had asked of her the unthinkable. To betray her sacred pledge. Sasha corrupted her, destroyed the only friend she had.

The walkie-talkie trilled.

She picked it up from the console and pressed the button and, though it was barely true, she said, "I'm still here."

And the voice on the other end said, "He's coming for you. Thorn is coming in his kayak. Fifteen minutes and he'll be there. Do him and it's over."

It was blacker than black. Everglades dark, with a sky cloaked by layers of clouds. A place so distant from man-made light, I could've been buried in a coffin a mile beneath the earth. A solid darkness I could feel against my skin, like a velvet hood, a suffocating gloom.

Human eyes don't adjust to that level of dark. Maybe some million-years-ago ancestor could've made his way just fine, but we moderns had lived too long in the dazzle of twenty-four-hour radiance. It was never ever really dark. Never ever as dark as that moment on the black water with the black sky above and the black black air before me.

In the last minute before pushing off from the Mothership, I climbed the spiral stairs to the wheelhouse, feeling my way through the blindness. The wind vane was unbroken, still mounted alongside the cluster of weather sensors on the roof. The electronic stuff was dead, but the vane still swiveled with the breeze.

I read the Braille etched into the base with my fingertips. Wind out of the north by northwest. I spent a minute up there taking readings to be sure it was steady enough to trust.

And now the wind was my only compass. I steered east, keeping the breeze at my left shoulder, the slightest oblique push from behind.

Even the smoldering red glow of Miami that was usually visible from fifty miles away was smothered by cloud cover. This was darkness that drank light. Absorbed it, and didn't give it back.

Not a glimmer on the water as I paddled. Not a flicker of raccoon eyes, or possums in the woods. No stars, no moon, not even a passenger jet circling over the Glades to make its approach.

Just the wind to tell me I was still on earth.

Blackness. No horizon, no up, no down.

The throb in my neck kept me company.

If I was bleeding to death, if I was about to die, then this was the place for it. The best place I could imagine.

CHAPTER THIRTY-NINE

Sugarman read out the coordinates, and Carter Mosley, compliant as a whipped pup, punched them into his GPS.

They lifted off, went west, then south. Neither spoke through the headsets. Sugarman rode shotgun, holding Mosley's .45 in his lap. He was just about pissed off enough to use it. Leaving Timmy Whalen bleeding back in the dark ran contrary to every value he had. Never abandon a fallen comrade. And he liked that woman, despite her moral failing. She'd acted out of love. Love of friend. The same emotion driving Sugarman at that moment.

They followed the lights of the coastline. Venice, Port Charlotte, Punta Gorda, Cape Coral, Ft. Myers, Estero, Bonita Springs—that narrow strip of illumination, the thriving Gulf Coast. At Naples they turned southeast to Marco Island, flew on, passing above the sprinkle of lights that was Everglades City, then ahead of them was darkness. A hundred miles of solid black.

Sugarman watched the numbers change on the blue screen of the GPS receiver. He tried to use that inner sonar system that sometimes worked for him, sounding the depths of his intuition. Was Thorn okay? Still alive? Still sending out pings?

It worked sometimes, but not tonight. He was not picking up anything.

* * *

Sasha slid into the ink.

Going swimming with the crocs, the gators, the cotton-mouths. Just another killer naked in the silky water.

She lazed on her back, floated, looking up at the godless night. Her hair brushed along her back. She swam toward the houseboat, the only direction Thorn could use to reach her.

She knew nothing about him except he was one of them, a kin to Bates or Milligan. She knew his face from earlier in the day but had formed no opinion. She could have slain him and Milligan this morning along the Wood River except for Griffin sleeping on the deck. Knowing Milligan was armed, she didn't want to risk a gunfight that might injure the boy, shorten his life by so much as an hour.

On that pass she'd seen nothing in Thorn's face that troubled her. One enemy was no different from the next. She'd never been one to scout the opposition, to put much stock in the pre-ops in Iraq, or back in wrestling days when the coach warned of an opponent's dirty tricks. The best things she'd ever done required no thinking. Her finest moments were totally unplanned.

She coasted backward through the dark. The water was thick as motor oil. Raising her head from time to time so she could listen, Sasha Olsen rode the tide, doing just enough to stay afloat. Waiting like the other killers, the crocs, the gators, the sharks, the spiders in their perfect webs, with patience that knew no end. Waiting for the twitch, the slightest quiver.

I knew damn well it had been thirty minutes. No wristwatch required. Maybe forty-five. I was sweating from the short, hacking strokes, taking painful care to make no noise. More paddling in one day than I'd done in years had knotted the muscles in my shoulders and back.

I'd always wondered how a pilot could lose his place so badly that he didn't know an upturn from a dive. Now I understood. No sky, no earth. Only the wind and gravity.

Ever-faithful gravity. The same planetary pull that weighted a body, kept the moon in flight. Unseen, it tugged at us, every atom, every second. And though I had tried and tried again to defy its authority, any act of revolt was a joke. Gravity wrote the rules. The best I could do was paddle, stroke by stroke, move forward through the dark.

A minute or two later, I set the paddle across my knees. Listened to the slosh inside nearby mangrove roots, though I couldn't see them, and couldn't tell if I was about to ram into their midst or was gliding past. I touched the Maglite in my pocket and was tempted. Just one quick blink to get my bearings. But I resisted. Even a flicker might be fatal.

I bent forward and felt between my legs for the reciprocating saw. It was a stupid idea to bring it. No idea at all.

A saw. A battery-driven saw. It would short out with the first splash of water. It was useless weight. But I'd brought it with a single scenario playing in my mind, a plan that might work if the little ball fell exactly in the right spinning slot. I liked the other scheme better. Rusty in the kayak, me towed behind. A flanking move, a two-on-one pincer attack. But that choice was gone. Now I had the saw. A reciprocating saw with a six-inch blade. Good for plunge-cutting holes in a wall, but little else.

A kayak. The dark. A woman with a rifle and a handgun. And me with a saw. In my haste and confusion, I hadn't thought to grab the dive knife or a steak knife or even a butter knife. I had brought the fucking saw.

I scanned the gloom and could distinguish nothing. I knew I'd traveled east at least that same mile I covered earlier in the day. It was possible I'd gone too far and passed by the inlet entirely. It was also possible I'd been betrayed by the wind—a slight shift might have steered me north of where I wanted to be, out into the open bay. Hell, it was possible I'd paddled right up to the edge of Sasha Olsen's bass boat and at just that moment she was reaching out to stroke my cheek.

I was lost.

So I did what anyone who's lost is warned never to do: I forged on.

Five minutes, ten. I was stopping to take another breather when somewhere off to my left I heard an unnatural squawk.

So dim I could barely separate it from the other night sounds. I held still.

Then out of the blackness I heard my name. I sunk the paddle in and turned the kayak on a swivel and began to push myself toward the human noise. Fifty yards, a hundred? The voice was so faint, nearly impossible to pinpoint in the void.

My name again. My name once more time. It was the handheld radio, the transmission so scratchy it sounded like the batteries might be going.

Again my name. And I adjusted my direction, homing in on the word. *Thorn, Thorn*. That family name, inherited from a long line of people who each in their own way had conspired to bring me to this exact place and moment. And again my name. *Thorn*, coming through the darkness.

This time when I heard her voice, it was distinct. Rusty. Rusty Stabler was calling out to me from nowhere I could see.

Arrangements had changed on the Mothership, some radical shift.

Again my name and I paddled toward it, toward Rusty's fragile voice.

Closing in, gliding, then lifting the paddle from the water, listening.

"Thorn? Can you hear me, Thorn?"

Oh, yes, I could and what I heard sent a dance of prickles across my back. She was weaker than when I'd left her. So weak it sounded like she was about to wilt away.

"She knows you're coming, Thorn. She's waiting for you. Watch out, Thorn. Watch out."

I was close to the bass boat but could not see it. Maybe twenty feet, maybe slightly more. The wind and water made estimates of sound all but impossible —increasing its volume, muting it. Bouncing it away from its source. But I was close. I was certain of that. Very very close.

I picked up the reciprocating saw, the fucking saw, and pushed the trigger, then let it go. A satisfying purr.

I floated, leaning forward, trying to peer through the black curtain, but could see nothing, not a gleam.

"Thorn." Rusty's voice was forlorn. Somewhere off my starboard side.

The saw required finger pressure to keep it running. Or some other pressure. I unwrapped the gauze from my throat, and felt the trickle of blood resume. I slid the paddle onto the floor of the kayak and made three quick wraps of the gauze around the reciprocating saw, tightening the bands down across the trigger, then making a hard knot. Keeping the saw lifted high in one hand, I drew myself up from the seat and slid overboard, and set the humming tool on the kayak floor.

The saw bounced nicely against the hard shell of the boat, and its noisy chatter would carry a hundred yards in every direction. I held on to the kayak's stern and flutter-kicked beneath the surface, pushing my simple decoy ahead of me. Then gave it a decent shove.

What Sasha would make of such a noise, I didn't know. I hoped it spooked her, hoped it drew her fire, or at least the beam of her flashlight. In either case, I didn't want to be nearby.

It coasted ahead into the night, the saw thumping and rattling.

"Thorn," Rusty called again. "She knows you're coming for her."

Why had Sasha Olsen left the radio on? Had she abandoned it? Was she dead or dying? Or was she using it to lure me to her?

Didn't really matter. I had no choice.

I swam toward Rusty's voice. Breaststroking, listening, careful to make no noise. I covered at least twenty yards before I sensed the bulk of the boat a half second before I saw it.

I extended my arms, dropped below the surface, reached out to touch its slick hull, then patted my way around to the stern. I couldn't recall the exact design of the craft, how high I'd have to heave myself to grab the gunwale and pull aboard.

I pushed myself under, went down feetfirst as far as I could manage, then swept the water past me, kicked hard, and breached with a burst of air—a war whoop meant to stagger her and jolt my own adrenaline as I went up and over the side.

I clawed for purchase on the slick fiberglass. It took longer than I wanted, far too long. Expecting the bullet in the brain, the white blast of death, I got nothing. I scrabbled up and over, coming down hard and clumsy on my hip and ribs, flopping on the deck like a foul-hooked trout.

"Thorn?"

I rose and banged into the console, made a quick circuit of the boat, swatting and punching at the empty air. I made another circuit to be sure.

She was gone.

She'd taken refuge out there somewhere in all that blackness. I heard the clack and clatter of the reciprocating saw bouncing around inside the kayak's hull thirty-odd feet away. Maybe she was tracking that, or maybe, goddammit, she was swimming to the houseboat.

Back behind the console, I located the golden screen of the walkie-talkie. It was sitting upright in a cup holder.

I squatted down behind the console. Keeping my voice to a murmur, I said, "It's me, Rusty. What's going on?"

"Thorn?"

"I'm here."

"You're okay?"

"I'm good. What's happened, Rusty?"

"Mona radioed her. Warned her you were coming."

I bit down hard on that, and couldn't speak for a moment.

"Thorn?"

"And after Mona called, what then?"

"Where's Sasha, Thorn? Did you get her?"

"She's not here. She's not on the boat."

I began patting the console, searching for the ignition.

"Mona's got a knife," Rusty said. "One of Teeter's ceramics."

"Are you safe?"

"I don't know. I don't where she is. I can't see a goddamn thing."

"But she has a knife, you're sure of that?"

"Oh, yeah. I'm sure. I bashed her with my flashlight, got

the radio away from her, then she found the knife somewhere and came back and slashed me once just out of pure spite, then disappeared. She's a twisted fuck."

"Aw, shit, Rusty."

"I'm okay. I'll make it."

"Listen, Rusty. Sasha could be coming. She could be on her way. I'll be there as quick as I can. Use the flashlight on her. Shine it in her eyes, then hit her."

I saw the glow fading in my hand.

"Rusty, can you hear me?"

Then the glow was gone. Quick as that. Back into darkness.

I patted down the console and found the ignition just where it was supposed to be. But no key. No key on the top panel. No key in the side pockets. No key.

I rose and looked out at the impenetrable night. I drew out the Maglite. I'd submerged it for a minute and doubted it still functioned. I flicked it on. Bright as ever. And remembered as I did it that Rusty's skiff was still unaccounted for. That's where Sasha could be. Set up her shooting blind somewhere nearby, just waiting for a target to appear.

Fuck it. I swept the light across the boat, found the front storage locker, and dragged it open. I stayed low and searched with short bursts of light, but the compartment was empty. No flares, no supplies of any kind. A brand-new boat, as yet unstocked with Coast Guard equipment. I checked the locker in the stern, the bait well. Nothing.

I listened but heard only the jangle of the saw using up its juice.

I dropped the Maglite into the pocket of my pants, then slipped over the side and began to swim. The kayak sounded like it was close by, maybe twenty feet, thirty. I kept my stroke quiet. Thinking of the bull shark, the croc, the gators. Thinking of Rusty, her exploded knee. And now a knife wound. Mona had been working all along with Sasha. A traitorous alliance I hadn't time to consider. Two twisted fucks.

I reached the kayak, pulled myself up, and slithered back into the seat.

I unwrapped the gauze from the trigger of the reciprocating saw and set it between my legs, then stooped forward and felt around for the paddle. Then felt around some more.

It wasn't there. The paddle was gone.

I drew out the Maglite and flashed it across the water, made a circle five feet out, another circle farther out. Saw nothing. Then the little flashlight dimmed and went dead in my hand. Everything I touched was dying.

A mile west the black night exploded with radiance.

The big bruiser. Its eighteen-million-candlepower beam was pointed directly toward the sky. The dazzling shaft of light shot straight up into the low swarm of clouds like the memorial to those skyscrapers no longer there.

A come-hither beacon for Sasha.

I plunged back into the bay and swam. Flutter-kicked as hard as I knew how and knifed toward the Mothership, churning the water behind me. Bull sharks be damned.

CHAPTER FORTY

Wing-embedded landing lights, and a single headlight under the prop spinner, that's all the Cessna had. Barely making a dent in the dark.

"I can't do this," Mosley said. His voice frail inside the headset. "A night landing on water. Never done it. My night vision is terrible."

"You're going to do it now," Sugarman said. "Put it down."

Sugar saw the single light ahead, looked to be that massive sixty-watt spotlight Thorn and he had picked out at West Marine a few months ago. The biggest baddest spotlight on their shelves. Natural daylight illumination, color temperature of 4,300 Kelvin. Rechargeable battery could go for eighty minutes, producing 1,100 lumens. Mother of all spotlights aimed straight up into the sky.

"Land this plane," Sugarman said. "Land it now."

Carter Mosley made another pass, dropping to less than fifty feet, then, panicked by the sight of mangroves rushing toward them, pulled up.

Sugarman leaned to his window and saw the Mothership was half sunk. Just as they passed, the spotlight on the houseboat's roof switched off and the shock of the sudden blackness pressed Sugarman back into the seat.

"Land it," he shouted into the tiny mike. "Circle back and land this goddamn plane."

* * *

A mile was farther than I'd swum in years and my heart was letting me know, banging body shots to my left rib cage like a nasty middleweight working me over from inside. I'd let my body slip, getting sloppy in middle age. Even the adrenaline charge was already wearing off.

I was two-thirds of the way across the bay when the airplane dropped from the clouds, loud and wobbling its wings, skimming close to the water like it meant to land. Then the pilot seemed to lose his nerve, pulled up sharp, and banked away. A drug drop or the park-service flyover. Hell, my thoughts were too scrambled to make a decent guess.

When I looked back at the Mothership, the spotlight cut off, and the black curtain dropped again before me. Blacker than before because my pupils had corrected for that glare.

I kept on swimming, trying to stay on the track I'd managed so far. It was only another ten or fifteen minutes if I didn't stray off course.

I toed off my boat shoes to get better snap in my kick, then fumbled open the top button and unzipped my shorts and swam right out of them. I didn't want to chuck that shirt, even though it was proving a hell of a lot less lucky than I'd believed.

Another five minutes and my arms were as heavy as if I'd been lugging a bag of cement up twenty flights. I wanted to stop but couldn't. Couldn't get Rusty's words out of my head. She'd been cut but claimed she was okay, an assurance I didn't buy.

I was lost in the rhythm of my stroke, taking a breath on every right hand reach, when something below me in the water brushed my leg. A gentle, whisking swipe.

It woke the jet-fuel gland and sped me up by double.

There was no creature living in those waters that I could possibly outswim. But that didn't stop me from trying. I pumped my legs, left a fluttering roil behind me. And whatever it was dropped away for a full minute.

Then it grabbed my ankle. Left ankle, and hauled me to a stop, then let go. I spun back on it, ready for a punch, a kick, whatever I could do. Go down scrapping.

I was panting hard and couldn't hear a thing beyond my breath.

I swiveled a one-eighty, faced behind me, came back almost at once. A spastic water dance. On impulse, I smacked the surface flat-handed, which I knew at once was a fuck-up, more likely to draw attack than spook.

She surfaced five feet away and I made out enough of her through the darkness to know who it was. Black gleam of hair, pale sheen of skin.

I was about to speak when she sunk out of sight. Then the hand gripped my right ankle and drew me down.

I got only the quickest breath and knew at once I would drown in seconds unless I broke her grip on the first try.

Her hand strength was staggering, a grasp that numbed the flesh. I relaxed and went along for another second, then tucked into a ball as tight as I could squeeze, and plowed my hands forward, turning an underwater somersault.

Halfway around, it broke the hold and I shot to the surface.

A few seconds later she bobbed up nearby.

"Better than your granny," she said. "Better than Uncle John."

I didn't waste my lungs on words, trying to drag in deep breaths as quietly as I could, stifling the gasps, not wanting to give her any reason to attack again so soon. Treading water, moving backward, little by little, opening up some distance.

"You ever timed yourself?" she said. "How long you can go? I have. Lying beside my boy, him struggling to get a sip of air, coughing blood and little specks of tissue. Five and a half minutes, that's my best."

I heard the plane off in the west. Closing in, but still minutes away.

"That's not record territory or anything," she said. "But it's longer than you can hold yours. I'll bet my life on that."

"What do you want?"

I saw her teeth and suspected a smile, but couldn't be sure.

"You going to offer me cash? That's what the rest of your people did."

"I don't have any money. What do you want?"

"You know," she said, "I don't want a damn thing. That's the weird part. Not a damn thing. Already had joy enough for a lifetime, until you people stole it from me, bone by bone."

I filled my lungs and filled them again, then ducked below the surface and frog-kicked away from her. I made what I hoped was a wide circle, trying to get back on path to the Mothership.

She was stronger than any woman I'd ever grappled with. Stronger than nearly any man. Just that grip around my ankle was enough to scare me. The flesh still deadened. I stayed down until my chest was ready to break open, then angled upward, ruptured the surface with a gasp and started swimming hard. I called out Rusty's name. Called it again. Then got back to swimming.

Rusty answered through the darkness.

"Thorn!"

I was off course by ninety degrees.

Rusty called again and I veered toward her and plowed on. Taking breaths on every stroke, leaving behind me a furious wake.

But Sasha cut me off. This time mounting my back and looping an arm around my neck and twisting me to the side, hauling me under, not so much with her weight, which was far less than my own, but using some kind of leverage, that precisely controlled force I remembered from a brief and unsuccessful fling at high school wrestling.

I twisted and writhed and tried to punch her somewhere solid. But she rode with me, and had me under and we were going down, her naked body pressed flat against my back, right forearm locking across my throat, left hand braced against the back of my head, jamming my chin against my chest. A neck breaker, a stranglehold from the playground, the barroom, the back alley, crushing so hard the sparklers began to fire up in my eyes.

I pried at the arm at my throat, dug my fingernails into her flesh. Her body was as slippery and hard as a bag of eels. I threw an elbow into her gut but it didn't faze her. I threw another with the same result. She tightened the pressure, wriggled for further advantage, using her weight and angle to keep me buried a few feet below the waterline.

I had no secret countermoves. I'd never drilled in breaking choke holds. For a loony moment I thought of the hero in that novel Sugar had pushed on me. That eight-foot-tall fantasy man had black belts in a dozen martial arts and could dispose of enemies with his little toe.

But I was going to die down there in the black depths, either by drowning or by broken neck. It was just a question of which came first.

The lights were winking out, brain cells bidding each other farewell, when the plane thundered across the water. Maybe twenty yards away, forty. I don't know how deep we were at that moment, but the plane's roar and shudder exploded in a chaos of bubbles.

It woke me from my defeat. I wrenched and bucked and fired an elbow backward, and this time I caught bone. The grip around my neck softened by some tiny fraction.

I twisted again, down to my last seconds of consciousness when I broke free, kicked to the surface. As soon as I got a breath, she was beside me. Breathing harder than before.

"Round two," she said.

But before she could duck out of sight, I snapped a right hand full in her face. Hit her again in the right eye.

That first punch dazed her. In that defenseless second I struck her with an overhand left and felt her nose crunch. I punched her twice in the forehead, then sent a roundhouse to her temple. No traction in the water, but the blows landed hard enough.

She slumped forward, sputtered. I grabbed her hair, hauled her face out of the water, and held her before me. She gagged and coughed and swatted at my arm. I slammed my fist into her mouth, slammed it one last time, then held her head underwater and counted off the seconds.

I was nearing sixty, watching a thin trickle of bubbles rise from her mouth, when Rusty called out my name, and swept the beam of the flashlight across the water.

I flipped Sasha on her back and hauled her by the hair through the dark bay toward the Mothership. I didn't know if she was dead already, or if I was drowning her as I towed her in. And I can't say I really cared.

Back at the ship, I heaved her onto the dive platform. She wound up facedown, head turned awkwardly to the side, looking out to sea. I didn't bother to right her. I squatted down and fingered her throat for a pulse. Got nothing and felt a black thrill.

"Mona's upstairs," Rusty said when I broke into the salon. She was biting off her words, a sharp wince at each breath. "She's got the Kyocera—Teeter's best sushi knife."

"Where'd she cut you? How bad?"

Rusty was crouched in the corner behind the upturned table, close to where I'd left her. She raised the flashlight and brightened it against her shirtsleeve. The cut was six inches long and the bloody trail ran from wrist to elbow. A defensive wound.

"Shallow," she said. "Not bleeding anymore. The bitch was pissed cause I got the radio from her."

"How the hell did you manage that? Your knee like it is."

"Teeter helped me. Gave me the juice."

"Bless his heart."

"The knee, it's really fucked."

"We'll get you a new knee."

She closed her eyes and swallowed. Turned her eyes down.

"Take the flashlight, Thorn."

"You keep it. We may not be done yet."

As I climbed the spiral stairs, the Cessna idled across the bay. It was Mosley's plane, the 185 Skywagon.

Which was fine. I wanted a word with Carter Mosley.

CHAPTER FORTY-ONE

All the crew cabin doors were closed. The passageway was dark, just a slash of illumination leaking in from the Cessna's distant landing lights.

I tried Rusty's cabin first. Turned the handle, threw the door aside, stepped into the darkness. The shades were open and the floatplane's lights threw diamond patterns on the wall. Teeter lay beneath his blanket, a dark bulk.

I rummaged through Rusty's drawers, searching for anything close to a weapon. But there were only clothes. All her hardware was on her skiff.

Teeter's cabin was empty too. His drawers were even more bare than Rusty's.

So she was in my cabin. In there with a knife. Waiting for me.

My fists were puffy, the knuckles gashed from Sasha's cheekbones and jaw. My palms were sliced from the barnacles on the mangrove branch as I'd swung away from the bull shark. The wound at my neck was throbbing again, and I'd been feeling an acid burn in my throat when I used my voice as though the tissues deeper down had been violated in some ugly way.

I was tired beyond imagining. Bruised, battered, hacked, and gutted. I didn't want another fight. Another bare-handed brawl with another woman. But I could hear the Cessna drawing close and suspected it had not come on a rescue mission. There was more fighting, more dying to come. I had to move.

Quietly, I turned the handle on my cabin door, raised my foot and kicked it, then went in fast.

She was sitting in the shadows on my bunk. She'd drawn the shades but there were threads of light showing at the edges. I made out a glimmer in her lap. Too dark to see her face, too dark to make out the size or shape of the knife, or how she was gripping it.

"That's Carter out there, isn't it?"

"Yes," I said. "It's his plane."

"He's come to take me away."

I held my place by the door. The cabin was only ten by ten. No room to maneuver. Even in that total dark I knew the space perfectly. On our shakedown cruises and from months of work, I'd navigated every inch of the space in every weather and every light. The sharp-angled deck gave her a slight advantage, however. I was downhill, she was up. Seven feet between us.

"Carter and I," Mona said, "have become very close."

"I see."

"We're kind of an odd couple, I guess you could say."

"You have Abigail's murder in common. That's something."

"I think we'll probably go to Costa Rica, maybe Mexico. Carter's been moving money in case the bottom fell out. I think it's fallen out. Don't you, Thorn?"

"Yeah, it's fallen out."

"This wasn't supposed to happen," Mona said. "Sasha went off the reservation. I lost control of her."

"She was just supposed to take me down and leave?"

"You or Dad, whichever was easier. That's all. Not all this carnage. This is wrong. I didn't want this."

"John wasn't in on it?"

I took a step to the right, a better angle of attack.

"Dad, the big hero. He goes out there in the kayak, thinks he can take Sasha down, or bargain with her, or whatever he was thinking. What a fool."

"Yeah," I said. "What a fool."

"I could try, but it'd be hard to explain all this to the cops. I've been sitting here working through plausible scenarios. You know, like Sasha Olsen did this all on her own. Revenge for her husband and kid. Put it all on her. Maybe that would fly for a while, but someone could start poking, look a little closer. Then there's Timmy. She'd be a problem. This is way past her threshold. If she caved, the whole thing would fall apart."

"It already has."

"Oh, I haven't given up. I'm optimistic. I've got a relatively good feeling, actually."

"Then you're insane."

"Oh, Thorn, I was hoping you'd be different. But you're not. You're as petty as the rest of them. Typical egocentric. Everything's about you guys. You spoiled, self-indulgent brats. But this is so much bigger. There are global problems at stake, huge issues we've got to solve. A lot of shit you and your parents caused, and now my generation's got to fix. We need the right people in place, and we need them fast. We can't dillydally while you all die off."

"Oh. That's how it works. Murder the old farts, make way for the enlightened kids. That's the plan?"

"Hurry things along, Thorn. That's all. Speed up the inevitable."

I heard voices down below and felt the shift of the plane's wake rolling under them. No more time to wait.

"What I told you about your parents, Thorn. That whole bit was true. Just so you know. I've tried to be honest. Tried to do the right thing. I'm sorry about this. I really am. Sasha lost it, and things just got off track. That's not how it was supposed to go."

I'd already started for her, was halfway across the cabin, when the blast staggered me, knocking me backward against the wall. I threw my arms up in front of my eyes, but it didn't help. I was blind and stunned and totally lost. The cabin was white-hot and whirling. Mona held the beam of the big bruiser right on my face, eighteen million candlepower, six feet away.

I hadn't shut my lids in time, and knew I'd be sightless for hours.

I put my head down and dove across the space.

Felt the prick of the blade in the meat of my right shoulder, felt the cold spread down that arm, then another prick, this one deeper. Teeter's fine sushi knife, so sharp, so well-balanced it could slice to the bone without hurting.

I thrashed my good left arm, spun and twisted against Mona's grappling. She wasn't half as strong as Sasha, not a quarter. I fumbled my hand in the white blaze of darkness, found the knife, took hold of it by the blade, that fine fine blade slicing into my palm, and twisted it out of her hand and felt the blood flow. But still no hurt, no pain. Such superb knives. So razor-perfect as they parted the buttery flesh.

I grabbed her by the front of her shirt and threw her across the room into the clothes locker, that teak dresser I'd spent two whole days installing.

I was across the cabin in a second, seeing the dazzle of sparks and red embers everywhere, the room clogged with fireflies. I found her huddled against the locker, patted her down till I located her arms, then hauled her to her feet, took her by the shoulders and shook her hard, shook her hard some more as if to wake her from her long idiotic slumber.

Sugarman saw a body lying out on the dive platform. A naked female lying on her belly.

Carter Mosley brought the plane as close as he dared and cut the engines, leaving the wing lights glowing.

As they both stripped off their headsets, Sugar looked at Mosley. He was staring at the body.

"Sasha?"

"Yes," he said. "That's her."

Sugarman leaned close to the small man. The rustic poet with his shrewd, predatory smile.

"Give me a reason to hurt you, Carter. The smallest reason. Please."

Mosley looked down at his lap.

Over on the Mothership, Rusty Stabler dragged herself

out of the stern door. One leg was wrapped in bandages. She held a long black flashlight in one hand.

"Rusty?"

"That you, Sugar?"

"Where's Thorn?"

"Up in the crew cabins. Somebody needs to get up there quick. Can't be me. I'm a little gimpy."

There was a twenty-foot span of water between them. No way to get to the houseboat but to swim. Sugar opened the door, then stopped, turned back, and pulled the keys from the ignition and put them in his pocket.

As he was preparing to make the jump, Thorn appeared on the upper-deck walkway. He was bloody and looked bad, and he was dragging along Mona Milligan, holding her upright by the nape of her T-shirt.

"Thorn?"

He raised a hand in greeting, shoved Mona on ahead with the other.

Mona climbed down the spiral stairs and Thorn followed. He said a word to Rusty, then climbed down to the dive platform. He took a loop of dock line from a locker, held on to one end with his bloody hand, and lofted about thirty feet of it out to Sugarman.

Sugar caught it. He held one end, Thorn held the other, then hand over hand they drew the two crafts together.

CHAPTER FORTY-TWO

That spring Sugarman took a half-dozen trips up to Sarasota to visit Timmy Whalen. She was a good woman, he said. She'd seen the light just when it mattered most, done the right thing. He obviously felt something for her. He came back after each trip looking calmer, happier. The relationship would have gone somewhere, I was sure of that, except that Timmy was going to be serving at least ten years in prison for aiding and abetting the murderer of Abigail Bates. Ten years was a long time to wait for someone you'd only known for a few days.

Rusty got used to her new knee in less than a month. She was up and around, prancing around on the docks, showing off her scars to the other guides. She recuperated at my house. I got to know a lot about that tattoo on her lower back—its symbolism, the meaning of nearly every swirl, every color, every hidden creature and Chinese character. But Rusty promised me there was more than half of it that was still her secret. She'd tell me if I was good.

I tried to be good. I really did.

In June, Rusty and Sugarman and I made the trip up to Sarasota to meet the folks at Bates. I'd done a crash course in corporate law with a fishing buddy of mine who used to be a financial planner for some big investment firm in Atlanta. Then he retired and came to the Keys and did financial planning for retired marijuana smugglers. He'd set them up in restaurants and motels and bars and showed them how to run responsible businesses. His name was Jimmy Fineman and he had a business degree from the Wharton School and lived on a thirty-foot sailboat anchored behind Snook's Bayside.

Jimmy was a financial Zen master. Just a few simple questions.

"Is it a public corporation or a family business?"

"Family," I told him.

"Good. A lot more flexible. Not so many rules."

"How do I extricate myself?" I asked him.

"Define extricate."

"Get out of this. Get my old life back."

"You want to sell the company or change it?"

"I don't know."

"Selling's easy, changing is hard."

"Maybe sell it, then."

"Then you lose all control. Whatever bad things they were doing, they'll still be doing."

"So change it, then. How does that work?"

"Like turning a battleship. Slow and easy. I'll talk you through it."

It took four more meetings, but he did. He talked me through it.

It was late June, and Sugarman, Rusty, and I were going to Sarasota to pick a new board of directors.

I was the only billionaire in Sugarman's car. I sat in the backseat. I was wearing my boat shoes, my quick-dry shorts, and my lucky shirt, now repaired. I looked like I always looked. Maybe that was how all billionaires looked, but I doubted it.

While Sugarman drove, I paged through the typed sheets. A list of questions the three of us had drawn up.

Five questions on each page.

We'd considered asking each of the applicants for the board to write a mission statement, but Rusty said that was likely to generate so much bullshit we'd have to spend a month wading through them all. And we'd still not have a clue who these people were, which ones would do a good job with correcting the course of Bates International. So we'd hit on the question idea. Ask them five simple questions.

Take the answer sheets back to the hotel that night, go over them, and make our decisions. We were looking for five people. We had twenty-two applicants, and most of them were Bates employees already. Some junior, mostly senior, some clerical people who'd heard the new owner was a maverick or a whacko and they might have a shot at a job they'd never in ten million years have a shot at otherwise.

I preferred the term *maverick*.

We stayed in a hotel on Siesta Key. Great powdery sand. Sugary. We had fish sandwiches and a glass of wine and got to bed early. All three of us were nervous. We'd never turned a battleship before.

Nine o'clock next morning we arrived at the corporate offices of Bates International, downtown Sarasota. The town had doubled in size since I'd been there last. Gotten fancy and crowded with traffic, lost all its sleepy charm. Like the rest of Florida. Hardly any sleepy charm to be found anymore. A security guard met us at the front desk and wanted to see ID's. I had none.

"No driver's license?"

"He's Thorn," Rusty said. "He owns this place."

The security guard's hand drifted toward his holster.

A woman in a white business suit arrived and saved us from certain death.

She escorted us up to a boardroom on the seventh floor.

Twenty-two people crowded in the room, some at the table, some standing. Rusty and Sugarman took seats. The woman in the white suit introduced everyone. They had important-sounding titles. They were CPA's, lawyers, investment advisers, head of the family office.

Sugarman asked what that was, the family office.

The woman in the white suit, Margie Banks, said, "The family office is responsible for all the Bates residences, in Cape Cod, Aspen, New York, and so forth. The cars and planes. Chefs, travel plans. You know, the personal stuff."

"Yeah," Sugarman said. "Personal stuff."

The walls were a tasteful yellow. There were a half-dozen portraits of the Bates family hanging on three of them. I made a circuit of the room while the others waited at the table and watched me. My grandparents and my great-grandparents had been cowboys. Lean men and women with squinty eyes and sharp cheekbones. They huddled around campfires, their horses tied up nearby. I bet they didn't have driver's licenses either.

I gave the speech I'd worked on in my head. I hadn't given a speech to that many people since high school. I was nervous and fumbled a couple of times, had to backtrack. Once Rusty had to prompt me. I did it without notes, five minutes. But it seemed like an hour.

Bates was a battleship. It had been heading in one direction, now we were going to make a slight course correction. But first, I understood we needed to pick a new board of directors. Five people to run the corporation. Five people.

Rusty handed out the sheets. Five questions for five people.

Everyone looked at the questions.

"Is this a joke?" one guy asked. He wore a very nice black suit with subtle pinstripes. He had a red tie and a blue shirt.

"You're excused," I said.

"What? You can't do that."

"Sugar, would you show him out?"

The man straightened his red tie and stalked out of the room. One down.

"Take five minutes," I said. "Short answers, one word, two or three at the most. Anyone need pencils or a pen?"

Nobody did.

Five minutes later we had the stack of pages.

I thanked them all for coming and they left. Several of them took a parting look at me. The maverick, the whacko.

"This is very unorthodox," Margie Banks said when everyone was gone.

"Did you fill out a questionnaire?" I asked her.

"Is my job on the line, too?"

"The five new board members will decide that. Maybe you'll want to be one of them."

Margie sat down and read the questions and filled out her answers quickly.

I thanked her, and then I took another look at my grand-parents and my great-grandparents. I could see some resemblance. They didn't look like they'd do well in front of a crowd of lawyers, either. Tough old coots.

We went back to the hotel on Siesta Key and we sat out at a picnic table and watched the twilight come as we read through the pages. A small band was playing on a stage nearby, tinkly calypso, a little reggae. Not bad.

Some people had left half the questions blank. Others had tried to scribble in as many words as they could manage in the space. Tiny scrawls. We rejected those.

A few had done a pretty good job. Succinct.

1. What was the last fish you caught?
2. What bait did you use?
3. Did you release it or eat it or do something else with it?
4. Name two rivers in Florida.
5. In a hundred years, how do you want to be remembered?

It only took us an hour to whittle the group down to six. Margie was one of them. She'd caught a bonefish in Venezuela on a fly and let it go. She got the Peace River and the Miami River. She wanted to be remembered as someone who'd left her campsite cleaner than she'd found it.

"Maybe she's bullshitting," Rusty said. "Giving you what she thinks you want."

"You know what?" Sugarman said. "Maybe you should put Rusty on the board, to keep a watch on these people." Sugarman sipped his wine and smiled out at the Gulf.

"Done," I said.

Rusty thought about it silently, looking off at the reddening sky.

"All right," she said after a minute. "These six and me."

"You'll do it, really?"

"I'll do it," she said.

"It'll mean coming up here from time to time."

"I can manage that. I could bring the boat up almost as fast as driving I-75. And have a lot more fun doing it."

"Done."

We shook hands. All three of us.

"Am I still a billionaire?"

"I think you'll have to sign some papers tomorrow," Sugar said. "Then you're free."

"Well, I should pay for dinner, don't you think?"

"Damn right," Rusty said.

Rusty walked down to the shoreline. She waved at Sugarman to join her. Somehow she talked him into dancing with her. When she'd danced him breathless, she waved me down to join her in another turn on the sand.

I went down to the shoreline and stepped into Rusty's rhythmic embrace. She had on a white skimpy top that showed off the freckles in her cleavage, and some kind of loose yellow pants that turned almost transparent in certain light. The pants rode so low on her hips, the tattoo at the base of her spine was fully exposed.

We danced for two more songs, barefoot, sloshing through the gold moon water. Her new knee didn't miss a beat, and I'm sure she felt more limber in my arms than I felt in hers.

"You look good together," Sugarman said when we returned to the table.

"We're too much alike for it to last," Rusty said. But she smiled at me, and I knew she was being ironic. Somewhat ironic.

"Tomorrow after we pick the board," I said, "we'll go see how the new school building is coming along."

Sugarman nodded.

"Leaving our campsite cleaner than we found it."

Rusty had another sip of her drink and was on her feet again.

"Another dance, kiddo? My knee's acting up, needs some action."

We went out to the sand again. We danced till the moon was low in the sky, and kept on dancing while the band packed up to go home.